The jolt of awareness his hand on her bare arm caused had both of them sucking in a quick breath. For one minute they merely stared at each other. He saw confusion and desire swirl in Natalie's eyes, and knew his own hunger was no doubt evident in his expression.

The moment their lips met a sort of electricity shot through her, startling her into gasping. Natalie's mouth opened on the sound, his tongue swept in along with oxygen, and it was like a backdraft in a fire: an explosive surge took place in her body, burning out every thought and worry and leaving only a desperate need for him. Natalie thought she heard Valerian groan, or maybe it was her. She wasn't sure, but he'd released her hands and they were now desperately reaching to touch whatever she could of his body.

Tearing his mouth away suddenly, Valerian nibbled his way to her neck, growling, "Natalie . . . God . . ."

"Yes," she gasped, arching her body and turning her head to give him better access to her neck and ear. Natalie then quickly turned her head back to claim his mouth once more when she couldn't bear the excitement he was causing her.

After their kiss, just being near her was enough to have his body humming with the desire to touch and kiss her.

By Lynsay Sands

LYNSAY SANDS

After
THE BITE

AN ARGENEAU NOVEL

AVONBOOKS

An Imprint of HarperCollinsPublishers

AFTER THE BITE. Copyright © 2022 by Lynsay Sands. All rights reserved. Printed in the United States of America. No part of this book may be used or reproduced in any manner whatsoever without written permission except in the case of brief quotations embodied in critical articles and reviews. For information, address HarperCollins Publishers, 195 Broadway, New York, NY 10007.

First Avon Books mass market printing: September 2022

Print Edition ISBN: 978-0-06-311155-4
Digital Edition ISBN: 978-0-06-309748-3

Cover design by Nadine Badalaty
Cover illustration by Larry Rostant
Cover images © Shutterstock; © iStock/Getty Images

Avon, Avon & logo, and Avon Books & logo are registered trademarks of HarperCollins Publishers in the United States of America and other countries.

HarperCollins is a registered trademark of HarperCollins Publishers in the United States of America and other countries.

FIRST EDITION

22 23 24 25 26 BVGM 10 9 8 7 6 5 4 3 2 1

After

THE BITE

Prologue

"**A**nything to report?"

Valerian glanced around with surprise at that question, and stared blankly at the man peering in at him through the open driver's side window of the SUV he'd just put into park. Garrett Mortimer, the head of the North American Enforcers and his boss, raised his eyebrows in question.

Giving his head a shake, Valerian didn't respond at once, but instead turned to share a "WTF?" glance with his partner, Tybo. He then shut off the engine, hit the button on the rearview mirror to close the garage door behind them, and then both men unsnapped their seat belts and started to get out.

"Nice to see you too, Mortimer," Valerian finally said as he closed the driver's door of the SUV. "Slow night, I take it?"

"That or his wife, Sam, is pissed at him and he came

out here to avoid her," Tybo put in as he walked around the vehicle to join them.

"Sam and I are fine," Mortimer assured them with irritation. "She's actually at Jo's right now, helping with some surprise they're preparing for Alex and Cale's anniversary."

"So, you just came out here to greet us because you were bored?" Valerian suggested with amusement.

Mortimer grimaced but didn't deny the claim. Instead, he said, "Lucian's coming around this evening and he'll want an update on any goings-on in the area. So . . ." He raised his eyebrows. "Anything to report?"

"Nothing," Valerian assured him, heading toward the door between the garage and the rest of the building. The structure was quite large, holding the huge multicar garage, an office, prison cells, and an area where the security dogs were housed. But the office—and the refrigerator there—was where Valerian was eager to get to. "It was quiet as death out there. Again."

"Good, good. Quiet is good," Mortimer muttered as he and Tybo followed him into the office.

"Hmm. It's been quiet since Dr. D. went after Thorne and Stephanie down in farm country four months ago," Valerian pointed out, walking straight to the refrigerator to retrieve a couple of bags of blood. He tossed one to Tybo, another to Mortimer, and then grabbed a third and popped it onto his fangs as they slid down from his upper jaw.

Valerian almost sighed as the blood was drawn up into his body and his tension began to ease. It had been a long shift and he'd needed this. He, like the other two men now also feeding, was what most mortals would call a vampire. But they preferred the term *immortal*. Unlike vampires, they weren't dead or soulless, and didn't run around preying on their mortal neighbors and friends. Well, not anymore anyway . . . usually. There were members of their population who did, but they were considered rogue, and were hunted and brought in for judgment by rogue hunters, or Enforcers, like himself and Tybo, who were basically vampire cops.

"It's too quiet," Mortimer growled irritably as he tossed his now empty bag in the garbage, and when Valerian turned raised eyebrows his way, the man explained, "It feels like the quiet before the storm." Grimacing, he added, "I'm not looking forward to the storm."

Valerian considered that as he tossed his own empty bag in the garbage and then asked, "Is there anything in particular you're worried about?"

"Summer is over. Fall is short and soon winter will be here," Mortimer pointed out, his gaze dropping to the file in his hand.

Valerian hadn't noticed what he was carrying, but now glanced at the file with curiosity and read "Angel-Maker" on the tab. He felt his body tense. "You think the Angel-Maker will start up again once winter is on us."

It wasn't a question, but Mortimer responded as if it had been. "Yes. I think the bastard will continue his games until we catch him. He won't stop on his own."

"The Angel-Maker?" Tybo glanced between them

with curiosity as he tossed his own empty bag in the garbage.

"That's what the newspaper named the rogue who was killing prostitutes last winter," Mortimer explained, setting the file on the desk and opening it to fan out the photos inside.

There were six pictures in all, each of a different female victim. They crossed a wide range when it came to looks. One was a small, thin blonde, another a chunky brunette, another a tall, voluptuous redhead, and so on. The Angel-Maker apparently didn't have a type. The only thing that connected the murders was that the women were prostitutes, all left completely bloodless, and found lying on the snowy ground, na-ked, flat on their backs with their hands clasped to their chests and the outline of wings impressed into the snow around them. From what they could tell, the killer made a snow angel and then posed the dead women in the impression in the snow.

Valerian supposed that was why the newspapers in Toronto were calling him the Angel-Maker. Although the long, rambling letters he'd sent to a reporter at one of the newspapers had probably encouraged it too. In them, the killer had gone on about turning whores into angels to save their souls. Like he was doing the women some kind of favor by killing them, he thought with disgust.

Sighing, Valerian let his gaze sweep over the pic-tures of the victims one more time.

"I didn't know the newspapers had a name for him," Tybo commented, his gaze still fixed on the photos.

"When I left to visit my family last winter, you said you were going to send someone to wipe the memories of those deaths from both the police and reporters in the know."

"I did. Eshe and Mirabeau went to take care of that," Mortimer told him. "But the reporter had already come up with the Angel-Maker moniker and the article had gone to print before they got to her. There was no sense erasing memories then. Though they did haze the memories a bit with the police and reporters so they wouldn't pursue it further and search for the killer. We don't need mortals stomping around getting in our way," he told them grimly. Closing the file, he added, "Not that it mattered in the end. The Angel-Maker hasn't killed since the last snowfall we had. That was just before you got back in April, Tybo. It's the end of September now, so there's been no new murders in nearly six months. At least, not that we know of," he added with a frown.

"You think he moved somewhere else?" Tybo asked. "Somewhere farther north, maybe? Where there might be snow for him to play with?"

"No," Valerian answered. "Mortimer has had me checking that once a month starting back in April when you were still on vacation. There have been no reports of similar deaths anywhere in the world." He paused briefly and then mentioned his own concern on the matter. "Although he could still be killing women and keeping them in a freezer or something until the snow returns and he can pose them the way he likes."

When Mortimer glanced at him sharply at that comment, Valerian shrugged and pointed out, "Serial killers don't usually just stop killing. They pretty much have to be caught to be stopped."

"Yeah." Mortimer peered down at the closed file unhappily. "Maybe we should look into whether any prostitutes have gone missing since the last victim."

"He could have changed his modus operandi for the summer," Tybo suggested. "Killing them, but not doing the whole wings-in-the-snow thing." He frowned slightly, and then added, "Or do serial killers not change their MOs?"

Valerian shrugged. "I'm no expert on the matter, but I did read an article once that said serial killers were both amoral and opportunistic. They may prefer brunettes, but if a blonde stumbles into their path and is an easy target . . ." He shrugged. "Good enough."

"So, they might change other things too if circumstances call for it," Tybo said thoughtfully.

"They might," Valerian allowed. "But there have been no other murders in North America where the victims were fully drained of blood since the last prostitute was found."

"What about accidents, or deaths thought to be accidents where the victims lost a lot of blood?" Tybo suggested. "He could still be killing, just not taking credit for it because he can't do his snow angel thing."

Valerian didn't respond, but his mouth was turned down at the corners as he considered the suggestion.

"What are you thinking?" Tybo asked when Valerian remained silent.

"I'm thinking that while he can't make snow angels without snow, he could have made chalk drawings of wings on pavement, or spray-painted wings on grass, or something like that," he pointed out. Valerian then shook his head. "But there's been nothing like that either."

"No, but he could also have done something less likely to be noticed, like leaving little angel necklaces or earrings or bracelets on them, or even placing little angel statues somewhere near the bodies," Tybo pointed out. "Investigators might not recognize the significance of them. Especially if Eshe and Mirabeau made the memories of the Angel-Maker's previous victims hazy in the minds of the police and reporters."

Cursing, Mortimer gestured for them to follow as he turned to lead the way out of the office.

"We're going to have to look into that," their boss said as they started across the yard toward the Enforcer house. "I thought serial killers stuck to a certain pattern and didn't deviate, so I assumed spring had put a temporary halt on his activities and we'd just have to pick up his trail again in the winter if he returned. It never occurred to me that he could just be following a different path now. I'm going to have someone look into the police files for any deaths since April where there was a lot of blood lost, and have them check to see if there's a mention of any kind of angel anything at the scene: necklace, statue, etc." Heaving out a sigh, he growled, "Lucian will be super pissed if the bastard's been killing all summer and we just haven't been taking notice."

Valerian cast the man a sympathetic glance. While officially Mortimer was the head of the North American Enforcers, he answered to Lucian Argeneau, who was head of the North American Immortal Council and made all their laws. Lucian was a hard-ass. Which was why Valerian hesitated before saying, "The Angel-Maker sent letters to a reporter for the last couple of snow angel killings. Have you had anyone check to see if there have been any more of those?"

"The reporter who got those letters accepted a job in the States. I guess the Angel-Maker story garnered some attention and got her the new position. The Angel-Maker would have to write to someone else. I have a person situated in the office keeping their ears open, but there's been nothing so far."

"Are they just keeping their ears open or reading minds too?" Valerian asked with concern, and pointed out, "Whoever gets the letters next might keep it to themselves until they release their own story. They wouldn't want another reporter jumping on it and stealing their story if it might get them an offer from a bigger paper in the States too."

Valerian could actually hear Mortimer's teeth grind together at the suggestion. His voice was resigned when he said, "I'll have my hunter read everyone to be sure that isn't happening."

"I could—"

"Your shift is done," Mortimer interrupted before Valerian could finish the offer to look into it for him. "In fact, your week is done. It's the weekend, Valerian. Go home and enjoy that new farmhouse of yours."

"He enjoys his farmhouse every day," Tybo announced with amusement. "He still has his apartment in the city, but pretty much lives in the country full-time now."

They'd reached the back door of the Enforcer house. Stopping with his hand on the doorknob, Mortimer turned back with surprise. "That's a hell of a commute, Valerian. The drive from your house to Toronto is three and a half or four hours one way depending on traffic. And your shifts are usually a good ten hours long. When the hell do you sleep?"

"I don't drive back and forth," Valerian assured him.

"He helicopters in," Tybo said with a grin. "He has his own helicopter and put in a helipad in his backyard at the farm. He flies out from there and lands on the roof of his apartment building in the city and then drives here."

"Your apartment building has a helipad?" Mortimer asked with amazement.

"It has two helipads," Valerian told him, and explained, "It's Harper's building. He put them in when he had the building erected. He lets me use one."

Mortimer stared at him blankly for a minute and then gave his head a shake and asked, "Why don't you just land on the airfield here?"

"I didn't want to interfere with flights landing or leaving," Valerian explained.

Mortimer opened the door with a laugh and led them into the house. "We aren't an airport with flights constantly coming and going, Valerian. You're more than welcome to park your helicopter here during your shifts. It would save you a good half hour each way from the apartment building every day."

"Thank you," Valerian said solemnly.

Mortimer nodded as they approached his office. "So, I'll let the boys know to expect your helicopter on Sunday night."

"Okay," Valerian said.

Mortimer stopped outside his office door, and was about to speak, but paused when the sound of a ringing phone drifted out to them. After glancing inside he grimaced and said, "I need to take that. It's Lucian."

Tybo gave a disbelieving laugh. "You have a special ringtone for Lucian?"

"No. I have caller ID on the landline and it pops up on my TV screen any time there's a call," Mortimer explained.

When the man then headed into his office, Valerian stepped up to the door to peer inside with curiosity, aware that Tybo was on his heels. They both eyed the television screen on the wall. There was no sound, but the television was on the news streaming channel, and a box opened across the bottom of the screen showing Lucian Argeneau's name and number as the phone rang again.

"That's nifty," Tybo murmured beside him.

"Close the door for me, will you?" Mortimer asked as he walked around his desk.

"Do you want us to wait in case he needs something done?" Valerian asked.

"No. Your shift is over. You two go on. Have a good weekend."

"You too," Valerian said, backing out of the doorway as Tybo began to pull the door closed.

"So," Tybo said as they headed back down the hall. "Any plans for the weekend? No, wait, let me guess," he added before Valerian could respond. "Golfing."

"You got it," Valerian said with a smile. He'd finished the last of the mild renos to his new house last weekend. All he intended to do this weekend was golf and chill. He wasn't going to even think about work or the serial killer called the Angel-Maker for the next forty-eight hours.

One

"The kitchen's done, boss. So unless you need my help with something else, I'm headed out."

Natalie glanced up from the architectural drawings spread out on the table in front of her and scowled at the pretty strawberry blonde weaving her way through the half dozen other tables in the golf club's large lower dining room to reach her. "Jeez, Jan. I hate it when you call me boss."

"I know," Jan said. A mischievous grin pulling at her lips, she added, "That's why I do it."

The words startled a laugh out of Natalie and she shook her head at the woman who was both her assistant chef and friend.

"So . . . ?" Jan stopped at the corner table where Natalie had set up and raised her eyebrows. "Is there anything you need help with before I go?"

"No. I'm good," Natalie assured her, and didn't

miss the relief in her friend's face at her answer. She wasn't surprised. It was Friday night, after all, and she knew Jan and her husband, Rick, had a date night planned. A 10 P.M. showing at one of the movie theaters in the city and a late dinner were apparently on the agenda.

"Are you going to close up now?" Jan asked, her gaze sliding over the drawings Natalie had been making changes to.

"Soon," Natalie assured her as she began to roll up the large sheets of paper. "Just waiting for Mr. MacKenzie to finish his round before Tim and I mow."

"The mysterious Mr. MacKenzie," Jan said, waggling her eyebrows.

"Mysterious?" Natalie asked with amusement.

"He books and pays for his eighteen holes online, and never steps foot in the club. None of us have even seen the man except from a distance."

"Roy sees him," Natalie corrected her. "He gives him the keys to his golf cart when he shows up."

"Yeah. Roy." She wrinkled her nose. "But the old coot won't tell us anything about the guy. What he looks like. If he's nice or not. Nothing. You should really let me swap jobs with Roy one of these nights so I can give Mr. MacKenzie the keys. Then I could give you the scoop."

"Roy in the kitchen?" Natalie asked with horror. "No. Never gonna happen."

Jan gave a fake scowl that quickly gave way to a grin. "That *would* be pretty bad."

Natalie didn't bother to comment, her mind was

taken up with imagining that scenario. Roy was old, ornery, and not someone she'd want holding a cleaver in the pressure cooker that was the kitchen at busy hour.

"It's a shame, though," Jan said now. "I'm really curious about our Mr. MacKenzie. I mean, what kind of man picks a sunset tee time?"

"It's probably when he gets off work," Natalie said with a shrug.

"Then why not golf in the morning, before he goes into work?" Jan said. "It has to be better than starting the course at twilight and then finishing it in full darkness, for heaven's sake. That's crazy! How does he even see his balls?"

Natalie opened her mouth, but before she could speak, Jan narrowed her eyes and snapped, "And don't say he drops his drawers and bends his head to look down. You know I'm talking golf balls."

"You spoil all my fun," Natalie complained on a laugh, and then said more seriously, "But what I was going to say is that I think he uses glow in the dark golf balls."

"Oh." Jan blinked. "Do they have those?"

"Apparently." Natalie stood and began to slide the drawings into the cardboard tube that protected them when she wasn't making adjustments to them.

"Why?" Jan asked with amazement. "I mean . . . glow in the dark balls? Surely there aren't a lot of people golfing in the dark who might need them?"

"Actually, I gather night golfing is a thing in some

places. I was reading an article about it and there are night golf courses in a lot of areas."

"Where?" Jan asked with open disbelief.

"Texas, Florida, Utah, Massachusetts," Natalie listed off. "There were other states mentioned, but I can't remember them all."

"None in Canada, though?" Jan asked. "Besides us, I mean."

"I'm not sure if there are any in Canada or not. The article I read was on American night golfing and the different places that offer it there," Natalie explained. "Anyway, we aren't really a night golf course ourselves. Those are all lit up with floodlights once the sun sets, and we don't do that. We just happen to have a client who likes to golf in the dark."

"And holds you up every night he does since you insist on waiting for him to finish before you mow the course," Jan pointed out with a scowl. "I don't know why you let him book so late."

"Because he spends a mint here," Natalie said patiently. "Valerian MacKenzie has booked for eighteen holes five or six times a week, every week since the end of June, and he rents a golf cart every single time."

"Yeah," Jan breathed, sounding resigned. But then she shook her head. "I wonder why he doesn't just buy a membership. That would have been a lot cheaper than paying every time."

"I know." Natalie frowned as she put the lid on the tube. "I did email and tell him that if he intended to continue to golf that often through the summer, a membership would be cheaper, but he continued to book online so I guess he doesn't care about the cost of—Why are you smiling at me like that?" she interrupted herself to ask.

"Because I'm pretty sure you're the only golf course owner in the world who would try to save a customer money at your own expense. His getting a membership would have cut into your profits and still you suggested it to him to save him money." Her smile widened. "It makes me proud to call you friend."

The words surprised another laugh from Natalie, but she didn't comment other than to say, "You should get going. Rick's probably foaming at the mouth waiting on you."

"Yeah." Jan glanced at her wristwatch before nodding and turning to thread her way back through the tables, but this time toward the smaller, upper dining room where the reception desk and exit were. "All righty, then. I'll see you tomorrow."

"Tomorrow," Natalie agreed. "Have fun tonight."

"You betcha," Jan responded easily, but then paused as she reached the screen door and swung back. "I almost forgot." Eyebrows rising in question, she asked, "A grocery list for the market in the morning?"

"Already emailed it to you," Natalie assured her, and then set down the tube and started around the table, saying, "But that reminds me . . . Wait here a sec." Not wanting to hold up the woman any longer than necessary, she didn't take the time to explain, but simply hurried into her office. After a quick dig through her purse, she returned to the dining area, holding out an envelope. "For you."

"What is it?" Jan asked with curiosity.

"A company credit card," Natalie announced. "I ordered it a while ago and it finally came in the mail today. I thought it would make shopping easier for you."

"Oh wow! Yeah, it will," Jan agreed, taking the envelope and opening it to retrieve the credit card inside. She peered at it for a minute, a smile tugging at her lips, and then raised her head and arched an eyebrow. "So, my plan worked. I've fooled you into trusting me."

Natalie just laughed and shook her head at the teasing.

"Jan got a company credit card?"

Natalie glanced around with surprise at that question to see Timothy, another employee, now standing behind the counter by the exit, waiting by the cash register. He must have returned in the few minutes that she was gone, but she hadn't heard the bell ring indicating that the door had opened. It wasn't the first time that had happened and she looked toward the door with a frown, thinking she needed to test it and see if it was the bell not working or just her being distracted enough not to notice it. If it was the bell, she'd have to fix it, she thought, and then turned raised eyebrows to Timothy.

"The nightcrawler is on the sixteenth hole, so I headed back to sign the guy out on the computer. Then I'll go out and wait to take the keys and put the golf cart away," the young man explained, answering her silent question. His word choice brought an immediate scowl to her face.

"Tim, I've told you. No nicknames for our clients. If he heard you and was offended, we could lose him as a customer."

Timothy grimaced and shrugged with unconcern. "Not a biggie. Then we wouldn't be stuck waiting on him to finish every night, and my Friday nights would stop being ruined. Besides, losing one customer wouldn't hurt."

"Oh no?" She arched an eyebrow. "So, if he stops coming, I can just take the money we would have made from him out of your paycheck, then?"

"What? No way! He comes nearly every damned night, and rents a cart every single time. I wouldn't have any money left in my paycheck if you—" His words died as she nodded solemnly. Looking irritated now, he muttered, "Fine. I won't call him nightcrawler again."

"Thank you," she said quietly.

Timothy nodded resentfully, and then glanced to Jan as she slid the shiny new credit card into her wallet. "So, do I get a credit card too?"

Natalie shook her head. "You don't need a credit card, Jan does. She shops for the kitchen daily on her way in."

"I shop for you," he countered at once. "Just last week you sent me to Home Hardware for that piece for the pump when the water feature broke down."

Natalie managed not to snap at him for his description of the issue. The water feature hadn't "broken down," at least not on its own; he'd helped, but she didn't bring that up and simply said, "That was the only time you've had to go buy something since I hired you two months ago, Tim. And that was only because it was an emergency. One trip to Home Hardware does not mean you need a company credit card."

"Or maybe you just don't trust me," he countered sulkily.

Natalie sighed inwardly at the accusation and the guilt it stirred in her. However, it was only a small bit of guilt, not enough to make her give him a company credit card to prove she did trust him, so she ignored his words and said, "If MacKenzie's on the sixteenth hole it should be fine to start mowing. Do holes five through ten. Those are farthest away from the last three holes where he is, so the noise shouldn't bother him. I'll wait for him to bring the golf cart back, then do the rest."

Tim was heading out before she'd finished speaking, but hesitated at the door. "I'll be done before you. Do you want me to help with your holes after I finish mine?"

Natalie shook her head. "I'll manage on my own. Just clock out when you're done. It's Friday night. I'm sure you have better things to do than mow the course."

"Oh yeah!" he said with a grin. "The Hoffman brothers are having a party, and now I might actually get there in time to have some fun."

"Good. Go," she said, and then moved around to stand behind the counter, her gaze sliding over the glass-fronted refrigerators that held the alcoholic and nonalcoholic drinks they sold to golfers. She'd have to restock it, as well as the snack stand, which held small bags of chips and such. Then she'd have to close out the cash register before she started to mow.

"You're too soft."

Natalie turned to find Jan now leaning against the opposite side of the counter, eyeing her with disapproval.

"Why?" she asked with mild amusement. "Because I'm letting him start mowing before MacKenzie's completely done the course?"

"That and because you're only making Tim mow six holes," Jan said solemnly. "That means you'll have to mow twelve yourself. It'll be after midnight before you're done."

Natalie managed not to grimace at those words, but knew they were true.

"It's fine," she said mildly. "It's Friday night, let him have fun. Besides, it's nearly nine thirty. Mia's gone to bed, Emily's here to keep an eye on things, so I'm free to mow."

"Yeah, but after mowing you have to put the equipment away and lock up. It'll be at least one before you get to bed and I know you get up at six in the morning. You need your sleep, Natalie."

"I can sleep when I'm dead," she said lightly, pulling a notepad out from under the counter and starting to write down what was missing from the drink refrigerators and the snack shelves so she'd know what to drag up from the basement where the items were stored.

"Dead might not be that far off if you don't start taking care of yourself," Jan snapped with clear frustration. "I know you're trying to save money for the addition you want to build, but your health is important. I wish you'd hire a couple more guys to handle the mowing."

Natalie sighed at the oft-repeated argument Jan gave her, and then rubbed the back of her neck to ease the tension tightening her muscles. "It's the last week of September, Jan. There's only another month or so left of the season. It's hardly worth hiring extra help for that short a time." Turning away from her, she started counting stock and making notes on her pad as she added, "After that, I won't have to mow anymore and will get loads of sleep."

Jan snorted. "Bull. Jimmy leaves for basic training at the end of October and I know darn well you plan to make the restaurant's take-out deliveries yourself rather than hire a replacement for him. You'll still be up late, just driving a car rather than the light reel mower."

"Don't you have a movie to go to?" Natalie asked, hoping to end the lecture.

Jan clucked her tongue with irritation, but did turn toward the door. "Fine. I'll go, but only because I'm late meeting Rick. I'll be discussing this with you again tomorrow, though, so don't think—"

Natalie looked around when Jan's words died on a sharp gasp. Seeing her staring out the screen door with wide eyes, she frowned slightly. "Jan? What is it?"

"Adonis," Jan breathed, moving closer to the door,

but making no move to open it. Instead, she stared fixedly out at something.

Curious, Natalie turned to peer out the window next to her, but the umbrellas on the patio blocked her view. Reminding herself to shut them before closing shop, she walked around the counter to join Jan at the door.

"What—?" she began, and then fell silent as her gaze landed on the blond man talking on his phone under the floodlight at the end of the path leading to the clubhouse.

"Is that MacKenzie?" Jan asked, her voice a little breathy.

"I don't know," Natalie said slowly, her gaze shifting over the man's figure in the dark clothes he wore. He was built like a Greek god. Muscular chest and shoulders in the black T-shirt he wore, and sculpted legs in the tight black jeans that rode low on narrow hips. She noted the golf bag slung over his shoulder, but quickly skipped up to the blond hair that was a little longer on the top than on the sides, long enough that several locks fell across his forehead as he lowered his head to listen to whoever was on the phone.

"Lift your head," Jan breathed. "You're too pretty to be looking down. Let me see your handsome face again. I—Oh there," she sighed as he lifted his head and began to speak into the phone. "Dear me. God was having a seriously good day when he made you."

Natalie couldn't argue that. God had outdone himself with this man. He was gorgeous, she acknowledged to herself as her gaze slid over his icy blond hair and sharp features. Then her gaze returned to the golf bag over his shoulder and she frowned. "That can't be MacKenzie. He booked a golf cart. He always does."

"So, he's another customer who likes to golf at night?" Jan asked, not taking her eyes off the man. "Is there anyone else booked right now?"

"No," Natalie admitted, her gaze sliding over the unknown man's face. "Valerian MacKenzie is the only one golfing right now."

"Then it must be him," Jan reasoned.

"Maybe," Natalie allowed. "But then where's his golf ca—?" Her question ended on a gasp when Adonis finished his call, and turned to glance toward the clubhouse as he slid his phone into his back pocket. It was Jan's alarmed squeal as much as the fact that the man's eyes landed directly on them staring out at him that had her leaping to the side and out of view.

Back plastered to the wall on the left of the door, she turned wide eyes to look at Jan, who was doing the same on the right-hand side. They were both breathing quickly and staring at each other with panic, and then Natalie gave her head a shake and pointed out, "We're acting like a couple of twelve-year-old girls."

"I know," Jan said, a grin suddenly busting out on her face. "Fun, huh?"

"Ridiculous," Natalie countered on a laugh, and stepped away from the wall.

"What are you doing?" Jan squealed. "He'll see you."

"You think he won't see us when he comes in here?" Natalie asked dryly, crossing in front of the door to walk around behind the counter again.

"Oh damn, you're right," Jan said with dismay, and quickly followed her.

The sound of the door opening caught her attention and Natalie shifted her gaze to it just in time to watch the Adonis enter. He was even more gorgeous up close. Taller and more muscular looking too, she thought as her gaze moved over his wide chest and thick arms. Not beefy, brawny arms, but nicely muscled. Beautiful, really, she thought. The man was a walking work of art.

"Good evening."

Natalie's eyes flickered back up to his face, but didn't quite make it to his eyes. His mouth was just so . . . and his cheekbones were . . . Realizing he had been speaking for a couple of moments and she hadn't heard a word he'd said, she forced herself to focus on what he was saying.

"—so, I thought I'd best let you know where I left it."

Natalie pressed her lips together, unsure what he was talking about. She took a moment, trying to find a way to avoid admitting she hadn't been listening, but then sighed and said, "I'm sorry. You thought it best to let me know where you left what?"

His eyebrows rose slightly, but he explained, "Your golf cart." When she didn't respond right away, he added, "As I said, it died on the seventeenth hole. Out of gas, I think."

"Oh." She blinked as her brain slowly processed what he was telling her, and then blinked again and said, "Oh no. I'm so sorry, Mr. . . . MacKenzie?" Natalie queried, just to be sure she'd grasped the situation and knew who she was talking to.

"Yes. Valerian MacKenzie," he confirmed.

"Right. Again, I'm so sorry. Roy usually makes sure every cart is fully fueled before releasing them to clients. I can't imagine why he—"

"Roy wasn't the one to set me up with the cart today. It was a young kid. Late teens, early twenties, dark hair."

"Roy left early," Jan reminded her, suddenly at her side in the crowded space behind the counter. "He had that appointment with the heart specialist."

"Right. Timothy set him up with the golf cart," Natalie muttered with a scowl, and then forced it away and managed a smile for MacKenzie. "I do apologize. Timothy doesn't usually take care of the carts. He must have forgotten to top up the fuel. I'll refund you for today's round and give you a credit for the next one to make up for the inconven—"

"That's not necessary," MacKenzie cut in to say. "I just wanted to let you know where your cart is."

"And I appreciate that, but you're a good customer and this *was* an inconvenience. I want to make it up to you," she said. "It'll be no trouble to you. You don't even have to be here for it. I have your credit card on record. I'll just refund your payment and—"

"No," Valerian interrupted the petite woman, and then offered a smile to temper the sharp word. She was a pretty little thing, her expression so sincere and earnest. She was trying to be fair, but in his opinion was offering too much. "I take some responsibility here too. I should have checked the gas gauge when I accepted the golf cart."

"You shouldn't have to," she responded solemnly. "That's Roy's job. Well, Tim's tonight since he covered for Roy," she added with a small frown, and then muttered almost to herself, "I'll have to remind him to check the fuel gauges on the carts to make sure they're full before he releases them next time. Although it's doubtful there'll be a next time."

Valerian's eyebrows flew up with concern at the possibility that the young Tim would lose his job over this.

Seeing that, and seeming to recognize where his thoughts had gone, the woman quickly explained, "Roy never takes time off. So, it's doubtful Tim will have to take his place again."

"Oh." Valerian relaxed. "Still, while I appreciate the offer to refund me for the night, that's a bit extreme and completely unnecessary."

She was shaking her head before he even finished talking. Knowing she was going to be stubborn about this, he quickly slid into her thoughts to give her a gentle nudge to make her accept his refusal and be content with it. However, Valerian was met by a brick wall. He couldn't get into her thoughts.

Startled, he blinked and then frowned and tried again . . . with the same results. Her mind was closed to him. Pulling his own mind back, Valerian gave his head a shake and then simply stared at the woman who might well be his life mate.

She was short. Or at least shorter than he would have expected his life mate to be. Valerian was six-foot-two himself, and he would have placed her at five-two or five-three, so a good foot or so shorter than him. She was also extremely thin, with her collarbones looking sharp and boney where the scooped neckline of her T-shirt revealed them, and there were pink, almost red bags under her eyes rather than the dark shade most people got. Even so, she was still lovely to him, with large green-almost-teal eyes, full, inviting lips, and long, wavy dark hair.

Lovely, but she needed food and more sleep was his diagnosis, and then Valerian tuned in to what she was saying and decided it was frustrating not being able to control her.

"—so, I'll process the refund later tonight. Right now, though, if you'll give me the key, you can be on your way and I'll go gas up the cart and bring it in."

Valerian stared at her blankly, his gaze moving from her expectant expression to the hand she was holding out over the counter. He then glanced down at the key with the Shady Pines Golf Course fob he'd forgotten he held.

"Oh. Right," he muttered, and held his hand out. Her fingers brushed his skin as she took the key fob from him, and they both gave a little start at the electricity it sparked between them. Valerian almost closed his fingers around hers in response to the visceral jolt, but the presence of the other woman stopped him just as he started to curl his fingers.

If his reaction had been to want to grab her and

hold on, hers was obviously the opposite. While the petite brunette had given a start at the initial jolt, she had then snatched her hand back and pressed it to her chest. Her other hand was now rubbing it as if to erase the tingling sensation they'd both experienced. She also took a step back from the counter, instinctively putting space between them.

Noting the avid curiosity on the face of the other woman—a tall, thin redhead with a narrow face, large green eyes, and freckles—Valerian forced a smile and said, "Good night," then simply turned and headed outside.

He had his phone out and was dialing Stephanie McGill's number before the door had quite closed behind him. Valerian listened to it ring as he crossed the patio at the side of the building where tables were set up for golfers to enjoy a meal or drink before or after their round. He was rounding the corner of the building by the time his call was picked up.

Two

"Finally," was Stephanie's enigmatic greeting when she answered the phone.

Valerian came to an abrupt halt in front of the club-house and echoed uncertainly, "Finally?"

"Yes. It took you long enough," she said, sounding amused now.

Valerian pulled the phone away from his ear to look at the face of it as if that would explain her words. He felt like she was speaking Dutch to him. Well, not Dutch. He spoke Dutch. Actually, he spoke several languages, but that was neither here nor there. Giving his head a shake, he put the phone back to his ear and asked, "It took me long enough to what?"

"To find your life mate," Stephanie said as if that should be obvious.

Valerian's eyes narrowed at the words. Life mates were like the pot of gold at the end of the rainbow for unmated immortals like himself. A precious, longed-for gift that each of them searched for. It could, and often did, take centuries or even millennia to find that one person, mortal or immortal, that they could not read or control and could live happily in peace with. Someone like the petite brunette he'd just met in the clubhouse was for him. Or at least appeared to be. The main sign of a life mate was the inability to read or control them, as had happened when he'd tried to read the brunette.

Of course, there were occurrences when an immortal couldn't read a mortal for other reasons. For instance, madness and brain tumors had been known to inter-fere with reading and controlling mortals. But judging by Stephanie's words, that wasn't the case here. The brunette was indeed a possible life mate to him. The word *possible* being inserted there because while he, as an immortal, recognized what she was and what they could have together, the brunette didn't and had the free will to refuse to be his mate, just as she would with any man, mortal or immortal.

Pushing that thought away for now, he considered Stephanie's words. "It took you long enough . . . to find your life mate." As if she had known all along that Natalie was his. And probably she had, he thought grimly. While Marguerite was usually the one who set up life mates with their partners, Stephanie had some skill in that area too. She also had some strange woo-woo going on with her. She could read absolutely everyone but her mate, even older immortals, and apparently she could read minds over the phone since she'd known why he was calling.

Or, Valerian considered, maybe this was a different branch of that woo-woo stuff Stephanie had going on. There was some suggestion she could see the future or something. That would explain her knowing that he would call about the brunette.

"How do you know why I called? Did you see it in my future?"

Stephanie snorted at the suggestion. "No, I didn't *see* it."

"Well, then how—?"

"Why else would you call?" she interrupted him to ask. "You've never called me or Thorne before, so I figured you'd met her. You have met her, right? At the local golf course?"

"Yes," he sighed the word.

"Finally," she repeated her greeting with exasperation. "I can't believe it took this long! I mean, come on, Valerian! You got crazy quick possession of the farmhouse, and have lived there all summer. It's now the end of September. As nuts as you are about golfing, I expected you to want to take a gander at the local golfing hole right away."

"I did," Valerian admitted, starting to walk again, heading for the parking lot. "I've been golfing here at the Shady Pines Golf Course since the day after moving onto the farm at the end of June. Thanks for pointing me in the direction of the farm, by the way."

"Well, you said you liked the area, and I noticed her

in town and was quite sure she'd be a mate to you, and then I heard from my neighbor that the farm down the road was for sale and—" He could picture Stephanie shrugging in the pause before she finished with, "It seemed too perfect. Obviously, you and Natalie were meant to be."

"Natalie?" he asked quickly. "Is that her name?"

There was a pause and then Stephanie asked, "Haven't you met her yet?"

"Yesss." He drew the word out with the uncertainty he was suddenly feeling. Valerian was ninety-nine percent sure they were talking about the same woman, but there could be other women working at the golf course besides the two he'd just met. Maybe he couldn't read the little brunette because she had a brain tumor and it was another woman Stephanie was speaking of. Which wasn't likely, he acknowledged. Still, it was just as likely as his actually meeting his life mate at all and while still so young. Valerian had only been born in 1790. The chances of finding his life mate before reaching four or five hundred years old was like winning the lottery would be for a mortal.

"Are we talking about a petite brunette?" Stephanie asked abruptly. "Pretty blue-green eyes? Owns the golf course?"

"She owns it?" he asked with surprise. He'd just assumed she was an employee there.

"Oh my God." Stephanie's voice was full of irritation. "You've been golfing there for three months and don't know her name is Natalie, or that she owns the golf course? How is that even possible?"

"It's possible because I never met her until tonight," Valerian said with irritation. "I book and pay for my tee time online. The only person I've ever met before tonight was Roy, the old guy who supplies me with a golf cart when I get here and takes the keys from me when I'm done."

"Be still my beating heart, an old fart immortal who actually knows about computers and how to use them," Stephanie said with wonder.

"I'm not old," Valerian growled as he reached the end of the walkway and started across the large parking lot toward his silver pickup truck. "In fact, by immortal standards I'm considered practically a child."

"Yeah, well, by mortal standards you're freaking ancient," Stephanie informed him. "And few immortals over one hundred even deign to look at computers, let alone know how to work them."

"That's not true either," Valerian assured her. "My parents . . ." His words died as the sound of women's voices had him glancing back the way he'd come. Natalie and the redhead were coming around the building, chattering away. Valerian stopped to watch them, his gaze focused wholly on the petite brunette.

"Valerian?"

"Hmm?" he murmured, watching the women separate with the tall redhead walking his way, while Natalie headed for the large outbuilding where the golf carts were kept. Probably getting gas to take out to the cart, he thought, his gaze following her until she disappeared into the large, barnlike building. He then glanced toward the redhead to see she'd gone to the smaller parking lot next to the clubhouse with an Employee Parking sign at the entrance. She was getting into a silver SUV. There was also an older-looking Corolla, and an even older white pickup truck parked there, and he wondered which if either belonged to his woman.

"Natalie," he murmured the name, testing it out. "Natalie. Nat. Nattie. No, Nattie is just—"

"Valerian?" Stephanie repeated, sounding a little exasperated.

Valerian grunted in response, but asked, "Natalie what?"

"Moncreif," Stephanie said with exasperation, before bursting out, "I can't believe you didn't at least ask her name! I don't know if it's because you're all so old, or because you're used to just taking control of mortals to get what you want, but you boys are seriously lacking in game."

"I have game," he protested at once. "And I don't just control mortal women to 'get what I want' as you put it. I haven't even been interested in sex in a good seventy years, but when I was, I didn't control women to get it."

"No?" Stephanie asked with interest. "What did you do?"

"I wooed them," he said firmly.

"Wooed?" Stephanie snorted at the thought. "You mean you let those extra-supercharged pheromones the nanos send out of you do all the work and caught the women when they fell in your lap."

"No, I—" Valerian paused, and then sighed as he

realized he had pretty much let those supercharged nanos do all the work. There was very little wooing needed when the women were drawn to you like moths to a flame.

Shaking his head, he changed tactics and instead explained, "I didn't exactly walk into the golf club thinking I'd meet my life mate, Stephanie. And once I realized I couldn't read her, I was too stunned to think to ask her name. Speaking of which," he added grimly, "a heads-up would have been nice. Why didn't you tell me you thought you'd encountered my life mate and that I'd find her at the golf club? Christ, she's been down the road from me for three months and the only reason I met her tonight was because my golf cart ran out of gas, forcing me to go into the clubhouse to let them know that and where it was. Otherwise, we might never have met at all," Valerian finished with a combination of anger and horror as he realized that was more than possible. If the golf cart hadn't run out of gas he could have continued booking online, and golfing here for years without encountering his life mate.

"Well, then I guess it was lucky that you ran out of gas," Stephanie said mildly.

Valerian scowled at that response. "Why the hell didn't you give me a heads-up?"

"Because if I'd been wrong about her being a possible life mate, it would have been devastating to you. Whereas if I was right, it would be a nice surprise. It *is* a nice surprise, isn't it?" she asked pointedly.

Valerian released a deep sigh, allowing his anger to flow out with his breath. Yes. It was a nice surprise.

It was like a lifetime of Christmases wrapped up in one moment of time. He just wished he'd known and met her sooner. They might already be mated by now. But he supposed he should be grateful Stephanie had steered him in this direction to begin with. After all, if she hadn't encouraged him to buy the farmhouse, they definitely would have never met.

"Isn't it?" Stephanie prodded.

"Yes. It is," he acknowledged, and then added a gruff, "Thank you, Stephanie."

"No need to thank me. I'm just glad you finally met her."

"Yeah," Valerian murmured, and turned to continue walking to his truck as a small frown started to pull his lips and eyebrows down. "Now I just have to figure out how to woo her."

"Yeah."

Something in her voice had his footsteps slowing and wariness creeping over him.

"What?" he asked with concern.

"I—It's nothing. Except . . ." A long sigh slid down the line. "Valerian, she won't be easy to claim. Expect to have to put in some effort."

Pausing beside his pickup, Valerian began to search for his keys as he said, "It's never really easy, though, is it, Steph? Or are you suggesting it will be harder than usual? Is there something in her background I should know about?"

"Yes, there is something both in her past and her present that might make it harder than most. But she should be the one to tell you about that," Stephanie said solemnly, and then advised, "Just step lightly and expect some resistance."

"Resistance, huh? Can you at least give me a hint or—ah, hell," he muttered when searching his pockets didn't turn up his keys and Valerian suddenly recalled where he last saw them.

"What?" Stephanie asked. "Is something wrong?"

"Yeah. No," Valerian answered, contradicting himself as he slung his golf bag off his shoulder and set it in the back of the pickup. He then turned on his heel to head back the way he'd come as he explained, "I just realized I left my keys on the dash of the golf cart and have to go back for them."

"Good," Stephanie said with satisfaction.

"What's good about it?" he asked with irritation.

"You might get another chance to talk to Natalie now," she pointed out with a grin in her voice. "Good luck, Valerian. Have fun. Don't do anything I wouldn't do."

The words were said in a singsong voice and were followed by dead silence as she ended the call.

"Don't do anything I wouldn't do." Valerian muttered the words to himself as he put the phone away. From what he'd heard, Stephanie and Thorne did things he *couldn't* do, let alone wouldn't do. Fair dues, the guy had wings, but sex in the air while flying? Yeah, that was something he definitely couldn't and wouldn't do. But maybe it was just gossip and untrue.

After all, life mates tended to pass out during sex, which wouldn't be good if they were a hundred feet up in the air, and Stephanie and Thorne were definitely life mates, as well as happy, something he'd never thought he'd be able to say about Stephanie McGill. In fact, for quite a while there, he, and most of the other Enforcers, had feared she'd go rogue and they'd have to hunt down the young woman and bring her in for execution. None of them had been pleased to have to consider that possibility. They'd all liked Stephanie and felt bad about what had happened to her. None of them had wanted the job of taking her down if the turn had ultimately driven her mad and she'd gone rogue.

But that wasn't a likelihood now that she'd found her life mate.

And now he had found his, Valerian thought. He just had to find out what there was in her past and present that might throw a wrench in his claiming her, fix it, and woo her into being his life mate. Easy.

"Right," Valerian growled with a shake of the head, and pulled out his phone to check messages as he started down the path to the eighteenth hole.

Three

Natalie spent the first half of her walk from the equipment barn to the seventeenth hole muttering to herself about the stupidity of males and how one young male in particular was becoming a pain in her arse. How could Timothy not check the gas in the golf cart before releasing it to a client? That was just . . . well, it should be common sense.

But to be fair, it wasn't normally Timothy's job, so he might not have thought of it, the objective part of her mind argued. *And he* had *been good about coming in early to fill in for Roy. And mistakes were to be expected when someone was new on a job.*

Natalie grimaced at her fair side. It was all true, of course. But this wasn't the first mistake Timothy had made in the last few weeks, and the mistakes he was making weren't small ones.

Every muscle in her body tightened as Natalie considered the two biggest mistakes. One had to do with the water feature Timothy had mentioned earlier. He had lost control of the reel mower, run off the course into the water feature, and hit the pump. That had cost her money and time. The other big mistake hadn't cost her anything in the end, but it could have killed her business. It happened just a week before the pump incident. She'd asked him to fertilize the turf. Timothy had filled the tank of the sprayer and had been heading out to begin spraying when Natalie arrived at the shop. She'd gone to check on the fertilizer and see if they had enough for another spray later or if she needed to order more and nearly had a heart attack when she saw all the empty containers of herbicide. Timothy had somehow confused one for the other and was about to spray her entire golf course with a chemical that didn't just kill weeds, but turf too. They used it to edge the sand traps to prevent the grass from spreading into the bunkers, and he was about to spray the whole course with that rather than the fertilizer.

Fortunately, she'd managed to catch up to Timothy before he got out of the parking lot. But had she not checked on him and happened to spot the mistake, he could have killed off every blade of grass on the course and put her out of business. The kid was giving her an ulcer.

By the time Natalie reached the eighteenth hole, she was too out of breath to even mutter her displeasure. She was hauling a five-gallon gas can that she'd foolishly filled to the top, which meant it weighed a good thirty pounds. That wasn't too bad. She probably would have managed it well enough if she were in better shape, and if the gas can weren't older than even she was. It was an ancient metal one with a handle that had twisted over time and was now digging painfully into her hand.

Had Natalie been using her head instead of fretting over the latest problem Timothy had caused for her, she would have filled it only a quarter full. She didn't need five gallons to get the cart back to the shop from the seventeenth hole. But she hadn't been using her head, and while the can had been heavy when she'd picked it up, it hadn't seemed too terribly bad. Now those thirty pounds were feeling like ninety and didn't seem so manageable anymore.

Wincing, Natalie set the gas can down. The plan was to shift her hold in the hopes of easing the pain the handle was causing, but the sound of rustling leaves to her right stopped her from picking it up again. Straightening quickly, she glanced toward the tree line that ran alongside the eighteenth hole. When she'd set out, the moonlight had lit the open path enough that she hadn't even thought of grabbing a flashlight. But the trees were just a dark blob along the side of the course. She couldn't even distinguish shapes, let alone sort out what was making that rustling sound. It could have been the leaves in the trees, or could have been leaves on the ground. They'd had a couple of cold evenings recently, encouraging some of the deciduous trees to start shedding, and the sound was similar to that of someone traipsing through dry, fallen leaves.

The rustling stopped abruptly now that she wasn't

moving, but rather than be relieved, Natalie felt a sudden prickling along her neck that made her heartbeat speed up. She listened for another moment, but when no other sound reached her ears, she told herself she was being silly. There was no one there. This was the country, after all, not a dark parking lot in the city where muggers or rapists might be lurking in the shadows.

"It was probably a stray cat, or a fox or something," Natalie muttered to herself, and bent to pick up the can again. She'd barely taken two steps, though, before the rustling sounded again. Someone or something was moving through the woods parallel to her. She tried again to tell herself that it was just a stray cat or fox, but other less benign options were now pushing their way into her thoughts. Coyotes, for instance.

Were coyotes known to attack people? Natalie wondered about that as she instinctively began to move a little more quickly. She was just telling herself that wasn't likely when she recalled the story that had gone viral some weeks back about a young girl who had been chased and attacked by a coyote while walking her dog. The dog, a little breed as she recalled, had fought off the animal, but had been wounded doing so.

"Brilliant," Natalie muttered to herself, realizing she was freaking herself out and now imagining a whole pack of coyotes trailing her along the course. The snapping of a branch caught her ear then and she instinctively stopped again and whirled to search the trees with eyes straining to see anything in the dark. Much to her surprise, the trees had thinned out here, and she actually could make out shapes now. Including what appeared to be a human form in some kind of long coat or cape ducking behind a tree trunk.

"Hello?" Natalie called out when the figure didn't reappear on the other side of the tree. Clearing her throat when she heard how weak her voice sounded, she tried to sound brave and a little annoyed when she added, "I know you're there."

Natalie waited, aware that the prickling had traveled from her neck to the back of her scalp now, and her heart was suddenly racing. It was a full-body scream of alarm, urging her to run. She managed to fight off the urge, but did turn and continue to the bend that led to the seventeenth hole. She was moving as quickly as she could, though, while lugging the heavy gas can, and her gaze was continually shooting to the side, scanning the trees as she went.

It was the sudden soft hiss of a voice that finally broke her last nerve. Giving up any attempt to seem unafraid and calm, Natalie broke into a run, the gas can banging against her leg as she went. But the rustling in the woods was keeping abreast of her and actually sounded like it was getting closer, as if whoever was in the woods was moving out of them after her.

Dropping the can with a yelp at this realization, Natalie put on a burst of speed and charged around the bend, looking back toward the woods now. That was a mistake. In her panic, she'd forgotten about the pond just around the bend, a trap before the seventeenth hole. Many golfers lost their balls in its depths. Tonight, it caught her as well.

Looking back as she was, Natalie didn't see it and re-called the presence of the pond only when the ground suddenly slanted downward at a sharp pitch under her feet. She swung her head around at once, briefly noted the dark shape of a person on the other side of the pond as she tried to stop her forward motion, but was distracted by cold water splashing over her feet as she tried to stumble to a halt. Her efforts were made use-less when she lost her footing and tumbled forward, her arms pinwheeling. Natalie felt the water closing over her just before pain exploded in her forehead and the world around her faded to black.

Valerian had just reached the golf cart when a yelp from behind had him turning to look around. His attention was immediately caught by the running woman coming around the bend from the eighteenth hole. He wasn't sure what was happening, but that yelp had sounded alarmed and the woman—Natalie, he realized—appeared to be in a full-blown panic as she charged forward. She was also looking back the way she'd come as if someone was chasing her.

Concerned, Valerian started around the large water feature between them, expecting her to run around it to him for aid with whatever trouble had come up. It actually took him several steps before he realized that she wasn't swerving to avoid the pond. In fact, it didn't appear to him as if Natalie even realized she was about to sprint into the water feature. Even as he realized this and opened his mouth to shout a warning, she hit the part where the land slanted downward toward the pond. Natalie turned her head then, her gaze briefly meeting his before her attention was taken up with her efforts to remain on her feet as she careened into the water. She was obviously trying to stop herself—her arms were pinwheeling and alarm was blooming on her face—but then she suddenly seemed to stumble and did a belly flop into the shallow water.

Wincing at the slapping sound as her body met the water's surface, Valerian slowed, trying to think how to handle the situation, because he was quite sure she would probably be embarrassed that he'd witnessed this. He pondered the matter for a couple of steps and then realized that Natalie wasn't bouncing back to her feet and wading out of the water as he would have expected. In fact, she appeared to be floating, as if she—

Cursing, Valerian burst into a dead run at immortal speed. He charged around the pond to where she'd fallen, and waded in after her, scooping her out of the water a few bare seconds after she went in. Even so, his heart was pounding like a drum, panic racing through his body. That panic didn't ease when Valerian noted the wound on her forehead as he carried her quickly back to the grassy bank. Laying her on her back there, he knelt to press his ear to her chest.

The relief that seeped through him at the sound of her heart still beating and her lungs taking in oxygen left him weak for a moment. He'd got to her quickly enough that she hadn't even taken in water. He sat up and looked over her face and the bleeding wound on her forehead, trying to sort out where she'd got it. There had been no one near her when he'd seen her going into the water, or even when he'd seen her running, but he glanced around now anyway, using his night vision to pierce the dark trees. He thought he caught a glimpse of a figure moving away quickly through the line of woods, but it was such a quick flash before the evergreens and oaks obscured it that he wasn't sure it hadn't just been a branch moving.

Valerian peered down at Natalie again, gathered her in his arms, and stood. He wasn't sure how she'd been injured. Even if there had been someone in the woods, they hadn't been close enough to hit her, and he hadn't heard a gunshot or anything. Besides, her injury didn't look like a bullet wound, more a jagged split, as if she'd hit her head on something. Perhaps in the water, Valerian thought as he headed for the eighteenth hole.

He spotted the gas tank a moment later. Valerian peered at the red can on its side in the grass, then took another look around, wondering why she'd dropped it and taken off running. Unfortunately, there was nothing that could answer that question and he supposed he'd have to wait for Natalie to wake up to solve the mystery.

Leaving that worry for now, he hurried on his way again, eager to get Natalie back to the clubhouse so that he could examine her wound. Then he'd have to take her to the hospital. Mortals were an odd breed, hearty in some ways and fragile in others. He wasn't taking any chances with this woman. He'd stop in the clubhouse to find a blanket or something to wrap her in to keep her warm, and then drive her to the hospital in his pickup and—

"Shit!" Valerian muttered suddenly, coming to an abrupt halt. His keys were still in the golf cart. Half turning, he glanced back toward the seventeenth hole, but he was almost to the clubhouse now. He could have her inside warming up in seconds.

Turning abruptly, Valerian continued along the path, thinking he'd get her inside, find something to wrap her in to warm her, then run back for his keys. Once back he'd pull his pickup as close to the door as he could and then go in to get her. It seemed like a solid plan to him and would have worked beautifully if a huge polar bear hadn't charged at him the moment he stepped out of the trees at the end of the eighteenth hole and started across the yard toward the clubhouse door.

He heard a woman whisper-hiss, "Sinbad, no," just before one hundred and fifty pounds of white fur launched itself at him. Valerian barely had a chance to brace himself before two huge paws landed, one on his chest and the other on the arm he had around Natalie's upper body. A long tongue then began to wash the face of the unconscious woman he was carrying.

"Sinbad! Get—Oh my God! What happened? Get down, Sinbad. Down! Is Natalie okay? What happened?"

Since the animal wasn't reacting at all to the almost whispered orders of the young woman rushing toward him with a cute little blonde cherub on her hip, Valerian took a moment to scowl at the beast and growled, "Down. Now," in a calm commanding tone.

When what turned out to be a very fluffy white dog immediately dropped back to all four paws on the ground, he nodded at the animal and then turned his attention to the young woman as she reached him. She was now clutching the sleeping child almost protectively to her chest, her wide anxious eyes shifting between him and Natalie.

"What happened?" she repeated as he read the name Emily from her mind.

Valerian hesitated, debating just taking control of what he could now see was really a young woman of about nineteen. But in the end, he held off controlling her and explained, "The golf cart I rented ran out of gas on the seventeenth hole. Natalie was going out to refill it and fetch it back, but fell in the water trap on her way. I think she hit her head."

When Emily continued to stare at him with uncertainty, he moved past her and headed for the steps to the patio as he added, "Fortunately, I'd left my keys in the cart and had gone back to get them. I was able to get her out of the water right away, but when I pulled her out, she had the head wound and was unconscious."

"She could have drowned," Emily said with dismay, rushing past to open the door for him when he reached it.

"Thank you," Valerian muttered. He took several steps into the room with the cash counter and a few tables, but then paused and glanced around at the small upper dining area. "Is there somewhere I can set her down? I didn't get my keys. I'll have to go back for them, and then we can take her to the hospital in my truck."

"Oh. The office." Emily rushed forward and led him through the restaurant and along a hall to a large office. There was a desk on one side and a sitting area on the other where a couch sat before a television.

Valerian waited patiently as the girl set down the now stirring little cherub she was carrying and rushed over to remove the coloring books and toys that were strewn on the couch. Once the faux leather surface was cleared, Valerian laid Natalie on it.

"She's wet," he announced as he straightened. "If you could find a blanket or something to wrap her in to keep her warm for the ride to the hospital while I go back for my keys, that would be—"

"Sinbad, stop that!" Emily interrupted him to snap, and he turned to see that the white beast had moved up to the couch the moment his back was turned and was solicitously licking the blood from Natalie's wound. Valerian stepped closer at once, intending to urge the dog away, but stopped when Natalie stirred and reached weakly toward the furry creature, muttering, "Sin."

"Natalie! Thank God you're awake!" The girl rushed forward, hip-checking Valerian out of the way in her eagerness to reach the woman.

Natalie heard Emily's words, but her mind was a mass of confusion and pain. She was also struggling to hold back Sinbad, the large white Great Pyrenees dog she'd got for security when she'd moved here nearly three years ago. The great beast was huge and hard to hold back as he whined and tried to lick her face. Managing to fend him off, she closed her eyes briefly, hoping the pain in her head would ease and allow her thinking to clear.

"Are you all right? What happened? This man said you fell in a water trap? Is that true?"

Blinking her eyes open as her memory filtered past the pain in her head, Natalie squinted at Emily and swallowed heavily, before managing a gruff "Yes."

Movement had her gaze moving past her daughter's nanny to the man towering behind her. She recognized Valerian MacKenzie and then her gaze drifted away and she saw that she was lying on the couch in her office. Confusion immediately returned then. The last thing she remembered was the water closing over her and then pain exploding in her forehead. Her voice was surprisingly weak and thready when she asked, "How did I get here?"

"He pulled you out of the water and carried you back," Emily explained, gesturing at the man looming behind her.

"Oh. Thank you for that, Mr. MacKenzie," Natalie mumbled politely, though she was still a little confused about what had happened.

"Call me Valerian," he said, his voice deep, smooth, and ridiculously sexy.

Natalie didn't respond; instead, she struggled to a sitting position, ignoring the protests of both Emily and Valerian MacKenzie that she should remain lying down. The rest of her memories were drifting back to her now: lugging the gas can out across the eighteenth hole of the golf course, headed for seventeen. The sound of someone trailing her from the woods to her side. How it had spooked her . . .

"Mama!"

That excited cry from her daughter gave her a moment's warning and Natalie managed to brace herself as the little girl launched at her, arms out and up in a demand to be picked up. Ignoring the pain it caused her, she lifted the two-and-a-half-year-old to her lap and hugged her briefly, then pulled back and glanced down when something poked her in the chest.

"What do you have there, sweetheart?" Natalie asked, frowning when she noted that her voice still wasn't at its full strength. In the next moment, that worry was forgotten as she spotted the small statuette of an angel that her daughter was holding. Natalie had never seen it before, and stared at it blankly, and then blanched as it sparked another memory in her head.

"Angel," she whispered faintly, and then shuddered as the word echoed down her memory in a growly hiss, the same growly hiss that she'd heard out on the course.

"What is it?" Valerian MacKenzie asked sharply.

"I thought I heard someone trailing me through the woods on the way out to the seventeenth hole, and then they hissed what sounded like the word *angel*. It spooked me," she confessed, almost embarrassed now to admit it. But that voice had sounded so malevolent.

A fine shudder ran through her again, and she muttered, "It was probably the wind . . . or you," she added, lifting her eyes to Valerian MacKenzie and narrowing them on him.

"I was nowhere near the woods," he assured her solemnly. "I had just reached the golf cart when I heard you yelp and saw you come running around the bend from the eighteenth hole. I didn't know what was happening, but you seemed in some distress, so I headed toward you just as you fell into the water trap. I fetched you out, and brought you back here. I was nowhere near the woods, and certainly didn't call you angel."

Natalie stared at him silently, unsure whether she should believe him or not, but her headache made thinking too much of an effort. She gave up on the worry and tore her gaze from the man to look down at the little statuette before raising her head again to ask Emily, "Did you give this to Mia?"

Emily adored Natalie's daughter and was always bringing little treats or inexpensive dollar store toys for Mia when she came to work. But the girl shook her head. "No. It was on your desk."

"My desk?" Natalie asked with surprise.

"Yes. I saw it there when I set Mia down to keep her out of the way while I removed her toys and books from the couch," she explained, and then grimaced apologetically. "I'm sorry. I should have moved it to the bookshelf or something where she couldn't reach it, but I was just in such a panic to clear the way so Mr. MacKenzie could lay you down."

"That's fine," Natalie said soothingly, knowing the girl thought she was angry at her. She wasn't, of course. What she was feeling was really confusion and concern. She had no idea how the statue had got on her desk. She certainly hadn't put it there. But just looking at it reminded her of her experience on the course, and the panic she'd felt when that word had come out of the darkness in that growly voice.

Mouth thinning with distaste, she held the statuette out to Emily. "Get rid of this, please."

"Get rid of it?" Emily asked with surprise, peering down at the statue as she accepted it. "Like throw it out?"

"Yes. Throw it out," Natalie said clearly. "I don't know where it came from, or how it got on my desk, but it's not mine. Throw it out."

"But . . . shouldn't I put it in the lost and found box or something? I mean, Jan or Timothy must have put it on your desk if you didn't," she pointed out.

Natalie frowned at that possibility. She knew Timothy hadn't. She'd been here all day until he'd gone to mow the course and he hadn't gone anywhere near the hall, let alone her office when he came in. As for Jan, she supposed the other woman might have put the statuette on her desk. At least she would have had more of an opportunity than Timothy to do it, but Natalie couldn't see why she would.

She'd barely had that thought when it occurred to her that she hadn't seen the statuette on her desk when she'd come into her office to fetch the credit card for Jan, and Jan had never left the dining area after that until they'd both walked out, Jan to head home and her to go fetch gas to fill up the golf cart and bring it back. So, the statuette had been left sometime after she'd headed out to walk to the seventeenth hole . . . where someone had hissed "Angel" at her through the darkness, spooking her enough to send her crashing into the water trap.

"I'll just put it in the lost and found box for now," Emily said, reclaiming her attention as she headed for the door. "After all, it could be someone's lucky charm. It probably fell out of their pocket while golfing and Jan or Timothy found it and brought it in."

Natalie opened her mouth, intending to insist she throw the damned thing out, but then closed it on a sigh. Emily would just toss it in the garbage can next to her desk, and frankly, Natalie didn't want it anywhere near her, even in her garbage. At least the lost and found box was under the counter where the cash register was. As far from her office as it could get without her actually throwing it in the burn pile or taking it to the dump. Which she intended to do the first chance she got.

Irritated that the cheap little plastic statuette troubled her so much, she tried to push it from her mind and glanced down at Mia. The little girl was slumped against her chest asleep, and the sight made Natalie relax as love poured through her. She was such a precious little girl, so sweet and lovely. *Sugar and spice and all things nice*, Natalie thought to herself with a faint smile. That was her Mia, everything good in the world, her one bright light and the only reason she was still alive at this point.

Valerian watched Natalie with the child he now realized was her daughter. He'd assumed the girl was Emily's child until she'd cried, "Mama," and thrown herself at his life mate. But he now knew Emily was actually her nanny, and Mia was Natalie's daughter. The shock of that knowledge had kept him mostly silent since Natalie had woken up. And it *was* a shock. Not a pleasant one either. It wasn't that Valerian had anything against children. Honestly, this one was an adorable little bundle. But wooing a mortal into agreeing to be a life mate was a difficult task at the best of times. The one ace in the hole that an immortal held to help them claim their mate was life mate sex, which was said to be crazy hot, addictive as hell, and overwhelming to the point it left both parties unconscious at the end. Valerian would have had no guilt at all in utilizing that to convince Natalie to become a part of his life . . . if it weren't for Mia. She was young enough to need constant supervision. Natalie would never forgive him if he seduced her, they both passed out, and harm came to an unattended Mia.

That was a problem he hadn't even considered. None of the daydreams he'd had over the decades about finding and claiming his life mate had included a scenario where his life mate had a child. Valerian was considering it now though, and what his mind was telling him was that life mate sex was off the table until he found a way to ensure it was done safely. For now he'd have to court Natalie the old-fashioned way, with a hands-off policy.

Valerian was still struggling with that when he realized that Emily had left the room. He focused on Natalie's face just in time to see it begin to almost glow with love as she peered down at her daughter, and was surprised to feel a pang of jealousy. He wanted her to look at him that way, which was ridiculous, he knew. They'd just met. But someday she *would* look at him that way . . . if he didn't screw things up.

Grimacing at that last thought, Valerian shifted his gaze to her forehead and frowned. "Your wound hasn't stopped bleeding."

Natalie glanced at him as if surprised he was still there, and then reached up to feel her forehead. A small wince pulled at her features as the light touch apparently caused her pain. "How bad is it?"

Valerian moved closer and bent slightly to examine the wound. There was a lot of dry blood crusted on and around it, and fresh blood still oozing out. The area around the tear in her skin was also beginning to swell and bruise.

Aware that Natalie was waiting for an answer, Valerian straightened. "Not as bad as I first thought. But head wounds are tricky," he pointed out, and turned toward the door. "I'll go get my keys from the golf cart so I can take you to the hospital to get checked over."

"Oh, that's not necessary," she protested. "I'm fine."

Valerian stopped and turned back to respond, just in time to see that while she'd started to rise from the couch with Mia in her arms, she'd only got halfway up and was now dropping back to sit on the couch again, her expression a little dazed.

Suspecting her attempt to rise had made her dizzy, he pointed out, "You took a bad blow to the head and lost consciousness. We should really have you looked at by a doctor to be sure everything is okay and you didn't sustain trauma that might be a problem later."

Valerian didn't wait for her to agree, but continued out of the office, nearly running into Emily as he entered the hall. The young woman jumped back in surprise, and then backed up several steps before whisper-hissing, "She needs to go to the hospital."

"Yes. She does," Valerian agreed mildly.

"But she won't go," Emily predicted unhappily, and told him, "I think she has some kind of phobia about the hospital and doctors from when her whole family died."

Valerian stiffened. "Her whole family died?"

"Yeah. Her husband, her three-year-old son, and her parents all died in a car accident three years ago. T-boned by a drunk driver, I heard," she said. "Mia was born six months later, and I honestly don't think she's even seen a doctor since then. I know she hasn't since I started working for her. Oh sure, she takes Mia for checkups and shots, but she never sees one for her own sake. Even when she burned her hand really bad in the kitchen last year. It was definitely an emergency room burn, but she wouldn't go. She just kept putting some salve on it and wrapping it up." Her mouth compressed at the memory. "It took months to heal, but she's damned lucky it did. I was sure she needed a skin graft or something and her hand would get infected and fall off. But it did heal. Finally, and with a nasty scar," she added grimly, and then sighed and said, "So I'm pretty sure she won't go to the hospital about her head."

"Well, if Mohammed won't go to the mountain," Valerian muttered, and pulled out his phone as he moved past the girl. He was aware that she was staring after him with uncertainty as he headed out of the hall, but didn't explain, and started to punch buttons on his phone as he crossed the larger lower dining room. He listened to the ring as he took the three steps up to the smaller combined dining area and check-in desk.

"You're supposed to be enjoying your time off, not calling into work," was Mortimer's greeting.

"I was," Valerian assured him as he walked behind the counter where golfers checked in and bought snacks. "But then a couple of things happened and now I need a doctor and possibly backup."

"What things happened?" Mortimer asked with concern.

"Well, first I met my life mate," he announced almost absently as he quickly scanned the shelves under the register for the lost and found box. It had only taken a quick read of Emily's mind to discover this was where it was kept.

"What?" Mortimer almost choked over the word in his shock. "You've met your life mate?"

"I have," Valerian said, a smile claiming his lips. He could hardly believe it himself. It should be a wondrous and amazing event, and it was, but . . . His gaze landed on a medium-sized wicker basket with a collection of miscellaneous items in it, including one small, cheap angel statuette. His smile faded. "But there was an incident and she's been injured."

"What kind of incident?" Mortimer asked at once.

Valerian plucked the small angel from the basket and held it up to examine. "I'm not sure, but it's possible that work followed me here."

There was a moment of silence as Mortimer apparently tried to absorb what he'd said, and then the man growled, "Explain."

Closing his fingers around the angel, Valerian walked around the counter and began to do exactly that as he stepped out of the building onto the patio.

Four

"Mama."

Natalie stirred at that soft whisper by her ear and slowly opened her eyes to stare sleepily at the sweet-faced little girl standing beside the bed.

"Awake, Mama?" Mia asked hopefully, her blue-green eyes wide.

"I'm getting there," Natalie assured her with a faint smile as she came more fully awake. "Are you?"

"Yes." The little girl laughed the word as if that was the silliest question in the world and then reached out to grasp the comforter covering Natalie and tried to pull herself up onto the bed.

Chuckling at her little grunts and huffs as Mia tried and failed to manage the task, Natalie caught her under the arms and lifted her. She then swung her over her body and dropped Mia on her back next to her in the bed and rolled over to blow raspberries on her belly where the top of her pajamas had risen to reveal her pale rounded tummy.

Mia squealed, thrashing under the tickling attack.

Laughing, Natalie tugged the shirt down into place and then dropped back in the bed and tucked the precious little girl into her side. "Good morning."

"Morning, Mama," Mia said, twisting against her until she could half lie on her chest and peer down into her face. "We get up?"

"You think I should?" Natalie asked with amusement.

Mia nodded solemnly. "Sin hungy."

"He is, is he?" Natalie asked, matching her solemnity.

Rather than answer, Mia turned her head and held her hand out, her fingers wiggling in demand.

Natalie turned her own head to follow her gaze, just in time to see their dog, Sinbad, rushing to join them on the bed.

"Oh no. No! Sinbad. God!" she gasped as he jumped up onto the bed and dropped half on top of her to lick her face. Only the comforter saved her from bruises and worse pain as his knees and elbows pressed into her breast, hip, and calf. Dear God, the dog was big and heavy. It was hard to believe he'd once been little more than a cotton ball no bigger than her hand. Although that hadn't lasted long. He'd seemed to double in size every time she'd looked at him for the first six months of his life. Now, nearly three years later, he was one hundred and fifty pounds, more than four feet long from nose to butt, and a good two and a half or more tall at the withers. That made him more than a foot taller than her when he stood on his hind legs and put his paws on her shoulders. Yet he was the gentlest, sweetest, most affectionate dog she'd ever encountered. At least he was with her and Mia. But he could be as protective as hell with them too, and most unfriendly with anyone he saw as a threat to either of them . . . which Natalie didn't mind at all. It was why she'd picked a big-dog breed. For protection.

"Eww. Stop that," she said on a laugh as Sinbad set about determinedly cleaning her face. Her laughter died, though, when his tongue reached the bandage on her forehead and a shaft of pain shot through her. "Ow. Okay. Enough," she said more firmly, reaching up to push his head away. When he wouldn't be deterred, she said desperately, "Who wants num-nums?"

Sinbad stilled at the magic words, even as Mia pushed herself up to a sitting position and squealed happily. In the next moment, both child and dog were moving. Grunting in pain as Sinbad pushed off her to get off the bed, followed by Mia scrambling over her, hands and knees digging into her chest, Natalie moaned, and then caught Mia before she tumbled her way to the floor. Helping her to land on her feet rather than her head, she sat up with a grimace and then pushed the comforter away and stopped to stare down at the jeans and Shady Pines T-shirt she was wearing. In bed.

"Mama! Num-nums!" Mia squealed demandingly.

Natalie turned to see her daughter clutching at the fur on Sinbad's side for balance as she scowled at her impatiently. The dog didn't seem to mind and appeared to simply be waiting calmly, but then he'd often acted as a furry walker for her daughter as she'd learned to stand and then walk, never seeming to mind her yanking and pulling at his fur to steady herself despite Natalie's attempts to prevent it. He was really the most patient dog, she thought, and then looked back down at her clothes again.

"Mama!" Mia complained.

"I'm coming," Natalie assured her, and got quickly out of bed, knowing that if Mia complained again, Sinbad would start barking to urge her on. Managing a smile for her daughter once upright, she hesitated, briefly considering changing into clean clothes, but that seemed a waste until she'd showered, so she decided to leave that for later and walked over to take her baby girl's hand. The moment she did, Mia released the hold she had on Sinbad, and the dog turned to lead the way to the bedroom door.

Smiling at the beautiful animal, Natalie scooped up Mia and headed out of the room. Sinbad was immediately at her side, his head swinging this way and that as he watched for any possible threat. To his mind, it was his job to be sure the way was clear of predators or stray stuffed toys—he'd been known to bark at those when found where they shouldn't be.

This morning Natalie found his protective nature almost reassuring as they crossed the dingy open space of the unfinished side of the basement to get to the stairs, though she wasn't sure why. But then she couldn't seem to remember much about anything at the moment. Why her head hurt, why she'd slept in her clothes . . . She didn't even recall going to bed the night before, which was troubling. Natalie was frowning over that as she carried Mia upstairs to the club's kitchen. As usual, Sinbad stopped just outside—knowing he wasn't allowed in—and sat down to wait as she continued on through the swinging door into the room.

The scent of coffee struck Natalie the moment she stepped into the kitchen. She then spotted a blonde woman by the coffeepot. About medium height and with a curvy figure, the woman was pouring steaming liquid into a cup. Still only halfway through the door, Natalie froze at once, her hands tightening anxiously around her daughter as she stared at the stranger. She had no idea who the woman was, but she did look kind of familiar, and Natalie was fretting over that when the woman turned and smiled at her.

"One sweetener and two splashes of Turtle creamer, right?" she asked, and proceeded to treat the coffee she'd just poured with what she'd just listed off. Concentrating on what she was doing, the woman asked mildly, "How is your head this morning? Any headache? Fuzzy thoughts? Blurry vision?"

Natalie almost sagged with relief as memories from the night before began to flood her mind and she recalled that the woman fixing her coffee was Dr. Dani Pimms.

Valerian MacKenzie, the golfer whose golf cart had died on the seventeenth hole, worked with Dani's husband, Decker. When Natalie had refused to go to the hospital, he'd called in a favor and asked his coworker's wife to drop by and take a look at her to be sure she was all right.

Natalie had at first been annoyed when Valerian had returned to the office and announced that his "doctor friend" was coming. She hadn't appreciated his overstepping and had been furious with him right up until Dani Pimms had arrived half an hour later. The woman had one heck of a bedside manner, or couchside manner in this case, Natalie supposed, since she'd still been on the couch in her office when Dani and her husband had arrived. The couple had barely entered before Natalie had felt herself begin to relax, and moments later she was sure that allowing the woman to examine her was for the best. After all, Mia needed her. It was better to make sure that the blow to the head she'd taken hadn't caused some unseen damage.

Her memories got a little blurry after that. She knew the woman had examined her, flashing light in her eyes and asking questions. She also had a vague recollection of being given a local anesthetic to numb her forehead, and then Dr. Dani stitching her up. Or perhaps she'd used some kind of glue. Natalie remembered her saying something about liquid stitches and surgical glue to keep the scarring down. She'd also given her some kind of painkiller for the headache. Finally, she'd helped her get down to her bedroom where Natalie had assured her she'd be fine on her own and get herself to bed. Natalie had then climbed into bed in her clothes, intending only to nap for a little bit and then go out to see to mowing the course.

That memory made her frown. Obviously, she hadn't

got the mowing done, which meant she'd have to attend to it now before the golfers started showing up and she was juggling running the check-in desk and the kitchen for those who wanted breakfast before golfing. Natalie's gaze dropped to Mia even as she thought that, but then she decided Mia would just have to come with her. It wasn't that big a deal. She'd done it before, but while Mia always found it entertaining at first, she tended to get bored and then either just dozed off or got whiny. Natalie was afraid it would be the whiny response this time, since the child had just woken up.

A cup of steaming coffee appeared in her line of vision, and Natalie blinked in surprise at it.

"It *is* one sweetener and two splashes Turtle cream, isn't it?" Dani asked.

"I—Yes," Natalie murmured, shifting Mia to her hip to free one hand. She took the beverage, but then glanced at Dani Pimms and asked with curiosity, "How did you know?"

"You told me last night," Dani said with a faint smile. "It was one of my questions to see if your thinking was clear."

"Oh." Natalie offered a crooked smile. "Guess I forgot that."

"I'm not surprised. There was a lot going on," Dani said sympathetically.

Natalie nodded and lowered her head to take a sip of coffee, but then paused and jerked her head back up. "You stayed all night?"

"I wanted to keep an eye on you," she said with a

shrug. "Besides, Decker and Valerian were out most of the night mowing the course for you."

"What?" Natalie gasped, nearly sloshing her coffee in her surprise. Setting it down on the prep counter next to her before she spilled it on Mia, she turned toward the door and then paused and swung back with confusion. She wanted to go check on her golf course and be sure it was okay. Mowing a course was not the same as mowing your lawn, and she was terrified of what state she'd find it in. But she needed to feed her daughter too, and Sinbad, so Natalie walked over to the small table she'd set up in the corner of the room when she'd taken over the golf course, and strapped Mia into her booster seat.

"Wait here, baby. Mama's going to get you breakfast."

"And Sinneee," Mia ordered.

"Yes, and Sinbad's too," Natalie assured her, and then moved to the large industrial refrigerator to retrieve milk and a container of Sinbad's homemade dog food that she whipped up for him weekly. Natalie didn't do it out of any concern that normal dog food wasn't good enough, but because it saved her money to use up the leftover vegetables and odds and ends of meat from the club restaurant rather than just toss them. Some weeks there were more leftovers than others, but there were always some, because she tended to overbuy a little rather than risk not having something that a customer ordered. And yes, all right, she did believe it meant the meals Sinbad was getting were probably healthier than dried bits of kibble, but that was just a bonus. She was equally sure she was saving money using up the leftovers like that.

"You seem worried," Dani commented mildly as she watched her scoop a cup and a half of the homemade dog food into Sinbad's porcelain dog food bowl.

"No, not at all," Natalie lied as she set the dog food in the microwave to warm it up a little, and then moved to collect cereal and a bowl. She could hardly admit that she was stressed about how the men might have mown the course. It had been kind of them to do it, after all. In fact, she could hardly believe they had. Valerian was a customer, for heaven's sake. He was someone she hadn't even met before last night, and they hadn't exchanged more than a couple of sentences since then. As for Dani's husband, he was Valerian's coworker, and presumably a friend to him, but neither of them should have felt responsible for mowing the course. The fact that both men had stepped up and done so to help her out was incredibly . . . well . . . kind. And it would be unkind of her to admit she was worried about what sort of job they might have done.

"I don't know how well you know Valerian," Dani began after a moment. "I understand he's golfed here for several weeks, but—"

"Months," Natalie corrected as she finished pouring cereal and milk into her daughter's bowl, slipped a spoon in, and then pushed it aside as she went to retrieve Sinbad's dog food from the microwave and carried it toward the door. "Valerian's been coming since July . . . or maybe late June," she admitted, unsure now when exactly he'd started coming. It had been around there somewhere, though, she thought as she pushed the door open, bent to set the dog food down in front of Sinbad, paused to give him a quick pet, then said, "Okay," and watched him dive into the food before she turned back into the kitchen.

"So at least three months," Dani said with a nod. "But I gather the two of you hadn't talked much before last night's . . . adventure," Dani finished delicately.

"No. We hadn't," Natalie acknowledged as she retrieved Mia's cereal and carried it to the table.

"Well, then he probably hasn't mentioned that his family owns more than a couple dozen golf courses, both in Europe and the US, and he grew up working on them."

Natalie turned swiftly, eyes wide. "Really?"

"Really," Dani assured her. "I guess he started out just helping around the courses as a boy, and then officially worked for his parents as a teen. And then, of course, he picked up the golfing bug so while his career took him away from it, he still golfs a lot and helps out on various courses when he visits family."

"Oh," Natalie breathed, tension she hadn't even realized was clenching her muscles now seeping out of her body. Managing a weak smile, she headed over to grab the coffee Dani had made for her and murmured, "Thank you for telling me that. I was a little worried they might have . . ."

"Mowed it like they'd do their front yards?" Dani suggested when she hesitated.

"Basically, yeah," Natalie admitted, watching Mia

scoop a spoonful of cereal into her mouth. She wasn't fully proficient at it yet—half the cereal in the spoon landed on the table—but her baby girl had an independent streak and threw a fit if Natalie didn't let her do it herself. Fighting the urge to take over and feed her, she peered down at her rapidly cooling coffee, thinking she needed it about now. She'd been up for several minutes already, but still didn't feel quite awake. Wondering if it was the painkiller Dani had given her, or a result of the head wound, she sipped at the coffee and then sighed as the creamy, sweetened brew filled her mouth and slid down her throat. God had definitely outdone himself when He'd created coffee, she thought . . . and the chocolaty goodness of her creamer of choice as well as sugar, or sweetener in her case. The trio was the bomb in her book, she decided as she took another sip.

"Are you hungry?"

Natalie swallowed the liquid in her mouth and glanced at Dani with a small frown. "I'm sorry," she said suddenly, setting the coffee down and moving to the refrigerator to start pulling out eggs, cream, and cheese. "You've been here all night and I didn't even think to offer you breakfast. You must be starved. I'll whip you up an omelet."

"That's not necessary," Dani said quickly. "I'm actually more concerned about you. You're awfully thin, Natalie. A good ten pounds underweight by my guess."

"Not ten," Natalie protested defensively.

"No?" Dani asked gently.

"I'm five foot three inches, and the charts say my ideal weight would be 104 to 127 pounds. I weigh more than ninety-four pounds," she assured her as she set down the items from the fridge and moved to grab mushrooms and onions next.

"So, what do you weigh?" Dani asked.

"Isn't that considered a rude question?" Natalie asked as she grabbed her best knife and set to work on the onions and mushrooms.

"Not from your doctor," Dani countered.

Natalie wanted to snap that she wasn't her doctor, but that seemed rude considering the woman had come to tend her last night, sewing her up, giving her medicine, and then had apparently sat up all night watching over her to be sure there was no cranial swelling or whatever it was they worried about after a head injury. Chopping furiously, she growled, "Ninety-five pounds."

"Ah. Underweight as I suspected, then," Dani pointed out gently. "I think it might be a good idea if we run some blood tests to be sure there isn't some underlying condition causing it."

Muttering under her breath about bloodsucking doctors, Natalie grabbed a frying pan from the hanging rack above her head and quickly scraped the mushrooms and onions she'd chopped into it, then found the butter, used her knife to cut off a portion, dumped that in the pan with the onions and mushrooms, and set them on the range. As she turned the knob to start the flame under the pan, Natalie said, "I'm just a little underweight because it's summer."

"Summer?" Dani asked uncertainly, apparently not making the connection between weight and the season.

"I'm super busy in the summer, making menus, mowing, fertilizing, watering, repairing items, running the till, taking orders, cooking . . ." She let her voice die off there and shrugged as she grabbed a mixing bowl from the same cupboard where she'd got Mia's cereal bowl. Walking back to the prep counter, Natalie added, "I'm up early, working late, and outside sweating most of the day away. I always drop weight in the summer."

"And apparently run yourself to a state of exhaustion," Dani said dryly.

Ignoring the comment, Natalie began cracking eggs into the bowl as she assured her, "By Christmas I'll be back up to one hundred again."

"Which will still be underweight," Dani pointed out. "And that's only if you haven't collapsed from exhaustion and died."

When Natalie snorted at the suggestion, Dani continued with exasperation. "Natalie, you're so pale I'm sure you're anemic, your skin is thin and dry, and your hair is very thin too. Have you been experiencing more hair loss than normal?"

Natalie glanced around at her with a jolt as she dropped the fork she'd been beating the eggs with and raised her hand self-consciously to her hair. She *had* noticed more of it on the shower floor lately, and her hairbrush too. Dear God, she wasn't losing her hair, was she?

Dani sighed at her expression. "I'm not trying to

alarm you, but you're showing all the classic signs of malnutrition and exhaustion. I think you're probably working yourself too hard and have been for a while."

Returning to beating the eggs, Natalie let her breath out, took in another, and then said stubbornly, "It's the time of year. The end of the season. I'm always exhausted and ready for a break by the end of September. Things will ease up soon. Golfing is pretty much over by the end of October, and then I can relax more."

"I'm not sure you can afford to wait another month," Dani said solemnly. "I'm afraid doing so could do irreversible harm to your health." When Natalie didn't respond, she added, "I'd hate to see Mia without a mother."

"So would I," Natalie muttered, pausing in her beating to stir the frying onions and mushrooms around in the pan. She then set the bowl aside, found a grater, and began to grate the cheese she'd pulled out before saying, "I'll try to take it easier."

"I happen to know a couple of guys who could help with that. They're both looking for temporary jobs for the next few weeks and love the outdoors."

Natalie glanced at her warily. She really didn't want to hire anyone else. She didn't want to cut into her profits. She was so close to being able to start construction on a new clubhouse. One where she and Mia could have a little self-contained apartment, a real home rather than just a bedroom in the basement, half her office for a living room, and having to use the club's kitchen for meals. Hiring on extra help would eat up profits meant to go toward the new building. But she supposed the money wouldn't do much good if she dropped dead. Poor Mia would have no one then.

Shoulders slumping, Natalie stopped grating. She gave the onions and mushrooms another stir, poured the eggs over them, followed that with the grated cheese, and then added some salt and pepper, before saying, "Fine. Give these guys you know a call and I'll interview and pick one of them to help out around here."

Five

"There's definitely a trail here. See?"

Valerian followed Decker's gesture and nodded solemnly. "Whoever it was drags their feet when walking. They left a shallow trench through the leaves." He followed the obvious path inside the tree line along the eighteenth green, noting how it moved closer to the edge of the trees as it went and recalled Natalie saying it sounded like they were getting closer.

"It stops here and moves off to the right, away from the eighteenth green," Decker commented a couple of minutes later.

Valerian paused and looked to the green on his left, noting that they were just past the bend with a clear view of the water feature by the seventeenth hole. The trees were thinner here and had been for a good ten or twenty feet. He swiveled his head to eye the direction the path went from here. Whoever had been following

Natalie appeared to have made their way straight out of the woods, heading away from where she was.

"What's that?"

Valerian glanced around at Decker's question to see him eyeing the seventeenth hole, or perhaps the pond, he thought as he followed the other man's gaze. Not seeing what had caught Decker's attention, he asked, "What?"

"This side of the pond. There's something yellow on the green," Decker explained just as Valerian spotted the splotch of color in the distance.

Curiosity piqued, Valerian decided to follow the stalker's trail later and headed out of the trees toward the pond with Decker at his side.

"The grass is dead," Decker said with surprise as they reached the pond and could better see the discoloration they'd glimpsed from the trees.

"Yes." Valerian's gaze slid over the large dead area just up the slight incline from the water. He stared at it, and then surveyed the area before he let his gaze return to the dead grass. His expression now troubled, he said, "I think that's where I laid Natalie when I pulled her out of the pond."

"Are you sure?" Decker moved to stand at the end of the good-sized patch of yellow and brown grass.

Nodding, Valerian dropped to his haunches to run his fingers over the edge of the discolored area. It was early enough that dew covered the ground, but whatever was on the dead grass was a little thicker than that. Rubbing his wet thumb and forefinger together, he raised them to his nose to sniff.

"Anything?" Decker asked, watching him.

"It's almost odorless," he announced. "But a faint whiff of . . ." Valerian hesitated and then said grimly, "It reminds me of the herbicide my father uses in the sand traps on his courses."

"So, it was deliberate," Decker said.

Something in his tone made Valerian glance at him sharply. Decker's features were set and grim. Eyes narrowing warily, Valerian straightened. "What is it?"

"Come look at the shape of the dead grass from here," Decker said rather than answer.

Eyebrows rising slightly, Valerian walked around to join him, then turned to look over the patch of yellow/brown grass again. The shift in position made a big difference. Standing at the bottom, approximately where Natalie's feet had rested last night, he found himself looking at what was the rough shape of a snow angel made with dead grass. It wasn't perfect, but he could see what it had been meant to look like.

"And you say you laid Natalie here?" Decker asked after a moment.

"Yes, but I doubt she had herbicide all over her back, and she certainly didn't raise and lower her arms or spread and close her legs to make a snow angel shape in the grass," Valerian told him solemnly.

"I didn't think so," Decker said, pulling out his phone.

Valerian didn't bother to ask who he was calling.

"Mortimer?" Decker said a moment later. "Yes. We've searched the area. Someone was definitely following Natalie from the trees, and we're pretty sure it wasn't the wind and she probably did hear someone whisper the word *angel* from the woods."

Valerian grimaced when he heard that. He hadn't thought it had been the wind himself, even when Natalie had suggested it. But he'd had to tell Mortimer that she'd offered it as an explanation when he'd called him last night.

"Why?" Decker said, obviously echoing Mortimer's question. "Because we just found a patch of dead grass shaped like a snow angel where Valerian laid Natalie on the ground last night, and that can't be a coincidence."

Definitely not, Valerian thought.

"What's that?"

Valerian was so surprised to hear that question in Natalie's soft voice he actually startled before turning sharply to see her walking toward him from a golf cart she'd parked several feet away.

"I didn't hear the cart," he said with surprise, and then frowned. "Why didn't I hear the golf cart?" The carts he was usually given here certainly weren't silent, Valerian thought, and glanced a little worriedly toward Decker. Fortunately, the man wasn't so wrapped up in his conversation that he hadn't noticed Natalie's arrival. In fact, even as he looked his way, the other man nodded a silent greeting to Natalie and walked toward the woods to continue his call with Mortimer in privacy.

"It's electric." Natalie explained away the silent vehicle, drawing his attention back to her as she reached his side. "I bought one to see how they run and how often they need recharging. If it's feasible, I might replace all the old gas ones with them."

"Oh," Valerian murmured, and then hoping to distract her from the patch of yellow-brown grass, he asked, "Did something happen? Do you need something? Or—"

"No. Dr. Dani mentioned that you boys mowed the course for me and I wanted to . . . thank you," she finished after a slight hesitation that made Valerian smile with amusement.

"You wanted to inspect the job and make sure we hadn't messed up your course," he countered knowingly.

Natalie didn't bother to deny it. Instead, she wrinkled her nose and shrugged. "Maybe. But she was right. She said you know your way around a golf course and obviously you do. From what I've seen so far, it looks great. Thank you for taking care of that for me. I really appreciate it, and I've decided to give you and Decker free memberships for the rest of this year as a thank-you."

Valerian frowned at the suggestion. First, she was offering to refund him for yesterday's round and give him a free round to make up for his golf cart running out of gas near the end of his eighteen holes, and now she was going to give them a free pass for the last month of the season just for one mowing? Decker wasn't a big golfer. Valerian doubted he would even use it, but he himself came to the course nearly every damned day. She was being far too generous. But before he could say as much, she clucked her tongue with agitation and asked, "Why is the grass dead here? What—?"

"I think I might have cut it too short," Valerian lied, catching her arm as she started to walk past him to examine it more closely. Urging her to turn back toward the golf cart, he added, "Don't worry, I'll cut that out and replace it with fresh sod. I know a great sod place about twenty minutes from here."

"I don't think that's from cutting too short," Natalie argued, trying to look back over her shoulder at the spot. "And the shape kind of looks like a—"

Valerian glanced at her quickly when she suddenly fell silent, and then stopped walking to take in her blank expression before glancing around to see Decker had finished his call and returned. He'd nearly reached them and had obviously taken control of Natalie. Valerian felt anger rise up in him at the realization.

"I know you're probably pissed," Decker said, his tone apologetic as he stopped beside them. "I was when anyone took control of Dani when we first got together, but I think it's probably better if she doesn't know about the angel mark. We don't want her terrified."

Valerian forced himself to relax and nodded. Natalie had seemed to be physically repulsed at just the sight of the tiny angel statue last night. He didn't think she'd react well to the snow angel shape chemically burned into the grass. While the little statuette could have been a lucky charm someone had dropped somewhere on the grounds and had been left in her office to take care of, there was no mistaking the angel shape in the grass as anything but a threat. Valerian had no idea if she followed the news in Toronto and had read the articles on the Angel-Maker some months back, or if she'd even make a connection now that so much time had passed, but he didn't want to take the chance.

She was a single parent who not only ran the golf course, but lived on the property with her young daughter. Something he'd discovered from reading Emily last night. He didn't want Natalie anxious and terrified on her own property. There was no need for that, because he had every intention of ensuring she had nothing to fear. If Mortimer didn't arrange for men to look into this, he'd take a leave of absence from work and take care of it himself. He wouldn't have her terrorized, and wouldn't risk losing her either.

"You won't have to take a leave of absence—Mortimer is on this," Decker announced, obviously having caught his thoughts.

When Valerian relaxed and grunted an acknowledgment, Decker added, "So, with your permission I'm going to change Natalie's memory a little so that she just remembers a blob of dead grass rather than one in the shape of an angel. After that, I'll give her the idea that we should return to the clubhouse to check on Mia so that she doesn't see it again until we can cover it up somehow."

Valerian nodded again, and then glanced toward the discolored patch and said, "New sod needs to be laid down."

"That sounds easy enough." Decker sounded relieved.

Valerian shook his head at once. "Not that easy. We

don't know how much herbicide was used, or how deep it went into the ground. The area needs to be dug up, and fresh clean soil put in before the rolls of sod can be laid."

Decker stared at the dead grass briefly as he considered that and then said, "I'll do it. I'm sure Natalie must have a shovel around here somewhere. And a wheelbarrow to carry the tainted dirt away," he added, walking down to examine the angel before saying, "I'll dig up a six-foot-by-six-foot square right away so that even if we have to wait on dirt or sod, the shape at least won't be there."

He started back up the incline to them. "I'll come back to the clubhouse with the two of you to find a shovel and wheelbarrow to take care of it right away. Then I'll follow that trail we found out of the woods. It probably ends as soon as it hits the green on the other side of the tree line, but it will at least give me an idea in what direction Natalie's stalker might have gone."

Valerian nodded and peered toward the woods with a frown as he considered the word Decker had used. *Stalker.* Like it might not be who he worried it was. "You don't think it's the Angel-Maker?"

Decker looked troubled for a moment, and then sighed and ran a hand around his neck with agitation. Staring back at the discolored grass, he rubbed his neck and said, "It's impossible to know. None of us had ever met any of his women before he killed them so we have no idea if he played little games like this with his previous victims." Letting his hand drop, he turned back and added, "But aside from having Eshe and Mirabeau search the victims' previous homes, Mortimer is going to have Enforcers interview and read the minds of any friends or acquaintances he can find of the previous victims to see if anyone remembers anything angel-related showing up in the women's lives before they died."

"A good idea," Valerian commented, his gaze sliding over Natalie's still face.

"He's also sending reinforcements," Decker announced. "Some will stay out of sight and watch the grounds, but two are going to take jobs here."

"Jobs?" Valerian asked with surprise.

Decker smiled at his expression. "Yeah. I was a little surprised too. But it seems Mortimer had just got off the phone with my wife when I called. Dani's concerned that Natalie is working herself to a state of exhaustion. She thinks she's malnourished, overworked, and on the verge of collapse, so used a little of our special persuasion and some guilt about her daughter to convince her to agree to hiring a couple guys to help out for the next few weeks. Dani even told Natalie she knew two trustworthy guys who could use a temporary job and would jump at the chance to work here."

"Did she?" Valerian asked with surprise. "Who?"

"Mortimer's trying to figure that out right now," Decker said with a grin.

Valerian smiled briefly in return, knowing that meant Dani hadn't mentioned names and had merely been leaving the way open for Mortimer to send in a couple of men who could be on site. Their poor boss was now no doubt going crazy trying to rearrange the men to free up for this job, he thought, but then sobered and said, "They should be guys who know at least a little about taking care of a golf course. We don't need someone who might accidentally destroy the green on her or something."

Decker's eyebrows rose at that. "Do we know any-one who knows anything about golf courses? Besides you?"

Valerian considered the question briefly and then nodded. "We do."

Ignoring the curiosity in Decker's eyes, he pulled out his phone and started away toward the trees so that Natalie wouldn't hear his conversation. He didn't need to give her more for Decker to have to erase, he thought, and said, "Go ahead and start fixing her memory. I'll only be a moment."

"You need to tell me what's going on."

Natalie glanced up from the papers on her desk at that firm announcement by Jan, and tilted her head in question. "What do you mean?"

"What do I mean?" The redhead snorted, and then said, "Explain that 'Pretty Parade' going on in the dining room. There must be at least half a dozen gorgeous male specimens out there. Not to mention two of the most beautiful women on the planet."

Natalie hesitated briefly, her gaze shifting to the

security monitor next to her computer. Putting in cameras and the monitor was one of the first things Natalie had done when she'd taken over the golf course. Aside from her full-time workers—Jimmy for delivering food orders, Roy and Timothy for the golf course, Ashley and Emily, who were Mia's day and night nannies, and Jan to help her in the kitchen— Natalie had two part-time workers, Maddison and Hailey. Both were local high school kids who worked Saturday and Sunday, helping in the kitchen and the dining rooms, which got crazy busy on the weekends. Having the monitors helped her keep track of where everyone was and what was happening. Most were images of the outside of the building and grounds, but the bottom three were all indoor shots. One of the larger lower-level dining room, one of the smaller upper dining area, and one focused on the space behind the counter where the cash register sat.

Natalie now peered at the small image of the large dining room on the monitor and pursed her lips. "Do you really think so?"

"Are you kidding me?" Jan asked with amazement. "Have you *seen* the customers in the dining room right now?"

"Yes, of course," she said quickly, and then bit her lip before admitting, "And honestly, when I greeted them and showed them to their table, I did think they were the most attractive people I've ever seen and sexy to boot, but . . ." Her eyes moved back to the monitor. "Looking at them now on camera, they just seem kind of normal."

"What?" Jan gasped with disbelief.

"It's true," Natalie assured her. "I mean, a couple of them are attractive enough, but the others are just average."

"You must be blind!" Jan exclaimed with amazement as she moved around the desk to look for herself. "Those people out there are . . . damn," she breathed as she stared at the security monitor.

Jan bent to reach for the smaller of the two mice on Natalie's desk and double-clicked on the camera view of the larger lower dining room. It immediately enlarged to fill the screen while the other images disappeared.

"Damn." Jan shook her head with bewilderment. "When I helped Maddy carry out their lunch orders, I could have sworn they were all models. But while those two men are above average in looks," she said, moving the cursor over a table in one corner, before shifting it to another table of two men in the opposite corner and adding, "These two are—Well, hell, my Rick's better-looking than both of them."

"He is," Natalie agreed. To be fair, the men were still good-looking, or at least they weren't ugly or anything.

Moving the cursor now to the table with two couples at it, Jan added, "And those two women *are* very pretty, but when I first saw them, I thought they were breathtaking."

"Yeah, me too," Natalie admitted, peering at the faces of the people on the screen.

Straightening, Jan finally said, "Crazy . . . I guess

this means personality really does add to attractiveness."

Natalie considered that, and supposed it was possible. It made as much sense as anything she could come up with to explain why people who had seemed almost supernaturally attractive in person just seemed average on camera.

"Anyway," Jan said now, turning from the monitor, "what's with the sudden influx of people?"

Natalie shrugged. "It's Saturday—we're always busier on weekends."

"Yeah, but not this busy. It's not even 11 A.M. and almost every table is taken. That usually doesn't happen until noon," Jan pointed out. "Besides, those two couples, and the other four men we've been discussing, aren't locals."

"We get the occasional city dweller here," Natalie murmured, reaching for the mouse and double-clicking on the image of the lower dining area. It immediately receded and the screen filled with all nine images again.

"One or two, sure, but not this many," Jan argued, and then her eyes narrowed on the bandage on Natalie's forehead. "Are you going to tell me what happened to your head?"

"I already did tell you—I fell and hit it," Natalie muttered, lowering her gaze to the paperwork she'd been working on before Jan had interrupted her.

"Emily said you fell in the water feature on the seventeenth hole and hit your head, and that if Valerian MacKenzie hadn't pulled you out, you could have drowned," Jan countered.

"Emily talks too much," Natalie growled with irritation. She really didn't want to talk about Valerian MacKenzie and how kind he'd been to her after her accident. She just knew Jan would take it wrong and start seeing things that weren't there. Hoping to change the subject, she asked, "And when did you talk to Emily? She doesn't start until four."

Mia's night nanny, Emily, worked from four until midnight, or later if mowing went late, Wednesday through Sunday. But Mia also had a day nanny, Ashley, who worked from eight until four those same days. Monday and Tuesday, though, were incredibly slow, so Natalie just kept Mia with her and mowed throughout the day when she had the time.

"Ashley had a 'thing' today and asked Emily to take her shift for her," Jan said with an expression and tone that told her what she thought of Ashley and her "thing." Natalie wasn't surprised at her friend's annoyance on Emily's behalf. Ashley often had a "thing" and convinced or guilted Emily into stepping in for her. It made for terribly long days for Emily, but she agreed to it, so Natalie didn't feel she had the right to intervene.

"Emily also said that you refused to go to the hospital last night," Jan added, apparently not as distracted from their conversation as she'd hoped. "She said Valerian called in a friend with a wife who's a doctor and the wife took care of you while he and the husband mowed the course."

When Natalie merely grunted an acknowledgment,

Jan said, "That was super sweet of him, taking care of you and the course like that. Wasn't that sweet?"

"It was very kind," Natalie said solemnly. "Neighborly even."

"Hmm." Jan sounded dissatisfied at the way she'd changed her words and then added, "Emily also said the way Valerian MacKenzie was looking at you she thinks he's interested."

This was exactly what she'd feared would happen. Jan was making connections that weren't there. Natalie lowered her head with a moan, and then said, "Emily is young with an overactive imagination. Valerian MacKenzie can't be more than twenty-five years old, while I'm thirty-two, with a daughter. He is not interested in me."

"Don't be silly," Jan said with exasperation, and pointed out, "I'm four years older than my Rick. Seven isn't that much more. Why wouldn't he be interested? You're a pretty gal. You're also smart and successful. You're a hell of a catch." She paused for a beat, and then added triumphantly, "And since you're finally hiring help, you'll actually have time to date him."

Natalie grinned crookedly at that and lifted her head so Jan could see it before saying, "You're a good friend, Jan. You always give my confidence a boost. But it doesn't matter if he's interested or not, 'cause the only thing I want to do with my extra free time is to sleep."

"Ah, baby girl," Jan said sympathetically, sounding for all the world like she was twenty years older than her rather than the two she was. Reaching out, she patted Natalie's cheek lightly and then straightened and headed for the door. "I'll give you a week to catch up on your sleep, but then I'm gonna start setting you up on dates. This will be the first time you've had some free time since I've known you and I plan on using it to find you a man. It's not good to go without sex for so long." Pausing with her hand on the door, she turned back to add, "If you don't use it, you could lose it."

"What?" Natalie gasped on a disbelieving laugh. "I'm pretty sure there's never been a case of a woman's vagina falling out, or hermetically sealing itself, from lack of use."

"There's a first time for everything," Jan said with a shrug as she pulled the door open and walked out.

Natalie shook her head at the very idea and then grimaced as she acknowledged that she would now be considered fair game for all the matchmakers in the area. Up to this point, they'd all left her alone because she was newly widowed and always busy. But Jan seemed to think she'd grieved long enough and it was time to find her a man. Natalie didn't doubt that a lot of the married women in the area were probably thinking the same way. Hell, they'd probably all gathered together and discussed it at church, bingo, the local summer barbecue, or whatever else passed for socializing out here in the country.

Natalie picked up her pen and twisted it in her fingers. She actually wasn't completely opposed to dating, and hadn't been for a while thanks to the counseling she'd had after the death of basically her entire family in a car accident three years earlier.

Natalie had been a mess after losing her parents, her son, and the father of her children. Grief had been like a black cloak, nearly suffocating her. The baby growing in her womb had been the only light in that darkness. Natalie honestly wasn't sure if she would have survived without her baby girl. First, she'd lived to give Mia life, and then she'd been determined to give her a *good* life. So, she'd spent the last three years working hard to make a go of the golf course. It was doing well now, partially thanks to the food she cooked in the clubhouse's restaurant.

That thought made her glance at the clock. She always handled the breakfast crowd on her own until Jan showed up at ten. Then the other woman took over while she came back to her office to handle paperwork for an hour before returning to the kitchen to start lunch prep. It was a daily juggling act, squeezing in everything she had to do to run the golf course as well as the kitchen, and she relied heavily on Jan to take over when necessary.

Fortunately, her friend had a lot of natural skill in the kitchen, and as long as Natalie explained the menu and dishes and stuck the day's recipes up on the board, Jan could manage it. Which was a good thing, because a lot of the income they were now generating was coming from the restaurant end of the business. They didn't just serve food in the small clubhouse restaurant, they also offered takeout.

She'd started that to keep money coming in through the winter when golfing was shut down. Natalie was hoping to add event hosting when she built the new clubhouse. She'd originally only intended to add a proper home for her and Mia, a small self-contained apartment. But when her food was such a hit with the locals, she decided to add a much larger kitchen and dining room as well, and even an events room where locals could hold wedding receptions, family reunions, or baby showers that she would of course be happy to supply the food for.

Natalie was hoping to start building the additions the following spring, which was part of the reason she'd been so resistant to hiring more help. She wanted to save every penny she could for the coming expenses. But Dani had convinced her that, as a mother, her health was important. Actually, she'd made her realize that she'd put her own health and well-being last on the list of priorities and really shouldn't have. She was all Mia had. Her little girl needed her, because if she died, there was no family to take care of Mia. She'd be put into the system, where anything might happen to her.

That wasn't something Natalie even wanted to think about, so she pushed it from her mind and peered down at the paperwork on her desk. She was trying to sort out what to order for the coming week. While Jan bought the meat and vegetables fresh daily, they still needed other items delivered like cooking oil, vinegar, spices, toilet paper, etc. Normally, she wouldn't even have to think about it and ordered pretty much the same things every week, but with how busy the club had been since opening that morning, she was having to adjust a couple of items.

Natalie quickly went over the changes she'd made to the list, and then glanced toward the monitor as she noted movement out of the corner of her eye. What had caught her attention was the arrival of a foursome of older men entering. Natalie recognized them at once. They were regulars, a good-natured group who were always friendly and chatty with her. Over the years since she'd inherited the golf course from her parents, she'd learned that they were all farmers, and had been friends since grade school. They'd also considered her father a friend since he'd often joined them in a drink after their round. One was a widower, another was divorced, but two were happily married, and all four had a son, nephew, or son of a friend they thought she should meet. Natalie always laughed off their offers to introduce her to one of these "fine young men." They always took this with good grace, but it didn't stop them from repeating the offer on each visit.

Just seeing them now made Natalie smile. They were all good-hearted, hardworking men who made her think of her father, and they came in every Saturday when harvesting didn't interfere. And every time they had lunch and then bought a six-pack of beer to "wet their whistle" while "walking off their meal" shooting eighteen holes.

Noting that neither Maddison nor Hailey were presently in the dining room to greet them, Natalie headed out to take care of them herself.

Six

"Natalie, girl! What happened to you?"

Natalie reached up self-consciously to touch the bandage on her forehead at that greeting from Mr. Copeland as she approached the men waiting patiently by the counter. She then winced as just the soft pressure from her fingers caused her pain. Letting her hand drop at once, she smiled crookedly and assured him, "It's nothing serious. Just my clumsiness. I took a tumble and bumped my head."

Mr. Copeland didn't look happy with this explanation and gave a soft, "Hrmph," that was echoed by the other men before he said, "Well now, you have to be more careful, Natalie. Take better care of yourself. We wouldn't want to lose you."

"No, we wouldn't," Mr. Jansen agreed, and then grinned and added slyly, "You can't marry my nephew Jake if you knock yerself senseless and die on us."

"Hey now, if Natalie's marrying anyone it's my son, Junior," Mr. Copeland said, a scowl on his face, but a twinkle in his eyes that showed they weren't being serious. That twinkle faded a bit now, though, as he added, "Besides, I wouldn't be recommending your nephew after what we just heard about his dealings with Beth when they broke up. He didn't treat her right."

"Not right at all," Mr. Larson agreed with a shake of the head. "Forcing her to sell her own house like that and move with her son to an apartment in town!" He turned and looked as if he was about to spit on the floor by his boots, but stopped at the last minute and offered Natalie a chagrined smile.

"He reminds me of that Snidely Whiplash character from the old Sunday morning cartoons who went after widows and orphans," Mr. Kincaid said with disgust. "He should be ashamed of himself, and you should give him a good hiding behind the barn, Ben. Or at least ban the little bastard from family gatherings."

Ben Jansen just shook his head unhappily. "His daddy should have done that years ago. Doubt it would help now."

"True enough," John Copeland said solemnly.

Hoping that was the end of that, Natalie chose that moment to say, "Are you heading right out to the golf course today, gentlemen, or—"

"Oh hell, no," Mr. Kincaid interrupted quickly. "Sweetheart, I look forward to having lunch here all week. You have the best damned food in the county. Even your sandwiches are special and tasty."

"Yes," Mr. Copeland agreed. "And those fancy meals of yours are mighty fine."

Natalie beamed at the compliment and quickly ushered them to one of her two remaining tables. She then stepped aside to allow them all to take their chairs before walking around the table, setting down the menus.

Her father used to serve diner-type food in the restaurant when he ran the place, but she had been a gourmet chef in a fine-dining restaurant in the city before taking over here and saw no reason not to use her skills. Fortunately, it had worked out. Natalie had at first worried that the food would be too fancy for a golf course in the middle of farm country where she suspected meat and potatoes was a staple, so it had been a pleasant surprise when her food was a hit. Oh, at first there had been a horrified expression or two and questions about what a pine nut or confit was, but for the most part, her clients had been surprisingly open to trying things, and usually ended up liking them. Now she did a steady business in takeout and delivery too, and not just on the weekends.

After getting their drink orders, Natalie headed to the check-in counter and the drink refrigerators. She was setting glasses on a tray when Hailey hurried up, looking a little flustered.

"Sorry, Natalie, Maddy and I were helping Jan in the kitchen and didn't hear the chime," the girl rushed out apologetically as she joined her behind the counter.

Natalie paused at her words, and realized she hadn't

heard the bell chime herself. That was something else she'd had installed on first moving in, a wireless door chime that sounded in both her office and the kitchen every time the door opened to warn that customers were arriving or leaving.

Frowning, she glanced toward it now, remembering that she'd intended to check and be sure it was still working. However, she'd forgotten about it in the crush that morning. In fact, she'd been so busy with the breakfast crowd and golfers that she hadn't noticed whether or not the chime had been dinging every time the door opened as it was supposed to do.

Reminding herself to check it after she delivered the drinks to the table, Natalie turned to retrieve the beverages the men had requested. While they took a six-pack of beer with them on the course, they always stuck to sodas and iced tea with their meals. She supposed it was to make sure their game wasn't affected by their imbibing too much before they even got onto the course. The foursome were fast friends, but also competitive as all get-out. She bent to retrieve a couple of Cokes from the bottom shelf, and then paused when the phone rang.

"I'll get it," Hailey assured her, and answered the phone. "Hello, Shady Pines Golf Course. How can I help you?"

Natalie straightened to put the sodas on the tray with the glasses and had turned back to the refrigerator for two iced teas when Hailey said in a much less friendly voice, "Oh. Hi."

Natalie's eyebrows rose slightly, but she assumed it wasn't a customer or Hailey would have kept up the cheerful, chatty voice, so simply fetched the two teas.

"What?"

Natalie straightened and turned to the girl at that cry.

"Oh my God, I'm so sorry," Hailey said now with sincerity. "Yes. Of course. Do what you have to do . . . I'll tell her . . . Again, I'm sorry. Hang in—" Hailey's voice died midsentence. The caller had obviously hung up as she spoke, because she then hung up herself.

"Who was it?" Natalie asked as she set the iced teas on the tray with the other items.

"Timothy," Hailey said.

"Ah," Natalie murmured, suddenly understanding the drop in Hailey's enthusiasm after her cheerful greeting. Timothy had been a little short and sarcastic with Hailey since she'd refused his offer of a date a couple weeks ago. He obviously didn't take rejection well. Natalie had intended to have a talk with him about it, but then he'd started avoiding the club when the girl was working so it hadn't seemed necessary.

"He was calling to say that his father died in a car crash yesterday."

"What?" Natalie gasped in shock, sounding just like Hailey had moments ago.

"Yeah," Hailey said with a grim nod. "He wanted me to tell you he probably won't be coming back to work since he has stuff he needs to do for his family and the season'll most likely be over by the time everything's settled."

"Oh," Natalie breathed, but just stood there for a

minute, her mind in chaos. She wasn't overly upset about his not coming back to work this season. How could she be? Timothy's father had just died . . . and in a car accident. She knew how shocking and life-altering that could be. "Poor kid."

"Yeah," Hailey agreed. "I mean, he's a dick, but I wouldn't wish that on anyone."

Natalie didn't comment. She was remembering the trauma she'd gone through three years earlier, and imagining Timothy must be going through the same thing now.

"This is for Mr. Copeland and his friends, isn't it?" Hailey asked suddenly, and didn't wait for an answer before picking up the tray. "I'll take it to them and get their orders so you can get to the kitchen."

"Thanks." Natalie stood there for a minute, her mind on what Tim and his family must be going through right now. But finally she gave her head a shake and pushed those thoughts from her mind. There was nothing she could do for him or his family to mitigate the pain. Of course, she'd have to call and find out where the funeral was and arrange for flowers to be sent, and she'd need Tim's mother's address to send him his last paycheck, but she wouldn't bother him with that today. Tomorrow was soon enough.

The sound of a dog's barking came muffled from outside, and Natalie glanced out the window next to her, but of course couldn't see anything thanks to the open umbrellas on the patio. She walked around the counter to the door and peered out. Her gaze slid over the tables on the patio, noting that there was only one couple outside so far. She wasn't terribly surprised that most people were choosing to eat inside today, though. Mother Nature had decided to put on one last blast of heat before giving way to fall and it wasn't only hot, but crazy humid. It wouldn't be too bad walking around the course where the slight breeze she could see moving the leaves in the trees would give some relief, but the patio was in a spot protected from the breeze by the building and the woods surrounding it. There was no breeze there to give relief. The air-conditioned interior would naturally be preferred.

Noting that the couple had nearly full drinks and had just started on their meals so shouldn't need anything right away, Natalie shifted her gaze to the back corner of the property. From the door she could only see part of the small playground she'd had set up there. She'd bought and paid to have it installed at the start of the summer to give Mia something to do besides watch television inside. It included a swing set and a small raised playhouse with steps up and a slide down, and sat in what was basically a twenty-foot-wide and twenty-foot-deep sandbox. Mia loved it, and Emily was more than happy to spend all day out there watching Mia play if it made the little girl happy.

Fortunately, the teenager wasn't foolish enough to leave Mia in the sun for hours on end. Usually, she had Mia play in the shade under the raised playhouse, which was happening now. Mia was happily using a little plastic shovel to put sand in a pail in the shady patch under the playhouse, while Emily sat watching from a few feet away, out of the shade and enjoying the sun.

Another bark drew her gaze to Sinbad, who was half into the bushes and woods that ran along the back of the yard, obviously after a squirrel or some other small creature. A smile curving her lips, Natalie started to turn away from the door and then recalled that she needed to check the ringer. Pausing, she swung back and opened, then closed, the door. Her lips immediately twisted with irritation when nothing happened. The damned ringer *was* broken.

Something else to add to her list of things to take care of, Natalie thought as she made her way back around the counter to retrieve a yellow notepad from one of the shelves there. She set it on the counter and grabbed a pen to make a quick note to herself to take care of the ringer, and then paused as she spotted the envelope on the countertop.

Setting down the pen, Natalie picked up the envelope. It was a card. The size and paper quality of the envelope made that obvious. The front of it simply said "Natalie." Turning it over, she saw that the envelope hadn't been sealed, the flap had simply been tucked inside.

Curious, she opened the flap and pulled out the card. The words along the top in large, dark calligraphy immediately jumped out at her.

In Loving Memory

As silly as it was, Natalie immediately thought of Timothy's father since she'd just heard of his passing. If she'd stopped to think, she would have realized that in memoriam cards were passed out at funeral homes during viewings and certainly wouldn't already be made up if the man had just died. Natalie wasn't really thinking, though, and opened it to find that in the spot where the picture of the deceased should be was a photo of her, and under it in bloodred marker were the words

OF YOU.

Natalie's heart stuttered in her chest and she slapped the card closed only to find herself staring at the angel under the header that she hadn't noticed on first taking it out of the envelope. It was a pale white with little strokes of gray the only thing giving it shape and distinguishing it from the white background. She stared at it, a roaring in her ears that almost covered the sound of the door opening. It made the voice that spoke somewhat muffled until the roaring suddenly subsided, leaving a resonating silence in her head.

"Natalie? Are you all right? What's happened?"

Her movements were almost robotic as she lifted her head to see Valerian MacKenzie in front of the counter. Natalie stared at him dully, only peripherally aware of the two men behind him, and then she felt a touch on her arm.

"Natalie, dear, can I see that?"

Movements slow and jerky, she turned her attention to the auburn-haired woman now standing next to her. When Natalie just peered back at her blankly, trying to sort out how the woman knew her name, and when she'd joined her behind the counter, the stranger gently took the card from her. She watched her read the front, then open it and look inside. The woman blanched at what she found there, and then her expression turned grim and she slapped the card closed and held it out over the counter.

Natalie followed the motion, at first thinking the woman was handing it to Valerian, but then she realized he and the men who had entered with him were not the only ones at the counter now. A tall, muscular, grim-faced man with ice blond hair that she recognized as another member of the out-of-town quartet took the card, perused the front without comment, and then opened it and grunted at what he found.

Eyes like chips of ice shot to her then, and he barked, "Where did you get this?"

Natalie wasn't sure if it was his demanding tone, or the coldness of his expression, but some of the numbness that had been holding her hostage dissolved at once. Her spine suddenly stiffening, she jerked her head up and speared the man with cold eyes. "I'm sorry, but who the hell are you?"

"Er . . . Natalie." Valerian moved up beside the man and offered her a soothing smile. "It's all right. This is Lucian Argeneau. He's here to help."

Since the name meant nothing to her, confusion now swelled up to join her irritation and she asked, "Help with what?"

"Is there a problem here, Natalie?"

She turned to see Mr. Copeland and his friends approaching the front desk, concern on their faces as they took in the group now surrounding her.

"Sit," the man named Lucian Argeneau growled and, when the men didn't immediately obey, snapped, "Now."

Much to her amazement, Mr. Copeland and the other three men immediately turned away to head back to their table as dutifully as children ordered away by parents.

Natalie gaped after them, a little shocked at their abrupt defection, and then eyed the man in front of her with dislike. "You're a guest in my club, sir. I'd appreciate it if you didn't speak to my friends and customers that way or I'll have to ask you to leave." Deciding that was a good idea, she added, "Are you done with your meal? I'll have Hailey bring you your bill."

"Uh, Natalie," Valerian said, moving closer to the grim-faced man so that he was in her line of vision again.

Natalie reluctantly turned her gaze to Valerian, her glare softening a little as she looked at him in question.

"I should probably introduce everyone," he said gently. "The couple next to you are my uncle, Julius Notte, and his wife, Marguerite."

Natalie turned to look at the auburn-haired woman

and the man behind her, unable to hide her surprise. Aside from the fact that Valerian had fair hair and skin while the man named Julius was dark-haired, olive-skinned, and with features that suited his Italian name, the man also definitely didn't look old enough to be Valerian's uncle. And his wife didn't look old enough to be his aunt either. They actually looked to be about his age, which wasn't unheard of but was still unusual, she thought as she automatically nodded in greeting.

"And this is Lucian's wife, Leigh," Valerian continued, dragging her attention to the petite brunette she hadn't noticed standing beside the block of ice that was apparently her husband.

Poor woman, Natalie thought, and blinked in surprise when Leigh suddenly grinned at her with amusement.

"They're here at my behest," Valerian explained apologetically. "To help with your situation."

That last word had her turning sharply on him, bewilderment uppermost in her mind. "What situation?"

When he opened his mouth, closed it again, and then looked frustrated, Marguerite suggested, "Maybe we should go somewhere more private to talk."

"Yes," Valerian said at once, looking relieved, and then glanced to her in question. "Your office?"

Natalie hesitated, thinking she didn't have a "situation" she needed help with, and she really didn't want to spend any more time than necessary with these people, or at least not with the tall, blond man named Lucian. Too much time in his company and she'd probably get frostbite, Natalie thought, and then glanced around with surprise when Marguerite and the man's wife, Leigh, both released short laughs that they immediately tried to cover up with coughs.

Lucian scowled from one to the other, and then shifted his icy gaze to her and said, "Office now."

Natalie was immediately annoyed at his high-handed behavior. She also wasn't sure if she really wanted to be trapped in her office with these people. Apparently, it didn't matter, because without really deciding to, she found herself turning and making her way to her office.

She tried to fight the urge along the way. Very aware that the others were following her, Natalie wanted to stop and turn to say, *No, we can talk right here*, but didn't seem to be able to. Her body didn't respond to the order she was trying to send it . . . and while this both confused and alarmed her for a moment, in the next she was completely fine with it, which part of her mind, some echo far in the background, found dismaying. But that feeling was so distant she couldn't seem to grab ahold of it.

Natalie was halfway across her office before this odd disconnect ended and she felt in full control of herself again. She didn't stop then, though. Instead, she continued across the room to her desk, eager to put the large wooden surface between herself and the others. Feeling that sitting would put her at a disadvantage, Natalie remained standing and simply watched the people who crowded into her office and surrounded her desk. Marguerite and Julius took up position on the left side of her desk, while Leigh, Lucian, and

Valerian stood in front, and the two men who had been standing behind Valerian at the counter were now on the right side of her desk.

Feeling boxed in, Natalie's mouth tightened, but she tried to act like she wasn't feeling anxious and a little intimidated and let her gaze drift over everyone before stopping it on the two men she didn't know the names of. They were both around Valerian's height, muscular, and had dark hair and eyes and olive skin like Julius, but while one had sparkling eyes and a cheeky grin, the other looked as grim as the ice man, Lucian. They were both attractive, though, as all of them seemed to be, and she wondered briefly if she'd find them as attractive if she were to see them on the monitor.

Letting that thought go, she turned to Valerian and raised an eyebrow.

Seeming to understand the silent question, he immediately performed the introductions. "Natalie, these are my cousins, Alasdair and Colle Notte. They are the men Dani mentioned would be interested in jobs here."

Natalie's eyebrows shot up as her gaze shifted quickly back to the cousins. Like everybody else in her office, these two looked somewhere between twenty-four and twenty-eight, tops, so they weren't Julius Notte's sons.

Natalie flickered her gaze back to the others. Valerian was watching her warily, Leigh was peering around her office with curiosity, Julius appeared to simply be waiting patiently, but Marguerite and Lucian were both staring at her with a concentration that immediately put her nerves on edge. It also gave her something of an immediate headache. It wasn't so much painful as . . . she was experiencing a strange ruffling or fluttering sensation in her mind. It made her think of someone riffling through a file drawer, thumbing through the files in search of something.

Which, Natalie thought with irritation, was a stupid description for the uncomfortable sensation she was presently experiencing. She let her hand drop from her forehead where she'd unconsciously been rubbing, and ran an expectant gaze over the group as a whole.

"All right," she said finally. "What situation?"

There was a brief silence where she noticed the people in her office all seemed to shift their gazes to Lucian. But he merely turned an arched brow to Valerian. It seemed obvious Lucian Argeneau was someone important, at least among this group, and they'd looked to him to explain. However, he was passing the job on to Valerian.

She didn't miss the fact that Valerian appeared less than pleased to be stuck with the task, and almost laughed at the way his eyes widened and his lips twisted slightly when Lucian looked at him expectantly. But after a hesitation, Valerian straightened his shoulders and faced her resolutely.

"Okay, you said someone was following you on the golf course last night." He waited for her to give a brief nod of acknowledgment, and then said, "And they said, 'Angel—'"

"It was probably the wind," Natalie interrupted with a scowl to hide her discomfort and embarrassment at the way she'd freaked last night and taken off running like a kid about to wet themselves. Natalie had walked the course at night over a thousand times since taking it over and had never felt the least discomfort doing so. But that voice last night . . . that creepy, chilling whisper growl of "Angel" had really spooked her. Dear God, she'd been in such a panic she'd run right into the damned pond and knocked herself silly.

"I'm pretty sure it wasn't the wind," Valerian told her solemnly.

When she merely shrugged uncomfortably, he continued. "And then there was the angel statuette that was on your desk."

Natalie stiffened at that. She'd actually forgotten about the cheap little plastic angel that Mia had apparently got from her desk.

"And now you've got a card with an angel on it and a message that is . . ." He paused and glanced at the card he still held as if searching for a word.

Probably one that wouldn't be too alarming, she thought. "Threatening?"

"Yes. Threatening," Valerian acknowledged. "There seems to be something of a pattern forming here, so I thought I'd better call in some help."

Natalie narrowed her eyes. "Thinking I heard someone whisper 'Angel' on the wind, and finding that little figurine, which is probably just a lucky charm someone lost on the golf course, do not make a pattern. You need more than two things to make a pattern."

"The card—"

"The card showed up after your aunt and uncle and

the others arrived. Before there was a pattern to suggest a situation," she said, her voice grim and suspicious.

"Where did the card come from?" Valerian asked rather than argue the point.

"I don't know," Natalie admitted after a hesitation where she briefly debated forcing him back to the point she'd made. Deciding to let it go for now, she said, "It wasn't there this morning, I don't think. At least, if it was, I only noticed it moments before you showed up when I went to get drinks for Mr. Copeland and his friends."

The words reminded her of how Lucian had snapped at her customers and she took the time to cast a dirty look in his direction. Not that he seemed to notice; he had gone from scowling at her, to scowling at Valerian, and now growled, "She doesn't recall the grass."

"No," Valerian sighed the word with something like regret. "We didn't want her unnecessarily alarmed, so Decker . . . helped me," he said meaningfully and then, noting the way she began to frown, quickly added, "To keep her from getting a proper look at the dead patch."

Lucian grunted in understanding and immediately turned to her.

Natalie froze when his ice-chipped gaze narrowed on her. For a brief moment she felt something like that ruffling or fluttering she'd experienced earlier, and then her memory of the splash of dead grass popped up in her mind. It was as bright and clear as it had been when she'd seen it that morning under the beating sun, only where she'd recalled it just being a blob, she now saw quite clearly that it had looked like a—

"Snow angel," she whispered with dismay, and noticed the way Valerian jerked in surprise, but she was busy reexamining the memory that was suddenly clear in her mind. It had been a big, life-sized, dirty yellow-brown snow angel surrounded by green. How had she forgotten that?

"Right, the snow angel was the third thing that made a pattern," Valerian said, drawing her from her thoughts.

Natalie looked at him, her mind now running through the events, someone calling out "Angel" in the dark, a plastic angel figurine on her desk, a snow angel made from dead grass in her course, and now the angel in memoriam card. Oh yeah, it was a definite pattern, and one she wasn't really liking. "You think it's the Angel-Maker."

Valerian wasn't the only one startled by her words. "You know about the Angel-Maker?"

Natalie eyed him with disbelief. "You're kidding, right? We do get the news out here in the country, and the Angel-Maker story was on every channel for a while. Of course I know about him."

"Of course," he said apologetically.

"What I don't know," Natalie said, ignoring his apology, "is why you would think it has anything to do with me. The Angel-Maker goes after prostitutes, and I am not now, nor have I ever been, a prostitute, so there's no reason for him to come after me."

"Not all of the victims have been prostitutes," Marguerite corrected gently. "The first victim was an un-wed mother of a two-month-old baby who lived in a building where a lot of prostitutes also lived. Many of them were her friends, and there is some suggestion she was considering taking up the profession to support her child. But she hadn't done so," she added firmly. "However, by the time the Angel-Maker sent his first letter to the newspaper and they realized there was a serial killer, there had been three women murdered, the first girl, who hung out with prostitutes, and two who actually were prostitutes. The reporters didn't bother to make the distinction and simply ran with the prostitute connection."

"I forgot about that," Valerian said with surprise, and then shook his head. "But it doesn't matter, Natalie isn't an unwed mother either. She's a widow. Her husband died while she was pregnant with Mia, but she *did* have a husband."

"I didn't," Natalie countered quietly, and when Valerian turned to her with surprise, she added grimly, "I am in fact an unwed mother."

Seven

Valerian stared at Natalie blankly for a minute, completely thrown by her words, and then shook his head. "Emily told me your history, Natalie. You're a widow. You were married to Mia's father. He, your son, and your parents all died in a car accident three years ago and Mia was born six months later."

"I did marry Mia and Cody's father," Natalie agreed, and then dropped into her desk chair before adding solemnly, "But I wasn't married."

"What?" Valerian asked with confusion.

Natalie was silent for a minute, and then she scrubbed her fingers through her hair with frustration before letting her hands drop to her desktop and lifting her chin almost defiantly. "I thought I was married."

"But you weren't?" Valerian asked slowly, trying to understand.

Natalie's mouth tightened. "I married Devin Daniels in Vegas seven years ago; we had a son a year later, and then, three years after that, when I was three months pregnant with Mia, a drunk driver T-boned the car my husband, my three-year-old son, and both of my parents were in." Her mouth twisted and her eyes closed briefly before she continued. "Not only did I lose my entire family, but at the hospital I learned my husband wasn't my husband. There was another Mrs. Daniels, and she'd been married to him for sixteen years, much longer than the four years we'd been married."

"Which made your marriage invalid," Valerian breathed as he grasped the situation.

"Right." Natalie lowered her gaze. "I wasn't his wife, just . . . the other woman with a fake piece of paper, using a name I had no right to."

"You'd taken his name after the wedding?" Valerian asked, because she went by Moncreif now so wasn't using his name.

"I had. But I changed back to my maiden name after moving here to the golf course," she admitted, and he saw the shame that flickered across her expression before she said, "It seemed like the thing to do. I had no legal claim to his name. We weren't really married."

Valerian was aware that everyone was looking at him, expecting him to say something, probably to comfort Natalie, but he couldn't. Mostly because he was afraid of what he'd say if he opened his mouth. The overriding emotion in him at that moment was rage. At Devin Daniels. He couldn't imagine how devastating it had been for her to lose her young son, her parents, and her husband in one fell swoop, and then on top of that learn that her husband wasn't her husband, and her life had been one big lie. The bastard had been a bigamist and a womanizer and . . . basically a piece of shit as far as he was concerned. And he couldn't understand how anyone could have done that. To anyone, let alone a woman as beautiful, and strong, as Natalie was. And she was obviously strong, because from what he knew, she'd had all of that crash over her and had simply picked up, moved out here, taken over the running of the golf course, and done it very successfully. All while dealing with her loss and grief and at first being pregnant, and then while raising a baby on her own.

"So . . ."

Valerian focused on Natalie again when she uttered that word, and watched her straighten her shoulders and raise her chin proudly.

"I *am* an unwed mother, and if the Angel-Maker's first victim was an unwed mother rather than a prostitute then I do match his victim demographic. I suppose that means it is him doing all this."

"It's a possibility," Marguerite said when he remained silent, still struggling with his emotions. "And as such, Valerian was right and it has to be checked out. I mean, someone calling out 'Angel' in the dark, the angel figurine, the snow-angel-shaped dead grass right where Valerian laid you the night before when he pulled you out of the water, and now the card *do* suggest something is going on. We just don't know if the Angel-Maker does these sorts of things ahead of attacking his victims or not." Pausing she looked at Lucian. "Do we?"

When Lucian immediately turned to him in question, Valerian forced his anger back and cleared his throat. Even so, his voice was gruff when he said, "Mortimer was going to have people check with acquaintances of the past victims to find out if any of them knew of things like this happening, but I haven't heard from him yet."

Lucian promptly pulled out his phone and punched in numbers, then walked across the room to the door to glance out into the hall as he waited for his call to be answered.

Valerian shifted his attention back to Natalie. She was still holding her head high, her eyes trained on Lucian as she waited. Valerian was simply staring at her when Leigh suddenly elbowed him, gave him a meaningful expression, and then glanced to Natalie and back. Realizing she was trying to tell him to say something to Natalie, he blurted, "Devin Daniels was a dick and I hope he's burning in hell."

Valerian knew at once that those words weren't the best. He didn't need Marguerite's and Leigh's gasps, or the groans from his male relatives, to tell him that.

Silently berating himself for the outburst, he eyed Natalie warily, sure he'd find anger there, or perhaps hurt, so he was a bit surprised when instead he found her biting her lip, the muscles in her face struggling as if she were fighting not to smile or laugh.

Hardly able to believe she wasn't upset with him, he

allowed himself to take a cautious breath and offered, "I'm sorry. That was inappropriate."

"Don't be sorry," she said with amusement. "He *was* a dick."

He was just relaxing when she added, "But . . ."

Valerian waited for her to continue. Unfortunately, it took her a minute, as if she was choosing her words carefully, and then she said, "But I wouldn't have had Cody without him and Cody was . . ." She shook her head and tears glossed her eyes as she was no doubt barraged with memories of her little boy, before she said, "Special. He was such a little sweetheart." She swallowed and cleared her throat, before adding, "So is Mia . . . and I wouldn't have had her either without him. I try to remember that. It helps me forgive him, which I had to do for my daughter. I never want her to feel less than because of who her father was or what he did."

Valerian stared, grappling with her words. He was centuries older than her and yet in that moment she seemed centuries more mature. "That makes you special, because I don't know if I could forgive a betrayal like that myself. Even for a child. But then, I haven't had my own children yet, so maybe that makes the difference."

"Maybe," Natalie allowed, but then her lips twitched with amusement. "Or maybe it's just the years of therapy I've had since the crash."

She allowed herself to smile then and he was helpless to keep from smiling in return. Dear God, she was beautiful. Valerian had met a multitude of women over the more than two centuries since his birth, but didn't recall thinking any of them were as beautiful as he found Natalie to be. Which told him she was definitely his life mate, because some of those women had been world-renowned beauties who in reality had probably been far lovelier than the woman before him. But in his mind, none of them could hold a candle to her. Valerian knew that could only be a result of her being his life mate. He also knew that because of that, she would always be the most beautiful woman in the world to him. Which meant he had to keep her alive, and somehow convince her to be his life mate, or he'd lose her and be alone and miserable for centuries, perhaps even millennia, if not forever.

"Er . . . Valerian?"

Blinking his thoughts away, he focused on Natalie in time to see her gesture for him to follow as she slid out from behind the desk. Curious, he excused himself to the others and followed her to the corner of the room. Valerian made sure to stay several steps behind her and stopped at once when she did to ensure there was enough space between them that he wouldn't accidentally touch her. So, he was more than a little alarmed when she turned, noted the space between them, and grabbed his arm to tug him forward to narrow that distance.

Fortunately, he'd donned a long-sleeved shirt over his T-shirt today when he'd headed back to the golf course to meet up with his cousins. He'd done so as protection against the sun since it was midday, but it now had the added benefit of keeping her hand from touching his skin.

Grateful for that, he released a little sigh of relief when she dropped his arm, only to suck in a sharp breath when she suddenly leaned up on her tiptoes and braced her hand against his chest to steady herself as she whispered in his ear.

Valerian stood there wide-eyed and heart racing as her scent enveloped him and her breath brushed against his ear.

"Wah wah wah wah wah," was all he heard. It was followed by, "Wah wah, and wah wah wah OPP." The last three letters, the abbreviation for the Ontario Provincial Police, knocked him out of his stupor and he jerked back slightly to get a look at her face as he asked with alarm, "What?"

She was at first startled by his reaction, and then seemed a little exasperated as she explained in a low voice, "Well, I know you said your family was here to help, but don't you think this is really something for the OPP? I mean, if—"

"No," he said sharply, and then realized he'd put more volume behind the word than intended. He took a breath before saying more calmly, "The police really don't have the manpower or even the tools to deal with this character if it's the Angel-Maker."

"And your relatives do?" Natalie asked dubiously.

"They are not all relatives," he corrected gently. "Leigh and Lucian aren't related to me."

"Whatever," she said impatiently, and then sighed and said, "Look, I appreciate everything you've done for me. You probably saved my life last night when you pulled me out of the pond. And carrying me back here and bringing in Dr. Dani was super sweet. But the Angel-Maker is a cold-blooded killer, a psychopath. The man bleeds his victims dry and then poses them naked like dolls for the world to see what he's done. I don't want to end up that way. I have a daughter to think of. I need the authorities on this. Professionals who can keep me safe and catch this guy."

"We *are* professionals," Valerian assured her the moment she paused to take a breath.

The words seemed to startle her into a pause that lasted the length of a heartbeat and then she clucked with irritation and pointed out, "You're a farmer, Valerian. And your cousins Alasdair and Colle signed up to mow my course. Those aren't the kind of professionals I need on this."

Before Valerian could respond, he felt a tap on his shoulder. He turned to see Leigh and Marguerite, and both of them were eyeing him with a combination of sympathy and pity.

"I think you should go keep the men company and let us explain the situation to Natalie," Leigh said solemnly. "Besides, Lucian is done with his phone call and wants a word with you."

He hesitated, but then glanced over to where Lucian had rejoined Julius and the others. When the man jerked his head in a silent order to get over there, Valerian sighed.

"Very well," he said, and then hesitated and asked Natalie, "Are you all right with my aunt and Leigh explaining things?"

She looked confused and a bit unhappy, but gave an

abrupt nod, so he assured her, "I'll be right over there if you need me," before turning to move away.

Natalie had to fight the urge to call Valerian back as she watched him walk away. She had no idea why. She barely knew the man, but felt more of a connection to him than any of the others, even the two women now moving to stand side by side in front of her. Forcing herself to face them, Natalie managed a polite smile and waited for one of them to speak.

"Hi," Leigh said brightly.

"Hi," Natalie responded with uncertainty.

"I realize this is all probably very frightening and confusing for you, and I want you to know I really do understand," she assured her. "In fact, I had a crazy psychopath after me some years back so have been in your shoes and can understand everything you must be going through right now."

Natalie blinked at that revelation. It was the last thing she'd expected to hear. "You did?"

"Yes. I did." Leigh nodded solemnly. "It was a terrifying time, and if it weren't for my husband, Lucian, I probably wouldn't have survived it."

Natalie looked over at Lucian Argeneau. He was presently surrounded by the other men, who were listening as he talked and merely giving an occasional nod. Their expressions, though, were serious and respectful. Even Valerian seemed to be showing him some deference, though she noticed his eyes sliding her way a couple of times, as if worried about her, or perhaps about how this conversation was going.

"My husband is the head of an organization that

acts as an umbrella over various agencies and departments," Leigh said now. "One of those agencies is a special branch of . . . law enforcement headed by a man named Garrett Mortimer. They hunt down . . . serial killers. Like your Angel-Maker and the man who was after me."

Natalie looked at Leigh with a combination of curiosity and suspicion. She hadn't missed the slight hesitation in the woman's speech before saying "law enforcement" and "serial killers" and wondered what had caused it. But then Leigh met her gaze and said, "Valerian works under Mortimer in that agency."

"What?" Natalie asked with surprise, and then she shook her head. "He's a farmer. He bought the old Wilkins farm down the road."

"Yes," Marguerite said now, joining the conversation. "But he rents the land out to someone else to farm and helicopters into work in Toronto five nights a week." She waited a moment to allow that to sink in. "In truth, you are very lucky he wanted a quiet place in the country and moved out here, not to mention that he loves to golf. It might have saved your life, and not just because he pulled you out of the pond. But because he suspected there was a connection here with the Angel-Maker last night and called the office at once, setting things in motion. It's the reason so many of us showed up today."

"The other out-of-towners in the dining room?" Natalie asked.

"Our men," Leigh said with a nod, and then added, "And so are Alasdair and Colle. They're Enforcers, just not in this area usually. However, Valerian arranged for them to come because he was concerned that anyone else working here might unintentionally damage your course and he didn't want that."

Eyes widening, Natalie glanced over toward the two men in question and supposed she shouldn't be surprised they both worked hunting down serial killers. She guessed it made sense to be in good shape for such a job, and these men were. They were both . . . big. It was the only word to describe them. Valerian was muscular, but these guys were brawny with thick necks and bulging arms.

"So, you see," Leigh said now, regaining Natalie's attention, "while the OPP really aren't equipped to deal with someone of the Angel-Maker's ilk, we are. We'll keep you safe."

"And hopefully catch the bastard this time," Marguerite said a bit grimly.

"This time?" Natalie asked.

"The men were on his trail last winter, but his killings seemed to stop when the weather warmed up and there was no more snow. They thought he'd gone to ground until the next snowfall. But obviously he's just changed his pattern to suit the weather with dead-grass angels rather than snow angels."

"And his hunting ground has changed too," Leigh pointed out. "All of his previous victims were in Toronto."

"True," Marguerite murmured, eyeing Natalie speculatively. "I wonder what brought him to this area, and how he latched on to you."

"Maybe he saw her in Toronto and followed her here," Leigh suggested.

"Have you been to Toronto this summer?" Marguerite asked.

The question surprised a short laugh from Natalie. "I haven't been to Toronto since university," she told them. "I haven't even left the county since moving here three years ago, and hardly leave the golf course at all now."

"Then he must have played golf here at some point," Leigh commented.

Natalie stiffened, but then realized it must be true. Dear God, the Angel-Maker was one of her own customers.

Eight

"There, that should do it," Valerian said, and shifted out from under the table.

Tybo offered him a hand to help him up, but Valerian waved it away and got up on his own, then moved to stand next to Alasdair behind the booth where Colle sat, now turning on the security monitor. He wasn't the only one to release a relieved breath when the monitor came to life with nine images on it, three of the interior of the clubhouse, and six of the exterior. They'd patched into Natalie's security system and ran a feed to the RV so that Colle and Alasdair could watch for anyone approaching the building.

The RV was his uncle Julius's vehicle, loaned to them for this job. Valerian had been surprised when he'd offered it, but was now very grateful. The RV, and running the security system patch out here, saved them having to put one man on every side of the house, leaving them more men to patrol the property.

Colle clicked on the image of the employee parking lot, bringing it to the forefront to fill the screen, clicked again, and it receded so that all nine images were visible once more.

"I think we're good," Colle said, relaxing back against the booth seat.

"Yeah," Valerian agreed, and then walked around to the end of the table to peer down at the blown-up satellite image of Shady Pines. Someone, probably Mortimer's wife, Sam, had found it on Google Maps, and somehow enlarged and printed it. They'd then used it to decide where to station the men so that the better part of the golf course and house were covered.

Valerian glanced over the image of the clubhouse itself, noting the red circles that had been drawn around the doors: the door to the gift store at the front that was usually kept locked, leaving people to have to enter from the dining room, the side door that was the main entrance, the kitchen door for deliveries, the sliding door off Natalie's office, and—

"What's this?" he asked, pointing to a circle at the back of the building. As far as he knew there was no back door.

Tybo moved up beside him to see where he was pointing, and said, "Oh, that's a bulkhead cellar door."

"You mean one of those double doors in the ground?" Valerian asked with a frown.

"Yeah. It opens to stairs down to a door in the basement," Tybo answered.

"Is it secure?" Valerian asked with concern. He'd thought he'd checked all the doors, but he'd done it from in the house and hadn't gone into the basement because he hadn't thought there could be an entrance underground. He'd never even thought of cellar doors; they were such an old-fashioned feature. But then this property used to be a farm way back when, and the clubhouse used to be an old farmhouse. He supposed he should have considered it would have things like cellar doors and such.

"Oh yeah, it's secure," Tybo assured him. "There's a heavy-duty steel padlock on it that's been there since before Natalie's father bought the place. She doesn't even know if there's a key for it anymore. She's never worried about it because it doesn't get used. She said the inner door comes out under the stairs. It's locked too and a bunch of boxes are stacked in front of it. No one's getting in that way."

Relaxing, Valerian nodded and took one more look at the image before saying, "Then it looks like we have everything covered."

"I'd say so," Tybo agreed. "No one's getting in without Colle and Alasdair seeing them, and the other men are patrolling the grounds. It should be all good."

"And even if someone does manage to slip past everyone, you'll be inside with Natalie as the last line of defense," Colle added. "I think we're covered here."

"All right." Valerian straightened and glanced around. "Then if there's nothing else we need to do, I guess I should go check in with the other guys before I go inside."

Natalie turned off the kitchen lights and jogged downstairs to check on a sleeping Mia. A smile of affection curved her lips as she looked in on her daughter. The little girl was sound asleep, splayed out in her little princess bed, her teddy bear clutched in one hand and half hanging off the mattress.

Movement drew her gaze down to where Sinbad was curled up in his dog bed next to Mia's. The movement had been him lifting his head. Recognizing her in the doorway, he gave one wave of his tail and then lowered his head and closed his eyes again, satisfied that all was well.

Natalie eased the door closed and returned upstairs. She'd entered the large lower dining room and was halfway across it before her footsteps slowed. Normally, she would be heading out to mow the lawn with Tim at this hour while Ashley or Emily watched over Mia. Now Colle and Alasdair were doing that, and Natalie had given Emily the night off because she was free to be with Mia herself.

Pausing, she looked around uncertainly as she mentally readjusted her thoughts, and then finally continued forward. Her gaze slid over the empty dining room, making sure everything was in order. She then mounted the short steps to the upper dining area and did a quick survey of it as she walked to the reception counter. A check of the drink refrigerators and shelf of snacks showed that they didn't need restocking.

Hailey or Maddy must have taken care of that before they left, Natalie thought, so turned her attention to closing out the till instead. Removing the cash drawer altogether once done, she carried it with her as she walked around to the door, intending to lock it, but then stopped as she realized she couldn't. Valerian was out checking on the other men and wouldn't be able to get back in if she locked it.

The thought of leaving the door unlocked left her uncomfortable, but she didn't really have a choice, so Natalie forced herself to turn and head to her office to count the day's receipts. Once that was done, she put the tray and money in the safe, and then stood in her office and looked around, feeling rather lost. She'd had the same daily routine for the last three years. It varied a little after the golf season ended, but then she had a different routine. Now . . . Natalie had no idea what to do with herself.

The realization was rather staggering. Here, after years of not having a moment to herself, she'd been given free time, and didn't have a clue what to do with it.

Giving her head an impatient shake, Natalie set herself to the task of cleaning her office, picking up Mia's toys and putting them in the toy chest in the corner, and then folding the throws and setting them on the back of the sofa. All in all, it took maybe ten minutes, and then she was once again at a loss as to what to do. Natalie just wasn't used to having spare time. Every moment of her day for the last three years had been taken up with tasks that needed doing whether it was mowing, working in the restaurant, doing taxes, or spending time with her daughter, which was the closest thing to relaxation that she enjoyed.

But now her workday was essentially done, her daughter was sleeping, and she had time she didn't know how to fill.

After standing there for several minutes feeling incredibly stupid, Natalie glanced around the office for inspiration and her gaze landed on the bookshelf. Walking over, she ran her gaze over the titles, but they were all business books: catalogs, how-to books for tending to the course, etc. There wasn't a single novel or fiction title. But then, she hadn't had time to read since university, so supposed she shouldn't have expected anything different.

Turning away from the bookshelf, Natalie found her gaze landing on the television. She stared at it for a minute, and then walked over to grab the remote off the coffee table and dropped onto the couch as she hit the button to turn on the TV. After flicking through the channels and not finding anything interesting, she switched to the Apple box and scrolled through her own movies before finally settling on *Tucker & Dale vs. Evil*. Perhaps not the best choice when she'd just found out she had a psycho killer stalking her, but it was a movie she often put on when stressed because it made her laugh.

She was only about five minutes in when Valerian came into the room. Natalie sat up at once and hit pause on the remote, then hesitated, debating whether she should turn it off and go to bed, or—

"Tucker & Dale vs. Evil?" Valerian asked, eyeing the paused screen as he walked around the end of the couch.

"Yes. You know it?" she asked, not hiding her surprise. It hadn't exactly been a big hit. In fact, Natalie had never even heard of it before buying it more than a decade ago, but the trailer had looked so entertaining at the time she'd decided to give it a try. It was actually a comedy/horror, and had some gory scenes, but the humor and wit more than made up for it to her mind. Besides, it wasn't really scary, at least she didn't find it so.

"Oh yes, I know it," Valerian said with a grin. "But I'm pleasantly surprised you do. It's a good movie, but I didn't think a lot of people knew about it."

"Yeah. Same here." Natalie grinned back.

Valerian hesitated briefly, his gaze shifting from her to the TV screen to the couch. "Is it okay if I watch it with you?"

"Yes, of course. Sit," she said, and watched him settle at the other end of the sofa before asking, "Everything okay?"

Valerian nodded. "Yes. Alasdair and Colle finished mowing the course, and then we patched into your security system so they can watch the cameras from the RV when they aren't patrolling."

Natalie nodded. She had no idea where the RV had come from. She supposed it was a company vehicle belonging to the agency, but it had shown up that afternoon and now took up half of her small employee parking lot. Natalie gathered Alasdair and Colle were staying in it to be on site at all times until this was over. Although the other men guarding the property might be using it as well between shifts. She had no idea. She hadn't met any of these men who were apparently patrolling her golf course to watch for any sign of the Angel-Maker.

Natalie suspected the four out-of-town men that had been in the restaurant at the same time as Lucian, Leigh, Marguerite, and Julius might be among them. She wasn't sure about that, but after the meeting in her office, Lucian had stopped at both tables and talked to the men before leaving with his wife and Valerian's aunt and uncle. She suspected Lucian had been briefing the men on what had been decided. Or really, what *he* had decided, because after she and the other two women had rejoined the men, Lucian had announced that Valerian would be staying in the clubhouse and there would be six men besides him on-site at all times, which included Alasdair and Colle, who would work here for cover and stay in an RV.

When Natalie had protested that she didn't have anywhere for Valerian to sleep, Lucian had merely pointed at the couch in her office. She hadn't protested further. Mostly because she wasn't stupid. It appeared that a psycho killer had set his sights on her. She would do whatever was necessary to keep her and her daughter safe. Not that the Angel-Maker had killed children before this, but she was the only family Mia had other than distant cousins Natalie hadn't met more than a handful of times as a child. She didn't want her daughter being raised by complete strangers. She also didn't want to end up dead.

"And then I checked in with the rest of the men," Valerian added, pulling her from her thoughts. "No one has seen or heard anything to be concerned about, but they're on the alert."

Natalie nodded and relaxed a little. She started to raise the remote, but then paused and asked, "You locked the door when you came in, right?"

"Yes," he assured her, his expression and tone serious.

Natalie offered an apologetic smile for checking on him like that, and then turned to start the movie going again.

They watched it in a companionable silence, broken only by the occasional chuckle or laugh, and it was nice, but she found herself looking at him a lot, often finding him looking back. It was during the last half hour of the movie that she noticed that he had started to absently rub his stomach. Natalie didn't think anything of it at first, but then suddenly realized that as far as she knew, he hadn't eaten since arriving at the clubhouse that morning with his cousins. He was probably starved. Since there was only about ten minutes left to the movie by the time that occurred to her, she didn't say anything until it had ended.

"Are you hungry?" Natalie finally asked as the ending credits started to roll.

Valerian blinked in surprise, appeared to consider the question, and then said slowly, "I could eat."

He didn't sound too sure, though, and she wondered if he was afraid that her cooking might suck. That's when it occurred to Natalie that as far as he knew, she just ran the golf course. He'd been out most of the afternoon and evening doing something or other with the men Lucian had left behind. He hadn't seen her working in the kitchen and had no idea about her background and training.

Well, he was about to find out, Natalie thought as she turned off the television. "Come on, then. I'll make us something."

As he followed her into the kitchen a moment later, Valerian asked with curiosity, "So, you use the restaurant kitchen for personal cooking?"

Natalie was surprised at the question, but then realized that he couldn't know this was the only kitchen. He hadn't really seen anything of the club except for the main floor, and probably hadn't seen all of that even. There was a small gift shop at the front he would have had no reason to go into, and he may or may not have seen the public washrooms off the lower dining area. He definitely hadn't been downstairs, though, so had no idea what was there.

"I don't have a choice at the moment," Natalie said finally as she walked to the large, old industrial refrigerator and opened the door to check the contents. As she perused what was available, she explained, "This place wasn't set up for anyone to live here when I inherited it from my parents. The basement was all one large concrete storage area with a little furnace room at the back when I got it." Pausing, she turned to ask, "Do you like steak?"

"I used to," he said and, when her eyebrows rose, added, "I mean yes."

Natalie eyed him for a minute, but then pulled out the large container of hanger steaks soaking in a soy marinade that she'd put in the refrigerator earlier for the next day. Reminding herself to drop a couple more steaks in later so she wouldn't run short tomorrow, she closed the door and set them on the counter. She then gathered a couple of sweet potatoes, some green and yellow wax beans, scallions, and garlic, and carried it all back to set on the prep counter next to the steak. Next, she grabbed a strainer, tossed the sweet potatoes and wax beans in, and took them to the sink to quickly clean the vegetables as she continued her explanations.

"When I first took over the golf club, I lived in my parents' home, which I also inherited. But it seemed a waste to pay heat and gas and electricity there when Mia and I spent so much time here."

"You kept Mia here while you worked?" Valerian asked with surprise. "Even as a newborn?"

"Of course. I was breastfeeding, so couldn't just hire a nanny." She paused for a minute and then admitted, "Well, I suppose I could have pumped milk and left it with the nanny to feed her while I was gone, but then I wouldn't have seen Mia at all. I was here from dawn until past midnight most days during golfing season and eleven in the morning until eleven in the evening the rest of the year." She finished cleaning the vegetables, used paper towel to pat them dry, and then carried them to the prep counter, grabbed a knife, and started slicing the sweet potatoes into fries.

"What can I do to help?" Valerian asked, stepping up beside her.

Natalie hesitated, but then said, "If you want to cut off the ends of the wax beans that would be good."

"My pleasure. Does it matter what knife I use?"

Natalie handed him hers, and went to fetch another.

"So, if you had no nanny at first, what did you do with Mia while you were working?" Valerian asked as they both began cutting up the vegetables.

"Sometimes she slept in her crib in my office, but most of the time I used a baby carrier," Natalie told him, and glanced up in time to see confusion cross his face. "It's kind of like a backpack, but the top is open and there are holes for the legs. I'd wear it in front while mowing the green and doing office stuff, but wore it so she rested against my back when cooking to ensure she didn't get splashed with hot oil or anything." She shrugged. "It actually worked pretty good for the most part."

"And you'd just take her home to sleep at night?" he asked.

Natalie nodded. "I did that for about seven or eight months. I moved out here during the last month or so of that year's golfing season. Stayed at my parents' place for the end of that season, and through the winter while it was shut down. But it only took about a month of the next season to realize working here and sleeping there wasn't going to work." She paused her cutting to grab a pot, fill it with water, and set it on the burner to start heating.

Returning to cutting, Natalie continued. "I was barely spending any time at the house. In fact, a lot of the time I'd just sleep on the couch in my office with Mia in her portable crib so I could get more rest. So, I decided to put a bedroom in here."

"I'm guessing that's in the basement?" Valerian asked.

"Yes. At the time, it was one big unfinished room with concrete walls and floors and some support beams down the center. It was full of golfing equipment, food, and stock items for the gift shop. It was all just sitting around in boxes willy-nilly. So, I had the walls insulated with that spray foam stuff so that it would be warm and dry down there. Then I bought shelves and organized all the stock on one side of the basement, and had a bedroom and private bathroom built on the other side." She smiled faintly. "It only took a few weeks to get it done, and then I moved in with Mia and sold my parents' house."

"I'm surprised you didn't just rent out the house," Valerian commented. "You might want to move back there someday once Mia is older."

Natalie shook her head. "I plan on putting on additions here. A proper apartment with its own entrance for me and Mia, and a larger dining room and kitchen for the club, as well as an events room for weddings and other celebrations that I can cater."

Finished with the sweet potatoes, she started to mince garlic and added, "The sale of the house gave me a good chunk of change to put toward the additions, but not quite enough. So, I stuck the money in low-risk investments and have been running the restaurant and golf course with as few employees as possible to save as much money as I can to put toward the additions."

"When do you think that will happen?" Valerian asked with interest.

"Next spring, I hope," Natalie said, unable to keep from smiling at the prospect of having a proper home for her and Mia. Their own apartment where they could lock themselves away from the world when not working sounded like bliss. She was also excited at the chance to be able to work a little less, because once the expense of the additions was out of the way, she wouldn't have to scrimp on staff and do the work of three people to save money anymore. Not that Natalie planned on sitting on her laurels and letting others do all the work for her, but it would be nice to work eight or ten hours a day five or six days a week rather than twenty-hour days seven days a week. She could spend more time with Mia that didn't include dragging the poor kid on the mower with her, or having her play in her office while she worked.

"I'm done with the beans. What next?"

Natalie glanced at the beans Valerian had taken care of and then at the pot of water. It wasn't quite boiling yet.

Setting down the garlic, she crossed the room to a shelf of bowls and picked one with a lid, then stopped to put the air fryer on preheat, before grabbing some spices and vegetable oil. Carrying them back to the counter, she set them down and picked up the strainer she'd used to rinse the vegetables.

"Can you put the sweet potatoes I cut into this, rinse them in the sink, and then pat them dry with paper towel?" she requested.

"As good as done," Valerian assured her, and moved off, leaving her to start slicing the scallions.

She'd finished the task by the time he returned. Thanking him, Natalie quickly dumped the sweet potato fries into the bowl she'd collected, measured in the spices and oil, slammed the lid on, and handed it back.

"Shake," she instructed, and then turned on the gas grill to heat up before walking over to check the air fryer. There were just seconds left on the preheat, and she turned to tell Valerian to bring the soon-to-be fries over, only to stop and step back in surprise when she found him right beside her.

"I'm guessing these go in there?" he said with amusement, removing the lid of the bowl as the fryer's buzzer went off.

Natalie nodded, and then watched as he pulled the drawer open, dumped the sweet potato fries in, closed it, and quickly pushed the correct selection of buttons to set it working.

"I have one at home for when my little sister, Aileen, visits," he explained when she raised her eyebrows. "I make wings and fries and whatnot in it for her when she comes."

Smiling, Natalie moved around him to head back to the prep counter. She didn't tell him she was impressed that he knew how to cook, but she was. In her experience, if a man wasn't a chef, he didn't bother with the task, but left it up to the women in his life. But maybe that had been only her, because she was a chef so they thought she should do it, Natalie considered, and asked Valerian, "How old is Aileen?"

"Twenty-two. She's at university in Toronto . . . much to my mother's dismay," he added with dry amusement.

"Why would that upset your mother?"

"Because she wanted her to pick a university closer to home. If not Scotland itself, at least England or somewhere in Europe where she could go home more often."

"Your family lives in Scotland?" Natalie asked, and knew her tone had been a little sharp when his eyebrows rose slightly.

"Yes," Valerian answered slowly. "Is that a problem?"

"No. Of course not," Natalie muttered, and turned quickly back to the counter. Grabbing tongs, she removed two steaks from the large container of marinading meat and set them on the grill. As it hissed and the flames roared up with excitement to sear them, she covered the remaining marinading steaks and returned them to the refrigerator. On the way back, she grabbed another bowl and filled it with water and ice cubes.

"What else can I do?" Valerian asked as she carried the bowl of ice water back to the prep table.

"Nothing. Just keep me company. It's all under control now," Natalie assured him as she dumped the wax beans in the now boiling water. Leaving them there for a minute she stepped away to collect apple cider vinegar and some spices, then lifted the boiling pot of wax beans off the range and carried them to the sink to drain them.

"Will they be cooked?" Valerian asked, eyeing the beans dubiously as she rinsed them.

"Just blanched. We're having a cold bean salad, not hot beans," she explained.

"Oh. I've never even heard of that," he admitted with surprise. "I thought salad was lettuce and stuff."

"It can be," she said easily. "But it can be shredded brussels sprouts, or blanched wax beans, or all sorts of things besides plain old lettuce."

"Hmm."

Natalie could feel him watching her, and felt her face heat up self-consciously as she next dumped the beans in the ice water.

"You really like to cook, don't you?" Valerian asked as he watched her whip up a vinaigrette using the apple cider vinegar, minced garlic, and spices.

"I trained as a chef," she said simply.

"Really?" Valerian asked with surprise. "I didn't know."

"Now you do," Natalie said lightly.

"Hmm," Valerian murmured. "What made you want to be a chef?"

"Self-defense mostly," she said with amusement and, catching his confusion, explained, "My mother couldn't cook worth beans. So, it was learn to cook or eat overcooked meat and vegetables boiled to the point they had no flavor or color left." Natalie shrugged.

"I started trying to cook. Found I loved it, and actually liked food."

Valerian smiled faintly and shook his head. "I thought from all the business texts on the shelf in the office that you must have been a business major at university or something."

"Good guess. I was," Natalie admitted with a chuckle. "At least at first. My father wanted me to get a degree that I could—as he put it—actually use, and not take something I could learn in home ec."

"Ouch," Valerian muttered sympathetically.

"Yeah." She smiled crookedly and then shrugged. "So, I took business at the local university for two years to please him. But while doing that I took an online course from the Auguste Escoffier School of Culinary Arts and got my diploma in Culinary Arts and Operations. It gave me a foot in the door to that university and during the second year of business I applied there for their Associate of Applied Science Degree in Culinary Arts." Natalie paused to grin at him before adding, "And I got accepted."

"I'm guessing it was a good school?" Valerian asked with a smile.

"Oh yeah. The best," she assured him.

"Were your parents upset that you gave up business for cooking?"

Natalie tilted her head from side to side in a so-so gesture as she drained the wax beans. She then threw them in the bowl with the vinaigrette and quickly tossed them, adding the scallions as she finally answered, "Not as much as I expected."

"No?"

Shaking her head, Natalie set the bean salad aside and grabbed the tongs to flip the steaks again. "I mean, Mom wasn't at all upset. She always knew I wanted to be a chef and encouraged me. In fact, she was kind of pissed off at my father for insisting I take business when my interests didn't lie there."

"But your father was upset?"

"Like I said, not as much as I expected him to be. I mean, he wasn't happy that I wasn't going into business as a career, but he felt I'd given business a fair try, and at least had that knowledge under my belt, so he didn't gripe too much." Natalie shrugged. "But it's a good thing I didn't have to count on him to pay my way through culinary school, because I'm pretty sure he wouldn't have paid. Fortunately, my grandparents— Mom's parents," she explained, "had left me money in trust for university in their will, so I was able to pay for it myself."

"And now you use it here," Valerian commented, eyeing the steaks hungrily as she stopped to flip them again.

Natalie bit her lip, and then admitted, "I was a chef in Ottawa for years before taking over this place."

She could feel Valerian peering at her and was almost sorry she'd mentioned it, but she'd already started so pushed on. "One of my professors at Auguste's had a friend in Ottawa who wanted to start a fine-dining restaurant, but claimed he wanted someone new and—as he put it—'exciting' as his head chef." She grimaced, and then told him, "The truth was he wanted someone cheap rather than have to pay the exorbitant wages an already established head chef would demand."

Pulling the steaks off the grill, Natalie set them on a wooden board to breathe, and then started making a dipping sauce for the sweet potato fries as she continued. "Anyway, my prof recommended me, so Gerry— that was the friend—flew down to Colorado a week before graduation to test me out. My prof had us both over to his house and had me make several dishes for him to try."

Natalie smiled at the memory as she confessed, "God, I was so nervous. I burned myself twice, cut myself once, and was sure nothing had turned out exactly right." She shook her head and said with remembered surprise, "But he loved it all. Offered me a job on the spot. A week later, I graduated and flew back to Canada, but to Ottawa instead of home. I was a chef."

"Living the dream?" Valerian suggested.

Natalie snorted. "Living the dream, my ass. He wanted the restaurant opened as soon as possible, but all he'd done was buy the building and decorate the dining room. He expected me to take care of everything else. And he wanted me to do it in two weeks!" she said with remembered horror. "I arrived on Monday and started on Tuesday. I lived out of a suitcase in a cheap motel for nearly a month. The first two weeks I spent scrambling to find an apartment around a crazy schedule of interviewing, hiring, and training staff, building a menu, and making sure the kitchen setup was up to snuff."

Valerian was listening wide-eyed. Even so, she didn't

think he understood how mammoth an undertaking it had been. But it was impossible to explain to someone not in the business, so she left it and continued.

"Then we opened, and my life became even more chaotic and stressful. But that's my own fault," she admitted with a shake of the head before glancing at him and admitting, "I'm a bit of a control freak. Well, I'm better now than I was then, but when I first started, I wanted to control everything. I was up at six in the morning to shower, dress, grab a coffee, and head into work. I had to be at the restaurant by seven," Natalie explained. "That's when the produce arrived. I had to take inventory, make sure everything was fresh and usable, and then oversee it being labeled and stored. Then I ran to the market for any fresh fish or meat I needed for that day. The rest of the morning was spent on mise en place."

"Mise en place?" Valerian queried with a frown as a buzzer drew her over to give the sweet potato fries a shake. "That means everything in its place, doesn't it?"

"You know French," Natalie said with a faint smile as she set the sweet potato fries back to finish cooking and returned to the prep table to slice the steaks into strips. "Yes. That's the literal translation, but in the restaurant industry it means pre-prep. Cutting and storing veggies, making sauces, cutting the meat into the portions you need for each dish, etc."

"Ah." Valerian nodded to show he understood.

"Of course, as the head chef I didn't do all of that by myself. Mostly I oversaw the sous chefs and stagiaires who did it. Although I did like to make my own sauces for recipes." She smiled crookedly. "Like I said, I'm a bit of a control freak as a chef. I like perfection, and some sauces are delicate." Natalie shrugged, leaving it at that, before continuing. "If the sauces weren't difficult and I trusted the staff to get it right, I'd often work on new recipes that we'd then taste test during the briefing before lunch service.

"We usually finished up with mise en place a good hour before lunch service. Then we'd all eat together while Gerry or I briefed everyone on the daily specials and such. After that the maître d' would announce if there were important bookings, or customers with reservations who had specific dietary issues. Allergies, and so on," she added to explain. "Then it was off to lunch service and the rush in the kitchen. I'd oversee everyone while also making certain dishes myself. Sometimes I'd have to have someone take over what I was doing, so that I could help if one of the areas was getting behind."

"Sounds hectic," Valerian commented. "Did you get time to relax after lunch service was over?"

"Not hardly," Natalie said with amusement. "Once the lunch rush was over, the kitchen had to be cleaned and mise en place for the dinner service took place."

"Sauces and vegetable cutting and stuff," Valerian said, wanting to be sure he understood.

Natalie nodded. "Dinner service usually ended around 11 P.M., although it sometimes ran as late as midnight, and then it was cleaning time again, but this time a thorough deep clean. This is also when we did marinades or started slow roasts if those were on the menu for the next day. I usually oversaw that."

A buzz from the air fryer caught her attention, and she took a bowl and walked over to retrieve the now cooked sweet potato fries.

She carried the bowl of fries back to the prep table and was pulling a couple plates off the overhead shelf when Valerian asked, "When did you . . ." He hesitated and Natalie suspected he was searching for words that wouldn't be insulting, but as she set the plates on the prep counter he finally said, "How long was it before you relaxed enough to let others take on some of the tasks for you?"

"When I moved here." She scraped half of one set of steak strips onto her plate, and then slid the other steak and a half of strips onto his plate. Setting the cutting board aside then, she offered him the bowl of sweet potato fries as she said bluntly, "Having a newborn to take care of kind of kicks your ass. I didn't have the energy to do everything, so it was let go of some of the control or . . ." She shrugged, because there had really been no alternative.

Valerian was silent as they both transferred the food to the small table where Natalie and Mia usually had their breakfast, but finally he pointed out, "But Mia wasn't your first baby. You had a son before her."

"I had a nanny and night nurse for Cody," she said quietly, avoiding his gaze as she felt old guilt swamp her. It was only when she'd stood looking down at her beautiful little boy in his coffin that she'd realized how little time she'd spent with him during his three years of life. His night nurse had taken care of everything at night, and brought Cody out for her to spend a little time with him before she left for work and the day nanny had arrived. Natalie had occasionally detoured home to spend a few minutes with him between the meat market and heading back to the restaurant, or sometimes, instead of working on new recipes before lunch, she'd rush home for a few minutes. But most often she didn't. The only time she really saw her son was on her days off, and then again, he had his nanny and night nurse, so she'd spend an hour here or there between personal shopping and nights out with her "husband."

Natalie had been a shit mother and knew it. She'd been too concerned with her career. She'd known it at the time even, but had thought it was just a temporary situation, and once she was more secure in her position she could slow down and make it up to him. She'd thought she'd have the time to do that. Instead, he'd died. Her beautiful, sweet little boy had never had her as a proper mother. Natalie had vowed not to make the same mistake with Mia. She was determined to be there for her daughter. But it wouldn't change her failure with Cody, she knew.

Not wanting to continue with this line of conversation and the depressing thoughts it caused her, Natalie turned abruptly and moved away to collect silverware for them both, asking, "What do you want to drink? Red wine would go nice with the steak."

"I'm not much of an alcohol drinker, but a glass wouldn't hurt."

"I have a nice shiraz in my personal fridge in the office," she said thoughtfully, and then started to set the silverware at their place settings and said, "I'll go grab it after I finish this."

"I'll get it," Valerian said at once. "You finish what you're doing."

He was gone before Natalie could protest. Not that she would have. She had no problem with his going into the little mini refrigerator in her office, so she finished setting the table. She was done when he returned with the wine. While he opened it and fetched two wineglasses, she quickly transferred the bean salad and the dip she'd made for the sweet potato fries to the table.

"So, if the dinner service lasted until eleven or midnight and you had to clean up afterward, you probably didn't get home most nights until midnight or one," Valerian commented as he poured the wine.

Natalie shook her head as she set down the bowls. "I never got out at midnight, and rarely at one," she assured him. "Once the others left, I had to go into the office, look over what I'd set for the next day's menu, and place my beverage and produce orders before I headed home to bed."

"And what time was that?" Valerian asked, pulling her chair out for her to sit.

Natalie blinked at the old-fashioned gesture, but then offered a smile of thanks and settled in the chair as she admitted, "I usually made it to bed around two or two thirty in the morning. But there were days I didn't get there until 3 A.M., and one time even 4 A.M."

Valerian blinked at this news, something like horror growing in his eyes. "And then you'd have to be up at six again the next day?"

Grinning at his expression, she nodded. "Six days a week. We were closed Mondays," Natalie explained, and thought she heard him curse under his breath.

"That's crazy!"

"It wasn't that bad," Natalie protested on a laugh. "And you have to remember I was young."

Valerian just shook his head, and took his seat. "How long did you work at this restaurant with those hours?"

"A little more than five years."

"Crazy," Valerian repeated with something like awe.

Natalie didn't bother to mention that her schedule was just as long and crazy now. Or had been until today when she'd hired Colle and Alasdair, which had taken hours of mowing off her plate.

"Surely other chefs don't work like that? You're the exception, right? Most chefs have more reasonable hours and balanced lives?"

"Not if they're a control freak like me," she said with a shrug. "I mean, I'm sure there are chefs out there who don't have to see for themselves that the produce is all up to snuff, or insist on picking their cuts of meat, and can leave that to someone else and come in later in the day. Maybe," Natalie added dubiously, because most chefs she knew were as controlling and obsessive as her. After all, every dish that left the kitchen was her responsibility. It was her name that would have been affected if it was subpar. And the same would be true for other chefs.

"Crazy," Valerian muttered as he picked up his knife and fork and cut one of the steak strips into a smaller bite-sized piece that he popped into his mouth. She watched in anticipation, a little afraid he might not like it. But much to her relief, his eyes immediately widened, and a moan of pleasure slid from somewhere in the vicinity of his throat. Once he'd chewed and swallowed, he looked at her solemnly and said, "You're a wizard. This is the best food I've ever tasted. And so tender too. Will you marry me? I have a castle in Scotland with a huge kitchen that you can play in all day if you like."

Natalie burst out laughing at what she was sure was teasing. "Sure. I always wanted to be a kept woman."

"I'll keep you," he assured her with a smile.

Natalie just shook her head at his tomfoolery and started to cut into her own steak, suggesting, "Try the bean salad. I'm curious to see what you think."

Valerian dutifully did as she requested, his eyes widening with surprise again. Once he'd swallowed and could talk again, he said, "That's really nice. I'll have to make this for my sister. She tends to prefer pizzas, and fries, junk like that," he explained, picking up his wineglass. "She swears healthy food tastes gross, but I bet she'd like this."

"I'll write down the recipe for you," Natalie said, but was glad he was now distracted trying the wine.

Her cheeks were warm, and she was sure they were flushed with the pleasure his compliments gave her. Cooking was something she worked hard at and took great pride in. It was always nice when it was appreciated. But by the same token, she was uncomfortable with the praise, so decided to shift the focus from herself to him. "Is Aileen your only sibling?"

Valerian swallowed his wine as he set down his glass, then shook his head. "I have three brothers. Two older, and one younger, then Aileen."

Natalie's eyes widened at this news. "That's a big family."

"Five isn't big," he said on a laugh. "I have relatives with a dozen or more children."

"Good Lord," Natalie breathed with horror. "I know that was normal before birth control, but I didn't think anyone had that many anymore. I mean, what woman would want to go through labor twelve times? And jeez, they'd spend nearly twelve years of their lives pregnant. Ugh!"

"Well, to be fair, twins run in our family, so it wasn't always that many pregnancies," Valerian assured her, picking up his wine again. "I gather you were an only child?"

Natalie's eyebrows flew up. "How did you know?"

"Emily said you lost your entire family in the car crash: your parents, husband, and son. There was no mention of siblings, so if that was the entire family . . ."

Natalie nodded, and picked up her own wineglass, but paused to say, "I always wanted brothers and sisters, and I guess I had a twin. But there were complications; my

twin died and Mom ended up having a partial hysterec-
tomy and couldn't have any more babies."

"So, twins run in both our families?" Valerian asked
with a sort of horror, and then gulped down the rest of
his wine almost desperately.

Natalie watched this with bewilderment. "Sounds
like it." Smiling faintly, she added, "Good thing we
aren't a couple, huh? We'd probably have a houseful
of identical rug rats running around with Mia riding
herd on them." Natalie chuckled at the idea as she took
a sip of wine, but suddenly had an image in her mind
of beautiful little twin girls with dark hair like hers,
and twin boys as fair as Valerian, running around with
Mia. The idea was oddly appealing until her sensible
side got wind of it and gave her a mental slap. Snap
out of it! They were just eating a meal together. This
wasn't a date, her sensible mind berated her.

Natalie set her wineglass down at that point, because if this was how her thoughts were when sober,
she wasn't adding alcohol to the mix. Deciding another change in topic was needed, she sought her mind
briefly for a safe subject and asked, "When does your
sister next visit?"

Much to her amazement, Valerian opened his mouth,
closed it, opened it again, and then cursed and suddenly
jumped up from the table to rush from the room.

Natalie stared after him briefly, baffled by his reaction to the question. But then it occurred to her that
perhaps he'd just realized that his sister was supposed
to visit this weekend, something he might have forgotten in all the excitement around here that day.

Worried that might be the case, Natalie stood to follow him out of the kitchen. She entered the lower dining area, fully expecting him to be out there with his phone to his ear. But he was nowhere to be seen. Her gaze slid to the exit, but the door was closed and she could see from where she stood that it was locked.

That was when the sound of violent retching reached her ears. Head swinging toward the public washrooms, Natalie started to hurry that way, but stopped abruptly halfway across the room with a shocked gasp. One hand immediately went to her stomach, and the other grabbed at the nearest table for balance, as pain shot through her gut so hard and sharp she nearly dropped to her knees. Clenching her teeth, Natalie pushed her fist into her stomach as she struggled with the pain claiming her. Sweat broke out on her forehead and upper lip, and her whole body started to tremble . . . as much from horror as the pain rolling over her in waves.

Dear God, she'd given them both food poisoning, Natalie thought with dismay, and then began to heave even as her legs gave out and she dropped toward the floor and sweet oblivion.

Nine

"You're sure it was poison?" Valerian's question ended
on a grunt as Decker slapped a bag of blood to his
open mouth. He was actually grateful for it since it
meant he couldn't talk. Speaking hurt his throat. It
felt like someone had run sandpaper on a stick down
his throat while he was unconscious, and for all he
knew they had. The last thing Valerian remembered
before waking up here on the couch in Natalie's office
was wrenching pain in his gut, a desperate dash to the
bathroom as his stomach contents tried to climb up
out of his body, and barely making it to the toilet before he started heaving . . . and heaving . . . and heaving, bringing up what had mostly been blood since he
hadn't eaten much before getting sick. Valerian must
have passed out then. Because the next thing he recalled was opening his eyes to find himself here with
Decker, and Dani bending over him.

"Very sure," Dani confirmed as she pulled more blood out of a cooler and stacked it on the coffee table. She paused at four bags, to add with a frown, "Although I don't know what kind yet. Colle's getting me a sample of your vomit as we speak. I'm going to send it to Argentis Inc.'s laboratories for testing." She returned to pulling out more blood bags. "I'm pretty sure, though, that if you were mortal you'd be dead by now."

Eyes widening with dismay, Valerian ripped the half-empty bag of blood from his mouth, uncaring that it sent the red liquid squirting everywhere as he rasped, "Natalie?"

"Christ, Val," Decker muttered, taking the torn bag from him and dumping it in the cooler to keep the room from looking like a slaughterhouse. "She's fine. Well, not fine," he added in a mutter as he grabbed a fresh bag of blood from the stack Dani was making. "But she'll live. I think."

"You *think*?" Valerian roared, and tried to get up, but he was surprisingly weak and one push from Decker was enough to keep him down.

"She will be fine," Dani said firmly to calm him. "She must not have got as much poison as you. I think it was in the wine. Did you drink more than her?"

"I . . ." Valerian thought back to the brief time they'd spent at the table. He hadn't even got to eat half of that lovely meal she'd made, he mourned, but pushed that aside to try to recall how much wine Natalie had drunk. He'd had a couple of sips, and then downed the rest of his glass when he'd realized twins ran in both their families. The idea of having children was frightening enough for a man who had spent little time around babies, but two at once? And they ran in both their families? That must double the chances of twins, he worried.

"Valerian? How much did she drink?" Dani asked impatiently.

"I think she only had a sip," Valerian said finally. "It was in the wine?"

"I'm pretty sure it was. It smelled off to me," Dani answered, and then sighed. "I'm not positive, though . . . and it might not be the only thing that was poisoned."

"We'll have to clear out the kitchen, then," Decker said grimly. "Remove every bit of food and drink in this place just in case."

"Yeah," Dani agreed. "Poor Natalie. She'll have to replace food, booze, spices . . ." She shook her head. "This is going to be a helluva big hit to her bank account."

Valerian frowned, thinking about Natalie's plans to build additions onto the club that included an apartment for her and her daughter, and worrying this would impact how soon she could do that. Unwilling to see that happen, he said, "I'll pay for it. Just have whoever clears out all the food keep track of what they take out, and order replacements."

Dani nodded, not seeming surprised at the offer, but Decker said, "Valerian?"

He turned to him, and then grunted with surprise when Decker slapped a fresh bag of blood to his fangs. "Shut up and feed. You are pale as death and weak as a kitten and need your strength to help keep Natalie safe now that the Angel-Maker has stepped up his game to murder attempts rather than just taunts and threatening cards."

Valerian grunted with irritation, but didn't fight the feeding. He was weak, and did want to get his strength back. Natalie needed him.

"Has he?" Dani asked suddenly.

"What?" Decker asked, glancing around at his wife.

"Has the Angel-Maker stepped up his game?" she asked. "Are we sure it's even him? He's never played games like this before that we know of."

"*That we know of,*" Decker repeated her words meaningfully. "We don't know, maybe he poisoned his victims before draining them."

"Which would mean you guys have been chasing a mortal, thinking he was immortal," Colle pointed out from the door, and Valerian glanced to his cousin to see him holding a baggie of what he suspected was his vomit in hand.

This was verified when Colle crossed the room and held out what turned out to be two bags side by side to Dani, saying, "One bag of Val's vomit as requested. But I scooped up some of Natalie's from the floor too in case you wanted that."

"Good thinking," Dani complimented as she took the bags. "Thank you."

"Why do you think the Angel-Maker is mortal?" Decker asked, and Valerian was grateful he had. He'd been about to rip another bag of blood off his fangs to ask that very question.

"Well, an immortal would hardly poison his victims; it would make their blood undrinkable," he pointed out. "So, if this is the work of the Angel-Maker—which the snow angel shape in the grass, and someone whispering 'Angel' seems to suggest . . ." Colle shrugged. "He can't be immortal."

Valerian frowned around the bag at his mouth, wondering if Colle was right and they might be chasing a mortal rather than an immortal. Not that it mattered to him. The bastard was after his life mate. He didn't care if he was immortal, mortal, or alien; Valerian was going to end the bastard before he hurt Natalie again. That thought had him worrying about her. Dani had said she would be fine. But what did that mean? She wasn't fine now? Was she writhing and crying out in pain even now somewhere in the club? And who was with her? Someone had better be with her, he thought grimly, and reached for the bag at his fangs, only to have Decker knock his hand away.

"Don't even think about it," Decker snapped. "You've already made enough mess. Just think your questions or comments and we will all hear them. Your mind's an open book right now. New life mate brain, remember?"

Valerian grimaced at the reminder that, no matter their age, immortals were somehow easier to read after first encountering their life mates. Even the oldest immortals who were usually completely unreadable to everyone became open books. Sighing, he relaxed back on the couch and let his worries and questions run through his mind.

"Natalie is not in pain," Dani assured him almost at once. "She would be if she were conscious, but I have her on an IV and put in something to keep her under until the worst of this passes."

That made him feel a little better, but not much as other worries surfaced.

"Yes, I'm sure she didn't get much," Dani said soothingly in reply to one of the worries swimming around inside his head. "Judging by your reaction to the poison, she'd already be dead otherwise. But this will probably lay her low for a day or so. Maybe more. And I want to monitor her until she's completely in the clear." She glanced at Colle then. "So I might be sleeping in the RV with you guys for the next couple of days. If I sleep," she added dryly.

"You will sleep," Decker said firmly. "Rachel's on her way down to help monitor her."

"She is?" Dani asked with surprise.

Decker nodded. "I called Mortimer while you were tending to Natalie. He said he'd arrange for Rachel, Alex, and Jo to come down."

When Valerian eyed the man with surprise, he explained, "Rachel will help Dani take care of Natalie, Alex will cook in her stead, and Jo is going to help guard her. Mortimer doesn't think it's good for her to be alone even for a minute after this, and I agree."

Valerian agreed too, but Jo wasn't needed for that. He fully intended on being at her side every moment of the day and night until they caught this bastard.

"Really?" Decker asked with amusement as if he'd spoken the words aloud. "And you think she'd let you be at her side all the time? Even in the bathroom, say? Or bed?" He arched an eyebrow. "Has your wooing progressed that far?"

Valerian scowled at him over the nearly empty bag of blood, and silently thought the words, *Go to hell*.

Decker chuckled at that and then reached for another bag of blood. Pausing with it in hand, he asked his wife, "Does he need to consume all of these?"

Valerian glanced at the stack of blood bags, and counted eight, which seemed a hell of a lot. He'd woken up with one on his mouth several minutes ago, and had gone through three before he could speak, as well as another one and a half since then.

"Yes," Dani answered as Decker pulled the empty bag from Valerian's mouth and slapped another on. She then added, "To start with. I'll check his vitals after he's finished them and see if he needs any more. I suspect he will," she added, and then straightened and said, "In the meantime, keep him lying down so he doesn't fall, hurt himself, and need even more."

"Yes, ma'am," Decker said.

She nodded, and then said, "We need to get that food out of the kitchen. I don't want to forget about it and possibly have someone else eat something."

"I'll see to it," Colle said, turning toward the door.

"Grab one or two of the guys from outside to help you, Colle," Decker said. "The food needs to be inventoried as it's removed so we can order in replacements."

Colle's answer was a nod as he walked out of the office.

Dani watched him go, but as he disappeared into the hall, she turned to her husband and said, "Maybe you should call Mortimer and have him start arranging replacement items for standard kitchen stuff. Otherwise, Alex will be coming down for nothing. She can't cook if there's no food," she added, and then suggested, "Tell him we'll need everything: cream, butter, vegetables, meat, spices . . . and a variety of sodas, alcoholic drinks, and snack items too. We should probably clear out the food by the reception desk as well."

"Good idea." Decker pulled out his phone at once.

Relaxing a little, Dani nodded and turned to head for the door, saying, "I'm going to check on Natalie."

"Okay, babe. Let me know if you need anything," Decker said as he punched in numbers. He watched her go, and then glanced at Valerian, narrowed his eyes, and answered the question even now forming in Valerian's mind. "Alasdair has been sitting with Natalie while Dani came back up to check on you."

Back up? From where? Valerian wondered.

"Natalie's bedroom downstairs," Decker answered.

When Valerian scowled with disgruntlement, thinking the bastard had got to see her bedroom before him, Decker grinned and announced, "We all have. Actually, you were in it and could have seen it too if you'd been conscious. Unfortunately, you weren't, but . . ." He shrugged. "Them's the breaks, right?"

When Valerian was less than amused, Decker rolled his eyes and said, "We carried you both down and put you in her bed at first, because we thought it would be

more convenient for Dani to take care of you both in
one spot. But she was concerned Natalie might wake
up and spot you consuming blood, so Colle and I carried you up here while she and Alasdair tended to
Natalie. I started feeding you blood while we waited
for Dani to come up. She sent Colle out to collect
vomit while she checked you and we continued to
feed you, and voilà!" He ripped the now empty blood
bag off Valerian's teeth and plopped another on before finishing, "You woke up."

Valerian grunted at that, but wondered what had
happened between his rushing into the bathroom and
their carrying him down to Natalie's bedroom. Who
had discovered them?

"Colle and Alasdair were—" Decker stopped abruptly,
his attention shifting to the phone at his ear as it was apparently answered. Raising one finger in a gesture for
Valerian to wait, he stood and started toward the door
saying, "Mortimer? We had a little incident here."

That was an understatement, Valerian thought with
disgust, and closed his eyes against the light in the
room for a minute.

Poison. In the wine. The thought made his eyes
pop open and he turned his head to glance toward the
small mini refrigerator in the corner. It was where the
wine had come from. He'd fetched it himself . . . and
opened it. It *had* been sealed. He distinctly remembered having to remove the wrap and cork. How the
hell could it have been poisoned, he wondered.

A syringe through the top wrap and cork would
have done it, he supposed. The hole would have been

tiny and unnoticeable. But when had it been done? The wine had been in the refrigerator in Natalie's office, a risky spot to perform such a task, he would think. At least during the day. From what he could tell, she spent her time floating between the kitchen, the dining room, and her office during the day. But at night she mowed the green. Or used to. She hadn't tonight, but the poison could have been injected before tonight. The night before, for instance . . . when the angel statuette had been placed in the office, he thought suddenly, and then shrugged the worry away. What did it matter? It had been done, he thought angrily, and then opened his eyes to see that the bag at his mouth was empty again.

Tugging it from his fangs, Valerian reached out to drop it on the coffee table, but then had to let his arm drop so his hand rested on the table briefly before he had the strength to grab a fresh full bag and slap that to his teeth. The blood he'd taken in had started to make him feel better. Valerian had still had sharp pain in his gut when he'd first woken up, and if there had been anything left in his stomach, he probably would have been still throwing up. But the pain had eased and gone entirely in the few minutes and few bags of blood he'd consumed since waking. He was still incredibly weak, though, and suspected Dani was right, and to completely recover he might need more than the blood she'd stacked on the table.

"Right," Decker said, putting his phone away as he reentered the room. "Mortimer's sending blood and food. He said he'd get it together and down here as quickly as he could."

Valerian grunted around the blood bag at his mouth at this announcement, relief pouring through him. He knew Natalie would be upset if the restaurant had to be closed while she was sick.

"Alex and Jo are apparently at the Enforcer house right now, just waiting on Rachel to arrive so they can set out," Decker informed him. "So, Mortimer is going to have Alex make up a list of what she thinks is needed in a restaurant kitchen and he'll source and send it."

Sitting on the coffee table facing him, Decker glanced at his watch and muttered, "It's nearly midnight now and the drive is a good four hours, which doesn't include having to get the food together." He didn't look hopeful, but said, "It might get here before the restaurant usually opens for breakfast."

Valerian just closed his eyes, wishing he could do something to speed the process along. He knew Mortimer would do what he could, but restocking a restaurant kitchen was a huge undertaking. He supposed they'd just have to hope for the best.

"So," Decker said, drawing his attention again. "As I was saying, Colle and Alasdair were playing cards when they saw you hurry across the dining room on the cameras. They said you were using immortal speed, which they thought was odd, but weren't really concerned until Natalie came out after you and then clutched her stomach and collapsed. They hurried out of the RV and ran around to try to come in, but the door was locked."

Valerian winced at that. A lot of good having them around was if they were locked out of the building. He should have thought to get a key from Natalie to give to them.

"Yeah. I didn't think of that either," Decker said as if he'd spoken his thoughts aloud. "We'll get them a key for the new lock. On the new door."

When Valerian's eyebrows rose, he explained, "They had to break in, so broke the lock, the door, and the frame. I told Mortimer I'd take care of getting someone in to fix it. I figured he has enough on his plate."

Valerian nodded at that, and then gave a start when Decker suddenly tugged the now empty bag off his fangs to switch in a fresh one.

"Anyway," Decker continued as he set the empty bag with the others. "They broke in, shouted for you, and ran to help Natalie. But when you didn't respond or come out, Alasdair went into the bathroom after you and found you lying in a pool of your own vomit— which was mostly blood—and still heaving even while unconscious."

Valerian grimaced around the bag at his mouth. He had no trouble believing it. His body would have used blood to surround the poison and get it out. Besides, aside from the stomach pain he'd been suffering when he'd first woken up, the taste in his mouth had, and still was, horrendous.

"Sorry, buddy. I never thought about that," Decker said suddenly, and stood, then hesitated and frowned as he pointed out, "There's nothing safe to drink here but tap water until we get the food replaced."

It was only when he said it that Valerian realized Decker had read his thoughts again. Or heard them. He knew it wasn't a case of having to read them. His thoughts were just exceptionally loud right now. He waved one hand weakly to tell him not to worry about it.

"Oh!" Decker said suddenly, and headed for the door. "Hang on. There's still an iced tea in the car from our drive down yesterday. I'll fetch it."

Valerian watched him go, and then just lay there wondering what iced tea tasted like. Until the meal Natalie had made for him, Valerian hadn't consumed anything but blood since the summer of 1950, and he hadn't eaten or drank regularly for a good ten years before that. Which was a thing with immortals. Living so long . . . shit got boring. Food and sex being most notable as things they just stopped bothering with. Of course, no one really needed sex to survive, but most beings needed food if they wanted to live. However, so long as they took in blood, immortals could do without the bother of eating, and did so when they reached the stage where eating seemed more trouble than it was worth.

Some immortals stopped eating shortly after turning one hundred, some closer to two hundred; Valerian had given up bothering with food at one hundred and sixty. Although he'd still indulged in sex on occasion for another couple years.

Of course iced tea had been around when he was

still eating and drinking. He just couldn't recall what it had tasted like, or how it would taste to him now that his appetites had reawakened.

Realizing the latest bag of blood was empty, Valerian pulled it from his fangs and dropped it on the coffee table. He managed to take a fresh one without having to rest his arm this time, but just laid it on his chest as he debated whether to pop it on or wait for Decker to bring back the iced tea and drink it first to get the awful taste out of his mouth. He was still debating when Decker hurried back into the room with a bottle of cinnamon-colored liquid in hand.

"I was thinking while I was getting the iced tea," Decker said as he crossed to the couch. He handed him the drink before saying, "We might want to replace Natalie's toothpaste and mouthwash too while we're at it. Those could just as easily be poisoned as anything else."

"Yes," Valerian sighed the word. It was something he should have thought of. Anything she might consume could have been poisoned and it was better safe than sorry.

Decker nodded. "I'll go take care of getting rid of those now."

"Thanks," Valerian said, his voice still raspy. Hoping the tea would take care of that, he unscrewed the lid of the glass bottle. Or tried to. He didn't have enough damned strength. And Decker was gone. Groaning, Valerian closed his eyes to wait.

Ten

It was pain that woke Natalie. A sharp sting in her hand pushed back sleep enough that she opened bleary eyes and looked down with confusion. The sight of a large bruise on the back of her hand, and the catheter of an IV that was dangling by a strip of tape, shocked her more fully awake. She followed the tube upward with her eyes to find a clear bag of liquid attached to a stand next to her bed.

Confused and a bit alarmed, Natalie sat up abruptly, and then froze as the room did a little spin around her. She felt like hell, like she had the flu, or was just getting over it, and didn't understand why. Sitting still, Natalie closed her eyes and took deep breaths until she felt a little steadier. She then cautiously opened her eyes. Much to her relief the spinning had stopped.

Releasing a little sigh, Natalie immediately shifted her attention to her daughter's bed across the room.

Finding it empty was almost more alarming than how she was feeling and the fact that she appeared to have been hooked up to an IV at some point.

She'd probably rolled in her sleep and dislodged it, Natalie thought as she tore the hanging tape off and let the catheter drop to the bed. The problem was she had no idea why she'd need an IV, or—more importantly— where her daughter was.

Moving slowly, Natalie slid to the opposite side of the bed and climbed out, then had to stop again as the room did another little dance around her. This time the vertigo was joined by nausea, and she swallowed to keep from heaving. In the next moment, she was grimacing as the action made her aware of an awful taste in her mouth. She also had something of a headache, she realized. It seemed obvious she had suffered some sort of illness like the flu, or—

Natalie stiffened as her brain finally began to function and memory started to creep in. The movie, making dinner with Valerian, his suddenly rushing off, her following . . . the sound of his heaving, and then her own stomach misbehaving—Dear God, she'd given them both food poisoning, she remembered with dismay.

Now worried about Valerian as much as her daughter, Natalie started moving again, making her slow cautious way to the bedroom door. She wanted to hurry, but wasn't steady on her feet yet, and the walk seemed to take forever as she left the room and crossed the storage area. By the time she reached the stairs, sweat had broken out on her brow and her legs were trembling with the effort of holding her up. She grasped the railing for safety's sake, and still found herself leaning her shoulder against the wall as she made her way upstairs.

Natalie was panting when she reached the upper door. She paused for a minute there and closed her eyes, trying to catch her breath and calm her heartbeat. It was going a mile a minute from just that short walk, and her head was spinning again. The food poisoning had obviously been serious, which made her wonder why she wasn't in a hospital.

Once she was no longer gasping for air and her heartbeat had slowed a bit, Natalie straightened and opened the door to the main floor. The hallway was empty, but she could hear chatter and laughter from the dining room. It was only then she wondered what time it was. However, while she was still dressed in the clothes she'd been wearing when cooking with Valerian, her watch was no longer on her wrist for her to check the time.

Supposing it had been removed when the intravenous had been put in, Natalie forgot about it for now and staggered up the empty hall. Her office door was open, but everything looked normal there, so she continued on to the kitchen.

The noise from the dining room grew louder as she got nearer and Natalie realized she would be visible to the diners once she reached the kitchen door. It made her look down at herself with concern. She was wearing the jeans and dark blue Shady Pines T-shirt she always wore while working, but they were wrinkled from sleeping in them.

Grimacing, she paused to tuck in her shirt with shaky hands, thinking that would stretch out the wrinkles. Natalie then also pinched her cheeks, and brushed her fingers through her hair. She was hoping that would make her look decent and not like the living dead she felt like, but suspected it probably didn't help much. Sighing, to herself, Natalie finally just lowered her head as she approached the kitchen door and then pushed it open.

As expected, the kitchen was utter madness. But it was even more chaotic than normal and she stared wide-eyed at the people rushing this way and that. Jan was there, cooking as usual. But there was also another woman in a chef's coat and toque, a pretty woman with brown hair cut in a shoulder-length bob who was working Natalie's station while yelling instructions at the men presently rushing about stacking food on her almost empty shelves and in equally empty cupboards. One of them rushed to the refrigerator with an armful of packaged meat, and opened the door revealing the nearly barren interior.

"What the hell?" Natalie gasped, wondering where all her food had gone. She hadn't thought she was overly loud, but the reaction was immediate: everyone seemed to stop and look her way.

"Natalie!" Jan pulled the frying pan she was cooking something in off the range, set it on the metal table, and rushed to her anxiously. "Oh my God, are you okay? They said you were sick, but you look like death warmed over. Should you be up?"

"I—What's going on?" Natalie asked rather than

answer her questions. "Where did all the food go? What—?" She paused and looked around with confusion as people started to move again, continuing with their efforts to restock her kitchen.

"Oh. It's . . ." Jan looked around, but then suddenly paused. For a minute, her expression actually went blank, and then she said, "I should get back to work. I'll let Rachel explain."

"Jan, what—" Natalie began, but her voice died because Jan had turned away and was walking back to her station.

"How are you feeling?"

Natalie turned sharply to find an attractive woman with long, dark red hair beside her. Unlike the other strange female in her kitchen, this woman was wearing street clothes, dress pants, and a white silk blouse. She was also eyeing her with concern.

"You shouldn't be up," the redhead said as she took Natalie's hand to examine the back where the IV had been. "Did you take out the IV yourself?" she asked at once, and then answered her own question. "No, you couldn't have, the midazolam would have kept you under." Shaking her head, she ran a finger over the bruising and muttered, "It must have got dislodged. You were moving about quite a bit in your sleep."

Clucking her tongue with irritation, the woman released her hand and shifted her attention to her face. "I'm sorry. It must have been distressing to wake up alone not knowing what was going on. I should have stayed with you, but I thought you'd sleep so it wouldn't hurt to help out here for a few minutes. Come, we'll get you back into bed," she added, urging her to turn toward the door.

Natalie resisted, asking, "Who are you?"

"Oh. Sorry, I'm Dr. Rachel Argeneau," she introduced herself, and Natalie's eyes immediately narrowed as she recognized the last name.

"Lucian is your . . . ?"

Rachel hesitated and then said slowly and almost uncertainly, "My uncle-in-law, I guess?" She then grinned and added, "Fortunately, I don't have to claim him as a blood relative. He's my husband's uncle." She eyed Natalie's grim expression and then said gently, "I know he can be a miserable old cur at times, but Lucian has a good heart buried under all that ice and bossiness. Way down deep under it," she added wryly, "but there nonetheless."

She waited a moment for Natalie to process that, but then asked, "Will you let me help you back to bed now? You've been very ill. Bed is the best place for you."

"What's happening here and where is Mia?" Natalie asked, resisting her efforts to again urge her toward the door.

Rachel stopped trying to force her out of the room and frowned slightly at her question, then glanced around and asked, "Alex? Do you know where Valerian and Mia are?"

The brunette in the chef's coat looked over, and then set aside the bowl she'd been stirring, and wiped her hands on the apron she wore over her chef's coat as she crossed the room to join them.

"Hi, I'm Alex Valens," she announced, holding out a hand in greeting.

"La Bonne Vie," Natalie murmured as she took the woman's hand. It was a restaurant in Toronto. Actually, a trio of restaurants run by a European-trained Canadian chef named Alex Valens, and considering the woman before her was wearing the typical chef's uniform and had the same name, she assumed this was that woman.

"Yes." She beamed at her for recognizing the name, and then explained her presence. "My sister called me about your situation here, and asked me to come help out until you get back on your feet."

"Your sister?" Natalie asked with bewilderment.

"Sam," Alex explained and, when Natalie looked blank, added, "She's married to Mortimer."

"Valerian's boss," Natalie said, recognizing that name.

"Yes." Alex smiled.

"Where is Valerian?" she asked now. The last Natalie knew of Valerian he'd been puking up her meal in the men's room, and that recollection now added him to the list of top three concerns she had. She'd somehow given the guy food poisoning with her cooking, for heaven's sake, Natalie thought, and then noted the way Alex was looking at her. Tilting her head slightly, she asked, "What?"

"Nothing. I just—" She shook her head and said, "Look, you obviously have no idea what's happened here, so I think we should explain."

"That would be nice," Natalie said, her tone a tad

dry, which made Alex grin slightly. But the grin quickly faded as Rachel promptly began to speak.

"There was poison in the wine you had with dinner last night," the redhead announced bluntly.

"Poison?" Natalie gasped with horror. "The Angel-Maker?"

"We assume so," Alex said quietly.

"Yes," Rachel agreed. "Fortunately, you apparently only had a sip of it?"

Natalie nodded.

"Well, that plus the fact that you probably threw up most of it, and that Colle and Alasdair got help here quickly, saved your life," Rachel assured her. "However, you've been very sick."

"Colle and Alasdair found us?" she asked.

"They were watching the cameras and saw you were in trouble in the dining room. They broke in to get to you, and immediately called Dani—my husband's cousin's sister," she explained, and when Natalie nodded, recognizing the name of the doctor who had taken care of her head wound, Rachel continued. "She came at once. You were apparently out of it and suffering incredible stomach pain from the poison, so she gave you a shot to knock you out, and then got you in bed and put an IV drip in to keep you hydrated. She added midazolam to the drip to keep you under and comfortable while the poison worked through your system."

Natalie was silent for a minute as she absorbed all of that, but Rachel had said that her only having a sip had probably saved her life. Valerian had downed a full glass, she recalled with alarm. "Valerian? Is he—?"

"He's fine," Rachel assured her.

"He's outside with Mia," Alex told her.

"But how?" Natalie asked with amazement. "He drank a full glass of the wine."

There was a pause as the women exchanged glances and then Rachel said, "He also vomited up most of the poison, and he's in better shape health-wise than you are at the moment, so recovered more quickly."

Natalie flinched a little at the bit about her health. It made her realize that she needed to take better care of herself. If she'd drank any more than the sip she'd had of wine, she might now be dead, leaving Mia an orphan. The very thought terrified her and made her want to hold her daughter close.

"I want to see Mia," she said abruptly. Although the truth was she wanted to see Valerian too. She wanted to see for herself that he was all right.

Rachel frowned. "You're not too steady on your feet yet . . . and do you really want to walk through the dining room looking so poorly? Why don't you let me tuck you back into bed and then I'll text Valerian and have him bring Mia to you."

Natalie grimaced. The other woman's words had just told her how bad she must look. But she really wanted to see for herself that Mia and Valerian were all right, so she straightened and turned toward the door. "I don't have to go through the dining area."

She wasn't surprised when Rachel followed her out of the room. Natalie *was* a little surprised, however, when the woman took her arm to support her as she walked back up the hall. As if she thought she couldn't manage it on her own. Perhaps not that crazy an idea, Natalie acknowledged when she realized that even with Rachel's steadying hand she was weaving a bit.

"In here?" Rachel asked with surprise when Natalie turned into the open office door.

A little breathless from just that short walk, Natalie nodded and crossed the room to the space behind her desk. She then had to pause to catch her breath.

"Is this—? I thought these were real bookshelves with real books," Rachel exclaimed with surprise as she reached out to touch the roller shade they'd paused in front of. It had been painted to look like wooden bookshelves with a selection of Natalie's favorite books on it. In Ottawa it had covered the sliding doors to her balcony, which stared out at another building next door and the parking lot around it. It hadn't been a very nice view.

Natalie gave a breathless chuckle and shook her head. "My mother . . . had them . . . made for me . . . for my apartment . . . in Ottawa." She glanced at Rachel and shrugged. "I love books."

"I guess so," Rachel chuckled at the claim, and then—without needing to be asked—bent to tug on the bottom so that the painted shade rolled slowly back up and out of view revealing the sliding doors and small deck that they had hidden. Rachel took in the view of trees and green grass beyond with appreciation. "This must be a nice spot to sit and enjoy a coffee."

"That's what I thought . . . when I saw it," Natalie said, able to speak with fewer pauses now as her breathing slowly returned to normal.

"It isn't?" Rachel asked, glancing at her with surprise.

Natalie shrugged. "I wouldn't know. The only time I have a spare minute to enjoy a coffee . . . on the deck is in the winter when it's too cold to sit out there."

"Well, you'll have time for that over the next couple of days," Rachel assured her, reaching out to unlock the door and slide it open. "Because I can guarantee no one is going to let you work until you're completely recovered."

Natalie raised her eyebrows at that, but didn't say anything and simply stepped out onto the deck when Rachel next slid the screen door open. Her gaze automatically took in the employee parking lot on the right with the huge RV in it. But Valerian's deep baritone voice, Sinbad's barking, and Mia's childish laughter had her swinging her head toward the back of the building. She smiled with relief when she spotted the trio under the shade of a large oak tree. She couldn't tell exactly what Mia and Valerian were doing, but they were standing side by side, facing the woods, waving their arms around while Sinbad looked on barking. Curious, she listened to what Valerian was saying, or singing, she realized, and her eyebrows flew up on her forehead. "Is he singing—?"

"'The Hokey Pokey,'" Rachel finished for her with amusement as they watched Mia trying to emulate Valerian as he put his right foot in, and then took his right foot out.

"Well, that's . . ."

"Adorable?" Rachel suggested when Natalie hesitated, searching for a word.

"Yeah," Natalie said with a chuckle, and it *was* adorable.

Despite Valerian's singing, Sinbad apparently heard them, because the dog suddenly stopped and turned to look their way, then headed over, tongue hanging out and tail wagging. Natalie couldn't help but smile at the silly-looking beast, and glanced to Rachel with surprise when the other woman took her arm.

"Are you afraid of dogs?" Natalie asked with concern.

"No. I'm just worried he'll jump on you and knock you over," Rachel said, her voice a little tight.

Natalie smiled at the suggestion. "He won't. I trained that tendency out of him as a puppy. It was cute when he was little, but I knew he was going to grow up to be big and didn't want him knocking me over once I'd had the baby and was carrying her."

"Really?" Rachel asked with surprise. "I'm sure Valerian said he jumped on him when he brought you back to the clubhouse after your fall in the pond. Val said he thought it was a polar bear coming at him."

Natalie chuckled at the description and scratched Sinbad behind the ears as he reached her and nestled his head into her stomach in greeting. "It was probably because Valerian was a stranger who was carrying me. He normally doesn't jump at all."

"Hmm," Rachel murmured, and reached out to run her hand over his head too.

Natalie grinned when the dog immediately moved away from her to bury his face in the doctor's stomach. "He's a bit of a slut for pettings," she told her with amusement. "And a big baby too."

"He's beautiful," Rachel sighed, burying her hands in Sinbad's soft thick fur and scratching him behind both ears. "My husband, Etienne, and I have been talking about getting a dog. I should call him and tell him to come down here so he can meet this big guy. He'd love him."

"He's welcome to come," Natalie said easily, and then glanced back to where Valerian was singing, "And you turn yourself around." He and Mia both immediately started to turn in a circle on the spot, but Valerian stopped dead when he turned to the point where his gaze landed on them on the deck. Hands still over his head from doing the Hokey Pokey, he stared wide-eyed at them with what could only be described as horror.

"Mama!" her daughter squealed with happy excitement as she too spotted her. The little girl immediately charged toward them as fast as her little body would let her.

"Mia!" Natalie squealed right back in the same tone. She didn't, however, run toward her as she normally would when they played this game. She simply didn't have the strength or energy, so instead she squatted down next to Sinbad, using a hand on his back for balance, and then held out the other toward her daughter. She really should have thought that through, Natalie concluded, though, when her tiny daughter threw herself into her arms, and her slight weight was enough to overbalance her. Arms closing around Mia to protect her, Natalie rolled back off her feet with a yelp, and cracked her head on the hard wood of the deck.

Eleven

"Are you all right?"

Rachel's face appeared in Natalie's vision as the flashing lights that had started going off when she hit her head began to disappear. Still, while she could now see, her brain was a little muzzy right up until Rachel's face was blocked by Sinbad's big white, furry one. His big pink tongue then came out to lash her face and Mia's, leaving the girl giggling helplessly on top of her.

The grimace of pain on Natalie's face slid away almost at once. She'd taken a good blow when her head hit the wooden deck, but Mia's laughter and the scent of baby powder left her awash in love and made that pain seem a small price to pay for her daughter's delight. Hugging her baby girl, she managed a smile for Rachel and murmured, "I'm fine."

"I've got you, my pretty!"

Natalie glanced around with surprise when Mia was suddenly lifted off her by Valerian. Sinbad immediately began to bark excitedly and jump around after Mia as Valerian lifted her into the air, crowing, "Ah ha ha!" He briefly swooped her around like she was a human airplane, before settling her against his chest with one arm under her bottom. With the other he reached out to pet Sinbad and calm him, before turning a concerned gaze to Natalie where she still lay on her back. Switching his attention to Mia, he raised an eyebrow and asked, "What do you think? We should help your mom up, huh?"

"Yes!" Mia shouted on a laugh.

Nodding, Valerian urged Sinbad out of the way and offered his hand. Natalie took it, then gasped when he tugged her quickly to her feet. Unprepared for the suddenness of it, or the strength behind the pull, she nearly overbalanced and fell forward, but Valerian stepped closer and caught her with an arm around her waist, so that she collapsed against his side instead.

"Sorry," Natalie muttered, struggling to regain her balance and move back a step.

"Nothing to be sorry for," Valerian said with a gentle smile as he helped her stand upright. "Should you be up?" Not giving her a chance to answer, he glanced past her to Rachel and said, "I thought Dani gave her something to help her sleep?"

"The IV came out and she woke up," Rachel said and, when Valerian arched one eyebrow in question, explained apologetically, "I'd gone upstairs to get a drink, and stopped for a few minutes to help with unpacking and putting away the food. It happened while I wasn't there to prevent it."

"I'm fine," Natalie said, frowning from one to the other. They were acting like she wasn't even there, or like Valerian was her parent or lover who had a right to know any of this.

"How do you feel?" Valerian asked, switching his attention to her.

Natalie opened her mouth but then paused as she noticed that Mia was playing with his face, first tugging at his ear, then his hair, then his chin, with a fascination probably borne of the fact that he was the first man she'd been this close to. The funny part about it was that Valerian hardly seemed to notice. His full focus was on her. Even when Mia used her little fingers to push his lips from a concerned line upward into a smile, he simply stared at Natalie, waiting for an answer.

Biting her lip to keep from laughing, Natalie shook her head and turned toward the sliding glass doors, automatically patting her leg in the sign for Sinbad to follow. The dog was at her side at once and she was more than grateful he was so obedient. She did not have the energy to chase after him. In fact, she needed to sit down. Now. Her legs were shaking like leaves and threatening to give out on her. Trying to hide how weak she was feeling, she stepped cautiously through the open door, asking, "How did you get stuck watching Mia? Where's Ashley?" Pausing just inside the door she glanced back sharply, adding, "It is Sunday, isn't it? I haven't slept for days or something, have I?"

"It's Sunday," Valerian assured her quickly, and

stepped through the door on Sinbad's heels. He then took her arm and urged her to the couch. "You'd better sit down before you fall down."

So much for trying to hide how shaky she was feeling, Natalie thought to herself, but then realized he hadn't answered her question. "If it's Sunday, Ashley should be here to look after Mia until four. Where is she?"

Stopping in front of the couch, she turned back just in time to see Valerian and Rachel exchange grim expressions. Tired of feeling like everyone knew something she didn't, Natalie scowled at the pair. "Did she just not turn up? Did she call in? Has anyone heard—?"

"She apparently went out of town for the weekend and had asked Emily to take her shift for her," Rachel said quickly, interrupting her.

"Oh." Natalie blinked, and then asked, "Well then, where is Emily? She doesn't usually just not show up. She's the responsible one of the two."

"Yes, well . . ." Rachel grimaced, and then admitted, "Emily was in a car accident."

"What?" Natalie gasped with shock and dropped to sit on the end of the couch, absently petting Sinbad when he, seeming to realize she was upset, crawled forward and nudged her hand with his nose.

"She's in the hospital," Rachel announced. "Her car went off the road into the ditch on the way home from here yesterday."

"How bad is it? Is she—?"

"She's okay," Valerian said quickly. "Well, not completely. She has a broken leg and pelvic bone. But it could have been worse and she will recover."

Natalie frowned at this news, and asked, "What happened?"

"They don't know," Rachel answered. "She took a nasty bump to the head and apparently hasn't regained consciousness yet. Dani is with her now and promised to call with an update as soon as she wakes up."

Valerian's gaze flickered to Rachel and away at that lie. While it was true the girl hadn't regained consciousness, they did know what had happened, or at least part of it. The left side of the little white Toyota the girl drove was scraped up, with bits of dark blue paint left on it. It suggested there had been another car involved. Either someone had hit her, or she'd veered into the left-hand lane and hit them. Whichever the case, it had led to her going off the road and crashing into the ditch. However it had happened, the other car hadn't hung around to wait for the police, nor had they even called it in, which made him suspect the other car had been at fault.

"Another accident and another employee gone," Natalie whispered in a troubled voice as she peered down at her dog.

"Another accident?" he asked. "Has someone else who worked here been in an accident recently?"

Natalie nodded. "Timothy called yesterday just before noon. His dad died in a car accident the day before and he had to go home to help his mother with the arrangements and everything. He doesn't think he'll be back before the end of the season."

"Timothy?" Rachel asked.

"He works the grounds," Natalie explained. "Well, he

used to work the grounds." Her gaze switched to Valerian, and she added, "He's the young guy who gave you your cart Friday night and forgot to check the gas."

"Ah." Valerian nodded, remembering a young man in what he would guess was his late teens or maybe in his early twenties. That was really all he recalled. Eager to get golfing, he hadn't paid the guy much attention.

"You don't think . . . ?"

Valerian pulled himself from his thoughts and peered at her in question when Natalie hesitated.

"I mean, two employees gone due to car accidents?" she said questioningly, and then shook her head. "I'm probably getting paranoid. After all the Angel-Maker hasn't attacked anyone but his targets before this. And Timothy wasn't in an accident, his father was, so the two probably aren't related and have nothing to do with what's been happening here. Right?"

When Valerian frowned and didn't respond at first, Rachel commented, "It *is* an odd coincidence. Two car accidents leading to two employees no longer being on-site." She paused briefly and then added, "I'm just not sure what the end game would be. If it was to isolate you and make you an easier target . . . well, even if we weren't here, you'd still have Jan, Hailey, and Maddison on-site. And . . . Roy, was it?" she asked.

"Yes, Roy," Natalie confirmed. "And the restaurant always has customers in it, so it wouldn't leave me isolated and alone anyway." Chagrin covered her face and she gave her head a slight shake. "Forget I said anything. I'm obviously very definitely getting paranoid. The two accidents must have just been a coincidence. Thank goodness," she added with a relieved smile. "Otherwise, I'd be worried about Jan, Ashley, and everyone else who works here."

Valerian smiled in response, but his mind was now turning paranoid as well as he considered it. Two car accidents one day after the other, each removing an employee from the premises, though in a different way. As Rachel had said, it might have been to isolate her, but for the fact that Jan, Hailey, Maddison, and Roy would still be here.

Until closing time, he realized now. After the restaurant shut down, everyone else would be gone, and normally it would just be Natalie and Tim mowing the course, and Emily here in the clubhouse watching Mia. But without those two here, she would have been left on her own with Mia if not for him and the others pretty much moving in here, which had only happened yesterday evening after closing.

"You're looking quite pale, Natalie. How do you feel?" Rachel asked suddenly.

"Other than a headache I feel mostly fine," Natalie insisted, but she sounded as weary as the little girl now dozing off against her side, Valerian noted.

"You should probably eat something," Rachel said. "How is your stomach? Does it hurt? Do you think you could keep down some broth?"

Natalie considered that and then shrugged. "I'm not really hungry."

"You threw up the last meal you had and have missed two since then," Rachel pointed out. "As malnourished as you are, you can't afford to not eat. We need to keep you healthy . . . for Mia's sake."

That made guilt immediately cross Natalie's face and she nodded reluctantly.

"Good." Rachel smiled at her and then turned to Valerian. "Can you stay with her while I go get my bag? I left it in her room." When he nodded, she added, "Then maybe while I examine her, you could see if Alex has any kind of broth or soup that would be easy on her stomach."

"Of course," Valerian murmured.

When Rachel hurried from the room, he gazed at Natalie to find she'd leaned her head back on the couch and closed her eyes. Mia was still tucked into her side, and Sinbad now had his head resting on her feet, his eyes also closed. It looked like all three were sleeping.

After a hesitation, he glanced around the room, and then walked over to the sliding glass doors to be sure Rachel had locked it when she followed him in. She had, so he then stood for a minute, peering out over the yard.

The clubhouse sat side-on to the road, its front facing the outbuildings and the golf cart parking area, as well as an open grassy area before the tree line that blocked the view of the course beyond. But Natalie's office was on the side of the clubhouse, facing the road. Not that the road was visible from here. The buildings were quite a distance in with a long driveway before one even reached the guest and employee parking lots. The side yard was a hundred feet deep, running the length of the building with a good-sized yard behind.

It also extended forty feet alongside the employee parking lot before the tree line curved in and it narrowed to a ten-foot-wide strip of grass between the edge of the driveway on the right, and a long narrow stretch of woods on the left as it ran the distance to the road. But it was dotted with trees that blocked any view of the road itself.

Valerian swept his gaze over the employee parking lot to the right, toward the front side of the clubhouse. He could see the back end of one of the big trucks that had brought the food Mortimer had arranged for. It had backed up to an access door to the kitchen to unload and was still there, although it looked like they had nearly emptied it. He could see only a couple of boxes left inside from his position.

Unable to collect such a large order that quickly, Mortimer had had the food sent in two deliveries. One had arrived right behind Alex, Jo, and Rachel that morning. It had been full of what Alex had thought she would need to handle the breakfast and lunch crowd. The woman had done a pretty good job at estimating what she needed too. They'd only had to run to the grocery store in the next town for half a dozen items after she checked the recipes Natalie kept pegged on a corkboard in the kitchen.

This second delivery, which had included both a refrigerated truck and this one he could see, held everything that had been removed from the restaurant, from spices to meat and frozen goods. Once finished unloading and packing everything away, the kitchen would be exactly as it had been before the poisoning.

Valerian grimaced as he thought of that incident. Physically he was fully recovered, thanks to the nanos doing their job, but mentally . . . he wouldn't soon forget the experience. Immortals didn't get sick and this was the first time he'd vomited in his long life. It wasn't a pleasant experience. Rachel had called it projectile vomiting, and had assured him that mortals didn't normally have as violent an experience as he had. It was the "normally" that hadn't impressed him. Even once in a lifetime was too much, and aside from feeling great sympathy for mortals, he also sincerely hoped he never experienced it again.

Tybo came into view with the truck's driver. The moment his partner stacked the last two boxes inside and carried them out, the driver lifted the ramp and slid it into place, and then began to close up the truck. Valerian watched for a minute, and then shifted his gaze to examine what he could see of the woods behind the building and running up to the road. He was looking for any sign of someone lurking and watching the office door or the building itself. Unfortunately, all but two men were presently helping to unpack the trucks and restock the kitchen, and those two men had to patrol a good hundred acres. He'd told them to concentrate on the space around the clubhouse itself, but it was a lot of area for two men to cover.

"Here we are."

Valerian turned around to see Rachel entering the room and Natalie opening her eyes and sitting up. She looked wide awake and alert, so perhaps hadn't been sleeping, after all, he thought, and then stiffened when she said, "You never told me what was happening in my kitchen. Why were my refrigerator and cupboards so bare?"

Much to his relief, Rachel answered the question. "We thought it was best to remove everything in case something else had been tampered with or poisoned. But the boys took an inventory of all the stock while removing it, and every last item has been replaced," she assured her quickly when Natalie began to look upset.

Her words didn't seem to reassure Natalie, and he understood why when she asked in a defeated tone, "How much did that cost me?"

"Nothing," Rachel told her. "The Enforcers—the enforcement agency will cover it," she said, trying to cover her slip as she told the lie he'd requested. Valerian didn't want Natalie knowing he'd paid for it himself. He didn't want her feeling beholden to him.

"The agency has good funding to cover such necessities," Rachel went on. "And it *was* a necessity. We didn't need a whole restaurant of vomiting or dead people here."

Valerian wasn't terribly surprised when Natalie began to shake her head. The way she'd tried to refund him for Friday night's round of golf and give him another round free just for the inconvenience of running out of gas, and then her intention to give him and Decker free passes for the rest of the season for mowing the course once, were enough to tell him a lot about her character. She wouldn't accept anything she had not earned, and would insist on taking responsibility for this, he was sure.

"It was my food, and it's my business. I'll pay for the replacements. Just tell me how much and I'll write out a check at once," she said grimly, shifting a sleeping Mia to lay next to her and starting to get up.

Rachel put a hand on her shoulder to stop her. "That isn't necessary. The food that was taken out will just be used in one of Alex's restaurants," she lied blandly, apparently recognizing this would be an issue for her. When Natalie immediately looked both shocked and horrified, Rachel quickly added, "Once it's checked thoroughly to be sure it's safe, of course."

"How can they check to find that out?" Natalie asked.

"They'll check the packages for tampering and . . ." Rachel hesitated and then her gaze became concentrated as she focused on Natalie and he knew she was using her skills as an immortal to make Natalie believe her and let the subject go. It only took a moment before her expression became more relaxed. Rachel then smiled and said, "So you see, there's really nothing to worry about. No one will be out anything other than time."

"Yes." Natalie nodded in agreement.

"Good, so let's check you over and make sure everything is okay," Rachel said cheerfully. Pausing then, she glanced to him.

Valerian immediately turned to pull the roller shade back down into place. Once done, he headed for the door, saying, "I'll go see if Alex has anything light for Natalie to eat."

Twelve

Valerian pulled his phone out once he was in the hall, but then reconsidered making the call he'd been thinking of. He wanted to talk to Mortimer about the car accidents and whether he thought they should be worried about the other employees, but wasn't sure if he was now just being "paranoid" as Natalie had put it. There was no evidence the Angel-Maker had ever attacked or harmed others around his victims. This really could just be happenstance. On the other hand, if it wasn't . . .

Deciding to ask the other men for their opinions, he slid his phone into his back pocket and continued on down the hall. A glance into the dining room as Valerian reached the kitchen door showed that it was finally starting to empty out with about a third of the tables now empty. Every table had been occupied since about eleven thirty that morning, including the tables on the deck outside. It seemed Natalie's food was really appreciated here, and it looked to him as if most of the county showed up for lunch on Sundays.

Valerian pushed through the swinging kitchen door and then stopped to survey the activity. While everything had been removed from the trucks, several boxes were stacked by the door and still being emptied and put away. He watched the men and women putting food away, and hoped it was getting put where it was supposed to go so that Natalie didn't have to waste her time rearranging later to what she was used to. But when he saw Colle directing one of the men, he relaxed. His cousins had emptied the kitchen, so should know where everything went.

"This is good. You should make this at La Bonne Vie."

Valerian turned at that comment to see Lucian leaning against the prep counter with a half-eaten lettuce-wrapped sandwich of some kind in hand. He was addressing Alex.

"I'd have to get Natalie's permission first," Alex said mildly and, when Lucian raised an eyebrow, explained, "I don't steal other chef's recipes and portray them as my own. So, I'd ask permission first, and then I'd put a credit on the menu to her and this restaurant."

Lucian merely grunted, then turned to Valerian as he approached. "Alex says she's awake."

"Yes," Valerian said quietly.

"How is she?" Lucian asked, and then took a bite of the lettuce-wrapped sandwich.

"Okay. Not great, but I think she'll be all right with

more rest and some food." Valerian's nose twitched at the scent that wafted to him. It smelled delicious and he wondered what it was, and if it was light enough for Natalie to eat. Maybe he could take them both some.

"They're peanut butter and chicken wraps," Lucian announced around a mouthful of food.

"Chicken Thai wraps," Alex corrected with amusement. "It has a peanut sauce so Lucian keeps calling it peanut butter and chicken. But the sauce is spicy so I don't think it would agree with Natalie's stomach at the moment."

"Oh," Valerian said with disappointment.

"I'll put some of the Thai wraps aside for you both to enjoy later once her stomach is more settled, and fetch you both a bowl of the chicken soup I made this morning for the lunch crowd from her recipe. I saved some for her when I saw it going fast," Alex added, and shook her head. "I didn't think it would be a popular item what with the temperatures outside being so high, but it's so darned good they apparently clean her out any time she makes it. Today was no exception."

"Some people order several containers to go and take it home to freeze," Jan announced, setting a plate with two Thai chicken wraps in front of Valerian with a smile. "To tide you over until Natalie can eat them too."

"Thank you." Valerian beamed at the woman and picked up one.

"Natalie has a real flair for cooking," Alex said seriously as Jan returned to her station. "Her recipes are fresh and tasty with something special always added. I'd hire her if I thought she'd give this up."

Valerian smiled at the compliment, his chest puffing up a bit with pride in his life mate's skills. Then he took a bite of the wrap and stilled. God in heaven, he'd thought the steak was good, but this . . . If a mouth could orgasm, his would have as the flavor filled it.

Valerian started feeling full only halfway through the first wrap. Not having eaten for so long, he supposed his stomach had shrunk to about the size of one of the peanuts in the dish he was eating, and he was no doubt stretching it out now, which was causing some discomfort. But despite that, he couldn't stop. It was *so good*. But once the first wrap was done, he eyed the second one with regret. He just couldn't manage that and suspected if he tried he'd end up making himself sick, an experience that was fresh in his mind and one he didn't want to repeat.

"I'll wrap it up and put it with the others I'm making for you two for later," Alex said sympathetically, noting his expression.

"Thank you, Alex," he murmured, and then felt a ruffling in his head and glanced sharply at Lucian. Valerian opened his mouth, but then just closed it again without speaking as he realized it would be faster if Lucian just read his concerns from his mind.

After a moment, Lucian finally said, "The car accidents could just be coincidence."

Valerian nodded, because he'd thought that himself. Fortunately, then Lucian spoke his other concern.

"But if it isn't and someone else gets hurt or killed . . ." Lucian shook his head unhappily. "That would be on us."

"Yes," Valerian agreed grimly. That was his worry too. He didn't want the death of one of Natalie's employees or friends on his conscience.

Cursing, Lucian straightened away from the counter and pulled out his phone. "I'll call Mortimer and have him send more men to keep an eye on Natalie's employees and ensure they're safe. Since you're staying here, I'll stay at your house and use it as a base."

When Valerian's eyebrows rose in surprise that he intended on sticking around for this case, Lucian looked down his nose at him and simply pointed out, "She's your life mate." It wasn't until he was walking away that Lucian added, "And a damned fine cook."

"Damn," Alex murmured as she watched Lucian walk out of the noisy kitchen. "I think my feelings are hurt."

"Why?" Valerian asked with surprise.

Alex shrugged and turned back to the bowl she was presently ladling soup into. "I've always thought of myself as a fine cook."

"You are," Valerian assured her quickly.

"You've never even tried my food," Alex protested with amusement. "Correct me if I'm wrong, but aren't you one of those immortals who hasn't eaten in centuries before now?"

"Not centuries," he protested. "Not even one, really. More like seventy years or so."

"Which means you haven't eaten my food," she pointed out.

"No. But I've heard the others raving about it," he said solemnly. "They say it's amazing."

"It is," Alex agreed. "But Natalie's recipes are . . ." She hesitated, searching for the right words, and finally said, "Exciting and exceptional. I can see why she's gaining more of a name for her food than the golf course, and I think her expanding and catering events here is a brilliant idea."

"How did you know about that?" he asked with surprise.

"Jan," she said, nodding toward the other woman. "We've been talking."

"Oh." Valerian nodded.

"And it seems Natalie's made something special here. The locals love this place now that she's taken it over, but they also care about her. So, I hope that if you do convince her to be your life mate you won't try to get her to shut this place down so you can drag her back to Scotland."

Valerian stiffened in surprise. "What makes you say something like that?"

Alex set down the bowl she'd just filled and picked up another one to start ladling soup into it before she admitted, "It's there in your mind, Valerian. You only left Scotland to find a life mate, and now that you have, you want to move back and be closer to your family."

Valerian grimaced. That was the hell of finding a life mate; your mind was easily read by everyone for the first year or more.

"And other than Mia, Natalie doesn't have real

family here anymore, so she might be willing to go," Alex continued.

Valerian was perking up at that news when she added, "But I think she'd always regret not going through with her plans, enlarging this place and seeing how successful it could be. And it would be good for her to have that success." Alex set the second full bowl down, and then faced him to say, "Because, trust me, I can see this place being somewhere people from hours away would book for weddings just for the food, and she deserves to enjoy that achievement for a bit before giving it up for you. Now, grab a tray to carry these on while I get some spoons for you two."

Valerian turned to look around for a tray as she moved off to fetch spoons, but his mind was on what Alex had said. She was right and wrong all at the same time. The truth was while he'd lately been thinking of returning to bonny old Scotland and the bosom of his family, for a lot of years that had been the last thing he'd wanted to do. In his youth, he'd determined to leave Scotland once he was old enough, break out on his own and enjoy some independence away from the watchful eye of his family. He hadn't been stupid about it, however. Valerian had got training and an education to be able to support himself, and had worked for a while to get experience and money together as well before striking out.

He'd spent the next century traveling the world, starting in Europe and then going farther afield, and eventually landing in North America. He'd kicked around the United States for a while until landing in New York where his cousins Colle and Alasdair were situated. He'd stayed with them for quite a while, which is how he'd got into being a rogue hunter, or Enforcer as they were officially called. His cousins were rogue hunters in the States, and had taught him the ropes when he'd shown interest. They'd trained him well in the job, including combat and their own version of detective work, which was basically critical thinking and paying attention to details.

Once he was suitably trained, Valerian had officially become an Enforcer and then found himself transferred to Canada some thirty years ago because more Enforcers had been needed up here. He hadn't minded and had actually enjoyed the job and the area, but as time passed, he'd begun to think more and more of Scotland and his family and that perhaps he might like to head back that way. It was a feeling that had grown over time, but then Marguerite's ability to match up immortals to their life mates had become an open secret and Valerian had found excuses to put off heading home to Scotland in the hopes one day he'd be one of the lucky ones she found a mate for. Instead, it was Stephanie who had done that.

"Here we go," Alex said lightly as she set two spoons, a package of crackers and two glasses of some bubbly orangish drink next to the bowls of soup he'd just set on the tray he'd found.

"What's that?" he asked, eyeing the iced drinks suspiciously.

"Orange juice and ginger ale," she said with a grin. "My mom used to give it to Sam, Jo, and me any time we were sick. She said the ginger ale settled the tummy and the orange juice had lots of vitamin C so was good for us. I thought Natalie might like some."

"Hmm," Valerian muttered, bending to sniff at the liquid with curiosity. It smelled interesting, but bubbles got up his nose and he quickly lifted his head to keep from sneezing.

"Oh, hang on." Alex rushed away, and he watched with curiosity as she fetched two bowls sitting on a corner of the counter.

"And what's that?" Valerian asked with interest when she added both bowls to the tray. One was a normal soup bowl, just a little smaller than the one holding his and Natalie's soup. But the other was positively huge, so much so that when she tried to add it to the tray, she nearly pushed half the other items off. Giving it up, she just set it so that it rested half on the tray and half on the back of his hand where he gripped the handles.

"Sinbad's food, and lunch for Mia," Alex explained.

Valerian eyed the contents of the larger bowl and pointed out, "Sinbad's food looks like stew." He didn't add that it looked bloody delicious, but it did. It smelled good too.

"Yes. Well, essentially it is," Alex confessed. "It's just stew without spices and salt."

When Valerian turned a disbelieving look her way, she gave a huff of exasperation. "His food was among the stuff we threw out. I had to make him more. Jan said Natalie makes a stew out of unsalted plain broth, and leftover vegetables and meat, and then throws in some brown rice to thicken it up. So that's what I did."

Alex eyed the bowl of stew with concern. "It should be all right. I checked every vegetable I put in it to be sure it wasn't toxic to dogs. I hope he likes it."

Valerian's lips twitched at her words. Today he'd seen the dog catch and eat a butterfly, try to eat and spit out a toad, and then chow down on the corpse of a squirrel that had to have been dead for at least a day, if not three. Sinbad did not seem to have a discriminating palate. Keeping that information to himself, he shifted his gaze to the smaller bowl and pointed out, "Mia's food looks the exact same as Sinbad's."

"It is," Alex admitted, and when he gaped at her, she scowled with irritation. "I didn't think to save enough soup for three bowls. Besides, Valerian, this is meat, vegetables, and rice. It's healthy, and I don't have time to make a ton of different dishes right now. Between the customers in the dining room and the take-out orders, we've been crazy busy. Now, come on. I'll get the door for you."

Shaking his head, Valerian followed her.

"Thanks, Alex," he murmured as he stepped out of the kitchen.

"My pleasure," she said lightly. He heard the quiet squeak of the door closing as he started up the hall. It wasn't until he was walking into Natalie's office that it occurred to him that he should have thought to get something for Rachel as well. Although, since the soup was gone, he suspected that would have resulted in another bowl of dog food landing on the tray, so perhaps Rachel would count herself lucky.

"Oh look! Valerian brought you guys lunch," Rachel

said with an amusement he could only imagine came from her having read his thoughts as he'd entered.

Rachel stood up from where she'd been perched on the arm of the couch while she chatted with Natalie about whatever women talked about when alone, and walked around the sofa toward him. "I ate earlier, so I'll just go see if I can do anything in the kitchen." Looking over her shoulder, she added, "I'll be back to check your vitals again in a couple of hours, Natalie. Between now and then I want you to eat, drink, and maybe relax and watch a movie or something, but rest. Doctor's orders."

Valerian stepped aside for her to leave the room, and then walked around the sofa only to stop with surprise as he saw the empty spot beside Natalie.

"Where's Mia?" he asked with a little alarm. Since everyone else had been busy with assigned tasks, he'd been watching the girl since she'd woken up that morning. At first, he'd thought it would just be for a little bit. They'd expected Ashley to show up, after all. It wasn't until Emily's mother had called to explain that Emily had apparently agreed to take over Ashley's shift but Emily had been in a car accident and they couldn't reach Ashley that he'd realized it was going to be an all-day thing.

Valerian really hadn't minded. He'd helped look after various relatives' kids over the years. None as young as Mia, but she was a sweetheart with her big smile and infectious laugh and hadn't been any trouble at all. Mostly he'd just had to keep her busy and entertained. Fortunately, for the first hour or so after getting up, she'd been content to just watch cartoons on the television while she ate the breakfast cereal Alex had brought her. Valerian had been grateful for that since he'd still been recovering from the poisoning.

Valerian had consumed more than enough blood by that point to power the repair of his body, but he hadn't felt that great yet. He'd been feeling much better, though, by the time Mia had grown bored with cartoons and wanted to go outside to play. His only problem then had been to find things to entertain her that didn't include the swing and slide out in the baking sun.

Valerian had pulled on all of his past experience with children to do that, including the Hokey Pokey Natalie had witnessed. But he'd had fun with the little girl. He liked her. He could only think that was a good thing since her mother was his life mate, or would be if he could convince her, he supposed.

"Our talking while Rachel examined me woke up Mia, and she decided to move to Sinbad's bed," Natalie explained.

She then turned an affectionate smile toward where the television sat on a wide credenza against the opposite wall. Valerian followed her gaze and stared blankly at the TV, before a snuffling snore drew his gaze down. A grin immediately claimed his features as he saw the little girl curled up in a fetal position on the large dog bed with a sleeping Sinbad's big white body curled around her. The dog's furry white upper leg was slung over her like a human would do, which amused him for some reason.

"Sinbad decided to join her," Natalie added, reminding him that the dog had been lying in front of the couch earlier.

"He's a good dog," Valerian commented before setting the tray of food on the table, careful to shift the dog bowl so that it didn't fall off the tray when he removed his supporting hand.

"Where did the dog food come from?" Natalie asked with concern, sitting forward on the couch to survey the contents of the tray.

"Alex made it. She said Jan told her you usually made his food with meat scraps and leftover veggies and stuff. Since they had to remove all the food, including his, she made up a batch for him, but she apparently looked up the vegetables she used online to make sure they weren't toxic for dogs."

"Oh." Her body relaxed a bit, and she managed a smile. "That was kind of her."

Valerian nodded in agreement as he began to remove the bowls of soup and their drinks from the tray to set them on the table. Straightening then, he hesitated, trying to decide if it wouldn't be easier to sit on the floor to eat at the coffee table, rather than hunch over it. While he was still debating that, Natalie grabbed the top of the table and tugged upward and toward herself. Valerian gaped, and then quickly dropped to sit on the couch to get out of the way as the top of the coffee table suddenly rose up and slid toward them revealing a storage area underneath.

"Well, that's convenient," Valerian commented as the table edge came to rest just inches from his chest.

"Yeah," Natalie concurred. "It comes in handy for

me and Mia to eat lunch and dinner when the kitchen is too hot or too busy for us to sit in there."

Valerian nodded and then glanced around the large room. He'd thought it did double duty as an office-cum-living-room, but it actually did triple duty as an office/dining room/living room. She'd really made the most of what she had available and he admired that.

"What's this?" she asked, picking up the glass of orangish liquid over ice and eyeing it with curiosity.

"Orange juice and ginger ale. Apparently, Alex's mother used to give it to her when she was sick as a child. She said the ginger soothes the stomach and the orange juice has vitamin C or something." He shrugged. "She says it's good."

"You've never had it before?" Natalie asked with surprise.

Valerian shook his head. Ginger ale had been around while he was still eating and drinking, but he'd never had it mixed with orange juice that he recalled.

"Oh well, you have to try it, then," she said at once, and assured him, "It is good. And my mom used to give it to me when I was sick as a kid too."

Valerian picked up his glass. The bubbles that had assaulted him when he'd sniffed it earlier had apparently dissipated because they didn't tickle his nose this time as he raised the glass to his lips. He took a tentative sip of the cold, sweet liquid and felt his eyebrows shoot up at the pleasant taste that crossed his tongue.

"Nice, huh?" Natalie asked with a grin, correctly interpreting his expression.

Valerian nodded, and took a larger swallow before setting it down and grabbing the spoons off the tray.

"Thanks," Natalie murmured, accepting the one he held out to her. "Is this . . . ?"

When she hesitated as she slid her spoon into the bowl, he said, "It's chicken soup made from a recipe you had on the corkboard? So, your recipe, I gather?"

"Yes." Natalie smiled faintly and took a spoonful to taste. Again, she relaxed and nodded slightly with apparent approval as she swallowed.

"Is it up to snuff, then?" Valerian teased lightly. "Alex didn't mess up the recipe or put in anything extra?"

"No. It's good," Natalie assured him, and then realized what she'd said and flushed. "I mean, I'm sure even if Alex had made her own version, it would have been good too. But . . ."

"But people don't come here for her version," Valerian said gently when she hesitated.

"Yes." She sighed with relief that he understood, and shrugged. "I appreciate everything your people have done. Trading out all my food to make sure no one else gets sick was no doubt a lot of work and a big enough deal, but getting Alex Valens in here to cook in my place is *major*," Natalie said with a sort of wonder, and then shook her head. "How on earth did they manage that? I mean, she's a big deal. Her restaurants in Toronto are super successful, and the scuttlebutt on the chef's group I belong to online is that she's accepted a contract for a recipe book. Between that and running three restaurants, she must be crazy busy."

"Well, her sister Sam is my boss's—"

"Wife," Natalie finished for him with a nod. "Yeah, Rachel said that. Still . . . I mean, come on!" Her eyes were wide and her tone suggested that the fact that Alex would step in to help them was crazy, and then her eyes widened even further, but with horror now. "Oh God!"

"What?" Valerian asked with concern.

"I don't think I thanked her," Natalie admitted with dismay. "I was so worried about where Mia was and if you were okay, I just didn't think of it."

Valerian was ridiculously pleased that she'd been worried about him. That meant she at least liked him, didn't it? He enjoyed that possibility for a minute and then gave himself a mental shake, and said, "I'm sure she understands and knows you appreciate her help."

"Maybe," she said dubiously. "But I should still thank her. Maybe I should just—"

Natalie had started to shift as if to slip out from under the tabletop now over their laps as she spoke, but froze when Valerian put a hand on her arm. The jolt of awareness his hand on her bare arm caused had both of them sucking in a quick breath. For one minute they merely stared at each other. He saw confusion and desire swirl in Natalie's eyes, and knew his own hunger was no doubt evident in his expression. For one second, he was tempted to tug her toward him and kiss her, but then a snuffling snore from Sinbad brought Valerian back to the situation at hand. He immediately released her and sat back, trying to give them both some space to recover, but had to clear his throat before speaking.

"How about we eat first, and then we can thank her

for lunch *and* for her assistance here?" he suggested finally. When she hesitated, confusion still on her face, but now joined by a little fear, Valerian added in a conversational tone that he hoped would relax her, "I don't know for sure if it would upset Alex, but it seems to me I remember Tybo telling me a story about how while eating a meal Sam had made him, he jumped up from the table to rush off to take a call or something and she was upset with him for letting the meal go cold after her hard work. I wouldn't want Alex to feel that way. Besides, you're terribly wan and your hands are trembling. You need to eat, Natalie."

She glanced down at her hands with surprise, and closed her fingers into fists when she saw that they were indeed trembling. Then Natalie let her breath out, shifted back to where she'd been before starting to slide out, and picked up her spoon. "I'll eat and then go thank her."

Relieved, Valerian picked up his own spoon. But his mind was on the sensations that had shot through him when their skin had made contact. He'd never experienced life mate sex before, of course, but he'd seen several couples who were new life mates and had witnessed their inability to keep their hands to themselves. They acted like addicts, constantly jonesing for the feel-good sensations that their pairing brought on. Valerian had to avoid it with Natalie, though. He couldn't take the chance that Mia might get into something she shouldn't and get hurt or even die because he and her mother were passed out on the sofa.

But damn, Valerian thought, he hadn't realized how

hard it was going to be to do this the old-fashioned way. Just touching her arm had given him a semi-boner and had awoken urges in him. He'd wanted to kiss her, but knew that was just the beginning, and if he'd given in to that urge, he had no doubt it would have led to touching, and then caressing, and eventually would have ended in two unconscious adults not watching a two-year-old. And that wasn't even taking into account that there was presently some lunatic out there burning angel shapes into the grass and trying to poison Natalie.

Yeah. No more touching, Valerian told himself firmly as he began to eat. But even as he did, he knew that was going to be incredibly hard now that he'd experienced just that little taste of what they could have together. He'd never in his life been aroused by just touching a woman's arm. He couldn't imagine what a kiss might do . . . but he wanted to find out.

Bad Valerian, he thought with exasperation.

"What?" Natalie asked.

Valerian turned a startled glance her way. "What, what?"

"You just said something," she explained. "It sounded like 'bad Valerian,' but maybe I misheard and you were talking about the soup or something."

"Oh God, no, the soup's amazing," he assured her, and then tried to find some explanation and simply went with the truth in the end. "I did say 'bad Valerian.'"

Her eyebrows rose slightly. "Why?"

"Uh." He stared at her nonplussed for a minute, but unable to think of an excuse, finally just admitted, "Because I wanted to kiss you."

Thirteen

Oh God, oh God, oh God.

Why had she asked him that? And why did his answer throw her poor brain into chaos?

Well, she knew part of the reason. Because just the touch of her arm had sent jolts of excitement through her and she'd wanted to kiss him too. It was only a small sound from Sinbad that had made her come to her senses.

Of course, his removing his hand from her arm had helped her fight the urge as well. While he'd been touching her, Natalie hadn't really been able to think clearly. Her mind had been too full of the uproar that simple touch had caused in her. Good Lord! Having his fingers touch the skin of her arm had been more arousing than some past boyfriends had managed with full make-out sessions or more. How was that even possible? Obviously, they had some serious chemistry.

But he'd called himself "bad Valerian" for that, and even admitted it to her. What was she supposed to take away from that? That mentally he really didn't want to kiss her and it was just a physical urge? Or that he wasn't interested in a relationship and thought it would be bad to start something up with a single mother? Maybe it was a work thing, she thought hopefully. Maybe Valerian didn't feel he should start something while he was supposed to be providing protection.

None of the options were good ones, but the last option was the least hurtful possibility. She could understand and even appreciate his professionalism if he didn't want to start anything while on the job. However, that just gave her hope, which was a bad thing. Natalie didn't want to hope that they could have something after all of this Angel-Maker business was cleared up. Because she didn't think it would work out, and she wasn't interested in being hurt again. But damn . . . with the chemistry so strong that just a generic touch on the arm had her hot and bothered, it might be worth the pain at the end to enjoy the pleasure it suggested they could experience in the short term.

Yeah, even Natalie knew that was messed up. She'd suffered enough emotional damage thanks to Devin and really didn't want to go through that again. Of course, no relationship was a given and there was always the risk of pain, but in her mind between Valerian's age and her responsibilities she just couldn't see it working. She was better to try dating someone her own age who could handle her responsibilities . . . and probably too she should wait until she had done the addition and actually had time to spend with someone to build a relationship.

Sighing inwardly, as she acknowledged that despite her attraction to the man Valerian just wasn't right for her, Natalie tried to think of something to say to end the awkward silence that had fallen over them since he'd admitted he wanted to kiss her.

"Who is Tybo?" she finally asked. Partially because it was the only thing she could come up with, but also because his story about the man had made her curious. She knew Sam was his boss's wife, but had no idea who Tybo might be.

Valerian paused with a spoonful of soup halfway to his mouth, and answered, "My partner."

Natalie nodded. "How long have you and Tybo been partners?"

"Decades," he answered before slipping the spoonful of soup into his mouth.

Blinking, Natalie turned to him with confusion. The man was not old enough to have been an enforcement agent for decades. Not unless he started at five, which was impossible, of course. Obviously, he was either joking or misspoke, so she asked, "Decades?"

Valerian opened his mouth, closed it, frowned, and then said, "Decade. Sorry. Did I say decades? I meant it's been at least a decade since Tybo and I started to work together."

"Right." Natalie relaxed a little, but not fully, because even a decade didn't make much sense, and asked, "Just how old were you when you became an enforcement agent? 'Cause you look about twenty-five. Twenty-eight, tops."

"Ah." Valerian nodded and smiled. "Yes. I've been told that before, but I'm older than I look," he assured her.

"How old?" Natalie asked at once.

"Older than you," Valerian said evasively.

"I'm thirty-two," she announced, sure he couldn't be that old.

He simply said, "I'm older."

Natalie arched one eyebrow dubiously, not believing that for a minute, but just as she opened her mouth to call bullshit, he said, "I was a foot soldier at eighteen with the 42nd Royal Highland Regiment of Foot."

Natalie paused, debating on whether to insist he just tell her his age, or address what he'd said. She had no idea what the regiment of foot was, though, and curiosity won out. "The Regiment of Foot?"

"An infantry battalion of the Royal Regiment of Scotland. It's also called the Black Watch," he explained.

"Oh." Natalie found herself blinking as she readjusted her view of him. Despite knowing he worked in law enforcement, she didn't really see him as . . . well, a gun-toting, macho-type soldier guy. In fact, she'd kind of assumed he was more a thinker, doing the psychological assessments of the criminal behind the acts. Natalie wasn't sure why. Maybe because he was so handsome. He looked like Prince Charming rather than some rough, tough action actor. Now she was imagining him in an army uniform, although with a kilt rather than pants. He said it was a royal battalion, after all. In her imaginings he had very nice knees. Shaking that image from her mind, she asked, "How long were you in the Black Watch?"

"Four years," he answered easily.

"And then you started to work with Tybo?" Natalie asked with a frown as she did the math in her head. Started the Black Watch at eighteen, stayed for four years, but worked with Tybo for a decade? He couldn't be the same age as her, could he? He certainly didn't look thirty-two.

Valerian hesitated, and then shook his head. "Actually, no. I kicked around for a bit first. Got some detective training and other skills that ended up being quite useful to a ro—an Enforcer."

Natalie noticed the slip, but had no idea what he had first started to say. Still she was more interested in his age, and estimated, "So, you're thirty-three or thirty-four?"

"Good guess," he said with a smile. "You'd make a good detective."

Natalie smiled faintly at the compliment, but shook her head. "Nah. I'd miss cooking too much."

"How long have you been a chef?" Valerian asked at once.

"Eight years," Natalie answered, but then returned to the subject at hand. "You don't look that old."

"You're not the first to say that," he said with a crooked smile. "Blame my parents and their parents before them. We all look young for our age, which sounds good, but is a terrible pain when everyone around you assumes you're younger than you are."

Natalie merely nodded and turned to scoop up some soup, but she was feeling a bit guilty since she'd assumed he was younger than he apparently was.

They ate in silence for a minute, and then Valerian asked, "So, you graduated from your cooking school at twenty-four?"

Her mouth full of soup, Natalie nodded as she swallowed, and watched him peer around her office.

"I guess your business courses came in handy, after all."

"Yes." Natalie smiled faintly, and admitted, "I'm sure that would make my dad happy. Actually, he'd probably gloat about it."

Valerian smiled in response, but asked, "Do you ever wish you'd completed your business degree?"

"I did complete it," she said, and when his eyebrows rose with obvious surprise, she frowned and asked, "Didn't I mention that?"

Valerian shook his head slowly. "No. I'm pretty sure you didn't."

"Oh." Natalie tried to think back through their conversation, and was a little surprised to find that she hadn't specifically said she'd graduated.

"In fact, you only mentioned doing two years before applying to culinary school. Did you do another year before going, then?"

"No." She shook her head. "I did three years of business in two and a little bit." When his eyebrows rose, she explained, "I took courses every term—summer, fall, and winter—to finish my degree. Including the summer after high school, and the summer before heading to Auguste's. I also took an extra course every fall and winter term, and got my business bachelor's in two years rather than the three it normally takes. I did the same at Auguste's. They had courses besides the main one: baking and pastry, plant-based culinary arts, and so on. I took as much as I could between the winter and fall semesters to learn all I could."

"I see," Valerian murmured, and he did. Her overdoing it in working hard was nothing new. It was how she'd lived her life for more than a decade. Maybe even longer, he thought suddenly, and asked, "Did you do a lot of extracurriculars and volunteer work in high school?"

"Yeah," she said with surprise. "How did you know?"

"Just a guess," he said mildly, and then asked, "Did you help out around here a lot too growing up?"

"Here?" Natalie looked confused for a minute, and then understanding crossed her face and she shook her head. "My parents didn't own this place when I was a kid. Dad was an executive for a big international food company. He traveled a lot for business while I was growing up."

"And your mom?" Valerian asked.

"She was a nurse anesthetist," Natalie answered, glancing to Mia and Sinbad when the dog snored loudly. Fortunately, it didn't wake Mia and the girl was still sleeping soundly.

"Long hours?" Valerian asked, almost sure the answer would be yes.

"Oh yeah," Natalie said, glancing back to him with a faint smile. "She used to complain that they never had enough staff at her hospital. She'd often get home from a twelve-hour shift only to get a call and have to turn around and go back because a car accident or something had happened and they needed her." Natalie shrugged. "They were both hard workers."

"And when did they buy Shady Pines?" Valerian asked.

"When they retired," she said, and then laughed. "I knew they'd hate retirement, and warned them that they should just try to scale back their hours rather than full-on retire. They were both getting burned out," she explained. "But they wouldn't listen. They'd saved enough to retire at fifty-five and they were retiring." She shook her head with amusement. "Of course they hated it. And then Dad saw that this place was for sale and decided it would make a nice retirement project, so he pulled their savings and bought this place."

"And your mom was okay with that?"

"Oh yeah," Natalie assured him. "As Mom put it, she was tired of sitting around contemplating her belly button."

"So, she didn't just back him up on it, she worked the golf course too?"

"Yes. She was as eager as him to have something to do. She said it was actually nice to work somewhere where she was busy, but where it wasn't life and death all the time."

"What?" Valerian asked with feigned alarm. "Not life and death? Was the woman mad? Golf is definitely a life and death thing."

Natalie snorted a laugh and leaned sideways to nudge his arm as she muttered, "Idiot."

Valerian took her teasing the way it was intended and grinned, but then his grin faded and he said, "Your childhood sounds . . . lonely."

Natalie turned to peer at Mia for a moment, her expression thoughtful, and then she sighed. "Yeah. Okay. After three years of counseling, yes, I can admit I was lonely as a kid. And yes, as my psychologist said I was probably doing all those extracurriculars and then extra classes and stuff to try to gain my parents' attention and approval."

"Three years of counseling, huh?" he asked solemnly.

"Hell, yeah!" she said as if that had been the only option. "I needed it too. I mean, losing my family was bad enough, but then finding out your husband isn't your husband, and lied to you about pretty much everything for a year of dating and four years of 'marriage' and you didn't have a clue, is pretty freaking mindbending." Her expression growing more serious, she admitted, "I was a complete mess when I moved here. Just utterly destroyed. Didn't trust anyone, including myself. I mean, how had I not seen that he had a whole other life?"

Natalie frowned at her own question. "But the doc pointed out that my upbringing had sort of made me the perfect victim for Devin to do that to."

"Because your father and mother were never around?" Valerian guessed.

"Exactly," she agreed. "Although more my father than my mother. As an executive, Dad had always seemed to be flying off to other countries for one meeting or another over acquisitions or mergers or whatever. Devin was the president of his company, so I thought of course he'd be gone even more." Natalie paused briefly, and then added, "And having been brought up pretty independent and used to being on my own, I never complained and even expected it."

"And you worked long hours too, so could hardly complain about his," Valerian suggested.

"Exactly," Natalie said. "I mean, jeez, how many men would put up with my hours at the restaurant? I thought I was lucky to have a husband as busy and understanding as him."

Valerian nodded solemnly, having no problem seeing how she'd ended up where she had. He watched the expressions flitting across her face, and then asked, "How did you two meet? I'm guessing it was at the restaurant in Ottawa since you spent most of your time there?"

"Yes." Natalie ate another spoonful of soup before telling him, "Devin stopped in for dinner one night while in Ottawa on business, and insisted on complimenting the chef after his meal. I was busy and didn't want to go out, but Gerry insisted. They were friends," she explained, her voice going grim.

"What?" Valerian asked with disbelief. "Your boss and your husband were friends?"

"Longtime friends," she said. "Roommates at university, Devin was his best man when he married, etcetera. Like thick as thieves. That type of friends."

Valerian narrowed his eyes and asked, "If so, then surely Gerry knew he was married?"

"Yes. He did," she agreed.

"And he didn't tell you?" he asked with disbelief.

"He didn't think it was his place to tell me," Natalie explained, her tone sarcastic. "At least that was what he said when I confronted him after the accident and I learned everything."

"Bastard," Valerian breathed.

"I couldn't agree more," she assured him, her tone light, though.

It seemed obvious to him that she'd dealt with that issue in counseling as well and had got over it, while he wanted to pummel this unknown man's face. Unable to do that, he instead asked, "Is that why you left the restaurant and came here to take over Shady Pines?"

Natalie shook her head. "Gerry didn't own the restaurant by that time. Devin had bought it just before we married." She frowned and then admitted, "I think now that's why he married me."

Valerian paused at this, and then shook his head. "I don't understand. Why would his buying the restaurant make him marry you?"

Natalie smiled faintly at his confusion and then peered at her soup briefly before saying, "I need to tell you about our relationship first to explain that."

"Okay," Valerian said at once, actually interested in hearing about it.

"Okay." Natalie blew the word out on a breath as she straightened and then started. "Like I said, the first time we met was because he wanted to compliment the chef."

Valerian nodded.

"But so was the second, and the third and the fourth." She smiled faintly, apparently at the memory, and then shook her head as if removing fond remembrances that had turned into a nightmare, and continued. "I think it was the sixth time that I finally told him he really needed to stop bugging me while I was cooking. That I appreciated the compliment, but I was far too busy to humor him, and that the next time he asked to compliment the chef, I'd refuse to come out."

"Good for you," Valerian said abruptly.

"Yeah," Natalie agreed. "So instead of continuing with the compliment thing, he showed up at the next after-party. He came with Gerry and—"

Valerian raised a hand to stop her. "Wait. What's an after-party? And when the hell did you have time to go to one with the schedule you had?"

"Oh." She paused briefly, looking bemused, and then explained, "Okay, so we all worked crap hours in our industry. We never had weekend evenings off ever. None of the restaurant workers did and that's when most people have date nights. But we in the industry were all in the same boat, and because of that, and because it wasn't like there was anywhere open at that hour, what usually happened was that once the cleaning was done, all the chefs and sous chefs and stagiaires, etcetera, would meet at a different restaurant every night for drinks and talking. Just to unwind, really."

"The after-party," Valerian said.

"Yeah. It was . . . fun. We'd talk about crap customers, or great things that happened. We'd laugh." She shrugged. "We got to wind down after work."

"And Devin came to one?" Valerian asked.

Natalie nodded. "Gerry brought him to one at our restaurant, which was kind of weird, but we all accepted it, and then he brought him to the next one at the next restaurant, and the next. I think it was at the fourth after-party that he asked me out." She looked down, and then raised her head and pushed on. "He seemed all right. He was good-looking, obviously successful, a friend of my boss, so I figured not a serial killer and probably an all right guy, so I said okay."

"When on earth did you find time for a date? I mean, from what you said you were working twenty hours a day, seven days a week."

"Oh." She smiled. "That was only at the beginning, while I was setting up the kitchens, and hiring and training staff and such. Once we were up and running, though, I had a little more time. I had Mondays and most of Tuesdays off. The restaurant was closed those two days."

"Okay." He nodded. "So you started dating."

Natalie nodded as well. "Yeah, and it was fine, but then he started bugging me to move into his house and—"

"He had a house in Ottawa?" Valerian asked with surprise.

"Yes. Although I honestly can't tell you how long he'd owned it," she admitted. "When we were first dating, we always spent time at my place. I didn't even think he had a place in Ottawa. I knew he lived in

Toronto where his business was, but then suddenly he took me to this great big house in a more expensive area of Ottawa . . ."

Natalie paused again, her expression thoughtful, but then admitted, "Now, knowing what I know, I half suspect he only bought it to move me into it, but it was all decorated and furnished when I first saw it and I just assumed he'd had it for a while to make his trips to Ottawa more convenient since he spent a lot of time there."

"You said he was bugging you to move in with him?" Valerian prompted, steering her back to her story.

"Yeah. Around six months after we started seeing each other he started bringing it up." Natalie grimaced. "I wasn't keen on the idea."

"Why?" Valerian asked at once.

"Well," Natalie said thoughtfully, "for one thing, I'd only known him six months of Mondays and Tuesdays, and not even every Monday and Tuesday either. And then there's the fact that I loved my apartment." Smiling she told him, "It was small, but perfect for me. It was right downtown, close to work, and set up just the way I wanted."

When he nodded, she continued. "But on top of that, Devin had told me pretty early on in dating that he wasn't interested in marriage." Turning to him she added quickly, "Not that I minded; I mean, I did plan on marrying someday and doing the babies and every-thing, but I figured I was young, and dating is a thing, so okay, marriage was off the table. This was going to be temporary. No problem."

Natalie didn't wait for him to comment, but then continued. "And that was the third reason. Knowing he didn't plan to marry I didn't think that moving in together would be a good idea. I was afraid things would get too . . . confusing?" She said it in an uncertain, questioning way, and then sighed and tried to explain. "I mean, we were dating. He didn't want to marry. That's fine, but if we moved in together, I might forget he didn't want a lifetime commitment and might let myself fall a little harder than I wanted to, if you know what I mean?"

"Having your own space helped you keep some emotional distance," Valerian suggested.

"Exactly!" She beamed at him. "Thank you. I've never been able to put my feelings about it to words, but that's exactly what it was." Natalie nodded with satisfaction, and took a drink of her orange juice and ginger ale.

"So did he eventually wear you down and convince you, or did he marry you to get you to move in?" Valerian asked.

"You're rushing ahead," she said with amusement.

"My apologies." Valerian grinned faintly at the reprimand. "Go ahead."

"Okay, so at the six-month mark he started talking about moving in together, which I was resistant to. Then about three months later he took me to see his house."

"The one you aren't sure he owned before that?" Valerian asked.

Natalie nodded. "That's when he really started putting on the pressure for me to move in. He started using our schedules as the reason behind it. We had so little time. This way he could spend every minute that he wasn't traveling for work with me. That kind of thing."

"And?" Valerian asked. "Did you cave?"

"No," Natalie said at once, and then shrugged. "I can be stubborn, and like I said, aside from liking my place, I didn't want to blur the lines emotionally when he had no interest in marrying." She turned her glass on the tabletop, and admitted, "Although I did concede enough to take some of my things over to the house and stay there when he was in town."

Valerian wasn't surprised to hear she had a stubborn streak. He suspected anyone who worked as hard as her had to have that. It kept her from giving up before she was done what she was determined to do. But knowing how things had ended, he half suspected that some part of her mind had seen or heard something that had made her doubt Devin was on the up-and-up. She might even have suspected he was married, considering he saw her only two days a week. A suspicion that was no doubt killed when he proposed.

"So," Natalie said now, looking upward thoughtfully as she ran through her memories. "About three months after that, maybe a year after we started dating, we were having lunch in a pub. We were talking while we were waiting for our meals when he brought up the fact that Gerry was looking to sell the restaurant."

When Valerian's eyebrows flew up, she nodded. "His mother had just died of a stroke. Gerry had a heart attack when he got the news and damned near joined her. That made him decide to dial back his responsibilities and maybe travel. Well, I'm sure the millions he inherited from his mother helped with that decision," she added dryly, and then shrugged. "Anyway, so Gerry was looking to sell, and Devin asked what I thought of his buying the restaurant. I told him honestly that it was probably a great investment. We were really popular by that point," she explained. "We'd had some rave reviews in the paper and online and were booked solid every service, both lunch and supper, for months in advance."

"Because of your amazing food," Valerian said with certainty.

Natalie chuckled and waved away the compliment. "A chef doesn't work alone. I had great support staff." Before he could argue the point, she continued. "Anyway, I pointed out that restaurants rise and fall all the time and while our restaurant was doing well, it could fall at any time, but it did seem a good investment at this point and I could always find a job elsewhere."

"What?" Valerian asked with surprise. "You would have left?"

"Oh yeah," she assured him. "Like I told him, I don't sleep with my boss. I wouldn't want to deal with the fallout: gossip, knowing looks, accusations of favoritism." She shook her head. "No, sir. I'd have been out of there like a dirty shirt."

"You could have just broken up with him and stayed," Valerian pointed out.

"Oh, like that would be better?" Natalie asked dubiously. "That would just cause even worse gossip, and hard feelings between the two of us. A boss with hard feelings would not be fun," she pointed out.

"True," he acknowledged.

"Devin got kind of quiet after that," she said. "And he had this troubled look, but when I asked what was wrong, he said, 'Nothing,' so I just thought maybe he'd actually wanted to buy the restaurant and was now displeased that he couldn't. But after a while he seemed to shake it off for the most part. I mean, we kept talking and eventually he seemed to relax again, although he did start drinking a little heavily," she said, before explaining further, "He wasn't usually much of a drinker, but that day he pounded back several."

"He'd already bought the restaurant," Valerian guessed.

Natalie nodded. "I didn't know that at the time, but yes."

"He must have been in a panic at that point," Valerian said slowly. "The restaurant was popular because of your food, but if you left . . ."

Natalie shrugged. "Another chef would have taken my place. Maybe even a better one. No one is irreplaceable, and I'm sure they would have done well enough. And even if the next head chef wasn't up to scratch, the restaurant already had a good rep and could have gone quite a while on it. Long enough to switch to another chef if that one didn't work."

Valerian thought she was being far too modest. The

restaurant's popularity had grown on her food, he was sure. Especially after what Alex had said, but he didn't argue the point.

"Anyway, as I said, he'd started pounding back the drinks and got pretty hammered, so I decided a walk would do us good and dragged him to the market. He was a funny drunk," Natalie added with amusement. "I mean, usually he was kind of straightlaced, the ultimate serious businessman, but when he'd had a few drinks, he'd relax and let his hair down, so to speak, and his hair was definitely down that day. He saw something funny in everything, from the fish for sale, to the vegetables, and had me constantly laughing. And then at one point, he said something—I don't even remember what now, but I remember it was funny as hell—and I laughed until my eyes started to water. Then, as I was wiping my eyes, I unthinkingly said, 'Oh God, I'll miss this when it's over.'"

Valerian's eyes went wide, but then so had hers, as if she was still surprised by what followed. He understood why when she said, "You'd have thought I'd slapped him. His laughter died abruptly, and he just kind of gaped at me, and then said, 'Why would it end?'"

"I said, 'Well, you were honest and told me you aren't interested in marriage and kids. But I am. So eventually I'm going to have to move on and find someone else.' And he stared at me for this full minute, and then said, 'Well, maybe I've changed my mind.'"

"What did you say then?" Valerian asked, finding himself leaning forward.

"Nothing," she admitted. "I think I just kind of gaped back at him. I mean, he really surprised me with that. He'd been so firm on the *don't even consider marriage, I'm not in the market, don't want kids either, etc., etc.*"

She let out a slow breath. "I think he shocked himself a little with that too, to be honest. But we left the market then and went back to the house. It was a Tuesday, and he lay down, claiming a headache from the alcohol. We didn't talk again that night, and the next morning was a rush as he headed to the airport and I went to work."

Natalie pursed her lips. "He didn't come back the following week, or the one after, and then he showed up the Sunday after that as we were finishing final cleanup. He was in Gerry's office talking to him until I was done, and then just as everyone from the other restaurants were showing up for the after-party, he hustled me out and into a limo. That was new," she added dryly, and explained, "Our dates had never been that fancy before then." She shrugged. "But it turned out this was special. The limo took us to the airport where a private plane was waiting, which I now know he owned."

"You didn't know he had a plane after you were married?" Valerian asked with surprise.

Natalie shook her head. "I think he found it handier for me not to know."

"How so?" Valerian asked.

"Well, if he wanted to leave, he could blame it on the flight being at a certain time and another one not being available in time to get him where he had to go. And he could also claim his flight was canceled to explain why he missed important dates like our son's first birthday, or our anniversary and such," she pointed out.

Which meant he had missed a lot of such days, Valerian realized, but didn't comment, and simply asked, "Where did he take you?"

"Vegas," she answered. "To get married."

Valerian nodded. That was exactly what he'd suspected. She'd said the other day that they'd married in Vegas.

"It was all very romantic and whirlwind. He didn't just rush me to the nearest chapel once we landed. He wined, dined, and romanced me first before convincing me to marry him. Not that he had to do that much convincing," Natalie admitted with a wry twist to her lips. "I mean, logistically, it was perfect. With my schedule I didn't have time to plan a big wedding. Besides, I didn't have a lot of family to attend a big shindig. Just my parents, really, and a couple of aunts and uncles out in British Columbia that I hadn't seen in at least fifteen years."

"Your parents were from BC?" he queried.

"My father was. But my mother was from Ontario. He met her when his company promoted and transferred him here," she explained.

"And your mother didn't have any family?" Valerian asked with more interest than she would understand.

"She had her parents at the time that they married, and maybe some cousins on her dad's side that they weren't close to, but no siblings or anything," Natalie said, and explained, "My grandmother had trouble carrying babies to term. Mom was the sixth or seventh pregnancy, and her miracle baby because she survived. They never had another." She paused briefly. "It was the same for my mom. I was baby five, I think, and the only one to survive to birth. It's something genetic, and I was afraid I'd have the same issue, but I guess I didn't get that gene. My son, Cody, was my first pregnancy, and Mia my second, and both came through just fine."

"But your grandparents aren't alive now, are they?" Valerian asked with concern.

Natalie shook her head. "Gramps had a heart attack when I was ten or eleven, and Grandma followed a year or two later of cancer."

Valerian relaxed and nodded. It would have been harder to convince her to leave elderly family behind to be his life mate, fortunately that wasn't a worry. But talking about her family made him think of something else. "What about his family?"

Natalie looked confused for a minute, and then understanding lit her eyes. "You mean, did I meet them?"

He nodded, worried that it had been another case of not thinking it was their place to talk about her marriage as it had been with her boss.

"I never met them," she said quietly. "He said they lived in Europe and didn't like to fly, but we'd visit eventually. Only eventually never came and it was all just a lie anyway. His family lives in Toronto."

Valerian was silent for a minute, recalling her reaction when he'd said his family was in Scotland,

and wondered if she'd thought he was just lying, as Devin had done. But she'd met four members of his family now. Perhaps it had just been a kind of trigger for her, though, he thought, and changed the subject. "I'm guessing you didn't register the marriage yourself once you were back from Vegas?"

"No. He said he'd do it," Natalie said quietly. "And later told me he'd received notice that it was now registered with some government body . . . the Office of the Registrar, maybe," she said uncertainly, and then shook her head. "Anyway, I remember asking if there was anything else we had to do? Or if we got any kind of certificate that came with it other than the one we got in Vegas, and he said no, just the email, so . . ." She shrugged. "I went back about my busy life."

"And then he told you he'd bought the restaurant?" he guessed.

Natalie snorted a laugh. "He said it was my wedding gift."

Valerian's eyebrows rose. "He put your name on the ownership?"

"Oh hell, no!" she said with amusement. "His company name was on it, but according to him, we were married now, so it was as much mine as his."

"But you weren't legally married," Valerian said slowly. "And when he died . . ."

"Technically, his wife would have been my boss had I stayed," Natalie said quietly. "She also owned the home I lived in, the furniture, the cars, the—" She closed her eyes. "Basically, just everything. Even the things I'd bought. I had no proof I'd bought anything in the house, and I did," she assured him. "It was totally furnished when I moved in, but the style was cold modern. I ended up redecorating the whole place, one room at a time to make it warmer, and then of course I did a nursery for Cody, and then his bedroom. I also bought new dishes, silverware, pots and pan, chef's knives . . ." She blew out a small breath. "It came to a lot of money over time, but I didn't keep receipts. I had no idea I needed to. And my car, Christ, I was pissed about that. I had a car when I married Devin, a nice one. A little Miata that I loved, but he insisted I should have a luxury car, so he traded it in and came home with a BMW sports car. His name was on the ownership."

"He was able to trade in your car?"

"I signed off on it so he could," Natalie admitted with chagrin, and then defended herself by adding, "He kept insisting I needed a safer car for Cody, and I didn't have time to shop for cars. It just seemed easier." Her mouth thinned out. "Well, newsflash, easy means getting screwed over. After the accident, I found I suddenly had nothing. Not even the credit cards in my wallet, or the money I'd made over the years."

"Wait, your credit cards and the money you'd made?" Valerian asked with disbelief. "How the hell did he manage that?"

"Because, frankly, I was an idiot," Natalie said with a self-deprecating laugh. "I had two credit cards when we met and great credit. But he thought it would be better if we had joint cards. So, he got me cards on his accounts. I guess supplementary cards, maybe? He had a credit card, and added me as a whatever, and they sent a card in my name, but it was actually on his account. He did that with three or four cards, and then suggested I dump mine, which I did because we were a couple and six credit cards was just ridiculous. I mean, they don't have enough slots in wallets for that many plus your driver's license, health card, etc.," she pointed out with disgust. "But that meant when he died, I had nothing, including credit. I hadn't rented for four years, or had a proper credit card of my own in that long. It was like starting fresh."

"Okay, but what about your money?" Valerian asked. "Your paychecks from working at the restaurant?"

"It was direct deposit rather than paychecks, and were deposited in what I thought was a joint account, but was actually a business account in his name that he gave me a supplementary debit card for. My money was deposited, and I had access while he was alive, but the minute he died—"

"His wife inherited it," Valerian finished for her, and then muttered, "The bastard."

Natalie shrugged. "Well, to be fair, he probably didn't expect to die so young or abruptly."

"But he did," Valerian pointed out grimly. "And that left you in a hell of a mess."

"It would have," Natalie said quietly, "if not for my parents leaving me everything in their wills."

"Ah," Valerian said with understanding. "And that's why you left and came here."

"Well, I sure as hell was not working in the restaurant for the actual wife of the man I had thought I was married to for four years," Natalie said with outrage.

Valerian hesitated, and then asked, "Did his wife never—I mean, she kept everything? She must have found out about you after her husband's death. Did she never offer you at least some money from—?"

"No," Natalie interrupted, and then sighed and admitted, "I mean, I don't know if she would have or not. I never asked for it or gave her the chance to offer." Her shoulders slumped and she admitted, "I couldn't even face her. He made me the other woman, and I was so . . . ashamed." The last word was a whisper he wouldn't have heard were he not immortal.

Valerian swallowed and had to fight the urge to take her into his arms. He couldn't imagine what she had gone through. It must have felt like horror upon horror. Losing her parents, son, and the husband she loved in one fell swoop to a crash, and then learning the husband wasn't legally her husband and she'd lost everything else too, even things she'd rightfully earned. He couldn't imagine the kind of strength it must have taken to navigate her way through that and come out the other side as strong and whole as she was today.

"So," she said suddenly, managing a crooked smile. "Now you know the gory details."

"It must have been awful to find out the man you loved betrayed you that way," Valerian said quietly.

Natalie gave another short laugh and corrected, "The man I *thought* I loved. It turned out I didn't even know the man I married in Vegas. He wasn't who I thought he was, and I never loved the real him because I didn't know him."

Valerian was silent for a minute, thinking, and then asked, "Were he and his wife separated or something?"

Natalie turned to him with surprise. "No. They were still together, apparently. Why would you—Oh," she interrupted herself with a sigh. "How did he fool both of us?"

Valerian nodded solemnly. It seemed an impossible thing to him for her husband to be able to have two families and neither know about the other. The logistics of time spent with each was just the beginning of the nightmare to his mind.

"Right." Natalie nodded and then said, "Well, like I said, he owned his own company, and we're talking a big international conglomerate-type thing, with various interests in tech, food, steel, etc. But mainly resorts and hotels all over the world. He was always either buying, building, or taking over some resort or hotel somewhere. If not the Caribbean, then Africa, or the US. He was always flying out to some meeting or merger, or to settle some labor dispute." She shrugged unhappily. "He explained that when we first started to date, and said he knew it would be difficult because he would be away a lot, but did I think I could handle it?"

The smile Natalie got then was self-mocking as she said, "And I was actually grateful."

Valerian sat up a little straighter. "What? Why?"

"Well, I told you about my hours," she pointed out as if that should explain everything, and Valerian supposed it did. But Natalie explained anyway. "I couldn't have a normal relationship. No average nine-to-five working guy would have put up with my leaving probably before he got up to go to work, and not getting home until he was in bed or at least headed there."

When Valerian nodded with understanding, she added, "And my only time off was Monday and part of Tuesday, which isn't your average weekend for most people. So, they'd see me for a couple of hours those nights and that was about it. I mean . . ." She grimaced slightly. "I know there are others out there who might have been able to get the same days off as me, but that would still mean they'd only see me a day and a half or a little more a week. Who would put up with that?"

I would, Valerian thought. He didn't say what she wasn't ready to hear, but he'd put up with that and a lot more. He'd already decided Natalie was worth any sacrifice. She wasn't just his life mate, she was also just . . . special. The woman worked harder than anyone he knew, but still managed to spend time with her daughter. She might have babysitters or nannies for Mia through the week, but Jan had told him she still spent a lot of time with her each day, taking her out with her on little jobs on the course and mowing sometimes, keeping her in her office while doing paperwork.

Jan said Ashley and Emily had about as much time off on the job as they spent working because Natalie would often tell them to go on break and take Mia off with her on whatever task she was doing. And she was doing a hell of a job with Mia too. The little girl was sweet-tempered, adorable, and—in his opinion—pretty darned smart for her age. She was also very polite, using *please* and *thank you* with him. And her giggles and laughter . . . damn, he'd never seen a child so full of joy as he had today while taking care of Mia. Natalie had obviously done an amazing job with her despite her long hours of work. If she agreed to be his life mate, Valerian thought he would be getting one hell of a woman, as well as a sweet little girl. If they'd allow him to adopt her as his own, he'd be proud to call her daughter.

"Devin did," Natalie said now, drawing him back to the conversation. "He made sure to show up for the Mondays and Tuesdays, and I was grateful to have someone who was as busy as me . . . It seemed perfect. I couldn't believe I'd been so lucky as to find someone who matched me so well that way and wouldn't feel neglected." Wrinkling her nose, she added, "You know the old saying, if it seems too good to be true . . ."

"It is," he finished dryly, and then considered the kind of life she must have had, seeing the man she thought was her husband only a couple days a week. How had that even worked? he wondered, and suddenly asked, "What about the holidays?"

"Ah." Sadness drifted across her face, and Natalie shook her head. "He didn't make a single Easter or Thanksgiving. He did manage to arrive on time for a late Christmas dinner with my parents and our son the third year. I'm guessing his real family must have had an early Christmas meal that time."

"How could he explain that?" Valerian asked with disbelief.

"Thanksgiving is only celebrated in Canada and the US and then they aren't even celebrated on the same day; Canada's is in October and the US has it in November. As for Christmas and Easter, there are a lot of non-Christian countries that do not celebrate those holidays and he had resorts in every single one of them, I think." She shrugged. "At least, that was the explanation he gave. Because they didn't celebrate it, he was expected to show up in these countries when they scheduled meetings at that time or risk losing the deal he was trying to make."

Valerian shook his head with disbelief. "You must wish you'd never met the man."

"What?" she asked, meeting his gaze with surprise. "Good Lord, no!"

Valerian's eyes widened slightly at her vehemence.

"I mean, yeah, he was a liar, and a cheat, and he made me the other woman, and I suffered horrible shame and misery over it all after he died. But I don't wish I could change a thing about our relationship. The car accident, yes. I wish I could go back in time and somehow warn my parents and save them and my son, or even him . . . possibly," she added dubiously, and then shrugged and added, "But I wouldn't erase my relationship and non-marriage to Devin. Not for a minute."

Valerian's eyes widened with surprise at both her words and her vehemence until she turned to look at where Mia was still curled up with Sinbad.

"Devin put me through hell at the end, but he also gave me two beautiful children. One I lost, my Cody. But Mia . . ." Her face softened with a smile full of love. "Every second of that hell was worth it to have Mia."

Valerian peered at the little girl sleeping on the dog bed, and couldn't help but smile. He understood. He also thought it was wonderful that she loved her so much despite what the girl's father had done. He'd lived a long life already, and seen enough women blame and take out their anger for the father on the child. But Natalie wasn't the type of woman to do that. She loved her daughter, and even seemed to accept what her husband had done and the situation he'd left her in as a worthy price to pay to have the little girl. He wondered if she'd always felt that way, or if it was a result of the counseling she'd had, and was about to ask her that when something heavy crashed on top of him.

Fourteen

Natalie gaped at the woman who had suddenly attacked Valerian. She was certainly fast. Natalie hadn't even seen her coming. She'd just leapt like a pole vaulter over the back of the couch, and landed in his lap with an impact that had Valerian grunting in surprise. The woman was now pressing kisses all over his face, and giggling at Valerian's gasping complaints and cries for mercy.

"Enough!" Valerian suddenly scooped the woman off his lap, stood, and dropped her so that she landed facing where Natalie had stood up.

"Hoy, you must be Natalie," the girl cried with excitement, and suddenly pushed away from Valerian to attack her instead.

Eyes wide and a little horrified, Natalie stared over the woman's shoulder at Valerian as she was caught up in a bear hug and lifted several inches off the floor in the kind of enthusiastic hug she used to give to Cody when the little boy had come running up for attention.

Valerian offered an apologetic grimace, and said with exasperation, "Aileen, love, stop mauling Natalie."

Recognizing the name of the sister Valerian had talked about, Natalie relaxed and even raised her hands to pat the girl's back in response to the embrace.

"I'm no' mauling her, brother," Aileen said with exasperation as she set Natalie back on the ground and stepped away to look her over with interest. "Lucian mentioned you were here protecting your LM and I wanted to meet her, is all."

"LM?" Natalie asked with confusion.

"Latest mission," Valerian said quickly.

"Right," Aileen said, slowly nodding her head with a wide grin. "Latest mission."

"Oh," Natalie said uncertainly, because Aileen's attitude was so odd.

"Lucian also said there was a niece," Aileen announced with excitement. "Where is the little cutie pie?"

"Niece?" Natalie asked with confusion.

"Lucian no doubt said you had a daughter and she misunderstood him to mean niece," Valerian rushed out, scowling again at his sister, before switching to a smile for Natalie and explaining, "Aileen's not from here so sometimes gets confused about language."

Natalie stared at him with disbelief. "Aren't you both from Scotland? I mean, her accent is Scottish, and you were in the Scots guard . . ."

"Well, yes, but it's the accent, you see; it can be a bit discombobulating at first."

"Ah," Natalie said, but narrowed her eyes because Aileen was rolling her own with every explanation Valerian gave. Turning her focus fully on the girl, she asked, "What year are you in at university?"

"Fourth," she said cheerfully. "I'm going for me master's in business."

Natalie turned back to Valerian and raised her eyebrows, not believing for a minute that someone who had lived and gone to school in Canada for almost four years could get discombobulated by the accent to that extent and mistake daughter for niece. Besides, she was pretty sure they spoke English in Scotland.

"Hoy, there she is!" Aileen exclaimed as she rushed across the room to where Mia and Sinbad were now awake and sitting up. "What a little beauty she is!"

Natalie's mouth was just softening into a smile at the compliment when Aileen dropped to her knees and cradled Sinbad's furry head between her hands to croon, "Aren't you a pretty girl, Mia? Yes, you are. You're gorgeous!"

Natalie's mouth dropped open at this, but then her daughter giggled and said, "He's Sinnee, silly. I'm Mia."

"What?" Aileen blanched with exaggerated dismay, and then released Sinbad with a kiss on the nose before turning to scoop up Mia and straighten with her in her arms. Peering down at her then, she nodded solemnly. "Well, aye, I should have seen it right away. Because you're even lovelier than Sinnee. Are you no'?" she asked, balancing her in one arm so she could tickle her belly with the other. "Are you no' a lovely lassie? Hmm? Pretty as a picture? Pretty little flower? Pretty as your mummy?"

"Yes!" Mia squealed on a laugh as the girl tickled her with each question.

"Aye," Aileen crooned, and then hugged her close. "You're a love, you are. You and me are going to be fine friends, do you no' think?"

When Aileen pulled back to meet her gaze, Mia nodded. "Yes. Please."

"Yes, please?" Aileen echoed with amazement, and then turned to Natalie and Valerian. "Gor I love her. I think I'll take her for ice cream if that's okay with you?" She barely waited for Natalie's nod before she headed for the door, chattering away to Mia. "Would you like ice cream? Alex was getting it ready for us. I like ice cream, how 'bout you?"

"With a cherry?" Mia asked, glancing over Aileen's shoulder to be sure Sinbad was following, which of course he was. Although he wouldn't go into the kitchen with them, he would wait patiently in the hall. To his mind, Mia was his to guard and he took that job seriously.

"Oh aye, I'll be sure there's a cherry on top for you, love," Aileen said on a laugh.

"Thank you." Mia's excited shout drifted back into the room as Aileen sailed out into the hall with her.

Natalie immediately turned to Valerian. "Your sister—"

"My sister—" Valerian started at the same time,

but they both then paused because he'd instinctively stepped forward, taking her hands in his in what was no doubt an effort to calm and appease her, but the effect was instantaneous. Like when he'd touched her arm, the simple act of his clasping her fingers sent shocking frissons of excitement through her hands, up her arms, and straight to parts of her body that were suddenly stirring with interest. Dear God, he was just lightly clasping her fingers, she thought with amazement, aware that her nipples were hardening under her shirt and bra, and that dampness was gathering between her legs like rain clouds on a humid day.

She started to look down, intending to check the front of her jeans and be sure she wasn't developing a wet spot, but her eyes got caught on Valerian's mouth. He had such a nice mouth. With one of those full, soft-looking lower lips that a girl just wanted to suck into her mouth and nibble on.

Natalie was so caught up in the idea that she didn't at first notice when that mouth started to lower toward her, and once she did, all she felt was a breathless anticipation. Was he going to kiss her? What would that feel like? Was he a good kisser?

Oh God, yes, he was, she thought on a gasp as his mouth covered hers and he proceeded to devour her. There was no buildup to passion. No little nibbling kisses to tease her into opening her mouth. The moment their lips met a sort of electricity shot through her, startling her into gasping. Natalie's mouth opened on the sound, his tongue swept in along with oxygen, and it was like a backdraft in a fire: an explosive surge

took place in her body, burning out every thought and
worry and leaving only a desperate need for him.

Natalie thought she heard Valerian groan, or
maybe it was her. She wasn't sure, but he'd released
her hands and they were now desperately reaching to
touch whatever she could of his body. That was only
his shoulders, arms, and butt since they were suddenly plastered to each other, their bodies writhing
and grinding together as his hands traveled from her
shoulders, down her back, and to her bottom to press
her even more tightly against him.

Tearing his mouth away suddenly, Valerian nibbled
his way to her neck, growling, "Natalie . . . God . . ."

"Yes," she gasped, arching her body and turning her
head to give him better access to her neck and ear.
Natalie then quickly turned her head back to claim his
mouth once more when she couldn't bear the excitement he was causing her. She sucked eagerly at his
tongue, and barely refrained from biting it with excitement when he grabbed her right leg behind the thigh
and pulled it up around his hip. Natalie moaned into
his mouth when he ground against her more fully. She
grasped desperately at his shoulders as her legs began
to give out.

Valerian caught her by the bottom at once and began
to back her up, toward the couch, she assumed, and
was proven right when he urged her down and she felt
the edge of the couch cushions against the backs of her
legs. Natalie turned then, so that they would lay on it
properly as he lowered her, and she felt the cushions
under her bottom, her back, and then—

She blinked her eyes open with surprise when something firmer, lumpy, and slightly higher stopped her head. Her eyes widened incredulously when she found herself staring up at a dark-haired man whose lap her head had apparently landed in. A moment of confusion claimed Natalie briefly as she tried to push back the passion presently soaking her brain so that she could understand who he was, how he had got there, and why? But it was hard to think with Valerian's tongue thrusting into her mouth, and his hands now gliding over her breasts between them.

"Hi."

Valerian froze, and Natalie, whose eyes had started to close despite herself as passion tried to drag her under again, blinked her eyes back fully open and stared at the man.

"I'm Tybo. You must be Natalie," he said in a cheerful voice.

Unable to answer with her mouth full of tongue, Natalie stared at him wide-eyed around Valerian's head, and then was suddenly pulled upright as Valerian leapt off her and the couch, taking her with him to stand on shaky legs in front of the man in whose lap they'd just been reclining on.

"Tybo," Valerian began grimly, only to fall silent as the man—his partner, if she was remembering correctly, which in her state wasn't a given—held out a cell phone.

"Lucian wanted to talk to you," he announced, waving the phone a bit. "I did cough and try to make my presence known," he added. "But you were both a bit distracted, so I sat down to wait. I knew it wouldn't be long. Life mates are reputed to be ridiculously quick about these things."

Scowling, Valerian snatched the phone out of his hand, and then hesitated and turned to Natalie. "I'm sorry. I have to take this."

"Of course," Natalie whispered. She then licked her lips as the attempt to speak made her aware of how dry her lips now were. She only realized what she'd done when she noticed the way Valerian froze, his eyes seeming to glow a silver green. Why had she never noticed the strange color of his eyes? she wondered. They were stunning. But the answer was simple enough: every time she'd looked at his face, her gaze had got caught on his lips. So, she'd avoided actually looking at him as much as possible. She was looking now, though, and those eyes of his were something else. If she didn't know better, she'd say the silver was increasing and the green fading beneath it as his face drew nearer.

Oh, he was going to kiss her again. That would be lovely, Natalie thought, and then jumped as Tybo cleared his throat loudly and said on a laugh, "Phone, Valerian. Lucian."

"Right." Valerian straightened at once, managed a crooked smile for Natalie, and then turned to hurry out of the room, putting the phone to his ear as he went.

"So," Tybo said, drawing her gaze back to him. "You and Valerian, huh?"

"Uh." Natalie felt her face heat up with embarrassment and didn't have a clue what to say. They weren't exactly a couple. He'd just kissed her. Well, okay, just kissed her was a bit of a milquetoast description for what she'd just experienced. Still . . .

Still what? she wondered. What was going on here? Was she now interested in a relationship with the man? Now that she knew he might be around her age or even a couple of years older? Now that she knew his kisses blew her mind? Now that she wanted to know if sex with him would be just as mind-blowing?

Was that last one even a question she needed to ask herself? Natalie thought with an inner sigh. 'Cause she was pretty sure the guy could rock her world in the bedroom . . . or the office, or the kitchen, or the dining room, on the golf course, in the equipment barn. Dear God, there were any number of places they could—

A chuckle from Tybo brought her meandering horn-dog thoughts to a halt and she glanced at him in question.

"Oh." Tybo waved a hand and shook his head. "I was just . . . er . . . remembering . . . something."

Natalie eyed him for a minute, and then dropped onto the opposite end of the couch from Tybo and smiled. "So . . . tell me about Valerian. Does he have a girlfriend or wife?" she asked, and then continued to smile sweetly as she added, "And bear in mind that I'll cut you up and serve you as stew in my restaurant if you lie to me."

"It's Lucian."

Valerian rolled his eyes at that response to his hello as he walked up the hall toward the dining room. "Yes. Tybo said."

"Hmm," Lucian grunted. "I heard him say it but wasn't sure you really comprehended at the time since I suspect your brain was lacking its blood supply."

"Why would my brain be lacking its blood supply?" Valerian asked with confusion.

"From all the moaning and heavy breathing I heard when Tybo carried the phone to you, I'm guessing you probably still have an erection," was his answer.

Valerian scowled at the accusation, and said through gritted teeth, "What the hell has that got to do with anything?"

"Well, where do you think the blood comes from?"

"What?" he asked with disbelief. "I don't know. What—?"

"My Leigh and the other ladies speculate it comes from the brain, and that's why we men are so prone to follow our dicks. Due to blood loss, we don't have the brain power not to."

"Jesus Chr—" Valerian began before Lucian cut him off.

"And considering the number of new life mates I've had on the payroll the last decade or so, and how useless and stupid they tend to be after meeting their life mates, I'm thinking she might be right."

Valerian gave a disbelieving laugh, and pointed out, "You were one of those new life mates not that long ago."

"Yes, I was," Lucian agreed easily. "But I took in extra blood at the time, which probably worked to counteract the effects of the BTDD."

"What is the BTDD?" Valerian asked with uncertainty.

"The Brain-to-Dick-Drain."

"Brain-to-Dick-Drain?" he bellowed with disbelief, and then realized he'd walked into the dining room during this conversation and was now standing in the center of it, shouting. The dozen or so diners presently spread out at five tables were all staring at him wide-eyed.

Cursing, he turned and headed back into the hall, hissing, "Look, Lucian, I presume you didn't really call to discuss the present level of the blood in my brain?"

"No," he agreed mildly.

"Well, why the hell did you call, then?" he asked with irritation, pausing outside of the kitchen.

"To warn you that Aileen is on her way there."

"Too late. She's here," Valerian growled, pushing his way through the swinging door and into the kitchen where his sister and Mia were presently sitting at the small table in the corner, giggling over bowls of ice cream while everyone else rushed around either cooking or putting away the last of the delivered food.

"Hmm. Well, I meant to call right after she left, but Leigh distracted me."

"The Brain-to-Dick-Drain?" Valerian suggested dryly.

Ignoring that, Lucian said, "I'll leave you with one thought."

"What's that?" Valerian growled with irritation.

"There's a madman out there trying to kill your life mate. Do you really think being in a naked, unconscious—and therefore vulnerable—heap is a good idea at a time like this?" Lucian ended the call by simply hanging up. But his point had been made.

Valerian slid the phone into his back pocket, and slowly scrubbed his face with his hands. He had a problem. Because Lucian was right. Being unconscious and vulnerable while there was a madman after Natalie was possibly the stupidest thing he could do at this time. And that wasn't even considering Mia, who he'd already decided was reason enough not to take things too far with Natalie, but to woo her the old-fashioned way.

Eventually, of course, they'd get to move on to the freaking awesome passion they'd enjoyed a taste of in the office just minutes ago. But only after ensuring Mia was somewhere safe with someone who could take care of her. And now he had to consider ensuring it was somewhere safe for Natalie too, where the Angel-Maker couldn't creep up on them. While he'd like to think having so many men guarding the golf course and clubhouse should make it safe, he knew better. One or more of the men could be knocked out or killed, leaving a hole in their protection for the Angel-Maker to slip through and creep up on them. He didn't intend to be unconscious and unable to protect his life mate if that happened.

Which is why he had a problem. Because Valerian really wanted Natalie. Now that he'd tasted the tip of what they could enjoy, it was going to be hell trying to behave himself. Just thinking about it had revved his boner back up to where it had been while kissing Natalie, and that was after shrinking quickly as Lucian had talked about his damned BTDD theory.

Valerian shook his head at the memory. Lucian Argeneau had always been the coldest, meanest hard-ass he'd ever met before Leigh. But now, every once in a while, the man—

"Surprises you?" Aileen suggested.

Valerian turned sharply to find his sister at his side.

"I like his BTDD theory," she told him. "But I'm thinkin' it's no' just a problem with immortals. For sure as shit I've met a ton o' mortal men with the same problem."

Valerian winced at her words. "I'd really rather no' hear about your ton o' men with BTDD."

Aileen's eyes sparkled with amusement. "Your accent's creeping back, brother. That only happens when you're upset."

Valerian merely scowled at her. He had worked hard at shedding his Scottish accent while traveling the world when young. Mostly because accents tended to draw attention, and attention was the last thing an immortal wanted. But it did creep back on occasion. Usually when upset as Aileen had just said.

"I could watch Mia so you and Natalie could—"

"No, thank you," Valerian interrupted before she could finish. "I can't take the risk while she's under threat."

Aileen shrugged and turned to walk to the table where Mia was waiting.

Valerian watched his sister and Mia chatter and eat their ice cream for a minute, and then headed back out of the kitchen with a sigh. If he were a smart man, he'd probably avoid Natalie, and have Tybo guard her until this Angel-Maker business was resolved. But he'd never claimed to be smart, and simply didn't want to. He was playing with fire, and knew it, but assured himself he could resist her. He just had to not touch her again. As long as they didn't touch, he was sure he could behave. Probably.

"Damn, I'm an idiot," he muttered to himself.

Fifteen

"Okay, so Mark and Gill are taking Aileen to Stephanie and Thorne's place," Tybo announced as he came back into the room. "She'll be safe there."

Valerian glanced up from the game pieces he'd been putting away, his eyebrows rising slightly at the names of two Enforcers who usually stuck to Toronto. "Mark and Gill are here?"

"They were," Tybo answered. "Their shift is done, though. Anders and Nicholas took their place and are patrolling now. That's why Mark and Gill were available to give Aileen a ride. They're heading to your place after to catch some sleep."

"I'll have to thank them." Valerian closed the game box and shifted his attention to putting away the cards Natalie had gathered and stacked.

"Where are Nat, the furball, and the little niblet?" Tybo asked, glancing around the room as if the trio might be hiding somewhere, an impossibility for Sinbad, Valerian was sure. The dog was massive.

"Natalie was yawning up a storm so I suggested she put Mia to bed and get some rest as well," he explained.

"And Sinbad followed?" Tybo asked with surprise.

Valerian raised an eyebrow at the question. "Yes. He never leaves Mia's side, or hadn't you noticed?"

"I noticed," Tybo assured him with a faint smile. "He's a good dog."

"Yeah," Valerian agreed. Sinbad was too fluffy to look threatening, but the animal was huge, and he suspected under all that cute fluffiness one would find the heart of a lion if Mia or Natalie were under threat.

"It was a good night," Tybo said, and Valerian smiled faintly and nodded.

After returning with Mia and Sinbad from their ice cream run, Aileen had asked for a tour of the golf course. Natalie had seemed surprised at the request until Valerian had reminded her that his family had several courses of their own. She'd then led them out to the equipment barn to get her electric golf cart, and driven them around the grounds. Aileen had insisted on Valerian taking the front passenger seat, while she'd claimed the backward-facing seats behind for her and Mia. Sinbad had thought it was a grand game and had chased after the cart, having no trouble keeping up with the slow-moving vehicle as Natalie had taken them around.

Afterward, Aileen had announced that she wanted to play the course, but not until sunset. When Natalie had raised her eyebrows and glanced at him, he'd told her their skin was ultrasensitive to sunlight and they tried to avoid it. Which was true, though not in the way she no doubt thought. Still, he was glad not to have to lie to her. He was also glad he'd given Natalie that explanation when understanding had crossed her face, and she'd commented that now she knew why he always golfed so late.

By the time they'd returned to the clubhouse, it was about an hour before dinnertime. Despite still not being fully recovered, Natalie had insisted on cooking for them rather than burden Alex with the chore. So, they'd headed to the kitchen and Aileen had sat at the table entertaining Mia, while Valerian had helped Natalie prepare their meal. Something called kefta with a kale salad, hummus, and naan bread.

Valerian had never had anything like it back when he used to eat, but it had been good. Although he'd had some concern when one of the tasks she'd set him to was massaging the kale with lemon and olive oil. He'd thought she was kidding at first, but she wasn't, and he'd wondered if the poison had affected her mind somehow. Who the hell massaged vegetables? But it had turned out and been tasty, so he supposed it was a thing.

They'd eaten in the office at the coffee table, the four of them sitting on the floor around it, with Mia settled on a couple of couch cushions to boost her to the height needed for her to eat there. They'd just been finishing when Tybo had entered. He'd been off catching some sleep in the RV so that he could help out tonight. The moment he'd mentioned he still had a few hours before he was supposed to get back to work, Aileen had insisted on playing board games and had roped him into joining them.

When Tybo had pointed out it probably wouldn't be very comfortable sitting on the floor for that long, Natalie had straightened with surprise and announced she had a folding poker table, and chairs. Muttering about why she hadn't thought of that before so they could have eaten at it, she'd led him and Tybo downstairs to find and fetch back the table and four folding chairs.

While he, Tybo, and Aileen had set up the table and chairs and searched through the games on the bookshelf, Natalie had put an animated movie on TV for Mia. The little girl hadn't lasted all the way through the movie before falling asleep curled up on the couch with Sinbad. But the adults had played games for hours, starting with Trivial Pursuit and running through two or three others, before ending with Cards Against Humanity. They'd played the last game the longest and Valerian didn't think he'd ever laughed so hard in his life.

He smiled at the memory. It *had* been a very good night. He didn't think he'd had that much fun in decades. Actually, probably not since the early nineteenth century when he'd been young and full of fun and mischief.

"Did I mention your Natalie is bloodthirsty?" Tybo said suddenly.

"What?" Valerian asked with a disbelieving laugh. Natalie was the least bloodthirsty woman he knew.

"Yeah. She asked if you were married or had a girl-friend and threatened to make a stew out of me if I lied," Tybo told him.

Valerian grinned at this news. "What did you say?"

"I said you had a gal in every port, and about ten wives back in some Arabic country I couldn't remember the name of," Tybo said with a shrug.

That made Valerian snort. "She didn't believe you," he said with certainty.

"No, she didn't," Tybo admitted. "But she did mention that since I'm such a bad liar she might only make sausage out of my sausage instead of the stew thing. She was pretty sure my meat was too tough even for stew anyway." He shook his head, his grin widening. "I like her."

"So do I," Valerian said softly.

"Yeah." Tybo didn't hide his envy as he added, "Lucky bastard."

Valerian merely nodded in agreement. He wouldn't offer the usual consoling crap that Tybo would meet his own life mate someday soon. He'd heard it often enough himself to know it wouldn't help.

"Should we fold up the table and chairs and put them away, or do you want to keep them out for meals?" Tybo asked as Valerian stood to put the games back on the bookshelf with the others stacked there. Natalie had inherited the games. They'd apparently been in her parents' house and she'd brought them here to the clubhouse when she'd sold their home. She'd never played any of them before tonight. Actually, Aileen and Tybo had been the only ones who had any experience with the games, but they'd explained the rules to them.

"No," he decided. "It'll give us somewhere to eat breakfast in the morning if Aileen returns."

"If?" Tybo asked with amusement. "She'll be here. The minute she called the house, got Lucian, and he spilled the beans about your meeting your life mate, it was guaranteed she'd leave school, head here, and stay until you succeed at claiming her."

"Why?" Valerian asked with surprise.

"Because she's afraid that you'll muck it up on your own," Tybo told him with amusement.

Valerian scowled at this news. "Well, she can't stay. She has classes."

"Uh-huh," Tybo said with dry amusement. "I don't think she cares. When it comes to her favorite brother's happiness or her classes, I guarantee she'll pick you every time."

Valerian didn't argue the point, mostly because he knew Tybo was right. Letting the subject go, he asked, "What time is Jo expected? She did go to get some rest this evening too so she'd be on the alert tonight, didn't she?"

"She did," Tybo assured him. "But she isn't coming."

"What?" Valerian asked with alarm. "Why not? She's supposed to stick to Natalie at night in case something happens."

"She was," Tybo agreed. "But Lucian reassigned her to guard Jan."

"Natalie's second in the kitchen?" Valerian asked with a frown.

"And her friend," Tybo told him, knowing he couldn't read Natalie and so might not know that the two women were close. "With two employees taken out by car accidents, Lucian thought—"

"I know," Valerian interrupted, not needing the explanation. He was the one who had taken the concern about the car accidents to Lucian. "What I didn't realize was that Lucian would do something as foolish as pulling Jo off Natalie and putting her on Jan instead."

"He didn't have a choice," Tybo said, his shoulders rising and lowering in a helpless shrug. "Mortimer only has so many Enforcers to work with. Besides, Lucian figured Natalie should be safe enough with you here inside the house, Colle and Alasdair patrolling the outside, and me watching from the RV."

"I thought Colle and Alasdair were going to watch from the RV?"

"Lucian actually wanted feet on the ground for this and two guys staring at the security screen was a waste of manpower, so he changed it to two patrolling around the house, constantly checking doors and windows, and one watching the security screen in the RV. We're going to switch out after a couple of hours. Colle and I'll change places and then Alasdair and Colle will change places so we all get a chance to sit down inside and have something to eat while watching the screen."

"Right," Valerian breathed. He'd rather have also had Jo inside with him. She could have slept while he patrolled inside half the night, and then he would have slept while Jo took his place on patrol. Now, he supposed he'd have to stay awake all night, just in case someone slipped past the boys outside.

"You don't need to stay awake," Tybo argued, not even making an attempt to hide the fact that he could hear his every thought. "We've got you, buddy. Nobody will get by us."

"Yes, but—"

"Besides," Tybo interrupted his protest. "How can you enjoy shared dreams if you stay awake all night?"

Valerian stiffened, his gaze turning sharply on the other man. "Shared dreams."

It wasn't a question, but more a realization. He'd forgotten all about shared dreams, another symptom of life mates. They shared their dreams. Usually they were sexual in nature from what he understood, and while not as overwhelmingly passionate as real sex with a life mate, they were supposed to be pretty hot. It was also another way to bond with a life mate, a safer way that wouldn't leave them in unconscious heaps. They would just be sleeping. That last thought made him frown, though. While he was a light sleeper and likely to wake up at the slightest sound, what if—

"Nothing's going to happen, Val," Tybo said patiently. "Man, we've worked together for decades. Surely you trust me enough to have your back by now?"

Tybo was younger than him, and was something of a jokester, but when it came to the job, he was good, and very serious under the lighter exterior he showed everyone. Valerian trusted Tybo to have his back.

"There you go." Tybo slapped his shoulder with a

grin. "So, go lie down on the couch and get dreaming. Natalie's waiting for you."

Valerian turned toward the couch, his excitement mounting as he grabbed up the pillow and blanket Natalie had left for him.

"Comfy?" Tybo asked once he'd punched his pillow a bit, and was lying down with the blanket pulled over him.

"Yes. Good night," Valerian said.

He'd already started to close his eyes in anticipation of the coming dreams when Tybo said, "Good, good. Except you need to get up and lock the door behind me."

Valerian's eyes popped open at once and he scowled at Tybo, knowing he'd deliberately let him get comfortable before pointing that out. Muttering, "Bastard," he tossed the blanket off himself and stood to follow him from the room.

Sixteen

"Is that your son with Mia?"

Natalie looked up with a start and had to shield her eyes from the sun with her hand to be able to see the face of the man looming over her.

"Valerian," she breathed with surprise, and then scrambled quickly to her feet and brushed off the sand clinging to her behind as she glanced back to Cody and Mia. They were at the shore's edge, giggling away as they scrambled backward on the hard-packed sand to avoid the approaching surf. Smiling with pride, she nodded. "Yes. That's my Cody and Mia."

"He was a handsome boy," Valerian said solemnly.

Natalie's smile faded at the use of "was." It reminded her that Cody was dead, and that this was a dream, one she often had in some variation or other. The three of them at the beach, the three of them playing in fall leaves, the three of them building a snowman . . .

"My therapist thinks these dreams are my way of dealing with my guilt for being a bad mother to Cody. In my dreams, I get to do all the things with him I didn't have time for in life," she told him suddenly.

"And what do you think?" Valerian asked.

"I think I miss him, and regret that I didn't spend more time with him while I could, that I spent most of his short life working and missed out on . . . so much," Natalie finished sadly, and then grimaced and pointed out, "Which is a lot more selfish than just guilt, isn't it?"

Valerian shook his head solemnly. "You're too hard on yourself. We all have regrets. Things we do or don't do, expecting to have the time later to get to it or fix it. Unfortunately, life doesn't come with a summary of events to come, and sometimes we just don't get the time we need."

"Yeah," Natalie murmured, and then deciding her dream was getting too heavy, she forced a smile and said, "So, like I said, my therapist thinks the kids are a manifestation of my guilt in dreams." She waggled her eyebrows at him. "I wonder what she'll make of your being in them."

"I suppose it depends on what you tell her about me," he said with a faint smile.

"Oh dear," she said, widening her eyes with feigned dismay.

"Oh dear?" he asked, uncertainly. "Why 'oh dear'?"

"Because I don't think she's ready for this," Natalie said with amusement. "I mean, it's been three years of dealing with boring crap like betrayal, and bigamy and whatnot."

"Boring crap, huh?" he asked with amused disbelief.

"Oh, trust me, I'm sure she gets that eight hours a day. People don't usually go for counseling to whine that after three years without sex they've met this incredibly handsome hottie they find ridiculously attractive, and who appears to like them at least a little. Enough to kiss anyway."

"Hottie?" he asked, beaming now.

"Oh please, like you didn't know that," she said with amusement. "I'm sure tons of women have told you you're gorgeous."

Valerian shrugged. "What other women think doesn't matter. What you think does."

Natalie nearly melted into a puddle there on the beach. He knew exactly what to say. But then, he wasn't really Valerian, just a part of her mind that she was trying to work something out with.

"I think I need more counseling," she muttered.

"Why is that?" Valerian asked with concern.

"Because I'm obviously very attracted to you, and I don't think it's a good thing."

Valerian stiffened slightly, the concern on his face deepening. "Because?"

Shifting impatiently, Natalie turned to walk toward the shore, noting absently that the children were gone. She and Valerian were alone on the beach now. But since it was a dream, it wasn't something to worry about, she supposed as she stopped at the water's edge and let the surf roll over her toes.

"Why is being attracted to me not a good thing?" Valerian persisted, following her.

"Because I have things I want to do—a business to run, a daughter to raise—and I don't want to get my heart broken." She listed the issues troubling her without hesitation. Dreams were to work things out, after all, so she may as well work on it.

Valerian was silent for a minute, and then asked, "What if I could guarantee you wouldn't get your heart broken?"

"No one can guarantee that," she said with amusement.

"I could," he assured her. "And I'd be happy to help you raise your daughter. I'd never get between the two of you."

What every mother wanted to hear, Natalie thought on a sigh. It was just too damned bad this was a dream.

"What are the things you want to do?" Valerian asked when she didn't respond.

"I want to make Shady Pines into something special, someplace people talk about and want to come to," she disclosed. "And I know I can do it, but it'll take work, and time and effort, and getting involved with you . . . It would be so easy to fall in love with you," she acknowledged. "And that might derail all my plans, then I'd always wonder . . ."

Natalie paused and frowned, but then admitted, "I think that must be what I need to work out and that you're here in my dream so that I can."

"Natalie," he began quietly.

"Look," she interrupted. "From what I've seen, you seem like a good guy. You have a very responsible job. You're protective, caring, concerned, an amazing brother, and dear God, the way you were with Mia already has me falling a little bit in love with you." Meeting his gaze she added solemnly, "You'd make a good father and I want that for Mia, but . . ."

"But?" he prompted.

"Can you really be as wonderful as you seem? I mean, I thought Devin was and look how that turned out." She shook her head. "I don't think I have it in me to go through something like that again. After the accident and everything came out . . ." She grimaced. "It made me doubt everything about myself: my intelligence, my ability to read people, my value as a person." Natalie peered at him solemnly. "It's taken three years of counseling to undo the damage. I'm just starting to feel whole and trust myself again. I don't know that I really want to risk getting hurt like that again."

"I would never betray you like that," Valerian vowed solemnly.

"Okay. So, what if you don't break my heart?" she asked at once. "What if we got together and everything is as amazing as that kiss we shared? There's no way a healthy relationship could survive with my hours. I'd probably have to make compromises, and the next thing you know I'd be doing what women often do and start making sacrifices for you, for our relationship. I'd be giving up my dreams and ambitions because they took too much time and energy and I wouldn't want you to feel neglected and possibly drive you away."

She closed her eyes briefly. "I never would have done that for Devin, but I'm not sure I wouldn't for you." She opened her eyes again. "All you did was kiss me, Valerian, but the chemistry was off the charts. I didn't want you to stop, and if Tybo hadn't been there I don't think we would have. So, what if we started to date? What if we became lovers? If we have that much chemistry in bed, I can easily see myself becoming addicted to it. To you. I'm not sure I'd ever want to get out of bed. I'd be like some pathetic heroin addict giving up everything to chase the dragon." She shook her head. "That can't be healthy."

"Natalie, I know it's a lot and scary because of that but—What's wrong?" he interrupted himself to ask when she suddenly looked to the side.

Natalie faced him again, a small frown plucking at her brows. "I thought I heard—" She paused and turned again, and this time found herself nose to snout with Sinbad, his white fur gleaming in the blue glow cast by the night-light next to her bed as he whimpered miserably.

Natalie suddenly wasn't there. Her abrupt disappearance from the shared dream was jarring enough to wake Valerian up. He opened his eyes to the dark office, wondering what had woken her, because that was the only explanation for the dream ending so abruptly.

She'd said she'd heard something, he recalled, and listened for any sounds that might clue him in to what had stirred her from sleep, but he didn't hear anything. Valerian was starting to worry that maybe someone had got into the house and slipped past him and down to the basement when he heard a door squeak open and the click of a dog's nails on the concrete floor downstairs and then start up the stairs. When he heard Natalie's soft voice murmuring something, he sat up and slid out from under the blanket.

Valerian reached the office door just in time to see the basement door open and Sinbad come trotting out, followed by a disheveled and sleepy-looking Natalie.

"Problem?" he asked as she closed the door.

Natalie turned with surprise, relaxing a little when she saw him.

"No." She smiled weakly and started up the hall. "I was just so tired I forgot to let Sinbad out before we went to bed. His whining woke me up. He needs a potty break."

"I'll take him," Valerian offered at once.

Natalie opened her mouth in what he was sure was going to be a protest, but then seemed to notice that she was in a thin cotton nightgown and stopped. "Oh. Right. The guys are out there, aren't they? Thank you," she added as he nodded. "I appreciate it."

Valerian smiled and then turned to follow Sinbad, who was already disappearing into the dining room. Judging by the dog's speed, he really had to go, Valerian decided as he caught up to the dog as he started to paw at the exit door by the reception counter.

"Here you go, buddy." Valerian opened the door and followed the dog out when he bounded across the deck for the steps.

"Dog duty?"

Valerian leaned over the patio railing at that amused

voice to see Colle coming along the side of the house on his patrol.

"Yes. We forgot to let him out before bed," Valerian said as he followed Sinbad down to the sidewalk and around onto the side yard. Pausing next to Colle, he peered up at the moonlit sky and then around the yard. "Nothing happening?"

Colle hesitated and then admitted, "Decker thought he heard someone in the woods out by him, but said it could have been the wind and he didn't see anything when he checked, and Bricker had the same, but speculated it could have been a coyote or just a branch moving in the breeze."

Valerian raised his eyebrows, and pointed out, "There's no breeze."

"Yeah. It's got everyone on edge, but might be nothing," Colle said.

Valerian didn't comment, but he did take a closer look at the surrounding area visible to him, which was mostly the yard, the equipment barn, and part of the golf cart building. The clubhouse was pretty cut off from the golf course itself by the woods all around it.

A wet nose nudging his hand brought Valerian back to the situation at hand, and he gave Sinbad a stroke as he asked, "All done already?"

The dog turned and walked back to the steps to the deck for answer.

"I'm thinking that's a yes," Colle said with amusement.

"Yes," Valerian agreed, turning to follow the dog's path. "Good night."

"Night," Colle responded, and continued on his patrol as Valerian crossed the deck and let Sinbad into the clubhouse. Valerian followed the furry beast in and stopped to lock up. He was a little surprised when he turned to find Sinbad had sat down to wait for him.

"Good boy," he muttered as the dog stood to cross the smaller dining room and led the way down into the larger one. Natalie was waiting in the hall by the basement door. She must have hurried back to her room while they were outside, because she now had a thin, short-sleeved light-blue summer robe on over her nightgown. Unfortunately, it didn't do the job he suspected she'd intended. The cloth was some sort of soft-looking, clingy material that hugged her figure and gaped at the top, leaving her white skin on display where the plunging V-neck of the pale blue nightgown didn't cover it.

Smiling when she saw them enter the hall, she murmured, "Thanks. I forgot about the guys patrolling or I would have thought to throw on some clothes before bringing him up."

"No problem," Valerian assured her as he and Sinbad approached. "He's a good dog."

"Yeah." She grinned down at Sinbad and ruffled the fur on his head when he stopped and sat in front of her. "He's a good boy. Aren't you?" she asked, and grinned when Sinbad leaned his head into her stomach.

Chuckling, she caressed the side of his head and then glanced up and went still, her smile slowly fading.

"Your eyes . . ." she murmured, and Valerian stiffened, knowing that they were no doubt turning silver as he watched her.

Natalie wasn't wearing anything deliberately slinky or sexy, but still managed to look incredibly alluring anyway. But then after their kiss, just being near her was enough to have his body humming with the desire to touch and kiss her. However, her words from the dream held him back.

Their shared dream hadn't turned out at all as he'd expected. Instead of dream sex, Natalie had revealed her worries and fears to him, and Valerian knew he had a lot of work ahead of him. He needed to gain her trust, and help her learn to trust herself. He also needed to ensure their relationship didn't interfere with her plans for the expansion of the clubhouse. Alex was right about that. She obviously needed that success. He suspected it would go a long way toward returning the self-confidence she'd lost when her dead husband's perfidy had come out.

"It must be the light," Natalie muttered now, sounding a little confused. Giving her head a small shake, she turned to open the door to the basement.

"Thanks again," she said as Sinbad headed down the stairs. Natalie started to follow, but stopped abruptly when the door handle, which was a lever rather than a knob, caught on the pocket of her robe in passing and held her up.

"I got you," Valerian said when she was forced to a halt and glanced around with confusion to see that she was caught on the door handle.

"Oh," Natalie murmured, and backed up a step to make it easier to unhook her. Valerian wasn't expecting it, and had started forward at the same time. They both froze and sucked in a quick breath as their bodies collided, her back pressing against his front. For one moment, they stood there like that, and then Valerian unthinkingly reached out to touch her arm to steady her as he took a step back. That was all it took. His hand on the bare flesh of her arm . . . again.

Valerian moaned deep in his throat and was quite sure Natalie did as well, and then she just leaned into him and he gave up the fight. Both hands now slid up and down her arms, and then clasped her waist to pull her back more firmly against him before drifting around her waist to hold there as he nosed her dark hair out of the way and nuzzled her neck.

Natalie gasped at the caress, her head lolling to the side to give him more access. When she then turned her head, her lips seeking his, Valerian gave her the kiss she wanted. There was no tentative stroking of lips, no slow buildup. His mouth covered hers with demand, his tongue thrusting out to slide between her already parting lips, and he explored her depths with a hunger and need centuries in the making. This was his life mate, the woman he'd been waiting for since his birth in 1790, or at least since he'd been told about life mates twelve or thirteen years later. He'd imagined her, dreamed of her, fantasized about her . . . But those shadowy images he'd had in his mind could in no way compare to the reality of a living breathing Natalie in his arms, her scent enveloping him, and the taste of her filling his mouth. She was so goddamned perfect, he thought as his hand slid up from her waist to find her breasts through the cloth of her nightgown and robe.

Natalie gasped into his mouth, her body arching to press into the caress as he felt excitement and pleasure shoot through him. It was her pleasure and excitement he was experiencing, alongside his own as he touched and kissed her, Valerian knew. He also knew he must have experienced this the first time he'd kissed her in the office, but it had all been so strong and new it had just been one overwhelming wave of pleasure crashing over him and he hadn't stopped to analyze what he was feeling. Now, he caressed one breast, and kneaded the other through her clothes, groaning with her as another wave of pleasure and excitement crashed through him on the echo of the first. Enthralled, he tweaked one nipple with the fingers of one hand, and let the other slide away and down across her stomach to glide between her legs, pushing the cloth of her robe and nightgown before it.

Natalie tore her mouth from his with a gasped, "Oh God," and began to twist her head against his shoulder as he caressed her, her hips bucking and pressing back against the erection that had sprung up the moment he'd touched her arm and only hardened and lengthened as this progressed.

Without her mouth to occupy his, he began to nibble and suck at her neck instead as he ground himself against her body and continued to touch her. But when Valerian felt his fangs begin to move in his jaw and slide down, he tore his mouth from her neck and froze briefly as he tried to force them back.

"Valerian," Natalie moaned in protest, writhing in his hold with frustration.

"What, love?" he panted, still struggling to get his fangs back in place. "What do you want?"

"You," she answered at once, and groaned when the fingers at her breast plucked at her nipple.

"What do you want?" he repeated, kneading her breast now and keeping his other hand still in an effort to try to maintain some control of himself. He wanted her, all of her. He wanted to sink his cock and his fangs into her at the same time and—

"Fuck me," she growled with frustration, grinding her bottom back hard against his erection.

For one second, Valerian froze, but it was only one second, and then he turned them both and pressed her front against the hall wall. Pinning her there with his body, he released her breast to unsnap and unzip his jeans with that hand while the one between her legs began to burrow through the cloth of the robe and nightgown to get to her naked flesh.

"Oh God, oh yes," she gasped when his fingers finally slid across slick skin. Waves of combined pleasure were now pounding over him on top of each other and their echoes, hammering at his mind, driving him on even as they were doing to her.

Hips bucking now, she cried, "Oh please. Valerian. Please, please, please, f—ah!" she cried out as he finally freed himself and thrust into her. He had to stop caressing her, catch her by the waist, and lift her slightly to do it, but then he surged into her in one stroke, her wet heat taking and sucking him in in welcome.

He'd been told that life mate sex was fast and furious, but being told didn't really prepare him for it ending as soon as he managed to get into her. But that's what happened. He thrust, she cried out, her body clenched around him, pleasure exploded between them, and they both began to shake and cry out with orgasm just as darkness crept over his vision, pushing awareness out ahead of it.

Seventeen

Natalie woke up and stretched with a sleepy smile. Damn, she felt like a million bucks in that moment, well-rested and . . . *content* was the word that came to mind. Like all was right with the world. At least her world. Sighing, she curled onto her side to peer toward her daughter's bed, and then stiffened when she saw that it was empty. Mia wasn't there.

Sitting up abruptly, she peered to the dog bed to see that Sinbad was missing too. Natalie quickly tossed aside her sheets and blankets to get up, only to pause when she saw the sticky note on her bedside lamp. Tugging it free , she read the message.

Good morning, sleepyhead,
I've got Sinbad and your Mia with me. She was awake and babbling, making Sinbad bark, and we were afraid they'd wake you so Valerian sent

*me down to collect them for breakfast. I promise
to keep Mia happy and entertained and Sinbad
out of trouble. Am taking them out to the RV for
breakfast with my cousins so we aren't under-
foot in the kitchen. Join us when you wake up
and I'll have waffles waiting. Or possibly corn
flakes if I make a muck of the waffles. Unlike
yourself, I'm not much of a cook.*

Aileen

A small chuckle slipped from Natalie's lips at the ending of the note. Shaking her head, she set the note on the bedside table and got up. If Mia was with Aileen, Natalie had no concern. The girl had seemed to fall in love with her daughter on sight and had pampered and spoiled Mia something awful the day before.

Natalie's smile and relaxed state lasted until she walked into the bathroom and saw the hickey on her neck. Freezing, she stared at that dark spot as memories of last night poured into her mind. It wasn't that she'd forgotten what had happened. In fact, Natalie distinctly recalled waking up in the dark in the middle of the night and remembering everything very clearly. The problem was, she'd woken up—not on the hallway floor upstairs, or even on the couch in her office—but in her bed, and because of that had managed to convince herself that it had all been a dream. A really hot, sexy, passionate wet dream, which had been easy to do because the whole thing had been so overwhelming and fast that it was kind of a blur in her mind and— Had she really fainted?

Dear God, she really was in bad shape if two minutes of passion had knocked her out, Natalie thought with dismay. It wasn't like it had been some hours-long, sweaty passion-fest. It had only lasted maybe two or three minutes.

The old joke about even an egg taking three minutes ran through her mind and Natalie grimaced, because she couldn't even blame Valerian for the shortness of it. He'd barely given her a kiss and a squeeze before she'd been ordering him to get to it . . . and then she'd passed out on him. Literally. His penis inside of her, and his body pinning her to the wall, had been the only things holding her up. Her feet hadn't even been touching the floor.

What had happened after she passed out? Natalie wondered about that with a frown. Obviously, he'd carried her downstairs and put her to bed, but before that? What had happened between her passing out and his putting her to bed? Had he realized she'd fainted and stopped? If so, then the poor bastard probably hadn't even found his own release. Dear Lord, she sucked as a lover.

Groaning, Natalie turned away from the mirror and stepped up to the shower to turn it on, but her thoughts followed her. She used to consider herself a good lover, but it had been three years since Devin had died and she hadn't been with anyone since him. Maybe she needed practice.

Natalie rolled her eyes at that thought, because she was pretty sure it was coming from parts of her body that were a little biased. Despite passing out at the end, it had been one hell of a ride. Now, though, she had to face the man after literally fainting on his dick like a Victorian miss. How humiliating was that?

For one moment, Natalie considered turning off the shower, climbing back into bed, claiming she still felt poorly, and avoiding him and everyone else until they caught the Angel-Maker . . . or until the Angel-Maker did her the supreme favor of killing her. But that was just the height of cowardice. She wasn't a Victorian miss, and Valerian wasn't the first man she'd had sex with. She had nothing to be ashamed of, Natalie assured herself as she checked the water to find it had warmed up. She continued the argument with herself as she started to step into the shower, telling herself that these things happened and she—Oh God, they hadn't used protection!

Natalie stopped with one foot in the shower as alarm shot through her.

Moaning, she turned her head and banged it lightly against the glass shower door several times, then paused with her forehead against the cool glass and tried to calm herself. She was freaking out over things that might not be an issue. Yes, she should have used protection. But hopefully Valerian didn't have any STDs. She'd have to ask him. As for getting pregnant . . . While Natalie did want more children, she'd prefer if it was while in a loving relationship, and not from a quicky in the hall with a man she'd only known for a couple of days.

With the happy, content mood she'd woken up with now completely blown to hell, Natalie let her breath out on a sigh and finished stepping into the shower.

It was Monday, if she had her days right. And Mondays were usually slow at Shady Pines, which was why she gave her employees both Mondays and Tuesdays off while she handled everything.

But she wouldn't be alone this week. Her business/home was presently overrun with Enforcers trying to catch a madman who had targeted her.

Which was fine, she assured herself. It wasn't like any of them knew what had happened between her and Valerian last night.

It took Natalie five minutes to shower, wash her hair, and shave her legs. Another two to pull on her clothes—underwear, bra, jeans, and a clean Shady Pines T-shirt. Two more to brush her hair and teeth and make her way upstairs, but a full six minutes to make herself open the door between the basement and the upper floor. Once she did, though, she felt like a complete idiot. The hallway was empty, as was her office when she walked past. All of her anxiety had been for nothing.

"So far," Natalie muttered to herself as she paused outside the kitchen door and girded herself to enter. Aileen's note had said she was taking Mia out to have her breakfast in the RV with her cousins. That meant Valerian was probably somewhere in the clubhouse, or out checking with the men patrolling her course. Natalie was hoping for the latter option; she really didn't feel prepared to face him yet. Mostly because she wasn't sure how she should act around him now. Should she just act like nothing had happened and she often slept around with stray men who wandered into her hall at night and caught her in her nightie? Or should she prostrate herself at his feet, thank him for the best orgasm of her life, and beg his forgiveness for passing out on his penis before he could have one too? What was the protocol in these situations?

"Idiot," she muttered to herself with irritation. Surely things hadn't changed that much in the eight years since she'd started dating Devin? There had been no talk of a relationship with Valerian, no date even. Obviously, she should just try to act casual and like he hadn't completely rocked her world when he'd screwed her up against the hall wall to the point of passing out. And like she wasn't now panicking because they hadn't used protection.

Natalie wasn't sure if that was the right move, but at least it was a plan, so she brushed her still damp hair back from her face, straightened her shoulders, and pushed through the swinging door into the kitchen.

"Oh hey, Natalie, you're up," Alex greeted her with a wide smile from where she was flipping an omelet at the range. "Valerian thought you might sleep late this morning. Guess he was wrong. How are you feeling?"

"I . . . er . . . good," Natalie said weakly, her eyes skittering around the kitchen. Not spotting Valerian anywhere in the large room, she relaxed a little and managed a real smile for the woman who had taken over cooking for her when she'd been poisoned.

"Are you hungry?" Alex asked.

"Oh, maybe. I thought—"

"Good, because I made those orange muffins of yours," Alex announced as she pulled the frying pan off the fire. She shifted the pan over to a cool burner, and then bustled across the room to the ovens to pull out a tray of muffins. "Jan said they were your favorite, so I asked her to find the recipe for me yesterday so I could make them for your breakfast today."

"Oh," Natalie said with surprise at the thoughtful gesture.

"Aileen took Mia out to the RV to have her cereal with the boys, so I'll just plate these and you can take them out with you."

"Lovely," Natalie sighed.

"I mixed up some of that vanilla butter Jan says you put on these muffins too. It's there in the bowl with the lid on the table." Alex nodded toward the table as she snatched a plate off the shelf and started to move muffins from the tin to the plate. "You might want to take that too. And a knife. And maybe a coffee," she suggested. "I'm not sure the boys have a coffee machine out there."

"Right." Natalie opened the silverware drawer to retrieve a knife, then grabbed a cup and carried it to the Keurig to make her coffee. As she waited for it to brew, she glanced to Alex and bit her lip briefly before saying, "I really appreciate your helping me like this. It was very kind."

"My pleasure," Alex assured her. "I've enjoyed your recipes a great deal. Speaking of which, I have a publisher interested in a recipe book."

"I heard," Natalie said with a genuine smile. "Congratulations. You must be pleased."

Alex grimaced. "Actually, I was, but it's turning out to be more of a pain in the ass than anything."

"Oh dear," Natalie said on a startled laugh, and then covered her mouth and shook her head. "Sorry. I'm not laughing at you. It's just the chef's groups are all atwitter about it, half of them dying of envy, and . . ."

"And yet I'm whining?" Alex suggested with a self-deprecating laugh. She then sighed. "Yeah. Like I said, it seemed a great thing at first. But now not so much."

"What's the problem exactly?" Natalie asked with curiosity, and then quickly added, "If you don't mind my asking?"

"I don't mind," Alex assured her. "And the problem is that they want at least one hundred and fifty recipes, but would prefer two or three hundred."

"Oh wow," Natalie said with surprise. That was a lot of recipes.

"Yeah," Alex said on a sigh. "I've been kind of struggling with it, but coming here actually gave me an idea."

"Oh? What's that?" Natalie pulled her cup from the Keurig as the machine finished spitting out the last of the coffee, and then moved to the refrigerator to retrieve her creamer.

"You have some amazing recipes," Alex said solemnly. "I mean, your Thai chicken wraps?" She stopped transferring muffins to a plate to give a chef's kiss, and then hurried over to the sink to wash her hands before continuing the transfer.

"Thank you." Natalie beamed at the praise.

"And that soy marinade for the steaks is amazing too," Alex added, and then gasped and exclaimed, "And oh my God, I tried a slice of your peach whiskey loaf when I made it and thought I'd died and gone to heaven."

Natalie was sure she was blushing now.

"I'd love to put those recipes in the book," Alex told her, and quickly added, "Credited to you and Shady Pines, of course, so people could find your restaurant."

When Natalie just stared at her wide-eyed, she said, "They're really good, Natalie, and it made me think that maybe I should consider including some of your original recipes to help get the number of recipes up to what they want."

"Oh wow," Natalie breathed. This was a big deal.

"The best part," Alex added with a grin, "is that the recipe book wouldn't be published for a good year and a half, and Valerian mentioned you were hoping to get the renos started in the spring. If so, they should definitely be done by the time the book comes out. It means if this book generates more customers driving down here to seek you out, you'd be prepared for it. I think it would be really good for business." She paused briefly, before asking, "Do you think you could get maybe fifty recipes together? That would be five breakfast recipes, five appetizers, five soups, stew, or chili recipes, five beef, pork, or lamb dishes, five poultry dishes, five pasta dishes, five fish or seafood recipes, five vegetarian or side recipes, five sauces, and five desserts?"

"Five?" Natalie grinned. "I could do ten in each category easy."

"That would be great," Alex said, sounding excited. "I could contribute ten each category too and we'd have two hundred, which should make the publisher happy. You'd have to be on the contract and the cover with me, though, if we're going halvsies. I'll call my agent and have her talk to the publisher to see what we can arrange. And here you are," she ended, setting the plate of muffins on a tray, followed by the knife Natalie had collected and the container of vanilla butter. "Set your coffee on there and off you go. Enjoy your breakfast."

Natalie set her cup on the tray, and accepted it from her, but then hesitated. She wanted to thank Alex for this opportunity and tell her how much she appreciated it, but the woman didn't give her the chance. Grasping her shoulders, Alex turned her toward the door and ushered her to it, then opened it for her.

"I'll let you know what my agent says after I talk to her. And grab at least two muffins the minute you set down the tray," Alex instructed as she urged her out of the kitchen. "The boys that still eat have huge appetites and you won't get any if you give them half a chance."

"That still eat?" Natalie asked, glancing around with confusion, but the kitchen door was already closed. Shaking her head, Natalie headed into the dining room, muttering, "Must have misheard her."

The dining room was pretty quiet this morning, with only two tables occupied. That was the norm, though, for a Monday morning. Natalie smiled and greeted her customers as she passed through. There was no one on the deck either this morning, but she saw two golfers heading out on a golf cart and wondered who had seen to that. One of the Enforcers, she supposed as she walked around the front of the clubhouse to reach the employee parking lot on the other side.

While Natalie did most of her work in the kitchen when it came to the restaurant, she had been known to work the tables on occasion when things got crazy busy. She was grateful for that practice when she reached the RV and had to balance the tray on one hand to free the other to open the door.

Natalie heard the clank of metal on glass through the RV's screen door as she reached for the door handle, and recognized it as the sound of a spoon on porcelain. Mia eating her cereal, she thought with a smile, but wondered why it was otherwise so quiet and Aileen and her cousins weren't chatting. Curious now, she opened the door, caught it with her hip, adjusted her hold on the tray to both hands again, and quickly walked up the steps with her tray.

Wanting to ensure the hot coffee didn't slosh out of the cup and onto the muffins, Natalie kept her gaze on the tray as she mounted the steps. It wasn't until she'd turned to start along the length of the RV that Natalie raised her head to look around. She then froze as her gaze landed on Colle standing directly ahead of her. It wasn't the water dripping from his damp hair, or the fact that he was wearing nothing but a towel around his waist, that caught her attention, but the bag of liquid hanging in front of his nose, mouth, and chin leaving only his wide, shocked eyes on view. The liquid in the bag was a deep dark crimson.

Blood, Natalie realized, and then shifted her gaze to the man at Colle's side when he made a choked sound. She recognized Tybo's horrified eyes over the bag of blood that seemed to hang suspended in front of his face too.

Confused, and more than a little alarmed, Natalie turned back the way she'd come and found herself staring at Alasdair, who stood just past the stairs, between the driver and passenger seats. Like Tybo, he was dressed, but he also had shocked eyes and a bag of blood at his mouth, though he had a hand supporting his.

"Nathalie, ith's othay."

She whirled at those words and this time noticed the people sitting in the booth. Mia and Valerian on one side, Aileen on the other. Honestly, Natalie wasn't sure how she'd missed them until now. She supposed the shock of seeing the other men—

Her thoughts died, her eyes widening with horror, as she took note of the fact that Aileen was holding a nearly empty bag of blood to her own mouth. Valerian had one too, but his was clasped in one clenched fist and squirting blood everywhere including on her little girl as he apparently squeezed the bag. That wasn't the worst of it, though. He also had bloody fangs presently on display, which she supposed explained his lisp when he'd spoken.

Cursing, Valerian closed his mouth for a moment
and then opened it again. The fangs were gone, but
there was still blood on his teeth and gums.

Natalie immediately dropped the tray of muffins
and lunged for Mia. Catching her under the arms, she
dragged her protesting daughter out of the booth and
turned to make a run for it. Natalie pulled up short,
though, when she found that while her back was
turned Alasdair had moved to the top of the stairs to
block her escape.

Eighteen

Clutching Mia protectively to her chest, Natalie took a step back and looked wildly around. Her only option was one of the side windows, but she wouldn't have time to open one. She'd have to jump through it. Could she do that without getting both herself and Mia killed? Maybe if she hunched herself over Mia and protected her with her own body, she could—

"Natalie. I need you to calm down," Valerian said, drawing her frightened gaze over her shoulder to look at him warily.

Much to her relief, he hadn't stood or moved closer to her. He was still sitting exactly where he'd been when she'd first seen him. In fact, no one other than Alasdair had moved. They all stood as still as statues, their gazes more concerned than alarmed, as if she were a wild horse who was kicking up a fuss and might harm herself if not handled carefully.

Swallowing, Natalie turned so that her back was to the sink counter next to the refrigerator, keeping all of them in view. But then she didn't know what to do. She had no idea what was going on.

"It's not what it looks like," Valerian said now.

"Oh good." She nodded a little hysterically. "Because it looks like I'm standing in a nest of vampires. But that's crazy, right? I mean, those fangs I saw protruding out of your mouth a minute ago weren't real, were they? Please tell me they weren't real," she begged.

Valerian hesitated, and then gave a resigned sigh and admitted, "I do have fangs, but—"

"Omigod!" Natalie closed her eyes with dismay. Opening them again, she muttered with disbelief, "I shtupped Dracula."

Valerian blinked, and then asked uncertainly, "Shtupped?"

"She banged you," Tybo clarified, and when Valerian just turned to stare at him, the dark-haired man added, "You know, a little of the old in-out."

"Thank you," Valerian said dryly. "I do know what banged means."

"Well, you didn't look like you did," Tybo said with a shrug.

"You really didn't," Colle agreed.

Valerian scowled at the pair of them and then turned to Natalie and offered an encouraging smile. "Sweetheart, I'm not—"

"Don't you call me sweetheart, I'm no Lucy," she snapped, and then realized with dismay, "Omigod, I *am*

Lucy. No one wants to be Lucy. Mina is the heroine. Why am I always Lucy?"

"You're not Lucy, Natalie. And I'm not Dracula, I'm Valerian MacKenzie. I am not some fictional dead and soulless guy running around turning Victorian virgins into vampiresses."

Natalie's eyes widened incredulously and she accused, "I fainted on your dick like a Victorian miss! Did you bite me? You must have bit me," she said with certainty, and shifted Mia so that she could free one hand to start feeling up her neck.

"I did not bite you. I would never bite you, Natalie," Valerian said, but then added honestly, "Well, not unless you wanted me to anyway."

Natalie glanced at him sharply, and sidled to the right along the counter to get closer to the door. Alasdair was still guarding the stairs, however, and she now swung her head around to examine him warily, wondering if she could slip past him if she was quick enough. He was one of those big, brawny, thick-necked guys. Probably physically slow because of all that girth, and no doubt had a brain the size of a pea in his noggin, she thought. Maybe if she looked behind him and gasped like she saw something there, he'd turn around and she could just nip out the door.

"No," Alasdair said.

"No?" Natalie asked with confusion.

"No nipping, slipping, or looking behind and gasping," he ordered.

"Did you just read my mind?" Natalie gasped with horror. "Of course you did. You're Dracula."

When Alasdair merely raised his eyebrows, it was Colle who said, "I thought Valerian was Dracula?"

"You're all Dracula," she growled impatiently, and then glared at Valerian. "What do you plan to do with me?"

When Valerian hesitated, Tybo said, "He was thinking marriage, babies . . . you know, the usual."

Natalie turned on the man with shock. "What?"

"Ty," Valerian growled with irritation.

"Just trying to help, bro," Tybo said apologetically.

Shaking his head, Valerian turned back to Natalie and tried a reassuring smile. "Please, just let me explain things. Once you understand, I'm sure a lot of your fears will dissipate."

Natalie stared at him. She was pretty sure nothing was going to make her fear dissipate. He had fangs. Apparently, they all did. And they drank blood too. Her dad used to have a favorite saying, "If it walks like a duck and quacks like a duck, it's a duck." Well, these guys had fangs like a vampire, and drank blood like a vampire. She was standing in the midst of a nest of vampires.

And she'd slept with one of them, Natalie thought with horror. She'd slept with Valerian, a bloodsucking vampire. Wow. That even beat out marrying a married man for bad taste in men. What was wrong with her? Why did she keep picking such horrendous assholes?

"What are you thinking?" Valerian suddenly asked with concern.

Natalie scowled at him, but then admitted, "That my manpicker must be broken."

"Your what?" Tybo asked on a disbelieving laugh.

"My manpicker," she repeated with a glare, and then said, "My guydar."

"Is she speaking a different language?" Colle asked, glancing at the other men with confusion. "What is a manpicker?"

"Maybe she meant manicure," Tybo said with a shrug, and asked Natalie, "Did you break a nail picking up Mia?"

"Oh my gawd!" Aileen snapped, ripping the now empty blood bag from her mouth. Slipping out of the booth, she rounded on Tybo. "She's no' talking about breaking a nail. She means she keeps picking married men and monsters for boyfriends."

"Valerian's not my boyfriend," Natalie protested quickly, as alarmed at the possibility that Valerian might think she was trying to claim a relationship as she was at the thought of anyone thinking she was the sex slave of demon seed. Good Lord. She was *not* Lucy.

"Well." Aileen turned to face her and said gently, "Maybe you two haven't verbalized what you are to each other, Natalie, but you do both like each other, and you did have sex, so I think it's safe to say you're in some kind of relationship."

"We're not in a relationship," Natalie said stubbornly. "Last night was an accident."

"An accident?" Tybo asked with amusement. "Like you tripped and fell on his penis, and then fainted from the shock of it?"

"Exactly," Natalie growled, glaring at the smart-ass vampire.

"Tybo, you aren't helping here," Aileen said with irritation, and then turned to her brother. "Valerian, you really need to start explaining. She's scared, and ready to throw herself through the window to get her daughter away from all of us."

Alarm crossed Valerian's face at this news. "Please don't do that, Natalie. I'm sorry you found out this way, and I know you're afraid, but I promise you, you're in no danger from anyone here."

When she merely stared at him, unconvinced, he added, "At least let me explain things first. If you still want out of here after I do that, Alasdair will move and let you leave. I promise."

Natalie hesitated, considering the situation. She might be able to keep Mia safe with her own body if she jumped out the window, but was pretty sure she'd do herself a lot of damage in the process. Probably enough that she wouldn't then be able to even crawl away from the RV, let alone carry Mia away to safety. So really, it might be better if she at least pretended to be willing to listen. Perhaps that would make the others relax enough that she would get the chance to escape more safely through the door. With that hope in mind, Natalie gave a brief nod.

"Thank you," Valerian said solemnly, and then paused, but finally he opened his mouth to speak, stopped, closed his mouth again, then opened and closed it a second time after another long pause.

When Valerian did that for a third time, Colle burst out with exasperation, "Oh, for God's sake, Val. It's not that hard."

"Isn't it?" Valerian asked grimly.

"No," Colle assured him. "Here, let me help you."

It sounded like more of an order than an offer, and Natalie watched warily as Colle turned back to her and offered a smile.

"We're scientific vampires, not the dead soulless kind. We were made—I mean, born—I mean—" He cursed, and then took a breath and tried again, "Our *ancestors* were born mortal, but got sick, or shot or something, and then some scientist guys came along wanting to try out these nanos they said would help them. The ancestors said okay and let them inject them with their nanos. But instead of just healing their wounds, or curing their ailments, the nanos did a lot more."

Natalie waited a moment when he paused, thinking there must be more, but when Colle didn't continue, she asked, "So these nanos turned your ancestors into vampires?"

"Right." Colle nodded.

Natalie stared at him with open disbelief for a minute, and then glanced around at the others in the room to see that they were all staring at Colle with expressions that were shouting, *WTF?*

Noticing that now, Colle said, "What?" and then just as quickly seemed to think he knew what the issue was and added, "Oh right, so this was a long time ago in Atlantis, and none of them were vampires there, because they were getting blood transfusions, but when Atlantis fell, the people with the nanos couldn't get blood anymore, and . . . some of them were *dying*," he told her with horror, and then shook his head and explained, "Because, yeah, while the nanos were still fixing things, they couldn't get blood anymore to support the nanos' work. So, the nanos gave them fangs, extra strength, night vision, and all the things that vampires are supposed to have, like the ability to read minds, and the ability to control their donors and stuff. Oh, and they also worked to keep them at their peak condition. So . . ." He seemed to do a mental review of what he'd said, and then nodded with satisfaction. "Yeah. That's it."

Colle smiled expectantly at Natalie now, but she had no idea what to say. Most of his babble sounded like the plot of a bad sci-fi movie. Nanos? Atlantis?

When she didn't respond, Colle glanced to Valerian and said, "I don't think she gets it."

"Gee, I wonder why?" Aileen said sarcastically.

"What do you mean?" Colle asked with a frown. "I hit all the high points, didn't I?"

Aileen just shook her head with disgust and turned to Natalie. "Me cousin has it mostly right. It did start in Atlantis. Our ancestors there were technologically advanced far beyond e'eryone else o' the time, and isolated too from the rest o' the world by the surrounding terrain, so did no' share that technology. And they did develop these bioengineered nanos they hoped would cure illness, heal wounds, and so on. But there was a flaw or two with what they came up with. The first was that the nanos used blood to power and replicate themselves as well as to do their work . . . and that can take a lot of blood," she pointed out. "More than a body can produce. Our ancestors dealt with that by givin' blood transfusions."

"And the other flaw?" Natalie asked, curious despite herself.

"To avoid havin' to make a couple hundred thousand versions o' the nanos, one fer each possible injury and e'ery illness known, they instead programmed the nanos with models o' both a male and female body at their peak condition. They then gave the nanos the directive to return their host body to that peak condition," Aileen said, and then added, "The nanos were supposed to repair any injury, or surround any bacteria or virus and remove it, and then shut off, break down, and be flushed from the body naturally once the job was done."

Natalie's eyebrows rose. "Why was that a problem?"

"Because the human body's at its peak between the ages o' about twenty-five to thirty, and those were the models they used. The nanos are basically computers, and computers are literal. So rather than just go in and find the illness or injury causin' the problem and takin' care o' that, they also . . ." She hesitated, and then said, "Well, I guess they saw the effects o' agin' as something to be repaired too."

"The fountain of youth," Natalie breathed with realization.

Aileen nodded. "That's what the scientists thought too. Cool, right?" She didn't wait for a response, but said, "Except the nanos never broke down and left the body like intended. I guess because the body is constantly under attack from pollution, sunlight, and even just the cells agin', the nanos never see their work as bein' done and stay active. So, while it does sort o' work as a fountain o' youth, the price is the need to take in extra blood to fuel them, which they managed with blood transfusions in Atlantis."

"What if you just stopped fueling them?" Natalie asked. "Wouldn't they break down and leave, then?"

"No. Well, no' without killing the host first," Aileen said with a grimace. "The nanos would use up every last drop o' blood in their host's body to try to keep doin' their work. I mean, *every last drop.* Once the veins were empty, they'd move into the organs to find what they need. It's incredibly painful."

"But blood transfusions fixed that issue," Natalie murmured.

"It did in Atlantis, but there were no transfusions after Atlantis fell. The Atlanteans who had been given this experimental treatment were pretty much the only survivors, and none of them were scientists or people in the medical field so there were no transfusions. The fall forced them to move out past their old borders and join a world far less advanced, and as Colle said, without the transfusions, they started in dyin'. The nanos couldn't allow that. Their directive was to keep their host alive and at their peak, so they presumably did what they had to do to get the blood they needed to do their job."

"Fangs," Natalie said grimly.

"Fangs, speed, strength . . ." Aileen shrugged, not continuing but Colle had already mentioned the other things. "Basically, anything that would make them a better predator."

"Including the ability to read and control the minds of mortals, their prey," Natalie said, her tone biting.

"It kept the donors from feelin' fear or pain, as well as prevented their rememberin' and becomin' a threat to our ancestors," Aileen pointed out unapologetically.

Natalie was silent for a minute, considering all she'd learned, but then a thought made her ask, "So you're all from Atlantis? You're like thousands of years old?"

"No," Valerian said at once. "Not anyone in this RV anyway. We're all descendants of the original Atlanteans."

"But you have the nanos?" she asked, trying to work it out.

"It's passed down through the mother," Valerian explained.

"So, your mother was an Atlantean?" Natalie asked uncertainly.

"No. My great-great-grandfather, Nicodemus Notte, was an Atlantean."

"Great-great-great-grandfather," Aileen corrected.

Valerian paused and appeared to be doing calculations in his head. But Natalie was doing some calculating of her own and the math wasn't working out. Her own great-great-great-grandfather had probably lived in around the early 1800s, but Atlantis was thousands of years ago or something. But then, the nanos were a fountain of youth, she recalled, and narrowed her eyes as she looked over the people surrounding her, before her gaze settled on Aileen.

"What year were you born?" she asked abruptly.

"2000," Aileen answered easily.

Natalie let out a little relieved breath. She'd answered without hesitation, so it was probably true. Which meant Valerian could be around her own age or a little older. Kids twelve or thirteen years apart wasn't unheard of.

"Me brother was born in 1790," Aileen said quietly, obviously having read her thoughts.

Natalie was gasping at that when she added, "Colle and Alasdair were born in 1699, and Tybo in 1920."

"Oh sweet Lord," Natalie breathed. "I had sex with a geriatric."

A startled laugh slipped from Aileen, followed by a cough Natalie suspected was a poor attempt to cover her amusement, and then the girl turned to Valerian and suggested, "Brother, maybe the rest of us should clear out so that you and Natalie can chat. You can tell her what you and the boys do . . . and talk," she said meaningfully.

"Yes, of course," Valerian murmured.

Smiling, Aileen moved toward Natalie and reached for Mia. "Why do I no' take her inside and get her cleaned up while you two talk?"

Natalie stepped back at once, her hold tightening on Mia, and the first sign of impatience flashed on Aileen's face.

Arms dropping, she scowled, and said, "Oh, come now, Natalie. I'd sooner cut off me right hand than hurt your little girl. Mia is a sweetheart. Besides, you're bein' irrational here."

"Irrational?" she asked with disbelief. Natalie thought she was being perfectly rational considering she was facing a bunch of vampires. And that's what they were. It didn't matter if it was because of some curse or science, they had fangs and drank blood.

"We prefer the term *immortals*," Aileen said stiffly. "Vampires are fictional monsters with no soul. We're just people with an affliction that forces us to take in blood because our bodies can no' produce enough to satisfy the nanos."

Natalie felt herself relax a little at that, but then frowned. Vampire or immortal, whatever they wanted to be called, they were predators, and she and Mia were their prey.

"And that thought right there proves you're bein' irrational," Aileen said dryly. "You saw that we all had bagged blood at our mouths when you entered. Why the hell would we do that if we could just run around biting mortals for free? 'Cause trust me, blood in a bag is no' free."

Natalie's eyes widened slightly, but she still wasn't giving up her daughter.

Aileen sighed, and then pointed out, "Me brother saved your life pullin' you out of that pond, and every single man at Shady Pines is here to keep you safe from the Angel-Maker. They are Enforcers. That's the official title, but most o' us civilian immortals call them rogue hunters. Because they hunt down immortals who have gone rogue and attack and feed off o' mortals," she explained, and then added firmly, "We're the good guys, Natalie, here to try to keep you safe from the bad ones."

Natalie shifted uncertainly. She wanted to trust her,

to trust them, but it was so much to take in. Vampires existed but were really immortals. They'd been around for thousands of years, coexisting with mortals who had no clue of who and what they were . . . And Valerian was over two hundred years old. Yet, knowing all that, she still couldn't look at him without wanting to experience the passion she had last night. Did she really want to be alone with him? Hell, no! But not so much because she was afraid of him anymore; instead, because she was afraid of herself and her inability to resist him.

Sighing, she shifted her gaze to Aileen. "I'll take Mia in, clean her up, and change her." She saw the disappointment on Aileen's face, and then added, "But you can come with me to help if you like."

Aileen burst into a smile at once. "Let's go," the girl said cheerfully, and whistled as she headed for the door.

Natalie was confused by that until Sinbad rushed out of the bedroom at the back of the RV to join them. She'd forgotten all about the big white dog. Apparently, he'd been napping during all the excitement, which kind of weirded her out. He was usually very protective if he sensed a threat, but hadn't reacted at all to these people. That actually went further to make her feel safe than all of Aileen's explanations.

"Natalie," Valerian said suddenly, drawing her gaze. "We have to talk."

"Later. Mia comes first," she said, turning quickly to follow Aileen and Sinbad out of the RV.

Nineteen

Natalie didn't relax until she was in the clubhouse and down in the room she and her daughter shared. Natalie knew it was foolish, but she locked the door after stepping inside with Aileen, Sinbad, and Mia. If this group was stronger than mortals as they claimed to be, any one of them could probably break through the door in an instant. She'd also basically locked herself inside the room with Aileen, who was also an immortal. But Natalie didn't feel threatened by the girl. And it just felt safer that way.

"We really will no' hurt you," Aileen said quietly as Natalie turned from locking the door. Following her to the bed when Natalie carried Mia there, she added, "Well, most of us would no' anyway. But Lucian might."

When Natalie glanced at her sharply at that, she explained, "He's one o' the originals from Atlantis.

He's old and powerful and . . ." She stopped and grimaced. "I'm no' explainin' this right, but basically, he'll do whatever it takes to keep our kind safe. But he would no' hurt you unless he saw you as a threat."

Natalie gaped at her with disbelief. "How could I possibly be a threat?"

"By tellin' others about us," Aileen pointed out solemnly. "The only reason we've survived without bein' hunted by mortals all these years is because nobody knows about us. We keep to ourselves. We do no' hurt people. We do no' feed on people. We use blood banks."

"What about before blood banks?" Natalie asked as she began to undress Mia, stripping off her blood-soaked top and shorts.

"Well, sure, in the past, before there were blood banks they had to feed on people, but they tried no' to do any damage, or take too much blood from any one person. That was just common sense. I mean, if you kill the dairy cow, you are no' going to get any more milk, are you?"

Natalie turned on her with disbelief. "Are you seriously comparing people to dairy cows?"

"Basically, yes," Aileen said mildly. "I'm no' tryin' to be rude, or insult mortals, Natalie, but we need blood to survive and mortals are our source for blood. Think on it like hemophilia," she suggested. "They have a blood disorder too, and often need transfusions because o' it. Well, so do we. The only difference is that we have fangs and were able to get the blood we needed even before blood banks. Hemophiliacs could no' do that, and just died in a lot of cases." She shrugged. "Personally, I'm grateful that me ancestors had fangs and all that jazz. If no', I would no' be here."

Natalie frowned over that as she moved to the dresser to grab fresh clothes for Mia. She was still thinking about it as she carried them back to the bed and picked up the bloodstained clothes and her daughter to take into the bathroom. She understood what Aileen was saying, and could see how mortals were like dairy cows for them, but it was still more than a little offensive.

"Mia's a beautiful wee lass," Aileen commented from the doorway as she watched Natalie set her on the sink counter.

"Thank you," Natalie murmured, but peered at her daughter with concern. She'd been oddly quiet through all of this. At least, she had after her initial protest when Natalie had pulled her from the booth in the RV. Too quiet, Natalie thought suddenly, noting the almost blank expression on her daughter's face. Turning narrowed eyes on Aileen, she asked, "Are you controlling my daughter?"

"You were upset and frightening her, so I just kind of veiled her thoughts to protect her from you," Aileen said solemnly. "Do you want me to release her now, or wait until you get the blood cleaned off o' her?"

Natalie swallowed and turned back to peer at her daughter, struck by the suggestion that she'd frightened her with her reaction in the RV. She didn't doubt it was true, but was sorry she had.

"After," she said, her voice husky. Clearing her throat,

Natalie grabbed a washcloth and turned on the taps. Once the water had warmed up, she soaked the cloth.

"What can I do to help?" Aileen asked.

Natalie hesitated, but then asked, "Would you rather wash her or dress her?"

"Dress her," Aileen said at once, a grin breaking out on her face that made Natalie feel better for making the offer.

"Okay," she said simply as she wrung out the washcloth.

"So . . . what do you think o' me brother?" Aileen asked as she watched Natalie quickly wash the blood from Mia's arms and face.

Natalie was silent for a minute, but finally admitted, "I don't know. I don't know what to think about any of you at the moment." Sighing, she added, "In fact, I don't know what to think about anything. It's a lot to take in."

"Yeah, I know," Aileen said, and when Natalie turned to look at her, one eyebrow arched, she grimaced. "Well, okay, I do no' really *know* what it would be like to find out about us because I am one and grew up with the knowledge. But I imagine it would be shockin'. I promise no one here means you or Mia any harm, though, least o' all Valerian."

"Why least of all Valerian?" Natalie asked with curiosity.

"Because you're a possible LM to him," Aileen answered easily.

Natalie glanced at her sharply. "Would I be right in guessing that LM doesn't stand for latest mission as Valerian claimed?"

"You'd be right," Aileen agreed.

Natalie nodded. "And would you like to tell me what it really stands for?"

"I'd love to," Aileen assured her, "but I can no'. I promised Valerian I'd let him explain when he felt the time was right."

"Great," Natalie sighed.

"I think if you'd stayed to talk to him, he would have told you," Aileen pointed out quietly.

Natalie was silent for a minute, and then grabbed a towel to dry her daughter and gestured for Aileen to get the clothes. The moment Aileen stepped up to dress Mia in the clean shorts and T-shirt, Natalie began to run cold water in the sink to soak the blood-stained clothes in. It wasn't until she had the items in the water and had tossed the washcloth and towel into the laundry basket that she said, "I don't think I'm ready to talk to Valerian. I think I need some time to adjust to all this."

Aileen glanced at her, and for a minute her gaze looked concentrated, but then she relaxed and turned her attention back to what she was doing as she dressed Mia. "I think you're right. I'll talk to Valerian. Suggest he stay out o' the clubhouse today and give you time to think and the space to do it. I'm sure he'll understand."

"I don't understand." Valerian scowled at his sister. "I mean, I know this has all probably been a shock for her, but the best thing now is for us to talk, to ease her worries. Not leave her alone to build them up in her head."

"Val, I read her mind. This is really for the best. Just give her the day to deal, and then tonight, you can have shared dreams and talk to her in an environment where she'll no' feel threatened."

"She feels threatened by me?" he asked with dismay. "How could she feel threatened? She's my life mate. I would sooner gnaw off my own arm than hurt her."

"I know that," Aileen assured him. "But she doesna."

"Well, she should. She's my life mate. Didn't you tell her that?"

"No," she said with irritation. "As I recall last night you gave me hell for even bringin' up LMs in front of Natalie and told me to stay out o' it. It was your business, and you'd explain it to her when you felt the time was right. So, I told her I could no' explain LMs to her, but I was sure you would when the two o' you talked. She said she wasn't ready and needed time to adjust to everything she's learned . . . and I think you should give her that time. At least for today. Then tonight, you can go into your shared dreams and talk to her. She'll feel safer in a dream."

Valerian scowled at the suggestion, but had to admit the idea wasn't bad. As much as he hated the idea of waiting to explain everything, it wasn't going to do him any good if she wasn't in a state of mind to listen. In a dream, she'd let her guard down and maybe be more open to what he had to say. Sighing, he nodded his head. "Okay. I'll steer clear of the clubhouse today.

But I'm sleeping in the office again tonight. I'm not leaving her unprotected."

"I would no' expect you to." Aileen patted his arm soothingly. "But do me a favor and spend this time really considerin' what you're goin' to say to her. I like Natalie, and Mia is a little love. As her aunt, I plan to spoil her rotten. I'll be very upset if you mess this up and lose Natalie and Mia."

Valerian just scowled at his little sister as she then headed out of the office. Her lack of confidence in him was more than a little dismaying. Especially since he had some concerns of his own about his coming talk with Natalie. It would be the most important conversation of his life. He would either gain her as a life mate, or lose her forever.

Sighing, Valerian ran a hand through his hair and headed out of the clubhouse.

Natalie stared at the ceiling, groaned miserably, and then rolled onto her side and stared at the wall instead. She'd spent the day locked in her office with Mia, Sinbad, and Aileen just to ensure she didn't run into Valerian. Aileen had assured her it wasn't necessary, and that he'd agreed to give her space, but she'd just wanted to be sure. She had wanted the time to consider everything. The problem was, she had considered a lot, but still hadn't come to any conclusions.

But then what was there to conclude? Yes, they'd

had sex, but he was a vampire, and she was food. And while she appreciated that these people were here to keep her safe and hunt down the guy who had targeted her, she wasn't completely comfortable having a dozen or so vampires around her daughter, friends, employees, and customers.

And still, she was attracted to the guy, vampire or not. How was that for sick and twisted?

Sighing, Natalie flipped in bed, shifting onto her other side to stare at the door now. Getting to sleep was absolutely impossible. It wasn't even eight thirty yet, but when she'd put Mia down, she'd gone to bed as well. Purely in a continued effort to avoid Valerian.

He could read her mind.

That was the thought that kept screaming through her head. Dear God in heaven, the thoughts she'd had about him since meeting him, especially since having sex with him. Thoughts she was still having despite knowing what he was. There really was something wrong with her, Natalie thought unhappily. Why couldn't she have fallen in lust with Mr. Copeland's son, Junior? He was a good guy, a hard worker, always polite and smiling . . . without fangs. But noooo, she had to fall for the guy with an "allergy to the sun."

That thought made her pause. If the vampirism was due to nanos, why would they have trouble with sunlight? Dracula had issues with it because of his curse or something, but these guys . . .

Fretting over that, Natalie closed her eyes and worried herself to sleep.

"Wow, this is—is that a coffin?"

Heart leaping into her throat, Natalie whirled around at that question and gaped at Valerian. Dressed in tight blue jeans and a white T-shirt, he looked totally out of place in the dark and gloomy castle setting. Besides, she'd kind of expected to find him in the coffin he'd mentioned, not wandering around like a tourist who'd got lost during a castle tour.

Fingers tightening on the candelabra of lit candles she was holding, Natalie turned back to the coffin she'd been creeping up on before Valerian had spoken, and reached out with her free hand to lift the lid, revealing that it was empty.

"What were you expecting to find in there?" Valerian asked, suddenly at her side.

Natalie let the lid drop closed and backed up several steps to put some space between them.

Valerian eyed her briefly, his gaze sliding over her in the flowing white nightgown she was wearing. Then he peered around the large dark room they were in. "What is this place?"

"You ought to know. It's your castle in Scotland," she said grimly. At least that's where she thought she was. He'd said he had a castle and she was there.

"This isn't my castle," Valerian assured her with amusement. "And I don't sleep in a coffin."

Natalie bit her lip, confused as to what was happening. She'd been sure she was in his castle.

"But I do like that nightgown," he added, his gaze raking over the thin, gauzy white material, and the low scoop neck that left so much of her pale skin on display.

Flushing, Natalie turned to walk away from him and then froze as she noted the changes to the castle she was in. Where the walls had been dark, damp stone, they were now snow white with a beige trim, and rather than it being night, bright sunlight was pouring in through large, arched windows that stretched a good eighteen or twenty feet up the high walls. Natalie was sure those windows hadn't been in the castle minutes ago. But then neither had the furniture now filling the room she stood in. Two long tables took up the center of the room, each with eighteen chairs around them, but room for more. However, there were also several smaller tables along the sides of the room as well, and a fireplace large enough to stand in at the opposite end from where they were.

"This is my castle," Valerian announced, pride evident in his voice. "Or at least the great room of my castle."

"The great room," Natalie whispered, turning slowly to take it all in.

"Would you like a tour?"

Natalie hesitated. Minutes ago she'd been in the middle of some gothic novel. The frightened girl creeping through Dracula's castle in her nightgown, a candelabra shaking in her trembling fingers as she approached his coffin. Now she was—

"Are those real candles?" she asked with amazement as her eyes landed on the huge chandeliers overhead. Three of them down the middle of the room hanging high over the tables. Each had to be five or six feet across.

"No. We switched to electricity after it became accessible to the public," Valerian said, following her gaze up to the lights. "But these were custom designed to look like the originals, which were real candles."

"Oh wow," Natalie breathed, her attention now moving to the arched designs in the high ceiling, and then finally to the walls. Eyes widening, she moved toward a mannequin wearing a high black furry hat, a red short coat, a blue, green, and black plaid kilt, and high white boots with black toes and red and black argyle trim around the top. "What's this?"

"My uniform when I was in the regiment of foot."

"The Black Watch?" she asked.

Valerian nodded.

Natalie peered at it, and then tilted her head slightly before commenting, "The skirt looks kind of short. Did it even cover your knees?"

"Good God, no," he said with a grin. "A kilt worn proper should no' reach below the top o' the knee."

Natalie turned to him with an entranced smile. "You sound so Scottish!"

"I am so Scottish," he reminded her with amusement.

"I know, but it's easy to forget because you talk like a Canadian most of the time."

"When in Rome," Valerian said with a shrug. "We don't like to draw attention to ourselves. Accents and anything else out of the ordinary draw attention."

"Right," she said softly, and then turned to move

on to the next display, a table full of items. It was utter chaos. At least it looked like utter chaos to her, weapons of every description and several uniforms all neatly folded so that all she could really see was their color and not much else. "What's all this?"

"Just different weapons and uniforms I've worn over the years," Valerian said with a shrug.

Natalie turned to him with surprise. "So, you weren't just a soldier for the Black Watch?"

"Actually, it wasn't called the Black Watch when I was a member. It was still the 42nd Royal Highland Regiment of Foot back then," he told her, and then added, "But yes, I've been a soldier in many wars."

"Which ones?"

"Well, the World Wars, of course. Very few people around back then weren't involved in WWI and WWII," he said.

"Right," she murmured, but was now picturing him in a scene from *Saving Private Ryan*.

"But there were a lot of other wars before those, like the Napoleonic Wars, the Hundred Days, the Barbary Wars, the Taiping Rebellion, the Crimean War . . ." He shrugged. "I can't possibly remember them all."

"Did you do anything besides fight wars for the last two-hundred-plus years?" Natalie asked with a sort of horror. Good Lord, imagining him marching around in a kilt was one thing, but this was sounding like a lifetime career of violent clashes.

"Of course," Valerian said at once. "I mean, there were a lot of wars, but most didn't last long. Some a couple years, some just months."

"So, what other things did you do?" she asked.

He paused and then said, "I was in California during the gold rush."

Natalie's eyes widened. "Did you pan lots of gold or whatever it is they did?"

"No. But I pulled in a lot of gold anyway," Valerian assured her. "I had a saloon as well as a store in San Francisco, and a lot of miners dropped their coin in both places."

"Did you have dancing girls?"

He nodded. "And a piano player, gambling, baths in the back, and rooms upstairs." He smiled as if at good memories. "Of course, I had to give up both businesses after about ten years."

"Why?" Natalie asked with surprise.

"Because we can't stay anywhere for longer than ten years or so. Our lack of aging would show," Valerian pointed out.

Natalie blinked at that. It was something she hadn't even considered. They didn't age. That would become apparent to those around them after a time. The thought troubled her.

"Anyway, so I stuck around there for about ten years, and then sold up and headed out to kick around for a bit, then went to work for the Pony Express."

"You gave up a cushy job as a saloon and store owner to ride for the Pony Express?" she asked with disbelief. "That's crazy."

Valerian chuckled at her expression, but shook his head. "I didn't ride for them. I was too big. Their riders were all built like jockeys today: short, slim, light on the horse. I was a stockkeeper at one of their relief stations." He grimaced. "That was actually a more dangerous job than being a rider. We lost a good fifteen or sixteen stock hands to attacks by Native Americans in the year and a half the Pony Express ran. They'd set the damned stations on fire with us in them. I was lucky not to be among that number."

Natalie raised an eyebrow. "So, you aren't really immortal? You can be killed?"

"Fire is deadly to us, but decapitating will do the job too if the head is kept away from the body long enough," he said quietly, and then teased, "Looking for ways to be rid of me?"

The question surprised Natalie. She hadn't even considered that, and frowned over the possibility he might think she would. Unsure how to address the question, she changed the subject and asked, "You said in the year and a half the Pony Express ran? I didn't know it existed for such a short period of time?"

Valerian continued to eye her for a minute as if debating whether to let go of the subject of her possibly wanting him dead, but finally explained, "The transcontinental telegraph killed it. It was cheaper to send a telegraph than send a letter via the Pony Express, so . . ." He shrugged.

Nodding, Natalie continued along the room, pausing at a grouping of old sepia photos on the wall. Cowboys and Native Americans, on foot and on horseback. "What's this about?"

"Those are from when I traveled with Buffalo Bill Cody's Wild West Show for a while."

"No," Natalie breathed, imagining him now in cowboy boots, chaps, and a cowboy hat. Oddly enough, she forgot the shirt and pants. He still looked good.

"Yes," he assured her. "I was mostly just support for the others. Bill wanted me to be a performer—I was a pretty good shot," Valerian explained. "But, as children, immortals have it drilled into us to avoid drawing any attention to ourselves ever, for the safety of our kind. So, I stuck to taking care of horses and whatnot."

Natalie moved closer to the pictures for a better look, and started scanning faces. She stiffened when she recognized Valerian among the group in one photo. He looked so stiff and old-timey, nothing like the relaxed man beside her. Shaking her head, she said, "So, you made all that money in San Francisco and then took jobs as a stock hand and then a stable boy? Why on earth would you do that? You could have opened another store elsewhere."

Valerian smiled faintly at the question, but rather than answer it, he asked, "How much do you enjoy owning and running the golf course?"

Natalie opened her mouth, closed it, and then admitted, "Not a lot, maybe. I mean, I enjoy working in the restaurant. Not so much the working all the time, though, and I'm so sick of mowing the green," she said. "But that's only temporary. Once the additions are out of the way I'll be able to take on more help and slow down a little myself."

Valerian snorted at the suggestion. "You won't. You might hire more help, but you'll still work around the clock. Owners always end up doing that, and they get all the stress too. Late shipments? Shipments of food that have gone bad? A bad drought that starts killing off your green?" He raised his eyebrows. "All of that stress falls on you, because you're the owner. At least it does if you're a good owner, and I'm pretty sure you're a good owner and won't pass the problems on to others."

Natalie frowned at this prediction, more than a little afraid he was right.

"Don't mind me," Valerian said. "Maybe I'm wrong. Besides, there are jobs more stressful than being a shop owner."

"Like what?" she asked, trying to be interested, but finding she was suddenly depressed and exhausted.

"Like being a doctor during an epidemic."

Natalie glanced at him sharply. "You're a doctor?"

"I was, but I wouldn't be considered one today," he said with a faint smile, and then explained, "I trained and then worked as a physician in the early 1900s."

"Yeah?" She was actually impressed and, when he nodded, asked, "How long did you do that?"

"From about 1899 to the end of 1919." He hesitated, and then admitted, "I had a small practice in a Texas town for a while. When World War I started, I became a medic in the army. But then I was transferred to a camp to treat the sick when the Great Influenza epidemic struck." Valerian paused briefly. "I enjoyed being a doctor at first . . . but the Great Influenza took all the joy out of it for me and is the reason I quit." Noting her confused expression, he added, "Some called it the Spanish flu pandemic."

"Oh yeah, that's the one where millions died."

"Somewhere between fifty and a hundred million according to the estimates," he said quietly, and shook his head, sadness clouding his eyes. "So many people lost their lives. Most of them young adults just on the cusp of life and we were as good as useless to help them, really." Different emotions played across his face as if his memory had taken him back there, in the thick of it, with too many people needing his help, and little in the way of help to offer.

Valerian gave his head a slight shake, as if trying to throw off the memories. "After that I needed a break from medicine, so I bought an apple farm in New York. I thought it would be quiet and peaceful, and it was."

"But eventually you quit that too," Natalie guessed.

Valerian nodded. "I still have the property, and have had various managers running it over the years, but yes, I did move on. But not to anything really interesting at first. Mostly I kicked around, visiting and helping out on various golf courses my family owned in the states. But then I ran into Colle and Alasdair. They were Enforcers in New York City."

"You said your cousins trained you," she reminded him.

"They did," he assured her. "I've never lied to you, Natalie. I may have avoided telling you things like that I joined the Regiment of Foot back in 1808, but I was always honest. I will always be honest."

"Thank you," Natalie whispered.

Nodding, Valerian started walking again, now heading for the door ahead. "My cousins trained me for a couple of years. I had a lot of battle experience from the wars, and I was a good shot, but dealing with rogues meant hand-to-hand combat at times too, and I didn't have much experience with that. They got me up to speed, and when they felt I was ready, suggested I sign up to be an Enforcer. I did, and worked in New York for a while, and then got transferred up here to Canada."

"How long ago was that?" Natalie asked at once. "That you got transferred to Canada, I mean?" He'd told her he'd worked with Tybo for a decade. Did that mean he'd be moving on again soon? For some reason the possibility alarmed her, when she should really be grateful. Her feelings for him were confusing and distressing. His moving on might actually be a great thing for her. She'd have to move on and forget about him.

"About thirty years ago now," Valerian said slowly, as if doing the calculations in his head.

Natalie immediately turned on him. "You said you'd never lied to me, but you told me you'd worked with Tybo for a decade."

"Actually, I first said decades," he reminded her gently. "But when you called me on it because I don't look old enough for that, I said 'at least a decade,' which isn't a lie," he pointed out, and admitted, "Although I suppose there's a vast difference between at least a decade and three decades. But in my defense, if I'd stuck with the decades answer, you would have thought I was either lying or crazy. I was kind of between a rock and a hard place."

Natalie was silent for a minute, and then sighed and started to walk again. He had a point. She probably would have thought him a nutter if he'd said three decades, and "at least a decade" wasn't actually a lie. Really. Still, she was now wondering what else hadn't actually been a lie, but not quite the truth either.

That was when Natalie realized how ridiculous she was being. This was a dream, obviously. She was usually aware of when she was dreaming, and that had to be the case now. In real life, a dark, haunted castle didn't suddenly turn into a beautiful, light and bright one in the blink of an eye. Which meant her mind was making up all these stories of what he'd been doing for two hundred years.

The only problem with that was she was learning things in this dream. She'd had no idea that the Pony Express had only been operational for a year and a half. So where had that come from? Or was it just something her mind had made up? She also hadn't known the Spanish flu had also been called the Great Influenza epidemic, and now didn't know if that was true or something else her mind had made up. It was very confusing.

"You seem a little distressed," Valerian said suddenly.

Reminding herself again that this was a dream and Valerian was just a representation of some part of her mind, Natalie almost didn't respond. But then she recalled that dreams were supposed to be your mind trying to work out issues, and her mind couldn't do that if she didn't participate, so she said, "I know this is a dream, and I'm just wondering why I chose all these different careers for you. What is my subconscious trying to work out with that?"

Valerian didn't respond at first, but when he finally did, his words seemed completely off topic as he announced, "LM stands for life mate."

Twenty

It took two steps before Valerian's words made their way through Natalie's mind. But once they did, she stopped abruptly and turned to face him. "Life mate?"

"Yes," he said solemnly.

Natalie stared at him, her mind running through the times Aileen had mentioned the term *LM* to her, or in her presence. To her it had seemed like Aileen was suggesting that was what she was for Valerian. Finally, she asked, "What is a life mate?"

Valerian moved forward, caught her hand, and led her out of the long, large room into an entry that her entire clubhouse would have fit in. Natalie barely got a glimpse of more whitewashed walls, and a huge table in the center with a large vase with peacock feathers arranged in it, before she was outside and walking across the most beautiful property she'd ever seen. If she ignored the long twisting driveway, it was like a huge park had been dropped outside the front door.

"You were told that immortals can read and control the minds of mortals," Valerian said finally. "But what they didn't mention was that immortals can also read the minds of other immortals if they're younger than themselves."

Natalie's eyebrows rose at this. "So, you can read Aileen and Tybo?"

"And my cousins can read all three of us."

"Hmm." Natalie frowned slightly. Knowing that they could read her mind had been probably as scary if not scarier than seeing their fangs. But she'd just assumed it was only a mortal issue. It had never occurred to her that immortals could read other immortals.

"It can make life difficult," Valerian pointed out.

"I can imagine," Natalie said dryly.

"But there is a way to block others from reading you."

That definitely caught her interest. "How?"

"Reciting nursery rhymes or something else will do it. Not that they can't read the nursery rhyme in your head. They will, but it keeps you from thinking of other things in their presence. However, it can be a bit wearing to constantly be having to guard your thoughts."

"I bet," Natalie murmured. "But what has this to do with life mates?"

"I'm getting to that," Valerian assured her. "So, basically immortals are constantly having to guard their thoughts from older immortals. No one wants to have to recite nursery rhymes constantly, so when they can, they avoid each other. Sometimes they'll spend their time with mortals to ease the loneliness, but that can be heartbreaking."

"Why?" she asked with surprise.

"Because mortals have such short lives. We can become attached and then it hurts when they die. Some immortals have even been tempted to turn a mortal friend to save them, and that can be a problem."

"Wait, so you can turn mortals into immortals?" Natalie asked with surprise, but then realized they would just have to share their nanos. After all, the originals were mortals who were given the nanos, so presumably new ones could be made the same way.

"Yes, we can, but we can only turn one in a lifetime."

Natalie's eyebrows rose. "So . . . what? You're like honeybees? Only you lose your fangs after biting instead of a stinger? Do you die from it too like they do?"

Valerian grinned at the suggestion and question. "No, we don't lose our fangs and die if we turn someone. Our only turning one is a law, not a physical issue. Our Council made it a law long ago to ensure that we don't outstrip mortals in population. We're also only allowed to have one child every hundred years to aid with that. Well, unless the birth brings on twins or triplets. They wouldn't fuss over that."

"Oh." Natalie considered that, and then said, "If these nanos are so great, why not let everyone in on the secret? No one would hunt you if we all had the option to be one. And it would save so many lives," she added, thinking of her son, Cody, and her parents. The car hadn't burst into flames in the crash, it had just been mangled like a pretzel. Her family would have survived the crash if they'd had nanos.

"The planet already has a population problem, Natalie. How much worse would it be if no one ever died, or the rare individual died?" he pointed out. "Besides, if everyone became immortal, where would we get the blood each one needed to survive? There would be no mortals to give blood at the blood bank." He shook his head. "These laws are for a reason."

"Right," she murmured unhappily, and considered what he'd said. "So, if you're allowed to turn one, why would turning a friend be a problem? Don't you get to choose who you turn?"

"Of course. But most save that one turn for their life mate."

"Ah. Finally, back to the life mate," she said at once. "You still haven't told me what that is."

"Well, a life mate is the one individual that an immortal cannot read or control. Some think it has something to do with the nanos, that they choose the perfect life mate and ensure they can't read each other, which makes sense, since while we can't read each other, our minds do merge in other ways," Valerian added thoughtfully, but then shrugged. "Whatever the case, an immortal can be around their life mate without the stress of guarding thoughts and whatnot. It means they don't have to be so lonely, and most unmated immortals *are* lonely," he assured her. "We avoid others when we can, mortal or immortal, because they are

exhausting. But that leads to loneliness, and sometimes to the immortal going rogue. A life mate prevents
that."

"And I'm a possible life mate for you?" she asked
slowly.

"Yes." That was it. The simple word without flour-
ishes or embellishments.

"How do you find out if I am?" she asked with curiosity.

Valerian looked confused. "If you are what?"

"Your life mate," Natalie explained. "Aileen said I
was a *possible* life mate for you."

"Ah." Valerian nodded. "You *are* my life mate,
Natalie. With you I could have peace, and joy, and all
the other perks that come when life mates find each
other. The word *possible* was included only because
you have free will. You can choose *not* to be my life
mate. So, while you are my life mate, you have a
choice so are still only a possible life mate."

Natalie stared out over the green grass and trees
dotted around, her mind in something of an uproar.
A life mate. To this man, she thought, and then sighed
and gave her head a shake. This was still just a dream.
Obviously, her mind was trying to cope with her attraction to Valerian, a vampire, and was throwing all
these things at her. Maybe to justify having a fling with
him, a vampire, which would be incredibly dangerous
to her thinking.

"And of course, there are other perks to life mates,"
Valerian said suddenly.

Natalie glanced at him warily, now seeing him as

the pleasure-driven side of her mind trying to convince her to sleep with him again. Not that she knew if the real Valerian even wanted to. The other night might have just been a fluke. She might have just been a handy willing body hanging around. If she'd even really been willing. Had he controlled her to make her want him like she had? The passion and need she'd experienced had been like nothing she'd ever before encountered. It certainly hadn't been normal.

"Did you—?" Natalie began angrily, and then hesitated as she recalled that he'd just said life mates couldn't read or control each other. So, she asked instead, "Can you really not read or control me?"

"No. I can't," he assured her, and then offered a crooked grin and added, "And believe me, there was a time or two I wished I could."

She peered out at the terrain again, her brain exploding with this news. "So not being able to read and control me is the only way to know that we're life mates?"

"No. There are other symptoms," he admitted and, when she glanced at him in question, explained, "Immortals grow weary of food eventually. Everything just starts to taste the same, and cooking and just the act of eating itself becomes a bother."

Natalie found that hard to believe. She loved food, and loved cooking. She couldn't ever imagine tiring of it.

"Sex too loses its excitement and interest at about the same time. Usually, somewhere around one hundred and fifty or so," he explained. "For me it was later. The last time I bothered with either was in the summer of 1950."

Natalie did the math in her head and worked out that he'd stopped eating and having sex at one hundred and sixty years old. Well, until the other night, she supposed. Good Lord! Was that the first time he'd had sex in like seventy-some years?

"Finding our life mates reawakens those passions," Valerian continued. "We start eating again, and enjoy sexual pleasure with them, which is something else. The passion between life mates is off the charts. It's desperate, and overwhelming, because while life mates can't read or control each other, for some reason their minds sort of merge during mating."

"What?" she asked with surprise. "What do you mean?"

Valerian paused briefly as if searching for a way to explain it. "I could feel every caress I gave you as if I was experiencing it myself, but I also felt your pleasure, as well as my own. It was amazing, but also overwhelming, because it just kept coming, wave after mounting wave of pleasure, growing with each moment. My pleasure on top of your pleasure, on top of mine . . ." He shook his head, looking frustrated at his inability to put to words what had happened, but he really didn't have to. Natalie knew exactly what he was talking about. While it had been something of a desperate blur of need and passion after the fact, now that he was discussing it, she distinctly recalled the pleasure that had shot through her when she'd ground her bottom back against his erection. She also recalled the mounting waves of pleasure as it had progressed, and how overwhelming it had been.

Feeling her body becoming excited at just the memory, Natalie took a deep breath to try to calm herself, and said, "So life mates make sex great again for immortals."

"They make sex amazing," Valerian corrected. "But only with them. Sex with anyone else would be like a dog chew next to a steak. Life mates never stray because of this. No other lover could bring about a passion so powerful and overwhelming." He chuckled. "Of course, that's something of a problem too. At least, at first."

"Why?"

"Because it's so overwhelming that the human mind cannot handle it, and for the first year or so after finding each other, life mates tend to pass out at the end of sex because of it. Which can be damned inconvenient."

Natalie whirled on him with wide eyes. "That's why I passed out?"

Valerian nodded. "I did as well."

"I thought it was because of my being so exhausted and worn out," she muttered, and then eyed him sharply. "Wait, you passed out too?"

"Yes," he admitted without shame.

"So you . . ."

"I joined you in orgasm," Valerian said when she hesitated to put words to it. "Like I said, our minds merge. I felt your pleasure, and when you orgasmed, I invariably orgasmed with you. Or perhaps I orgasmed and dragged you along for the ride," he said with a crooked smile.

"Oh," she breathed, and then shook her head. "This is crazy. I mean, this is a dream. Where the hell am I coming up with this stuff? Passion so overwhelming that both parties pass out?" She snorted. "I should write this down when I wake up. Maybe I could try my hand at writing fiction."

"Shared dreams is another symptom of life mates," Valerian announced.

Natalie had started walking again, entering the woods that surrounded the property and leaving him behind. But she slowed now and turned reluctantly to face him. "Shared dreams?"

"You are asleep and dreaming. But so am I. We are sharing the dream, Natalie. This isn't your imagination."

Natalie stared at him silently, unsure what to think. Was this her mind trying to convince her that this wasn't a dream? Or wasn't all her own dream anyway? And if so, why?

"This is my castle," Valerian said solemnly. "In your dream when I joined you, you had envisioned a dark, gloomy place nothing like the reality, so I thought of my home and brought you here. This isn't your dream, it's our dream."

"So, you just jumped into my dream?" she asked uncertainly.

Valerian sighed and ran a hand through his hair, then straightened his shoulders. "Aileen said you needed time to sort yourself out. I didn't want to give it to you. I thought you should have all the facts first. But she insisted. She also suggested that you would feel less threatened in a shared dream and more likely to listen. So, I left you alone today, hoping that we could talk in our shared dream tonight. And we did. Are," he corrected himself with a crooked smile.

Natalie swallowed, her brain struggling with his words. "But how do I know this is a shared dream? How do I know I'm not just dreaming and making that up?"

Frustration crossed Valerian's face briefly, but then he said, "Well, we could have a code word."

"A code word?"

"Yes. Pick something for me to say when we first see each other while awake, and I'll say it. You'll know then I was here with you in our dream."

"Oh." Natalie smiled faintly. "Yes, that could work."

Valerian nodded and took her hand again, urging her to continue forward as he asked, "What word should we use?"

"Hell, if I know," Natalie said with amusement.

"It should be something no one would normally just say out of the blue," he pointed out.

"Yes," she agreed, and was searching her mind when they stepped out of the woods and into a clearing on the edge of a lake. Natalie stopped walking to gape at the beautiful scene: a sandy beach ahead, cool clear water beyond, and rolling mountains in the background. She was enchanted. "Where are we?"

"My home," he answered, squeezing her hand gently as he peered out over the water with pride.

"Yes, but where is your home?"

"The Highlands of Scotland."

"Highlands," Natalie murmured, and then smiled. "The code word could be Highlands."

"Highlands," he agreed.

They were silent for a minute, simply enjoying the view, and then Natalie glanced at him uncertainly, and said, "Valerian, if we are life mates—"

"We are," he assured her. "If you choose it to be so."

She looked away toward the water again. "But what does that mean? What would happen? What do you want from me?"

"I want . . . you," he finished finally. Taking her hand, Valerian turned her back to face him and cupped her face in his palm. "I don't want to rush you. I know as a mortal this is all happening incredibly quickly, and I do want to give you time to adjust and feel safe and comfortable. But I don't need that time. I know that if the nanos have decided we are life mates, we would be good together. But aside from that . . ." Valerian hesitated, and then admitted, "I think you're amazing, Natalie. You're brilliant, and beautiful, hardworking, and kind. I would be proud if you eventually agreed to marry me. I want to spend my long life with you and Mia. I'd adopt her as my daughter if you were both okay with that, and I'd support and help you both in any way you wish. I'll live at the Shady Pines with you if you'd prefer to finish what you started there,

or we could live in Scotland, or we could divide our
time between the two. I will endeavor to give you
whatever you want. I will live to make you happy.
I would never hurt you, and would give my life for
you without hesitation."

Natalie stared up at him wide-eyed. Every word
he'd said had plucked at her heartstrings. His including Mia had really touched her too. He saw her and
her daughter as the package they were, and accepted
that without issue. But his promise to never hurt
her . . . She wanted so badly to believe it. To believe
him. And to believe this wasn't just a dream she was
having alone.

Caught up in her thoughts as she was, Natalie was
a little startled when he suddenly bent to kiss her, and
at first didn't respond. Unlike the other night, passion
did not suddenly explode and overwhelm her, turning
her into a desperate ball of need. Instead, a slow burn
started as his lips brushed over hers, and she found
herself opening her mouth to him and stepping closer.

A little sigh of pleasure slipped from her lips as his
tongue slid past them and his arms wrapped around
her, drawing her closer still so that their bodies met.
Natalie then wrapped her own arms around his shoulders and actually joined in the kiss, turning the heat
up. Awake or dreaming, the man could kiss. It was
hard to believe he had such skill after seventy years
without indulging in carnal pursuits, and she moaned
and sucked at his tongue when his hands began to
move over her body.

Natalie gasped into his mouth when one hand found

a breast and squeezed her through the thin cloth of her nightgown. Arching into the caress, she clutched at his shoulders, and shifted against him, groaning a "Yes" when his leg slid between both of hers and rubbed against her core.

"Valerian," she gasped in protest when he broke their kiss, but then a surprised grunt left her lips when he scooped her up and carried her a few feet to . . . a bed?

Natalie glanced around with confusion to see that the water and clearing were gone and they were now in a large bedroom decorated in sky blue tones. The bed he'd set her on had dark blue curtains, and that was the last thing she saw before Valerian climbed onto the bed and lowered himself half on top of her.

Natalie wrapped her arms around him again in welcome as he began to kiss her, then moaned and writhed on the bed as he caressed her. He never actually removed his clothes or hers, but suddenly they were gone and she didn't question it, but simply took advantage and began to run her own hands over his body.

Tearing his mouth from hers, Valerian began to nibble his way across her cheek to her ear, and murmured, "I want to make love to you."

"Yes, please," Natalie begged, and his hand immediately began to slide down her stomach.

"Oh God!" she gasped when his fingers slid between her thighs to find and caress her core.

"Do you like that?" he asked, nipping her earlobe now.

"Yes," Natalie panted, her legs squeezing tight around

his hand. She twisted her head on the pillow, wishing he'd kiss her again. But instead, his mouth drifted from her ear, down her neck, and to one breast to claim the nipple.

Natalie moaned and groaned by turn, her body dancing under his attention, and then he let her nipple slip from his mouth and began to kiss a trail down her stomach, following the same path his hand had taken a moment ago. When he reached the top of one thigh, and urged her legs apart, Natalie spread them willingly, and then cried out when his head disappeared between her legs and he began to lash her very center with his tongue.

Gasping, panting, and crying out by turn she twisted her head and then squawked and sat up abruptly when something wet and foul smelling was suddenly in her mouth. Blinking away the sleep now, she looked around in confusion until a whining sound drew her gaze to the dark shape of Sinbad next to the bed. Her bed, in her room.

It didn't take Natalie long to figure out what had happened. She must have been making sounds in her sleep while she was dreaming, maybe even thrashing around a bit in real life as she had been doing in her dream, and Sinbad had gotten distressed thinking there was something wrong and had tried to wake her up. No doubt by licking her face. Hence the foul-smelling wet thing that had landed in her mouth. Sinbad had really bad doggy breath.

Sighing, she reached out to pet the dog. "It's all right, Sin. I'm fine. It was just a dream."

Sinbad leaned his head into the caress as she scratched behind his ears, and then turned to walk back to his bed.

Natalie considered asking if he needed to go outside, but he'd had a potty break before bed, and usually didn't need to go in the middle of the night. Besides, he was already curling up on his bed and settling in.

Sighing, Natalie laid back on the bed and peered into the darkness. She loved Sinbad, but really wished he hadn't woken her up when he had. That dream had been . . . Wow! was all she could think of.

Maybe if she went back to sleep, the dream would pick up right where it had left off, Natalie thought, and then frowned as she became aware of a bad taste in her mouth. She didn't know if it was from moaning and groaning in her sleep and drying her mouth out, or from having Sinbad's tongue lash through it as he woke her up. But since she knew the dog ate dead things when he came across them, she suddenly was rather grossed out that his tongue had landed in her mouth even if only for a second.

Grimacing, Natalie tossed her sheet and blanket aside and slid out of bed to make her way to the bathroom. She kept a glass in there in case she or Mia woke up thirsty in the middle of the night. Unfortunately, she wasn't quite fully awake yet and managed to knock the glass over when she reached for it. It bounced off the tap handle, broke, and rolled into the sink like a drunk rolling off a curb.

Cursing, Natalie grabbed the base of the glass that was still intact, and then began picking up the upper pieces that had broken off. She dropped them into what remained of the base, and then hesitated about what to do with it. Tossing it in the bathroom garbage probably wasn't a good idea. Mia might get into it if she woke up first and came in here. She'd have to take it upstairs and throw it out, Natalie supposed. But she needed to fetch another glass down here anyway, so . . .

Shrugging, she turned and slipped back into the bedroom. A quick glance showed her that Mia and Sinbad were both sleeping, so she tiptoed out of the room. Not wanting to make any sound that might wake the pair, Natalie didn't close the door all the way, but left it cracked open. She then made her way through the dark unfinished basement to the stairs by the glow of the one night-light she'd plugged in by the stairway the first year she'd moved here. Stubbing her toes and stumbling into walls on a journey like this once had been enough to convince her a night-light was needed.

The hallway was dark and silent when she got upstairs. Not wanting to make noise and possibly wake up Valerian, she didn't close the door here all the way either, but left it cracked open and tiptoed up the hall. Natalie did glance through her open office door as she passed, but couldn't make out anything in the darkness. She supposed, though, that Valerian was asleep in there. Even if her dream had just been her own and not a shared one, it was the middle of the night. He would be sleeping.

The kitchen door made a slight squeak as she opened it, and Natalie winced at the sound, but slid inside and let the door close again.

"Natalie?"

She gave a start at the sound of her name and quickly found and flipped on the switch next to the door. Natalie then stood blinking as the lights flashed on. Once her eyes had adjusted to the sudden explosion of brightness, she found herself staring at Valerian, who was at the kitchen sink with a glass in hand. He was also shirtless, wearing only his jeans that were partially undone, revealing black boxers with a white trim that had -*vin Kle*- imprinted on it. Calvin Klein, she thought, and then raised her gaze to his face.

"What were you doing standing here in the dark?" she asked with a little irritation. The man had nearly given her a heart attack, for heaven's sake.

"Sorry. I didn't mean to startle you," he said at once. "I was just getting a glass of water."

Valerian turned the tap on even as he said that, and Natalie started across the room, saying, "Okay, but why didn't you turn the light on?"

"Didn't need it. Night vision." He held the glass under the running water, and then glanced around, smiled, and said, "Highlands."

Natalie froze with disbelief, hardly aware when the already broken glass she was carrying slipped from her suddenly numb fingers and shattered on the floor in front of her. She was vaguely aware of Valerian's concern and that he turned off the tap and rushed to her side. She heard "Wah wah wah" followed by something that included "Cut your foot" and then he was scooping her up off her feet. Natalie stared at him as he carried her over to the table where she and Mia usually had breakfast, but her mind was bouncing around inside her head like a ball in a pinball machine as everything that had happened in her dream now rushed through her mind.

Once he'd set her down, Valerian moved away to clean up the mess she'd made. Natalie watched him, the word *Highlands* echoing through her head.

Dear God, it had been a shared dream. Did that mean all the lovely things he'd said were true? Did he want to spend his life with her? And if so, what was she supposed to do about that? Cripes, he was a vampire, scientific or not. How could they ever have a relationship? And what if he wanted to turn her?

Her thoughts stuttered to a halt, and Natalie blinked when he was suddenly in front of her again. This time she was aware enough to notice his scent reaching out to envelop her. She had no idea if it was cologne or pheromones, but it was damned delicious and she unthinkingly reached out to touch his chest. Her fingers barely grazed his skin before excitement vibrated up her fingers, through her arms, and then shot out to every corner of her body. It was all she did, but it was enough. Valerian was suddenly on her. His mouth claiming hers, his arms encompassing her and pulling her to the edge of the table so that her legs rested on either side of his and their bodies met from the hips up.

Natalie moaned with both need and despair. One part of her mind thought this was a terrible mistake. She was already confused, and this wasn't going to help. But the other part of her mind and every part of her body did not care. Her hands certainly didn't care as they squeezed and kneaded his pecs and biceps before dropping and sliding around to find and squeeze his behind, urging him tighter against her. Her mouth didn't care as she opened to him and kissed him back with a hunger and need that sprang up fully formed and demanding. And her legs didn't care as they wrapped around his upper thighs, trying to pull him closer still.

She felt him tugging at the boatneck of her nightgown, and released his behind to help him pull it over one shoulder and then the other so that it dropped to pool around her waist. Natalie then gasped and shivered as he broke their kiss and leaned back to cover her bared breasts with his hands and knead her excited flesh.

"God, you're beautiful," he growled, watching her face as he caressed her.

Natalie stared back through slitted eyes, her body humming with need, then snaked her hand out to catch him behind the head and pull him down to her. She'd only meant for him to kiss her, and he did, but he also urged her to lie back on the table with his kisses, so that he was leaning over her. She felt him drag her nightgown up so that the hem was tangled around her waist with the top of it, and then his hand was there, between her legs and gliding across her damp flesh.

Natalie cried out into his mouth, her heels digging into the backs of his legs as her hips thrust up into the caress, and then Valerian tugged his mouth away with a curse and dropped his mouth to her shoulder, his hand stilling.

Natalie hesitated then, unsure what was happening. Her body wanted more, *she* wanted more. Was he stopping? Had he lost interest? Well, screw that, she thought suddenly, and withdrew one hand from where it had been clutching at his shoulder, to snake it between them and find his erection through his jeans and boxers. Oh no, he hadn't lost interest. The man was as hard as a rock, and jumped when she rubbed him through the material.

Natalie had to close her eyes as pleasure suddenly shot through her as well at the touch. Egged on by the sensation, she released the hold she had on his other shoulder and quickly pushed his jeans and boxers over his hips, then found him again, this time without the material between them.

They both groaned and jerked as she took him in hand and stroked him. One stroke, and they were both trembling like leaves in a wind. With a second stroke, Natalie was sure she was on the verge of orgasm.

Growling, Valerian straightened, urged her hand out of the way, found her opening, and thrust into her. Natalie screamed at the pleasure that immediately exploded at her center and shot outward, and then grabbed the edges of the table and held on as he thrust into her again. It only took three strokes to push her over the edge. The pleasure that had been beating at her brain for whole seconds now became a tsunami as her body began to shake and quake, almost convulsing, and then the lights shut off in her head.

Twenty-One

Natalie woke up on the sofa in her office. For a minute, she was confused as to what she was doing there. The last thing she remembered—

"Oh shit," she muttered as what had happened in the kitchen filled her mind.

God, she could still smell and taste Valerian, and he'd felt so good, and it had been so hot . . . and then she'd orgasmed and passed out again. But then he'd said that was what happened with life mates. The pleasure was so overwhelming their minds couldn't handle it. Valerian had said that both parties passed out after, but she guessed he must have woken up first and carried her in here. But where was he now? She sat up and peered around.

The office was empty.

Natalie was trying to figure out where he could have gone when Valerian entered the room. He was walking slowly, with his head down, his gaze fixed on a tray he was carrying as the glasses and silverware on it clanked together. He was several feet into the room before he looked up to see that she was awake and sitting up on the couch. A smile immediately claimed his lips.

"Oh hey, hi. You're awake," Valerian greeted her, beaming a smile as he walked around the couch. "Perfect. I brought us food and some of that orange juice and ginger ale stuff, but I wasn't sure about the amount for each so I hope I didn't put too much juice in or something."

Natalie looked him over as he set the tray on the coffee table and began to remove items from it. His pants were back in place and done up, but he'd donned a T-shirt as well. That thought made her peer down at herself and her eyebrows lifted when she saw that the only thing she was wearing was the blanket covering her. She had no idea where her nightgown was.

"Your nightgown fell off when I picked you up off the table. I fetched it after I laid you on the couch. It's folded and on your desk."

"Oh," Natalie mumbled. Pressing the blanket back against her body and ignoring her embarrassed blush, she tried for nonchalance as she asked, "So, you said it was shared pleasure . . . and that means you passed out too?"

His lips twitched and he turned to look at her with a plate in hand. "Is that your way of asking if I orgasmed?"

Grimacing, she nodded. "Both times I've woken up

somewhere else after. First in my bed, and then this time here on the couch. If we both passed out . . ."

"I did orgasm and pass out," Valerian assured her. "I just woke up first. I have no idea why. It could be because I'm immortal, but nobody's ever mentioned it as being a factor, and I haven't taken a survey of other immortal life mates to see who woke up first."

Natalie considered that and then asked, "Are possible life mates always mortal?"

"No. Immortals can be life mates to each other. There are less problems when that happens." When her eyebrows rose at that, Valerian explained, "I mean, because both immortals know about life mates, they usually simply accept it, and there is little chance either will have to be convinced of how wonderful the relationship will be. With a mortal . . . well, there is the whole having to explain about immortals, and convince them that while similar to vampires, we aren't vampires and so on."

Natalie nodded, thinking that was exactly what was happening with her.

Valerian sat down on the edge of the couch where her legs were still resting and met her gaze. "I know you thought it was only a dream when I said what I said earlier, but I really was there, and I meant every word of it. I respect and admire you a good deal, Natalie. I also think you're incredibly beautiful. I would never hurt you. I would never be unfaithful. I would give my life for you. I would be pleased to claim and raise Mia as my own daughter. And I would be happy to live wherever you wanted."

Expression solemn, he added, "I understand this is a big decision, and I won't try to rush you, but please allow me to remain in your life while you make it. I have complete faith in the nanos. If they chose you, that's enough for me to know we could be exceedingly happy together. I've seen it too often. And you've seen the results too."

Natalie blinked with surprise at that. "I have?"

"Yes. Dani and Decker are life mates, as are Uncle Julius and Aunt Marguerite, and Anders and Valerie, and—"

"Who are Anders and Valerie?" she interrupted.

"Oh, actually, I guess you haven't met them yet. Anders is here patrolling the grounds, but Valerie only dropped by to take him back to my house to sleep. She's spending the night there with him and then returning home early tomorrow morning for work. She's a vet," he explained.

"Oh," Natalie murmured, and then asked, "So were Dani and Decker both immortals?" She didn't know about his aunt and uncle, but from what she'd seen, Dani and Decker did have a wonderful relationship. You could just see their love when they were together.

"No. Dani was mortal."

"And Decker used his one turn on her?" she guessed.

"Actually, no, she was turned by a rogue," Valerian admitted with a small frown, and seemed to want to say more, but then dropped the subject and said, "My point is, I know we could be happy together, but I understand if you need time and I'd like to actually date you, so you can get to know me better to help you decide."

"Date," Natalie murmured, the word almost sounding alien to her. It had been eight years since she'd dated, and even then she hadn't done it much. She'd been too obsessed with her career. If a man couldn't fit into her schedule, and tried to convince her to fit his, she turned him down. Now . . . well, until Valerian and the others had arrived, she'd had even less time for dating.

"Yes, date," Valerian said, and guessing by the way his lips were twitching with amusement, he knew it wasn't something she'd considered much. "I know you're a very busy woman, but perhaps we could have little picnics with Mia here on the grounds. You have to eat, and it's probably safer to stay here where the men are standing guard. Or," he added, "we could have more game nights like the other night with Aileen and Tybo. I really enjoyed that."

He didn't give her a chance to say yes or no, but then added, "Speaking of eating, I made us some sandwiches."

Valerian picked up one of the plates off the tray and turned to offer it to her, saying apologetically, "It's just peanut butter and jelly. I considered using your air fryer and making proper food, but I wasn't sure what was needed for the restaurant tomorrow and what I could use, so just stuck with PB&J." He shrugged slightly. "It was always a hit with Aileen."

Natalie smiled at his expression as she accepted the plate. "I love peanut butter and jelly. Thank you."

His smile suggesting he didn't believe that, he picked up his plate and settled next to her when she moved her legs for him.

They ate in silence at first and Natalie found herself thinking about what he'd said. She liked that he was including Mia in his suggestions. He wasn't ignoring the fact that she came as a package deal. If she were being honest with herself, she actually liked the idea of dating too, but it was also scary as hell. Because despite the fact that he was a vam—immortal, Natalie corrected herself midthought, and then tried again. Despite that, she did like him, more with every encounter. And that game night he'd mentioned? It hadn't been a date, but had been surprisingly revealing. During Cards Against Humanity, she'd learned they had a similar sense of humor when every time the answer she'd picked had been his, while the ones he'd picked had been hers. They'd been partners during Codenames, and he'd had no problem guessing which card or cards she was giving the clue for, and again the reverse had been the same when he'd given clues. Every time. It was as if their minds worked in sync.

On top of that, Valerian was polite, caring, and good with Mia. Add the mind-blowing—albeit quick—sex they'd had twice now and Natalie suspected she could fall for this guy hard, if she hadn't done so already, and that was scary as hell. Because he had fangs and drank blood.

Is that really so bad? Natalie asked herself now. They claimed they didn't bite mortals; in fact, Valerian's job was actually to hunt down immortals who had gone rogue and did bite mortals, so . . . So what? another part of her mind intruded to ask. Now she was so desperate to get laid that a vampire was looking good?

Natalie grimaced at the inner comment and countered that at least she knew that about him. She'd been married to Devin for four years and hadn't known he had another wife. If fangs and the occasional need for blood were Valerian's biggest flaws, it beat out a bigamist any day.

"What happened to wake you up?"

Natalie glanced at him with confusion, and then realized he was talking about what must have been her sudden disappearance from their shared dream. "Sinbad. I must have been making noises or something."

"Ah." Valerian smiled. "He's a good dog. You've trained him well."

"Yeah. Well, it wasn't hard. He's a guard dog by nature. His breed was bred to guard sheep," she explained.

Valerian nodded, and then reached out to brush her cheek next to her lips. "You have a little peanut butter right here."

Natalie froze in response to the shock of excitement that immediately shot through her when his fingers brushed her skin.

She thought Valerian might have experienced the same thing since he immediately closed his eyes and sat completely still, as if almost afraid to move.

"Playing with fire," he muttered with a little exasperation, and then removed his hand and opened his eyes. "When awake, I can't even touch you without wanting to—"

His words died abruptly when Natalie reached out to touch his face. She knew she shouldn't but simply couldn't resist, and ran two fingers over his lips as he spoke, and then let them rest there when he stopped. She loved his lips. It was that simple. She wanted to feel if the lower lip was as soft as it looked to her, and it was, she thought, and then gasped when his lips opened and he ran his tongue over the pads of her fingers.

Yeah, vampire or not she wanted this man, Natalie acknowledged to herself. Just the rasp of his tongue over her fingertips had her reacting like Pavlov's dogs. Only rather than salivating, liquid was pooling low in her belly and making its way to where it would be most useful.

Squeezing her legs together as he sucked her fingers into his mouth, Natalie closed her eyes briefly, and then opened them and reached for his T-shirt. She wanted to touch him. She wanted to run her hands over his chest and—Her thoughts died as Valerian realized what she was doing and took over the task, dragging his T-shirt off over his head. He had to release her fingers from his mouth to do it, and Natalie sat with her hands clenched in her lap, eyes wide as inch after beautiful inch of his naked stomach and chest were revealed to her.

The man was perfect. Wide shoulders narrowing down to a trim waist that just seemed to make his pectoral muscles look huge in comparison. She simply couldn't resist touching that pale flesh and almost expected it to feel like the marble it looked like, but it was flesh and bone, and she sighed as her fingers ran over him and excitement as well as pleasure ran through her. His pleasure, she knew. The shared pleasure he'd told her about. It made her want to experience more, and she let her hands drift down across his flat stomach toward the top of his jeans. Valerian caught her hand then, and leaned forward to kiss her.

Like before, all hell broke loose inside of Natalie at his kiss. Her body went crazy, her nipples popping up like a pair of jack-in-the-boxes, and an ache starting between her legs as she swelled and dampened there. But it was the passion it stirred in her that was most notable. While the dream sex they'd started had built up slowly, this was far from slow. She was immediately almost mindless with need and couldn't get enough . . . of anything. She wanted to touch him everywhere, wanted their naked bodies pressed together from toes to head, never wanted him to stop kissing her.

Natalie could hear her own moans, groans, gasps, and little mewling sounds she'd never before heard come from her mouth as she arched and writhed against him. She was so caught up in the sensations he was causing in her she never noticed when he tugged the blanket away from her body and left it to slither to the floor as he covered her breasts with his hands. The first touch brought a cry of startled pleasure from her that his mouth muffled, and then he released her breasts, caught her at the waist, and lifted her to straddle his lap so that he could claim first one nipple and then the other with his lips.

Finding the sensations roaring through her almost unbearable, Natalie clutched at his shoulders and flung her head back, her hips shifting over him and simply adding to the maelstrom of feelings. Her heart was hammering, her breaths coming in short, shallow gasps, and she was beginning to fear she'd faint again without doing more than run her fingers over his chest, so she reached down between them to unsnap and un- zip his pants. Natalie snaked her hand inside the heavy material of his jeans to tug his underwear toward her, freeing his erection. Natalie sighed into his mouth with relief when it sprung up and right into her palm.

She closed her fingers around him and stroked him precisely once, and then froze as a tsunami of pleasure rolled over her, and her body began to convulse with her orgasm.

It was the ringing of his phone that woke Valerian. Opening his eyes, he blinked sleepily and then peered down at Natalie in his lap. They'd done the whole im- mortal postcoital faint thing, or maybe it was a during- coital faint since they really didn't get to enjoy a full orgasm, but passed out midway through because of how overwhelming it was. Although they hadn't actually got to coitus this time, he recalled.

When his phone rang again, Valerian started search-

ing for his phone. It was in his pocket. With Natalie in
his lap he couldn't get to it. Lifting her, he stood and
laid her on the couch, then tugged up his boxers and
pants and did up the snap to keep them in place before
going for his phone.

Noting that the caller was Tybo, Valerian hit the
button to answer even as he reached down to grab up
the blanket from the floor and quickly covered Natalie
with it.

"Val?" Tybo asked when he didn't speak.

"Yeah," Valerian said in a whisper as he straightened from covering Natalie. He then moved toward
the rolling shade with bookshelves painted on it so he
wouldn't wake Natalie as he asked, "What's up?"

"That's what I was about to ask you."

Valerian's eyebrows rose at the unexpected response.
"What do you mean?"

"Uh, well . . ." There was a pause and then Tybo
suggested, "Maybe you should go check on Natalie."

"What?" Valerian turned to peer at the woman
asleep on the couch, and almost smiled at how sweet
she looked in sleep.

"The kid just toddled out of the clubhouse holding
on to the polar bear by his fur, and I'm pretty sure
Natalie wouldn't let—"

Valerian didn't hear anymore, he was heading for the
door to the hallway at a dead run. Dear God, this was
exactly why he hadn't wanted to indulge in life mate
sex to win Natalie. It left Mia alone and unattended.
But what the hell was she doing up in the middle of the
night?

That question was answered as soon as he started into the dining room and saw early-morning sunlight streaming in through the windows. They'd obviously been unconscious for several hours. It had been a little after midnight when Natalie had come into the kitchen, and two thirty when he'd woken up and carried her into her office. He'd then made the peanut butter and jelly sandwiches, and they'd only managed to eat half a sandwich each before attacking each other again. All of that couldn't have taken more than fifteen or twenty minutes. Which meant that he and Natalie had been out for a good four hours, since the clock on the wall read 7:04. And who knew how long they could have continued to remain asleep had Tybo not called?

Nope. Nope, nope, nope. Indulging in life mate sex was now off the table. He couldn't risk Mia again like that. They'd just got lucky that the boys were here at the moment to catch her wandering off. Had they been alone . . .

Valerian didn't want to even think about that and merely ground his teeth together as he stopped abruptly at the clubhouse door . . . that was still closed and locked.

Lifting the phone back to his ear with one hand while he unlocked the door with the other, Valerian barked, "Ty?"

"Still here," his partner assured him.

"How the hell did Mia get out? The door is still locked. Or was," he added as he opened it.

"The doggy door. Sinbad came out and she crawled right out after him," Tybo answered with amusement.

"What doggy door?" Valerian asked with amazement, his gaze moving over the solid door he was opening.

"It's in the wall behind the counter," Tybo told him. "I suspect it used to be a milk door or something in the days when they had delivery and the clubhouse was just a little farmhouse."

Valerian turned to the counter and leaned over to look behind it.

"Sweet Jesus," he muttered, taking in the little wooden door. It was a foot off the ground and about two feet in height and a foot and a half wide. There was a dead bolt on it that probably made it at least a little secure when in place, but it wasn't engaged now. Mia must have opened it.

Well, that wasn't safe, he thought with irritation, and how the hell had they missed it? Straightening, he opened the screen door and stepped outside, then looked at the dog/milk door again. A table and chairs situated in front of it had helped conceal it, he saw.

Shaking his head, Valerian left it for now and turned to look for Tybo, spotting him at once. The younger immortal was standing on the grass on the other side of the railing that ran around the deck. Valerian didn't bother with the stairs, but walked to the railing and vaulted over it, landing right next to his partner.

"Morning," Tybo said with amusement, taking in his attire. Valerian had no shoes, no shirt, and his jeans were snapped up but his zipper was down. He suspected his hair was probably also a mess, since Tybo grinned when he looked at it.

"I was sleeping," Valerian growled, reaching down to quickly do up his zipper as the other man walked around him before returning to his side.

"Uh-huh," Tybo said. "And Natalie?"

"She's sleeping," he said shortly.

"And were the two of you sleeping together, or did someone else put those scratches on your back?" Tybo asked conversationally.

Valerian glanced swiftly over his shoulder, but there were no marks. Tybo was messing with him, he realized, and snapped, "Where's Mia?"

When the other man pointed toward the path to the eighteenth hole, Valerian saw the little girl and her dog. She had one hand on Sinbad's back for balance, and was toddling along, stopping every few feet to pick a flower from the edging of mums that lined the path.

"I was going to fetch her back in, but Sinbad growled any time I got near her," Tybo told him with a wry smile. "Let's hope you have better luck."

Valerian grunted and started forward, but hadn't taken more than a couple of steps when a gunshot rang out and Mia and Sinbad both went down. He didn't even think; Valerian shouted and ran for the girl, planning to throw himself on top of her. But she straightened again just before he reached her, another flower in her hand. It was as she added it to her growing bouquet that she noticed Sinbad on the ground, dark red blood on his white fur. Even as Mia began to scream, Valerian was snatching her up and spinning to carry her back toward the clubhouse, sheltering her with his body as much as he could. He passed Tybo on the way. The man was heading over to help Sinbad, but had his phone out and was talking rapidly as he looked around, trying to spot the source of the shot.

Valerian had nearly reached the stairs to the deck when he spotted Colle coming around the corner. He'd obviously seen everything from the camera screens in the RV and had rushed out to help. Valerian immediately changed direction to meet the man.

"Take her to the RV and try to calm her down," Valerian growled, passing the still screaming child to him.

"Shouldn't I take her into the clubhouse to Natalie?" Colle asked with surprise.

Valerian shook his head. "I don't want to wake her until I know how bad Sinbad is. I don't want her any more upset than necessary."

Nodding, Colle turned to carry the little girl back the way he'd come. Valerian followed him to the corner to watch until the man had Mia safely inside the RV and then turned to run back to where Tybo was kneeling over Sinbad.

"How is he?" Valerian asked, dropping to his haunches beside the other man.

"I'm not sure," Tybo admitted, and then barked into the phone. "The shot came from the back corner of the yard, closest to the eighteenth hole."

Leaving him to his call, Valerian urged the hand Tybo had on Sinbad's side away to see the wound, and then quickly covered it with his own hand to try to stop or at least slow the bleeding. In the quick glance he'd got, it looked like Sinbad had taken the bullet in the upper leg or shoulder, which might not normally be deadly, but it was bleeding pretty bad, and Valerian was worried that an artery had been hit.

"I need everyone to converge on that area and start searching. Don't let the bastard slip past you," Tybo growled into his phone, and then ended the call even as Valerian reached for his own phone. "Who are you calling?"

"Anders," Valerian said grimly. "I'm hoping Valerie hasn't left yet."

"Right. She's a vet. Good thinking," Tybo muttered, eyeing the back of the property.

Valerian punched in Anders's number, but muttered, "What the hell is going on? The Angel-Maker has never gone after children before."

"He didn't," Tybo said with surprise. "He shot the dog."

"He hit the dog, but he was aiming for Mia," Valerian said grimly as he listened to his call ringing through. "He only missed her because Mia bent down to pick a flower."

Cursing, Tybo pulled out his phone again as Valerian began to speak to Anders.

Twenty-Two

Natalie woke up on the couch again, completely naked except for the blanket covering her *again*, and thought this was becoming a habit. Shaking her head at the thought, she sat up and glanced around, but *again*, Valerian was nowhere in sight. Her gaze sought out the clock on the shelf, and her eyes widened with surprise when she saw that it was after seven. It was Tuesday, another slow day here at Shady Pines, but Natalie would usually be feeding Mia and prepping for the breakfast crowd by now.

That thought in mind, Natalie got up and wrapped the blanket around herself before recalling that Alex was cooking for her again today. It was the last day the other chef would be taking over the chore. Alex had offered to carry on for a couple more days, but Natalie had refused, assuring her that she was fine now. She didn't want to take advantage of the woman after her kindness in helping out.

Stifling a yawn, Natalie hurried around the couch and headed for the door. She needed to shower, change, and get Mia and Sinbad upstairs and fed. Actually, she thought, maybe she should throw on some clothes and let Sinbad out to potty first, then take her shower and get both her daughter and the dog breakfast. Alex should be here by then.

Satisfied with that plan, Natalie hurried into the hall, but slowed when she saw that the basement door was open. She'd left it cracked open last night, she recalled, but now it was wide open. Wondering if Valerian or someone else had gone downstairs for something, she left it open and flicked on the basement light as she started down.

A grimace crossed her face as she reached the bottom and made her way across the unfinished section of the basement. She really hated this part of the building. It was cold and kind of creepy. But it was only used for storage, so putting the money into throwing up walls and whatnot to make it prettier had seemed a waste when she was saving everything she could for the renovations and additions.

Telling herself those renos would start soon, Natalie continued on to the bedroom. Like the basement door, the bedroom door was now wide open as well. It gave her pause and then had her moving a little more quickly when she saw it.

Natalie's heart nearly stopped when she stepped

into the room and saw Mia's empty bed. Then she saw that Sinbad's bed was empty too and relaxed. The dog wouldn't have let anyone near her that he didn't know, and the fact that both her daughter and Sinbad, as well as Valerian, were gone meant the three were probably together. In fact, she wouldn't be surprised if Valerian was in the kitchen with Mia, giving her cereal.

Except that Sinbad hadn't been in the hall outside the kitchen when she'd left the office, Natalie thought. She shrugged that concern away. Aileen had taken them out to the RV yesterday morning for breakfast, to keep them out of the way. Perhaps Valerian had done the same thing today. Which was really sweet, Natalie thought as she dropped the blanket she'd wrapped around herself and headed into the bathroom for a quick shower.

Thoughts of Valerian and how sweet he was followed her into the shower and Natalie grimaced at her sudden change in tune. Yesterday, she'd been horrified and thinking him a monster. Today . . . Well, he was still a vampire, and that should completely repulse her, but it didn't seem so bad this morning. Or more likely, after last night, she acknowledged. Sex with the man was just so . . . soooooo. Her body tingled just at the memory. It was so amazing, and overwhelming and awesome.

And addictive. Even now she wanted him again, and was wondering when they'd next have the chance to be alone. But aside from that, just look how he was with Mia. Entertaining and looking after her daughter while Natalie had been sick after the poisoning. Even doing the Hokey Pokey with her, for heaven's sake. Would a monster do the Hokey Pokey?

"Not hardly," Natalie said to herself as she shampooed her hair. So, he had fangs and needed blood to survive. Like Aileen had said, they were kind of like hemophiliacs, just with fangs that had helped them get the blood they needed before blood banks had arrived on the scene. She could deal with that if it meant a caring father figure for Mia, and a sweet, considerate partner for her who gave her crazy wild monkey sex.

"Oh yeah, you've got it bad," Natalie said to herself with dry amusement as she rinsed her hair. And she didn't care. She wanted Valerian. She liked Valerian. She might even love him a little . . . or more. There was absolutely nothing about him that she disliked other than that whole vampire thing, and Natalie was softening on that too. So . . . dating sounded delightful. Picnics with Mia, game nights with Tybo and Aileen, maybe even a movie night if she could work it into her schedule. Or maybe she should change her schedule a bit. She gave everyone else Mondays and Tuesdays off. Maybe next season she would close altogether on those days, Natalie thought as she turned her attention to washing her body.

The thought was almost a startling one. Her, Miss Driven-to-work-herself-to-death, closing up the golf course and restaurant for two days a week? Shocking.

Her counselor once suggested that she worked so much to avoid thinking about her past and her losses, or perhaps even as punishment for marrying an already married man. She now wondered if that weren't true. If so, then apparently she was finally accepting and getting past her losses, or had decided she'd punished herself enough. Whatever the case, it felt good to make this decision. She needed to take care of herself to be a good mom, and she deserved a life as well.

Yep, Natalie decided, she was going to agree to date Valerian, and if things continued as they were, she'd probably agree to a life with him. Whatever that entailed, she thought with a grimace. He had mentioned about turning a life mate, so imagined he'd want to do that to her. Natalie just wasn't sure how she felt about it. Although, really, it was just a medical thing. Wasn't it? They'd probably give her a shot of the nanos and send her on her way like they did with flu shots.

Maybe she should just agree to be his life mate now, she thought suddenly. He'd said that life mates were happy and were never unfaithful, and Natalie did believe that she was a life mate for him. She felt his pleasure during sex, and had shared dreams with him, after all. That had to be pretty special. And if she did agree to be his life mate, she wouldn't be depending on her own judgment in this instance, which had already proven flawed with Devin. She would be putting her faith in the nanos' choice, since he'd said it was believed that the nanos chose the life mate. That was actually something of a relief to her since her man-picker had failed her so miserably before.

Taking all of that into account, why wait? As addictive as sex with him was, Natalie suspected he'd be here every night anyway.

Considering that, she rinsed herself off, and then turned off the water and opened the shower door to grab a towel. She dried herself off as she left the bathroom and crossed to her dresser, then dropped the towel and pulled out underwear and a bra. She'd managed to don those and was looking through her closet when she heard a thud from the storage area.

Pausing, Natalie turned to the bedroom door, wondering what that had been. Someone getting something from the food stocks stacked on the shelves in the unfinished side of the basement seemed the most likely answer. When she didn't hear anything else, she decided it must be, and turned back to pull a pretty white summer dress out of her closet. Her Shady Pines shirts and jeans had pretty much been the only thing she'd worn for the last three years since moving here. They were her work uniform, and Natalie was always working. But today she wasn't, and felt like wearing something prettier and more feminine.

Not to impress Valerian, of course. Oh no, she thought mockingly, knowing that was exactly what she was doing. Because seriously, who didn't want to look attractive for their man? Natalie pulled the dress on and quickly did up the buttons that ran down the front, only to undo the top two again and peer at herself. Was that too low? Too obvious? She didn't think so.

Natalie looked down at the dress, imagining how convenient it would be for sex. Tug her panties aside and . . . voilà! Fast and furious strikes again, she thought, and shook her head at herself. Before Valerian, if anyone had told her she'd enjoy two-minute escapades in the bedroom, Natalie would have laughed in their face. But now she was wet just at the thought of it.

"Ah, you're pathetic, Nat," she murmured to herself, and then added, "But happy," as she walked to the bedroom door and opened it.

She'd taken two steps out of the room before spotting the young man by the stairs. Stopping, she stared at him blankly.

"Timothy? What are you doing back at work? You should be with your family at a time like this," she said, and then moved forward to catch him in a quick hug. Looking over his shoulder as she did, she saw the shifted boxes and open cellar door under the stairs even as she whispered, "I'm so sorry about your father."

"You should be."

Natalie blinked in surprise at his words, and then pulled back to look down when something poked her sharply in the stomach. For one minute she just stared at the knife handle sticking out of the front of her dress and the blood beginning to soak the white cloth. And then she stumbled back, her gaze lifting to Timothy with confusion. "I don't understand. Why—?"

"Because you killed my father, you whore," he said furiously.

"He's going to be all right."

Valerian breathed a sigh of relief at that announcement from Valerie as she examined Sinbad.

"You did a good job of stopping the bleeding," Valerie praised.

"Lots of practice with field surgery back in the day," he said quietly.

She nodded. "Well, I suspect you saved his life. But I need to take him to the nearest animal hospital to remove the bullet and patch him up."

"There's a veterinary hospital about twenty minutes away in Glencoe," Valerian said as he bent to scoop up Sinbad. "But I don't know the exact address."

"I'll look it up on my phone and punch it into my GPS," Valerie assured him. "It'll be fine."

"Do you want one of the men to go with you to carry him in?" Valerian asked as they walked to her car in the parking lot. Fortunately, Valerie had still been at his house when he'd called Anders. She'd come at once, managing to get there in only a couple of minutes.

"Oh please," Valerie said with a snort. "I'm immortal too, you know. I can lift him no problem."

"I know you can, but should you?" he asked solemnly, thinking of the don't-attract-attention rule.

"Right," she said with a sigh. "I'm not supposed to show people I'm super strong. Fine, if you can do without one of the men, I suppose I'd better take one."

Valerian was just worrying about whether he should risk reducing the men he had here when Tybo said, "Lucian's sending everyone back from the house to help hunt for the shooter. They should be here any minute; we could send one of them with her."

"Good idea," Valerian agreed as he waited for Valerie to open the back of her SUV so he could lay

Sinbad inside. The dog was asleep now. Valerie had given him a sedative first thing so that she could examine his wound without getting bit. He suspected it was seeing the way Tybo had had to hold the dog's muzzle closed and away from him as Valerian had done what he could for the animal that had convinced her a sedative would be smart.

"And here they come," Tybo said a moment later as Valerian eased Sinbad onto the blanket Valerie had laid out in the back of the vehicle for him.

Straightening now, he turned to see several SUVs and one car barreling up the driveway toward them. Focusing on the car, he frowned, not recognizing the vehicle.

"Is that a customer?" Tybo asked beside him.

"I don't know," Valerian admitted, and asked, "Has anyone spotted our shooter?"

Tybo shook his head. "They'd call if they had. But every last man on the property is searching the tree line behind the clubhouse. They'll spread out from there if they don't find anything."

Valerian grunted at that, and then focused on the car again. While the SUVs were turning into the larger visitor's parking lot, the car was continuing on to the employee parking lot. Nope, not the employee parking lot, he realized when the car drove right onto the grass in front of the clubhouse and a woman in a business jacket and skirt jumped out and ran to the front door of the building and tried to open it.

"Well, this is interesting," Tybo commented.

"Hmm," Valerian muttered, and headed over to stop

the woman from smashing a fist through the window as she began hammering on it when it wouldn't open.

"Is there something I can help you with?" Valerian asked as he neared her.

She whirled around at his question, her expression at first panicked. But then she took a deep breath, forced herself to calm, and said, "I need to speak to Natalie Daniels. I believe she owns and runs Shady Pines?"

"You mean Natalie Moncreif," Valerian said, his gaze narrowing on the woman as he slipped into her thoughts.

"I—Yes, yes, of course, I'm sorry. I forgot she took back her maiden name. I just—I really need to talk to her," she said almost desperately.

Valerian was silent as he read her thoughts, and then asked grimly, "To warn her about your son, Anthony?"

The woman gave a start of surprise at his words. "How do you know about Anthony?"

"Who's Anthony?" Tybo asked next to him.

"Anthony Daniels is Devin Daniels's only surviving son," Valerian explained, having read the knowledge from the woman's mind.

"Natalie's dead not-husband Devin?" Tybo asked, obviously having heard about Natalie's nonmarriage from someone.

Probably Colle and Alasdair, he thought, and said, "Yes. This is Devin's wife, Sheila."

Tybo gave a low whistle, and then turned to the woman. "So, what do you want with Natalie? If you plan on giving her hell for marrying your husband, you can just shuffle on. It's not her fault your husband was a bigamist."

"I know that," she said wearily. "And I have no intention of giving her hell. I need to warn her. I'm afraid Anthony . . ." She paused, looking torn, but Valerian had already read the worries in her mind.

"He stole an experimental drone from a tech company your family owns and you're afraid he's going to use it to hurt Natalie." Ignoring her shocked expression, he turned to Tybo and added meaningfully, "They're trying to make an armed drone that can shoot at static and moving targets from the air, like the ones the Israelis are developing."

"So, we're not looking for a person, but a drone, and our rogue here isn't the Angel-Maker but a mortal?" Tybo growled.

"The Angel-Maker?" Sheila asked suddenly. "Anthony was obsessed with the news stories about that guy. He read everything written about him, including the junk on the internet, half of which probably wasn't true."

Valerian shared a glance with Tybo, and the other man said, "He was probably hoping the Angel-Maker would take the blame."

"Yeah," Valerian sighed.

"This Anthony kid could be operating the drone from anywhere," Tybo pointed out, and then asked Sheila, "How close does the operator have to be to the drone to control it?"

She hesitated, and then shook her head unhappily.

"I'm sorry. I don't know. I don't have much to do with that project. It's just one of many companies we own. I'd never even been there before this morning. The only reason I was called in was because the theft was caught on camera and one of the security guards recognized the thief as my son. The guard used to work security at my husband's office and recognized Anthony from when he used to visit his dad there."

Nodding grimly, Tybo pulled out his phone and walked away, punching in numbers.

Valerian turned back to Sheila Daniels. He'd read from her mind that she really didn't hold any ill will against Natalie for marrying Devin. She placed the blame squarely where it belonged, on her dead husband's shoulders. Her son, however, didn't feel the same way. He'd become obsessed with Natalie after learning about her. Hating her for "luring his father away from their family" and upset at the possibility that Mia might have a right to half of his inheritance.

Sheila had ignored his obsession at first, hoping that eventually he'd get over it. She'd been wrong. Without her knowledge, the moment he'd gained his inheritance on his twenty-first birthday this last spring, Anthony had hired a private detective to track down Natalie. But thanks to her having changed back to her maiden name, it had taken until the middle of this summer for the detective to find her.

That, or he'd just claimed that to milk more money out of the job, Valerian thought. Whatever the case, the moment he had the information, Anthony had taken off. Not knowing that he'd hired a detective, and tracked down Natalie, Sheila hadn't worried at first. She'd thought he was just traveling and partying as the young do. But his continued absence had begun to bother her, and a week ago she'd searched his room at home and found the detective's report.

She'd spent days debating what to do about it. But last night there was a break-in at the tech company that was one of many businesses the family owned. When security had called her in at two o'clock this morning and shown her the security camera video of her son stealing the latest prototype of the rifle-bearing drone, Sheila had panicked. She'd suspected he would use it to try to hurt Natalie, and get himself arrested in the process. She'd rushed back to her home to get the address of Shady Pines from the detective's report, and then had driven straight here to warn her.

A little late, Valerian thought grimly, because he was pretty damned sure that the rifle-bearing drone was what had shot at Mia but hit Sinbad. Anthony was trying to take out his half sister.

"I have the men looking for a drone now as well as a young man," Tybo announced grimly, returning to his side. He glanced from Valerian to Sheila Daniels and asked, "What are we going to do about her?"

"We let her talk to Natalie," Valerian decided. He knew Natalie carried a lot of shame and guilt for marrying Devin Daniels. He could only think it would be good for her to hear that the first Mrs. Daniels didn't blame her for their husband's bigamy. Maybe it would help her heal.

Turning, he glanced toward Valerie's SUV to see

her just pulling away with Decker in the vehicle with her. Relieved to know Sinbad would be operated on soon, he turned back to Sheila Daniels.

"Come with me and we'll go find Natalie," Valerian said, and started around the building toward the side entrance. His gaze moved to the trees as he walked, and he could see men moving through them, searching the ground and the air for a drone. Valerian was just grateful they weren't being shot at. Not that it would kill any of them, but it would be an inconvenience. He supposed this meant only Mia was his target.

And Natalie too, Valerian realized as he led Sheila Daniels into the clubhouse. If Anthony had poisoned the wine, he hadn't been targeting Mia there. Two-year-olds didn't drink wine.

"Oh!"

Valerian turned to see that Sheila Daniels had stopped just inside the door and was staring at a corkboard full of pictures on the wall above the snack racks. Moving back to her side, he saw there were a couple of flyers advertising specials, and a whole lot of pictures tacked to it. Pictures of customers golfing and diners in the restaurant, as well as pictures of the kitchen staff, Roy and Timothy washing the golf carts, and Natalie and Mia riding a lawn mower.

"That's my son, Anthony," Sheila said with quiet horror. "Why is he wearing a Shady Pines shirt?"

Valerian stared at the picture of Timothy and Roy as she pointed to it, and felt the skin on the back of his neck crawl.

"He's been working here for two months. This past

weekend he called and said his father had died in a car accident and he needed to help out his family so wouldn't be back," Valerian told her grimly.

Sheila Daniels pulled her hand back, her expression frightened. "What is he doing?"

Valerian didn't respond. They both knew what he was doing. He could see it there in her mind. She just didn't want to admit it to herself.

Turning, he continued across the upper dining area. He'd left Natalie asleep in the office. Naked, Valerian recalled, and suspected she wouldn't be happy to meet Sheila Daniels in that state.

"Wait here," he said in the hall outside of Natalie's office. Thinking he'd probably have to send her back to the dining room so Natalie could go downstairs and get dressed, he hurried across the room to the couch. But when he walked around in front of it, Natalie was gone.

She must have got up already, he realized. She was probably downstairs dressing. Valerian supposed he'd have to sit Sheila in the dining room and go look for Natalie. He walked back out into the hall, but Sheila Daniels wasn't there. Frowning, he headed back into the dining room, but she wasn't there either. Scowling now, he walked to the exit door and stepped out onto the deck. Tybo was talking on his phone, but when he saw Valerian, he said, "Hang on," then pressed the phone to his chest and told him, "They found the drone."

Valerian merely nodded, and asked, "Where's Sheila Daniels?"

Tybo's eyebrows flew up. "She went inside with you."

"She didn't come back out?" Valerian asked sharply.

Tybo shook his head.

Cursing, he spun on his heel and hurried back inside, aware that Tybo was now following him.

"Your father?" Natalie shook her head with confusion. "Your father just died in a car accident. I didn't even know him. I—" She peered down at the knife again, and put her hand to her stomach, careful not to touch or nudge the knife itself. It had barely hurt when he'd stabbed her, but it did now with a sharp burning sensation that was increasing with every breath she took. Natalie was starting to shake too, her legs trembling and threatening to give out on her. And there was a lot of blood, spreading in a circle on her white dress like a blooming red rose as her life blood ran out.

"My name is Anthony Daniels," Timothy said coldly.

"Daniels?" Natalie echoed with bewilderment, raising bleary eyes to peer at him again.

"Devin Daniels was my father," Timothy told her, and then spat, "He was fucking married, but you just had to shake your ass in front of him and lure him into marrying you too, huh? Hoping for a big payday, were you?" he asked with disgust. "Well, there's no money for you and your little bastard, bitch. I'm putting you both in the grave with him. Where is Mia?"

Natalie shook her head. Her vision was blurring to

the point she couldn't make out his features anymore. He was just an unfocused blob before her. She was panting, and breathing was becoming hard, beginning to hurt, yet the wound was nowhere near her lungs so she didn't understand why it should. But then her thought processes were slowing too. It felt like her brain was full of cotton, or maybe mud. She couldn't seem to understand what was happening. Timothy was Anthony? Devin's son. Why did he want Mia?

"Never mind, I'll find her myself," Timothy/Anthony growled, and suddenly stepped forward and yanked the knife from her stomach.

Natalie wanted to shriek in agony, but didn't have the breath for it, and simply dropped to her knees, gasping for air and clutching at her stomach as blood began to pour out as if a tap had opened.

"Anthony!"

Natalie lifted her head to see Timothy hesitating with his knife raised as if about to plunge it into her chest.

"Put down the knife, Anthony."

Natalie followed the voice and peered at what looked like a blonde woman on the stairs.

"She's a whore!" Timothy spat. "She ruined our family! Dad died because of her and her whelp! They both deserve to die."

"No, she doesn't," the woman snapped. "She was as much a victim as anyone. She didn't know he was married."

"So what? I'm supposed to just be okay with this bitch and her daughter taking my money?" Timothy growled, lowering his knife and turning on the woman with fury. "I heard you and grandfather talking about giving her and her brat money. *My* fucking money. I'm the son and legal heir."

"Oh, Anthony," the woman said, sounding weary, and then there was silence except for the sound of footsteps and Natalie opened eyes she hadn't realized she'd closed and found that she'd somehow fallen and was now lying half on her back and half on her side on the cold concrete floor. She knew she was dying, and panic tried to claim her, but it was a far-off feeling. Mostly she was experiencing worry for her baby girl, regret for all the highlights she'd miss in her life, sadness that she wouldn't get to tell Valerian that she'd decided to be his life mate, that she couldn't now be that for him.

Natalie felt hands on her, and heard voices. She was pretty sure whoever it was was talking to her, but she didn't have the energy to try to decipher what was being said, and simply let herself drift into the comforting darkness creeping over her.

Twenty-Three

Natalie could hear Mia's voice as she slowly woke up. Her little girl was chattering away to someone. Probably Sinbad, she thought as she finally managed to push her eyes open. Good Lord! She felt dry as dust! Her eyes were crusted with guck, and her tongue felt like shoe leather in her mouth, and tasted bad too. What was up with that? she wondered, and turned her head to look for her daughter. She didn't have far to look, Mia sat on the bed next to her, holding up her fingers as she counted out loud.

"One, two, four, five, three," she said solemnly, and then beamed triumphantly at the man sitting cross-legged in front of her.

"Very good," Valerian congratulated. "Very close. But let's try again." Holding up one finger after the other just as she had done, he said, "One, two, three, four, five. Now you try."

"One, two, three . . . five, four," she finished happily.

Valerian chuckled at her glee, and then glanced to Natalie and froze briefly, his eyes widening. "You're awake."

Mia turned to look at her, saw that her eyes were open, squealed happily, and launched herself at her.

Natalie tensed for impact, but it never came. Valerian caught the little girl by the waist and set her down gently next to Natalie instead, saying, "Give Mommy a cuddle. But gently. She was hurt, remember?"

"Mama hurt," Mia agreed, and snuggled up to her, then kissed her cheek. "All better?"

Natalie chuckled at her hopeful expression, and assured her, "All better."

"Sinnee hurt too," Mia announced.

"What?" Natalie asked with surprise.

"Hey," Valerian said lightly, drawing Mia's gaze to him. "Who wants ice cream?"

"Me!" Mia squealed, pushing off Natalie to hop on the bed next to her on her knees and clap her hands.

"How about I take you to get some, then?" Valerian suggested, scooping Mia up and getting off the bed with her. Carrying her around the bed, he smiled gently at Natalie and said, "I'll be right back and we'll talk."

Natalie nodded with understanding. Obviously, whatever he had to tell her was not for young ears. Sighing, she watched him carry her daughter out of the room, and then noticed the IV stand next to the bed. Eyes widening, she stared at it, noticing that a half-full blood bag hung from it, and a tube ran down and disappeared under the blankets covering her. Natalie pulled her hands out from under the blanket and stopped when she saw the catheter in her arm.

For a minute, she was completely flummoxed, and then the memory of Timothy stabbing her flashed across her mind.

"Anthony," she corrected herself in a whisper. Devin's son. He'd wanted to kill her and Mia. Something about money, she thought. Her memory got a little fuzzy after she'd dropped to her knees. But Natalie distinctly remembered the little jerk stabbing her, and her thinking she was dying. Apparently, she'd been wrong about that, and they'd managed to save her, Natalie thought, and started to push down the blanket and sheet covering her. All it revealed, though, was the pale blue nightshirt she was wearing. She was about to tug it up to look at her stomach when she heard footsteps coming back down the stairs. Natalie quickly pulled the blanket and sheet back up and watched the door until it opened and Valerian entered with a bowl of ice cream in hand.

"Where's Mia?" Natalie asked, watching him approach the bed.

"Eating ice cream with Aileen in your office," Valerian answered as he set the bowl on the bedside table. He then took her completely by surprise by catching her under the arms and lifting her to a sitting position, and holding her there while he stacked pillows behind her.

Natalie stiffened, waiting for pain to rip through her stomach, but it didn't come. She peered down at her blanket-covered stomach with a frown, wondering why it didn't hurt.

"Sinbad was shot," Valerian announced as he finished seeing to her comfort.

That managed to distract her from her own wound, and Natalie's head shot up at this. "What? How? When?"

"Three days ago," Valerian told her solemnly, and picked up the bowl of ice cream to walk around the bed and climb in next to her. Once settled there, he continued. "Timothy, or Anthony really, used a rifle-mounted drone to do it. He was actually aiming for Mia, but she chose the perfect moment to bend down to pick a flower to add to the few she'd already collected for you, and Sinbad got hit instead."

Natalie's eyes widened with horror at how close she'd come to losing her daughter, and then she asked, "Is he . . . ?"

When Natalie hesitated, not even wanting to put her fear to words, Valerian assured her, "He's fine. He was hit in the shoulder. Fortunately, Anders's wife, Valerie, is a vet and was at my place. She operated on him, removed the bullet, patched him up, and said he'll be fine once he's healed. But he won't be able to manage stairs for a while, so he's up in your office right now. Hence the reason Aileen and Mia are eating in there. Mia wanted to take Sinbad ice cream too to make him feel 'all better,'" he added with an affectionate smile.

Natalie found herself smiling as well, but then her smile faded and she said, "Timothy, I mean Anthony, stabbed me."

"Yes." The word was clipped and angry. "Shooting Mia was to serve two purposes. One, to kill Mia, of course, and the other was it served as a distraction. All the men converged on Mia and Sinbad, or the area the shot came from. Even Colle left the RV and the security cameras and rushed out. It left Anthony free to approach the clubhouse from the other side and slip in through the bulkhead cellar doors and attack you."

Natalie stiffened at this news, recalling that the door under the stairs had been open and a couple of boxes out of place. That must have been the sound she'd heard from the bedroom while dressing.

"I read from his mind that he'd cut the old padlock off the cellar entry some weeks ago and replaced it with one he had a key to," Valerian explained, and then added, "He'd also gone downstairs his last day here, unlocked the inner door under the stairs, and stacked the boxes in front of it again, so that he could get in later." He blew out a breath. "Emily apparently saw him in the basement by the door, and he worried she would say something sooner or later, so he drove her off the road, hoping to kill her."

"Oh God," Natalie breathed. "He must have hated me so much."

Valerian hesitated, and then said, "It seems that while Sheila Daniels, his mother, never blamed you for marrying Devin and considered you as much a victim of her dead husband as she was, and rightfully so," he added firmly, "Anthony had other opinions. At least, that was his claim. Although, frankly, I think he's just a greedy little shit who didn't want to share his inheritance."

"Oh," Natalie sighed. She did remember him going on about paydays and money and whatnot, and suspected Valerian might be right. But was less concerned with that than—"He didn't get away, did he?"

"No," Valerian said, relaxing a little.

"Was he arrested?" Natalie asked. "Will there be a court case?" The answer to the last question was the one she wanted most. If she was going to have to get up in court and recount her fake marriage, and the loss of her entire family . . . The very idea was enough to make her nauseous.

"No," Valerian said quietly. "Lucian arranged a three-on-one for him. Anthony's presently in a psychiatric hospital, under observation."

"What is a three-on-one?"

"It's where three immortals repeatedly erase the person's memories, until they are completely gone."

"So, he won't remember trying to kill me?" she asked slowly, thinking that wasn't much of a punishment. How did they know he wouldn't just try again now that he didn't remember trying already?

"He won't remember anything," Valerian corrected. "Right now, he's a blank slate. A tabula rasa. He doesn't even remember how to eat or walk. For some mortals who go through it, they remain that way, a vegetable, forever hospitalized. But others can be trained to walk and talk again, and eventually become a decent person. Hopefully," he added dryly, and then shrugged. "We won't know which way it'll go for him for a while."

"Oh," Natalie said weakly, not sure how she felt about that. It was better than having to fear his coming after her again, but—"Wait," she said, lifting her head suddenly. "I heard a woman's voice while I was lying on the floor. She stopped Timothy/Anthony from stabbing me again."

"His mother, Sheila Daniels," Valerian said quietly. "She found you just as he was about to stab you for a second time. Fortunately, she stopped him long enough for us to catch up and take control of him. But he'd already stabbed you once."

Natalie nodded. She didn't think she'd ever forget that. The pain had been excruciating. "I thought I was dying."

"Natalie," Valerian said with concern, but she raised a hand to silence him.

"I need to tell you, Valerian," she said when he fell silent and waited. "When I thought I was dying, I—one of my regrets was that I didn't get to tell you yes."

"Yes?" Valerian asked uncertainly.

"Yes, I'll be your life mate," Natalie explained, and then rushed on. "I think I might love you. I mean, I like you a lot, and the sex is great, and you're so good with Mia, and good to me too, and I know this means I might have to go through the turn, but it can't be that bad, can it?" she asked a little worriedly. "I'm thinking it's just a shot, right? One of your scientists gives me a shot with nanos in it and ta-da! I'm immortal, and maybe suffer a few flu-like symptoms for a day or two and then I'm fine?"

"Uh . . ." Valerian's mouth was twitching with amusement, but she wasn't sure why. "No. It's not just a shot."

"It isn't?" she asked anxiously, and then her eyes widened. "You don't have to bite me, do you?"

"No," he assured her. "Actually, I had to bite myself. The nanos are inside of us and can't just be retrieved and given to someone else. Their whole objective is to take care of their host so they fight being removed from the body. Poking a needle in would just make them scram from the point of insertion. You kind of have to catch them unaware. So, an immortal has to rip their wrist open and quickly press it to the mouth of the mortal so that enough nanos get caught up in the first unexpected wave of blood and rush into them."

"Oh gross," Natalie said with disgust.

"And I'm afraid a day or two of flu-like symptoms is not what follows," Valerian added solemnly. "The nanos set to work at once on repairing, in your case, thirty-two years of damage caused by pollution, sun, childbirth, and whatnot. It's excruciatingly painful. Fortunately, the turnee rarely remembers more than bad nightmares afterward."

"Oh dear," Natalie breathed, not sure she had the courage to go through what he was describing.

"Do you remember any bad nightmares?" Valerian asked.

Natalie glanced at him with confusion. "Me? Oh . . ." She blinked in surprise. "Actually, yes, I did have a few nightmares, I think. Mostly a lot of blood, and fire and . . ." She shuddered at the memory. "It must have been from being stabbed."

"Hmm," he murmured, and handed her the ice cream. "Would you like some?"

Mouth still incredibly dry, Natalie nodded and accepted the bowl. Hoping it would take the nasty taste out of her mouth, she immediately scooped some up, and then moaned with pleasure as she slid it into her mouth. Not only did it taste good, but the dryness was immediately gone as the cold delicacy melted in her mouth.

"Hey!" she gasped with surprise, nearly spitting it out in surprise when Valerian began to tug down her blanket and sheet.

Pausing he lifted his head, and smiled sweetly. "Trust me."

Swallowing the ice cream in her mouth, Natalie nodded uncertainly and watched him pull the bedclothes down to lay across her hips. She bit the spoon to keep from saying anything when he then reached up to undo the buttons of her nightshirt. He was quick about it, opening it all the way to her lower stomach, before tugging the right side apart to reveal the red, angry scar there.

"It hasn't fully healed yet," Valerian said as Natalie gaped at the scar. Not scab, or fresh wound, but scar. "The nanos have been busy the last three days with everything else they had to do, I suppose, but the scar should be completely gone in a couple more days to a week."

Natalie lifted her head to look at him. "The nanos have been busy?"

"You were dying by the time we got to you, love," he said gently. "I didn't have a choice. It was turn you or lose you. Which is why I'm so damned glad you said you wanted to be my life mate." He smiled crookedly. "I would have turned you whether you were willing to be my life mate or not. I couldn't let you die. You might only think you love me, but I know I love you. To me, you are the most courageous, beautiful, and brilliant woman on the planet, and—" His words died abruptly when Natalie gave a start and squawked.

She gave him an apologetic grimace and then peered down at herself. She'd been so enthralled by what he was telling her that she'd apparently let her bowl tip, and a half scoop of ice cream had slid out and dropped onto her upper chest. It was now sliding slowly down the slope of her breast.

Natalie glanced around but the box of tissues that usually resided on the bedside table was missing. She was about to try to scoop it back into the bowl when Valerian suddenly ducked his head and took a good third of her breast, including her nipple and the ice cream, into his mouth.

Gasping, Natalie sat a little straighter, and then moaned as he swirled the ice cream around and sucked her nipple. It was like nothing she'd ever experienced and she could have wept when he stopped and lifted his head to meet her gaze.

His voice was gruff with passion when he said,

"Now that we're life mates and you're turned, I think we should marry."

Natalie blinked at the announcement. It was the last thing she'd expected him to say. But he wasn't done.

"I just know I won't be able to stay away from you. I'll be here all the time, probably naked and on top of you in your bed, or on your sofa, your desk, your kitchen table . . ." He shook his head. "That's no way to behave with a little girl like Mia around. We need to marry, and I need to hire a nanny"—Natalie opened her mouth to protest at once, but he held up a hand to silence her—"to make sure Mia stays safe. Not to look after her all the time," Valerian assured her. "Just someone to be a backup to make sure she doesn't wander off or electrocute herself or something while we're in our postcoital faints."

"Oh," Natalie breathed, realizing that could be an issue. Sighing, she nodded.

"You'll marry me?" Valerian asked, sounding surprised.

Apparently, he'd expected to have to talk her into it, she realized, so said, "No, but I'll hire a nanny."

When Valerian's mouth dropped open, she burst out laughing. "Of course I'll marry you. Jeez, I've already been turned. That's pretty much as good as married anyway for immortals, isn't it? Besides, I don't want Mia growing up thinking it's okay just to use men for sex and send them home. I want her to respect men."

When Valerian blinked at that, his brain apparently unable to compute what she'd just said, Natalie smiled and slid her hands up his leg, toward his groin, and murmured, "You didn't get all the ice cream."

He glanced down, just in time to see her dump another scoop onto her chest.

A startled laugh slipped from Valerian's mouth, and he met her gaze again. "I love you."

"I love you too," Natalie whispered, and as he ducked his head to begin to help clean up the mess she'd made, she knew it was true. Valerian was a good man. He would accept and love Mia as a daughter, and would do his best to ensure both of them were happy. She could envision a future full of love, laughter, and a lot of amazing sex. What more could a girl ask for?